The
Stone's
Heart

Books by Jessica Thorne

The Queen's Wing

The Stone's Heart

JESSICA THORNE

bookouture

Published by Bookouture in 2019

An imprint of StoryFire Ltd.

Carmelite House
50 Victoria Embankment
London EC4Y 0DZ

www.bookouture.com

ISBN: 978-1-78681-754-9
eBook ISBN: 978-1-78681-753-2

To Dad, thanks for all the stories

Chapter One

Petra

Golden sunlight filters through the windows and I shift the tablet around so I can continue to read it. Anthaese sunlight seems richer and thicker than the sunlight of my homeworld, far-off Vairian, on the other side of the galaxy. There's a knock on the door of my office. I have an office now, with a desk and everything. Someone insisted. One day I will find out who and then they'll regret it.

'Enter,' I snap, pushing the tablet back from me and locking the screen. To my surprise, when the door opens, Bel's standing there.

Well, more correctly, Princess Belengaria Merryn of Vairian, Duchess of Elveden, Countess of Duneen and betrothed of the ruler of this world, the Anthaem, Conleith stands there. She's slight and beautiful in a strangely fae sort of way, her golden-toned skin like polished waeywood, and her hair black as raven feathers. She smiles nervously. It obviously isn't a day of many formal appointments because I'd know if it was, and secondly, she'd be wearing a much more elaborate dress than a simple Vairian-style robe in cream and blue, a keen reminder of our home. A very different world from here.

'Bel?' I wait as she comes inside and closes the door behind her. Just Bel, on her own, which is frustrating. She's wearing her knife belt, of course. It's a habit, one of which I approve. The slipping-away-from-the-guards-I-assign-to-keep-her-safe is a lot less endearing.

I get to my feet and give a bow but she rolls her eyes. 'Oh, stop it.'

'What can I do for you, your Highness?'

The monarchy isn't hereditary here. They pick the best and the brightest, and in Bel they have a shining star. I know that better than anyone.

She takes a seat by the window. It looks out over the city, rather than the gardens and from it you can see the rebuilding work, still underway. They're doing everything they can to replicate the original, unique style of the buildings, matching, to the best of their abilities, those scattered across the surface of Anthaeus, elegant and beautiful, those precious few settlements, on this otherwise wild and sparsely inhabited planet. It will take years, but we'll do it. It's not everyone who gets to watch a new world being built out of the ruins of the old.

'I have a favour to ask.'

As if I could deny her anything. 'Of course. Just ask.'

She doesn't though. Not at first. Her attention is captured by the view.

The Rondet soar through the skies, glittering and wondrous. The non-human sentients – the preferred term according to the xenobiologists who keep trying to study them – look like a mix between insects and dragons, their crystalline forms catching the light, their four wings bearing them effortlessly. Awake from their hibernation, the three survivors of a lost race reborn range far and wide through the skies. Bel woke them from their long sleep in the darkest hours of the invasion. We would never have won without them.

Human life is flourishing too, though our losses in the war were great. The surviving colonists are resettling in the capital, Limasyll, although many stay in the newly-discovered subterranean cities – feeling safer there, more comfortable among the ancient architecture which they study and emulate, just as the first settlers did. Their numbers are few, the death toll higher than we imagined at first. We still don't know the total lost.

Anthaeus sits at the farthest edge of a network of planets and a loose alliance of worlds holding its own between two powers, the Empire to one side of us, Gravia on the other. Both of them wanted control of Anthaeus. The Empire tried negotiation, the Gravians invaded, and ultimately, both failed. The Empress seems content – for now, anyway – to allow my homeworld of Vairian, through Bel, to be her hand here. Vairians are soldiers, through and through. We fought the Gravians on our own world and drove them off. Since then we've been the Empress's attack dogs, the shock troops of the Empire, even if we are among the newest worlds aligned to it. Sending Bel here as Con's betrothed was her way of reaching out to take control of Anthaeus as well. They spoke of her duty to Vairian, her father's duty to the Empire, the need for peace and unity, and all the other flowery language of diplomacy… when you got down to basics, Bel was handed from one world to another without any choice in the matter.

But it wasn't that simple. Nothing is ever that simple.

I don't think the Empress realises how completely Anthaeus tends to make those who come here its own. Perhaps no one does. Spend any time on this world and it draws you in, and gives you a new home.

Bel and Con, beautiful as night and day, complementing each other in all things, rule a court filled with wonders. Con was always an engineer at heart, and now his inventions are changing the galaxy. Bel's courage is the foundation on which he builds. Their people adore her like a living saint, as much as they did Con's first wife, Matilde, an idea which makes her blush and laugh at the same time. But you can see how much it means to her. How much she loves them back.

Eventually Bel lets out a heavy sigh. 'You aren't going to like it, Petra. But I really need you to do this for me.'

I sit in the matching chair. 'Bel, I'm at your command. You know that.'

It must be to do with the wedding.

Their wedding – *the* wedding – was interrupted by a Gravian invasion the first time they attempted it. Bel and Con went through hell to get this far again, but this time it's a formality, more like a celebration for the new Anthaeus and its restored freedom. A statement of their victory. It has to be perfect. Jondar will see to that, and Thom is almost as bad.

Master of the Court of Anthaeus, Prince Jondar of House Henndale, is the most uptight control freak I've ever encountered. How my fellow Vairian turned Anthaese general, Thom Rahleigh, puts up with him outside of working hours, I don't know. Perhaps because he's secretly just as bad.

And as for them, Thom and Jondar were handfasted in a traditional Vairian ceremony combined with a full Anthaese marriage. It was horribly complicated, overly elaborate and a lavish affair but they loved every minute of it. I pointed out that perhaps they should have let Bel and Con have their wedding first but Thom told me it would take too long and he wouldn't wait. So that was that.

So here I am and here I stay, serving my princess, leading my troops, rebuilding a world anew. I'm not a soldier any more but a general, which just means more paperwork and less time. But awards had to be handed out, promotions bestowed. There were medals. It doesn't sit well with me, if I'm honest. I've seen how fast everything can change, how quickly all those honours can be taken from someone. When the interstellar networks tell the story of the defence of Anthaeus, they speak of heroism and valour. Who wants to hear of death and agony, of sacrifice and destruction? They don't speak of the aftermath.

Bel laces her fingers together, a sure sign that she's nervous. So it really is something I won't like. To be honest, I'm intrigued.

'I'd rather not make it a command, Petra. It's difficult and it's not something I'd ask lightly.'

It's sounding worse with every second that drags by. I'm imagining ball gowns, tulle and so much lace. Probably in a very bright colour that definitely isn't my preferred black.

'What is it, Bel?'

She bites on her lower lip and looks guilty. It's really bad then. Worse than ball gowns. 'Zander's coming to the wedding.'

Oh.

I desperately try to find something polite to say instead of what I'm thinking. He's her brother, after all. He was invited the first time.

But it's Zander. Ball gowns would be easy in comparison.

'Of course he is. Crown Prince Lysander is—'

'Stop it. I know, he's a pain. We've all heard the latest stories. I need you to keep an eye on him. He has a habit of getting himself into trouble. And I know this might be awkward but...'

She knows. Of course she knows. She finds out everything. She looks so little and helpless and suddenly she has you in a headlock with a knife at your throat and a gun in your back. Not that she would need either one.

Zander and me. There's a history. Not just my refusing to follow his orders when they conflicted with my duty to her. But so much more. Back at home, all through training and on a hundred missions.

'I'm at your service, your Majesty,' I tell her, because what else can I say? She's my queen and if she wants me to babysit her big brother, well then… I'll babysit.

Zander and me.

This is going to be a disaster.

*

Thom isn't any help. When I tell him he just looks at me blankly.

'Well of course he's coming. He's her brother.'

'Yes, but…'

How am I meant to explain? When I was a kid I never even thought of romance. Why would I? Long before the Gravians invaded Anthaeus, they came to my world. The war between Vairian and Gravia lasted many years and I was born into that, grew up in its chaos and destruction. I'm a war orphan like so many others, there and here. When I was a kid, all I wanted to do was grow up as fast as possible so I could fight too, so I could mete out some sort of revenge on those who took everything from me. Or at least, the Gravian ones.

And oh, I did. Back home, and in every other warzone the Empress sent us to. Vairian troops, the best, disposable. The dogs of the Empire, despised by everyone but entirely necessary, all the same.

'You mean that *thing* you two had when we were posted on the Noble Hawk?' Thom asks.

It feels like a punch to the gut.

That thing. I can't believe he'd refer to it like that. *That. Thing.*

I carefully rein in the shock before I reply. 'That. And the fact that last time he spoke to me I disobeyed a direct order.'

Thom shrugs. 'So did I.'

'You aren't his ex.'

He laughs then. 'It was years ago. Besides, *General* Kel – Zander is a Crown Prince now. No matter what he's done in the past, or what he's got up to recently, he's going to be shone up and married off to the most politically expedient bidder. You know that, don't you?'

He gentles on the last few words. Thom isn't the ignorant oaf he sometimes pretends to be. It isn't just marriage to Jondar that's softened him up. He always had that side to him. He just doesn't show it very often. Not even to his friends.

'Of course I know that, *General* Rahleigh.' I lean on the title a little for emphasis. Just as he did mine. To be honest we're still both bemused by our rise in station. The rank feels strange. He may have expected it one day but I never did, not with my family history. But Con decided and once he decides something he's even more stubborn than Bel. 'Even after all the drinking and ancestors know what else Zander got up to on Cuore... You've heard the stories.'

The Empress summoned him to her palace world before the Gravians invaded Anthaeus, and in my less charitable moments I wonder if he used the battle for our liberation as a way to avoid facing her. Whatever the reason, after the war he ran out of excuses. Zander went to Cuore because he had no choice but to go. Our world is her vassal world, and as Crown Prince he had to swear fealty. And he stayed for months, allegedly indulging every vice I've ever heard of. Sad to say, it didn't even surprise me.

Thom shrugs. 'A few, yeah. They weren't easy to avoid. Look, he's never been one to take orders, that's all. And the Empress isn't one to take his sort of carry-on lightly. I can't imagine it went smoothly, can you?'

'Do you think she kept him there to punish him?'

It isn't a good thought. Zander could have annoyed her so much that she deliberately kept him on Cuore. And he retaliated by – well, by being Zander. Being even worse.

'Who was punishing who, do you think?' he asks.

Our eyes meet and we almost laugh. Even among the regular troops Zander was known as a hellraiser, long before his rise in station. Not just known, *notorious*. The amount of times we've pulled him out of a bar or a brothel, the number of besotted girls we've had to carefully turn away… I pity whoever is doing that job now.

I should never have made a fool of myself with him. But we were young and there were battles to fight. And no one ever knew who would be coming back. The sheer unadulterated joy of being with him was enough for me.

Then he told me he loved me.

I applied for reassignment within an hour.

*

The Vairian shuttle spirals down to the landing strip, its stocky bulk gleaming in the afternoon sunlight. Someone thought to decorate the reception area with streamers of silk which billow out, rippling in the wind it kicks up. As it touches down there's a rush of activity overhead, birds taking off as one, startled by the noise, and by Rhenna, of the Rondet, soaring low over the field, all four of her glistening wings spread wide.

Bel laughs with delight to see her. 'She's curious.'

I shift nervously. 'Aren't we all? What do you think happened when he went to Cuore? He was there for months.'

She just shakes her head. 'I'm sure it went fine.'

I'm not. We heard the stories, just like I said to Thom. How could we avoid them? The interstellar networks love gossip almost as much as a war, and a bad boy, heart-throb, handsome prince, especially a new one, meant hits all over their feeds. They told tales of scandal after scandal, drunkenness, debauchery, and a hundred broken hearts. They detailed all the ways he disgraced himself and, by extension, Vairian in lurid details.

I believe every tall tale. Perhaps Bel doesn't.

I sometimes wonder if I know her brother better than she does. Or if she is just in denial. I knew him at his worst – or at least his previous worse, before this new low – but to her he was always a hero. That's the way of things. I wonder if he is really here for the wedding? Or something else? I wouldn't put anything past him. But I don't get a chance to pursue any questions. The door to the shuttle opens and Zander steps out.

But it's not Zander, not the Zander I knew. This is Crown Prince Lysander Merryn of Vairian, plus a lot of other titles he's acquired. Too many to follow. Vairian's Playboy Prince.

He's still arresting to look at, his height, broad shoulders, a perfectly proportioned physical specimen. He'd never get away with everything he does without that. His eyes. And that smile.

I've learned to be so very wary of that smile.

He turns it on the assembled well-wishers now, like a weapon.

Three of Bel's ladies-in-waiting absolutely simper. A number of the guards as well, although they manage to look suitably contrite when I glare at them. They're lucky Thom chooses not to notice.

The smile does not affect me. I'm immune.

And I'll keep on telling myself that.

I recognise Daria with him, her tall, solid presence as much a staple in his entourage as ever. Her black hair is close cropped and functional and she doesn't seem to have aged at all since I saw her last. She is to

Zander what Shae was to Bel, once upon a time – bodyguard, confidant, best friend. She never liked me, of that I'm certain. But then, she once served with my father.

As Bel makes her way towards them – because would it hurt her just once to stay put like she's told? – I follow as nonchalantly as I can. We've almost reached him when, with a noise like a fist hitting concrete, Rhenna slams herself down on the ground between us.

Two hundred pounds of gleaming, crystalline dragon-like alien body blocks Zander's path and, incredibly, he doesn't instantly retreat. I knew he was brave, but this borders on foolhardy.

'What's she doing?' I ask Bel.

She's already frowning, with that slightly distant look in her eyes which tells me she's talking to the remaining female member of the Rondet. It's clearly a disagreement at best.

Thom says that communing with them is like hearing someone whisper in the back of your mind. I haven't had the pleasure. And I'm not entirely sure I want to. Psychic bonds with non-human minds? No thank you.

'She's curious. And a bit… oh, *ancestors*, Rhenna…'

Zander stands his ground, looking up at her, part in wonder and part in defiance. His guards fan out, unsure of what they should do. No one prepared them for this. Even Daria looks shocked. How do you prepare someone for meeting ancient non-human lifeforms who until recently were thought extinct? Zander doesn't move when Rhenna takes one step and then another forward, and thrusts her slender, deadly muzzle towards his face. Her tail lashes back and forth.

'Bel?' I ask. 'What is it?' I've never seen Rhenna so defensive before. She's acting out of character and I don't like it.

But Bel just looks exasperated. Whatever Rhenna is telling her, she doesn't like it.

'Last time Zander was here he tried to make me leave with him. She's not... not too happy to see him.'

No, really? She looks like she's about to bite his head off.

'What do we do?'

'I'm trying to talk to her but she's so stubborn.'

Well, she ought to know stubborn. And as for Zander...

He stands there, gazing at the enormous, hostile creature as if he's looking at a wonder. Which, of course, he is. But the gleam in those hazel eyes shows no hint of the fear he ought to be feeling right now. That stupid Merryn family bravery again, that ability to sail through a crisis while everyone else runs away like people with brains.

It'll only take a moment to go to hell. It'll only take an instant for Rhenna to crush him or tear him limb from limb. I've seen her do it.

Admittedly, that was with Gravian invaders. But still, there have been rumours, accusations, missing livestock, even tales of missing children. I don't believe a single one of them. But stories grow. It's only a matter of time before the finger points more directly to them. Or for the Vairian guards to decide she's a threat to their Crown Prince and try to protect him by attacking her. She wouldn't take well to that.

I can't just stand here. Instinct compels me into action. I throw myself forward, leaping over her tail and dodging under her wings. But I'm too late. I know it even as I start to move. I'll never make it in time. I'm far too late.

Zander lifts his hand and presses it against the hard, shining surface of her muzzle.

I skid to a halt between them, ready to block her, or him, ready to keep them apart. Ready to let her attack me instead of him. But Rhenna barely notices me. She leans in against his hand, her multifaceted eyes glinting as they gaze down at him. Is she in his head too? I can't tell. I only know she doesn't deign to talk to me.

Abruptly, she purrs. It's unmistakable. The rumble passes through my chest like an earthquake, shaking my lungs against my ribcage.

She looks at me, instead of him. Her eyes are so many colours. They shift and glow, almost hypnotic. She's studying me.

Then she shies back from us, gathering her muscles, and leaps for the sky, all four wings outspread. The blast of wind throws my hair back from my face and I bring up my hand to shield my eyes as she flies away.

'Beautiful,' says Zander. He means it too, his dazed expression fixed on the native Anthaese in flight. A smile drags its way over my face to hear the awe in that single word. 'Hello, Petra.' His tone doesn't change but flows on, surprisingly calm. 'That was dramatic.'

The old me would have bristled and become instantly defensive. Part of me still tries to. I haven't grown that much. I get it under control as fast as I can.

'Have to make an entrance, Zander. Wasn't that always your rule of thumb?'

I glance at him, unable to help myself. Ancestors, he's only got better looking in the intervening years. How is that possible?

'Well, your dragon certainly understands that. Was she marking her territory?'

Or was I? The unspoken words are a glint of amusement in his hazel eyes.

'She's not *my* dragon, your Highness,' I tell him and step away to give a curt bow. 'She's not a dragon at all. They are the native species here, the ancient Anthaese. This is her world. We're the interlopers.'

Just then Bel arrives and thoroughly distracts him by throwing her arms around his neck in an act of royal impropriety that will scandalise the uptight, etiquette-obsessed Anthaese nobility.

Or perhaps not. They're almost used to her now.

The interstellar media, on the other hand, will have a field day – one look at the dismayed expression on Jondar's face tells me that. He tries so hard to be understanding with Bel, but now that there are two Merryns in residence he hasn't a hope. I make a mental note to tell Thom to talk him down. He's the only one who can. Maybe he can give him some further tips on handling Vairian royals. They aren't the same as Anthaese. We come from very different worlds, people shaped in entirely different ways.

'Kel,' Daria says with a curt nod to me. 'Well handled.' I accept the unexpected compliment with a dip of my head. 'Do they often do that?'

'Not often. But then, they do what they like most of the time.'

Daria gives a short laugh. 'Well, we're used to that, aren't we?'

Bel is already talking nineteen to the dozen to her bemused and suddenly somewhat helpless older brother, introducing him to various dignitaries. He does well, considering he's Zander and he would probably rather be heading straight to a bar if I remember correctly.

And then, before I realise what's happening, all attention is on me again.

'And you remember *General* Kel,' she says blithely. The devious little monster. She even gets the tone just right. Rubbing it in. I'm a general now. *Her* general.

'*General Kel.*' He rolls the words around on his tongue like he's tasting them. Well, he might be the crown prince but he never made general. Admittedly he could probably appoint himself general now if he wanted to but that wouldn't be the same. And I'm an Anthaese general rather than a Vairian one so he probably doesn't really class it as a proper general. And... and he's smiling at me. Why is he smiling at me?

Oh ancestors, yes. Procedures. Politeness. Speak, Petra.

'Crown Prince Lysander,' I say, and give a formal bow. No matter what Jondar says, I do not curtsey. I straighten, standing to attention, and I wait for it, a barb or some kind of low blow. Just to knock me off my perch.

'You and Thom are heading up the newly restored military, I believe?' he replies.

'Yes, your Highness, Vairian and Anthaese veterans serve together now.'

He gives a laugh, amused but curt all the same. 'You can't be a veteran at your age, Petra.'

I freeze a bit inside. I'm older than Bel, but not by much. And given all we saw during the invasion we certainly qualify as veterans. A veteran isn't defined by years.

I should have let Rhenna eat him. Bel would get over it. She has two more brothers after all.

But it's Bel who answers, her voice uncharacteristically sharp. 'You would be surprised by how young some of our veterans are, Zander. We lost entire generations to the Gravians. This was not a clean war. But then neither was the one at home... or have you forgotten? Now, come on. We need to get back to the palace. Con is waiting.'

Con didn't come out to meet Zander. For many that would be a slight but Zander doesn't even appear to notice. Con is run off his feet these days. If he's not overseeing the rebuilding projects, he's rolling out another new invention, arranging financing for another orphanage, or trying to muscle in on the archaeological work in the hidden city.

'*Waiting*' might be an exaggeration.

*

There's no sign of Con when we get there. We pause on the wide, sunlit terrace leading in to the audience chamber, which was once no more than a minor receiving room. It's still a building more beautiful than anything on Vairian and that gives me a small thrill of pride in my new home. Bel tries to hide her annoyance and Jondar is barking into his coms in what he thinks is a subtle manner. Luckily, Thom arrives on the scene and the next thing he and Zander are laughing and swapping war stories. It's all loud and male and while I'm used to that, it seems suddenly out of place and alien in the refined atmosphere of Anthaeus. I'm not part of it now. Why Thom still is and I'm not, I don't know. I stand stiff and formal, off to one side, watching them.

'General? Is there anything you need?' Dwyer pops out of nowhere. Whoever had the stupid idea of getting me an office also had the stupid idea of assigning me an equerry, a fifteen year old war orphan who is frighteningly efficient and reminds me way too much of myself at that age.

'No, Dwyer. Just… watching.'

'Flight command sent through a message. An Imperial ship is in orbit and requesting permission to send down a shuttle.'

Now he has my attention. 'What ship?'

He checks the tablet in his hand, scrolling through the information there. 'It's um… it's…'

'Spit it out, Dwyer. What other ship?'

'The Gallacian. Out of Cuore.'

There's no ship from Cuore due in now. I'm sure of it. I make eye contact with Jondar. He frowns and makes an excuse to whoever he's talking to before crossing to me.

I tell him.

'The Gallacian?' He gives me a blank look and Dwyer clears his throat.

'It detoured off its registered itinerary to call in here, by Imperial command, for a group of passengers to disembark. That's so strange. Why would they—?'

'What passengers?' Jondar asks warily.

Dwyer hands him the tablet.

I don't think I've ever heard Jondar use language like that before.

Chapter Two

Bel

By the time we return to the palace, I'm actually ready to strangle each and every one of them. Rhenna for the over-possessive floor show, Zander for being Zander and Petra for acting weird. I'm not just upset, I'm furious. Not that I can let anyone see that. And of course, Con is nowhere to be found.

Because why would he be where he's meant to be? He's the ruler of this absurd, obstinate world. So of course he's missing.

I march through the gallery, my hands in fists at my side. Various people take one look and get out of my way. Only my bodyguard, Beq, follows me, keeping a discrete distance. I'm still aware of him though. He's not that inconspicuous.

I make my way to the other side of the remaining wing where Con has his study now. He wanted to be close to the site of his old study, as if something of the former lingers here. I climb the narrow, winding staircase.

I feel Aeron's mind brush against mine. So he's there too – in spirit if not in body –peering through Con's eyes at his inventions. As one of the Rondet, we've communed before, but it's Con he's closest to. They have the same interests, the same enquiring minds.

The door is closed and there is no sign of the guards who are meant to be outside it. Which means he invited them in again. He's probably using them as brute strength or guinea pigs. I give Beq a look and he finds a point on the wall to study intensely rather than meet my eyes.

Great. They always stick together.

I ought to hammer on the door until he opens it. There's no one to see. I'd barely be making a scene. But Anthaeus is rubbing off on me. Instead I use the coms unit on my wrist, ornately decorated like a bracelet and a gift from him. I love it for its beauty, its ingenuity and the thought behind it.

But right now I'm less than enamoured with him.

'I know you're in there, Con. Open the door.'

The response is a not so regal curse and I hear someone running to the door. It's dragged open and his guard Kelvin stands there, six feet of muscles, bright red with embarrassment to match his red hair. He's unable to meet my gaze in his guilt. Behind him, taking up the secondary defensive position I see Con's other guard, Dex, looking if possible, even more sheepish.

The room is small and cramped, space being something of a premium shortly after the liberation. It's a far cry from the enormous, glass-domed top room that used to be his study. That doesn't seem to be a problem for my engineer though. He has it crammed to the ceiling with every bit of equipment he could salvage and he only keeps adding to the collection.

Con is bent over something on the bench, lights all trained on it and a huge pair of magnifying goggles on his face. His hair is everywhere and he's wearing the same simple linen shirt he put on for breakfast.

'Bel! Come and look at this.' Con's voice rings out in delight and despite my annoyance there's a thrill inside me at the sound. He looks like a child on the morning of his birthday and he's holding out his hands to encircle something that looks like a lump of Anthaese crystal.

'You're meant to be at the reception. Zander just got here.'

The glee on his face dampens. He glances at Liette, one of his assistants, who doesn't make eye-contact with me. She's a pretty girl in her early twenties, golden haired with cornflower blue eyes that look over-large in her slender face. She obviously idolises Con. If I was a jealous person I might have issues – if Con was less trustworthy than he is. I know a hopeless crush when I see one. I really ought to let him in on the secret but I think he'd die of embarrassment rather than deal with it. Besides, she'll find someone else. Both Con's guards are very attentive, not that she's noticed yet.

'Oh, love.' He sets the piece down carefully and makes his way over to meet me. 'I'm sorry. Flight command sent through reports of a number of anomalies around Kelta which could indicate incursion. Probably just smugglers but we need to check them out. Could just be related to the meteor shower we're expecting, but just in case, I came here to read them through, where it's quiet. And I had some work to finish. I lost track of the time.'

With anyone else, I'd say that was extremely convenient, but no, I can see that's exactly what happened. I can't stay angry with him.

'I'm surprised Jondar didn't have Kelvin and Dex lock you in the audience chamber.' If the two of them could make the ground open up and swallow them right now, they'd do it. They look so shamefaced that all I can think is that it's a good job I found them and not Petra. 'How could you forget *again*?' I sigh. I try not to sound too accusatory but sometimes it is hard. It's not like this is the first time.

'I sent Jon to the landing strip. I just needed a bit more time to finish this.'

I cross my arms over my chest. 'Con, that was *hours* ago.'

He looks up, eyes magnified on the other side of the thick glass so they look like they take up half his face. They are so green they're like precious stones.

'Oh,' he says. 'I'm… I'm sorry, Bel. Just… just let me…'

He fumbles with the goggles and his equipment, trying to finish whatever he's in the middle of and tidy up.

'The readings on the crystals are still off,' his assistant Sorrell chimes in as she appears from the smaller test room behind him. 'We've only got forty-five percent and I'm pretty sure we should be getting at least— Oh! Sorry, your Highness.'

She's the star of the university's earth-science faculty with a speciality in both geology and engineering. She's not quite seventeen and has a slight, boyish figure. Con found her making bombs and booby traps during the occupation. She was very good at it.

'It's all right, Sorrell,' I tell her. It's not her fault. I understand them getting caught up in their work, but he has other responsibilities. The reason for taking on Sorrell and Liette was so he wouldn't get so completely absorbed he forgets everything else. 'I'm just collecting the Anthaem.'

He gives me a guilty grin, and it doesn't matter that he's infuriating, maddening and so intelligent that he gets lost in the pathways of his brilliant mind. It's not that I don't understand his excitement, but we have so much more to do. He sometimes just gets so carried away with it all. Or possibly uses it as an escape.

Rebuilding a world isn't just about building new things. It's about diplomacy and strengthening ties. It's about conversations and deal-making and all the things that bore my fiancé to death.

I should have words with Jondar about it, find some way to manage it all better but I don't want to replace the wonder with the mundane.

Con still wakes up screaming, his torture at the hands of the Gravians always a shadow behind his eyes. There's nothing I wouldn't do to try to banish it.

My heart twists around inside me as I look at him and all I can think of is that we are finally going to be married in a few days.

'Can I just check this?' he asks. So serious and solemn that I know if I refused he'd leave it instantly. And thinking about it and what it might contain would torment him for hours until he got back here. I could never do that to him.

I nod and his grin widens. He knows I'd let him away with anything for that smile.

Sorrell offers him the tablet and Con grows more solemn as he examines it.

'There just isn't the same energy transfer. Keltan crystals would give more, otherwise we'll have to dig deeper.'

'What are you working on?' I ask. I should know better – I hardly ever understand the answers. Con tries to simplify it for me but he gets excited just explaining it and I can't always follow the leaps he makes.

'It's a new way of connecting the crystals in a network and using them to amplify each other, but using much smaller pieces. They work on the same principal as a neural pathway, right? We see that with the Rondet. So we should be able to programme them to allow us to help with body trauma, both physical and mental. They can be the connection too. We could embed them in a subcutaneous layer, or even just—'

I strain to understand. I like physical things: techniques, actions, reactions. He makes weapons that are better than anything else the galaxy has to offer. His shielding technology and the solar power cells have revolutionised the industries, not just here but throughout the galaxy.

Luckily Jondar reminded him to patent them. With the two of them working together the Anthaese treasury will never fall short. The projections following the occupation were terrible, but he just refused to let the worst happen. We lost such a large section of the population, mainly those of working age. Those who remain are mostly young, without experience of much besides fighting for their lives. And there were so many injuries and trauma. He's not only looking for a way to protect them, but to heal them too.

'You're talking about putting crystals into people?' I ask.

'Well… sort of…' Which means yes. Of course it does. He grabs my hand and pulls me over to the bench. Held in a cradle, like a net of slender gold wires, there's a disk no bigger than my thumbnail. It has a ring of crystal shards around the edge, a delicate knotwork of wires and minute electronics in the middle. It's rather beautiful really, reminding me of the elegance of my coms bracelet. It's like looking down on a maze from the sky.

Liette clears her throat. 'It can treat paralysis, or involuntary tremors. It can work on the mind too, locking down post-traumatic-stress episodes or lifting depression. It just needs enough power from the crystals. Con thought if we used them as an interface, it gives a double benefit.' She's so eager to please, so determined to make me understand. Clearly she sees that as a trial.

So many Anthaese suffer after effects of the war against the Gravians. The occupation was brutal, especially for those interned and used as slave labour. And for those like Con.

A terrible thought occurs to me.

'How have you been testing this?'

The guilty silence from all of them, scientists and guards, says it all. Liette however, doesn't have the self-preservation instincts Con does. 'We take every precaution, your highness—'

'It stops now,' I tell him, ignoring her. 'What gave you the idea?'

I peer down at the thing again as if it will answer me when he won't. And suddenly I know. It doesn't look Anthaese, not when you strip away the surface. It doesn't look Imperial either.

'Con? Is this based on Gravian Mecha technology?'

The three of them exchange another guilt-ridden look. Con's the only one who meets my eye. The two women suddenly find their work intensely interesting.

'Only a little. The idea is sound and I'm not going to use it to raise a zombie cybernetic death squad or anything, Bel. But look, the technology isn't to blame. And it's brilliant. It can cut off the emotional link to the body in milliseconds, stopping a traumatic incident before it fully takes hold. It can restore physical movement and—'

'Con, I'm not debating this with you. I know you mean well, but... Mechas?'

Speaking of emotional reactions, I can't even look at anything remotely connected to Mechas without thinking of what the Gravians did to Shae. What they did to so many of our fallen, taking their bodies and resurrecting them with technology to fight on their side, turning our friends into our enemies and their mindless slaves. Destroying all that made them human. To see something similar here on Con's workbench sends a shiver through me. Not to mention the idea of him connecting himself up to it.

'It isn't operational,' Sorrell says gently. She's trying to help, trying to comfort me, I think. 'Not for more than a minute. That's the problem. The crystals we have aren't strong enough to make the neural-physical link and sustain it for more than sixty seconds.'

'We ought to try the ones further north, the ones from Montserratt for example,' Liette says, reaching for the tablet. 'The readings there were always stronger. And the Gravians certainly concentrated there from the first. I should go up there.'

'Yes,' I say blandly. 'Maybe you should.' Anything to get her to stop talking.

Con passes her back the tablet. 'As Sorrell says, it's not working yet.'

It's the *yet* that does it. It's not working *yet* but it will. If I believe in anything, I believe in his ability to solve a problem. Even when he should leave it alone.

I spin on my heel and go. Even when I hear him calling after me, I don't hesitate or turn back. I know I came to fetch him but now I really don't care any more.

I don't stop until I'm in the gardens. At the Wall of the Lost in the palace gardens, I pause instinctively. Once it was an actual wall, a memorial of images and ephemera, fluttering pieces of paper left by people from all over Anthaeus, everyone who fought for its freedom and survived, to preserve the memory of the dead. Everyone lost someone in the invasion. There were no bystanders. The new wall is a smooth sheet like glass. Pictures flicker and glow inside it, powered by crystals and sunlight and the ingenuity of my husband-to-be. It's like looking at ghosts in a mirror, held there forever in a moment. Some of the pictures are static. Others have been animated or use archival footage, and personal video. Matilde walks down the staircase into the ballroom which is now forever gone. Like her. Shae's picture is still just a photograph gleaned from a file somewhere. He never liked to have his image taken.

The pain on seeing him is still there, but it is duller and more regretful now – a might have been and a never was. Another lifetime.

'Bel,' Con's voice is soft, hesitant. He followed me then. At least there's that.

Our guards stand at a remove, trying to give us space, as much as they can. I force my breath to be calm, but I can't force a smile.

'You need to change. It's a formal reception.'

'I will.' His hands close on my shoulders and he pulls me back against him. He's warm and gentle and even when I'm angry I can't stay that way with him. 'I will be careful, Bel,' he says, his voice a whisper against my hair. 'I promise.'

I relent. I believe his promises too. Because he's never actually broken one. Not when it mattered. He pulls me into his arms and kisses me until all I want to do is forget about brothers and banquets and everything else.

Eventually I force myself to pull away and rest my face against his chest, listening to his heartbeat. I never want to move. But...

'We're late,' I tell him, aware that my voice is a little hoarse.

'Of course.' He smiles down at me and I see the man I love now, still looking after me. 'But we can stay a while if you want.'

He shares me with a memory. Shae will never leave me. But then, in Matilde, I share him with a ghost he lost twice over. Perhaps that's why we fit together.

But I know it isn't just that. He is a wonder to me. I can't imagine life without him. Strange to think that, once, I dreaded marrying him and coming to this – his – world. Now the day cannot come quickly enough. Less than a week.

We wait a moment longer while Dex, Beq and Kelvin pay their own respects and then make our way up through the gardens. New life is everywhere. Spring has brought the rich foliage back anew and the colours are more vibrant than ever before. So many birds have taken up residence. I don't remember the gardens in their many terraces being so full of song.

Jondar is waiting for us at the palace level, his face lined in concentration as he scrolls through data on a small handheld tablet.

'Oh good, finally,' he says. 'We've a thousand things to go through. I was just coming to find you. We have a problem.'

Con gives me a helpless look but he's brought this on himself. 'You shouldn't have been hiding for so long,' I tell him gravely.

The look of betrayal is almost comical. 'You're meant to be on my side, love.'

I laugh. I can't help it. 'I am, always. Now go help Jondar and I'll see you for dinner with Zander.'

'Not just Zander, I'm afraid,' Jondar interrupts us. He does look worried – *actually* worried. Not just his usual harried self.

Con sees it too. 'What is it? What's wrong?'

'An Imperial ship has arrived, the Gallacian. It's carrying a party from Cuore.'

Con frowns. 'We aren't expecting anyone from Cuore.'

'The Empress decided differently. She has sent us a new ambassador to "honour you for your wedding", a temporary one but with full powers. Lord Valentin Teel will be with us shortly.' Jondar's features are frozen, giving nothing away. It's a bad sign. A really bad sign.

'Well,' says Con, and that strange kind of cool mask slips over his face, hiding the man I love from me. 'We would be well advised to meet him as soon as possible. Crown Prince Lysander first though. My future brother-in-law takes precedence. Lord Teel will be welcome to join us this evening. In the interests of diplomacy.' Not *the new ambassador*, I notice. Con hasn't accepted him as that yet. Certainly not as the voice of the Empress here. Ambassadors are not Con's favourite thing. He remembers the Gravian ambassador, Choltus, far too clearly. He also remembers, as I do, that the Imperial ambassadorial representatives did nothing to help us at all.

Jondar's face twists almost in pain. 'Con…'

'Family first, Jondar.' He smiles, a thin hard smile. 'And my wife-to-be has not seen her brother in far too long.'

'Very well, Anthaem. I will make arrangements.' Jondar gives a formal bow and finally relaxes. 'And Bel, Arianne is looking for you, by the way.'

I swear and in spite of all that is happening, Con snorts with less than regal laughter. Not very kingly at all.

There's no putting this off. I head for my quarters to find my chief lady-in-waiting and discover what I've done wrong this time.

Chapter Three

Petra

They've billeted Zander and his company in quarters not far from mine in one of the remaining older structures, the kind formed from curves and arches, decorated with painted tiles and lush fabrics. I had a team sweep the rooms for security threats last night and double checked myself this morning. Bedchamber, sitting room, bathroom, balconies and terrace. The views are much better than mine, out over the gardens with their riot of colour and life. It's opulent, or as opulent as they can make it after the invasion where many of the Anthaese treasures were stripped away and stolen. But then, they're creative in so many ways. You'd never guess.

Zander's ship, the Valiant, remains in orbit and I'm sure there's a full crew there too. As it is, Daria is nearby with five guards billeted in the adjoining quarters. I don't know any of them, but given the looks they cast my way, they know me. Or at least they know of me. It's not comfortable. I wonder what they've heard, but then I decide I don't want to know.

I retreat to my own quarters as soon as possible. I've never run away from anything in my life, and I'm not running away now either. Tactical retreats are not the same thing.

Dwyer fusses around me. He has tomorrow's dossiers ready and waiting.

'Will there be anything else, ma'am?' he asks. Where I come from only members of the royal family have equerries and the Merryns don't seem to bother with them at all. Here it's royal household and senior ranking officials and I was firmly told not to argue about it by Jondar, with Thom smirking away behind him, in that infuriating way he does. Besides, Dwyer is only fifteen and I think he's here to learn from me – ancestors help him. Even so, there's something hard and unyielding in him that I recognise. He's seen too much in his short life. Slight and fair, his grey eyes are like flint.

War orphans. We've that in common, although I'd never let him know it.

'Nothing else for tonight, Dwyer,' I tell him.

He doesn't move. When I look up from the paperwork, he's frowning at me. 'Aren't you going to change, ma'am?'

Oh ancestors, he's been listening to Jondar. Or Arianne. Bel's chief lady-in-waiting is eager to get her hands on me now that Bel is playing by her rules and being queenly.

'Dwyer, how well do you know me by now?'

He at least has the good grace to blush.

'You're dining with the crown prince of Vairian. You're representing the military of Anthaeus.'

He's given up trying to fancy me up for Con and Bel, but this is a bold new tactic. I try to read his face and then I see it. Hero worship. Great. Just what I need.

'I've dined with him before. And in far less attractive circumstances than here. The food wasn't anything to write home about either.'

He fidgets. I know I make him uncomfortable when I talk like that. Even now I make so many of the Anthaese uncomfortable. Bel has a way of charming them, as well as being their hero. Which, I'm told, by extension I am as well. They just can't seem to cope with my determination to stay away from their elaborate gowns and refusal to play the girl. My intent is, against all odds, to just be me. Stubborn to the core. Even a fifteen year-old soldier who has seen far too much death can't handle it.

I relent, just a little. 'Oh fine, lay out my formal uniform. You can put on all the extra shiny bits you want to as well. Go on. Hurry. It'll take me at least half an hour to get it all on.'

He gives a smart salute. I guess I'm lucky it's not a bow. I'm going to regret this. Tonight and the next time there's an event like this. He vanishes into the dressing room where I hear the rustling of clothes and a suspicious amount of clinking.

I know what Zander is going to say. I just know it.

*

'That's a *lot* of medals, Petra.'

I made Dwyer take off half of them already. I just don't need Zander's judgement, especially when he's wearing an Imperial star on his left lapel and an Order of Clatheen sash. Like he earned that. Plus the ceremonial sword hanging at his side is the very definition of overkill.

I almost make a crack about his oversized weapon. Almost.

'She isn't wearing most of them,' Bel adds unhelpfully as she sweeps by in a gown that looks like it was spun from starlight on water. I feel like an oaf, standing there. A particularly plain oaf. And it would be much worse if I tried wearing something like that. She's tiny and delicate. I'm… well, I'm not. I'm made for war. Normally I wouldn't care. It wouldn't occur to me at all…

But nothing here is normal.

I hazard a glance up into Zander's face and our eyes snag on each other. Damn it. Why is he staring at me?

'Conleith and Belengaria are too generous,' I say carefully.

'From what I heard you earned every one. And more.'

I narrow my eyes and he grins. What is he up to? As a server goes by he refreshes our glasses with a sparkling wine from Melia. It tastes of sunshine and gooseberries, like the ones they grew in my village near Elveden, and makes me momentarily homesick.

'Zander?' I ask as quietly as I can. 'What do you think you're doing here?'

'Attending my sister's wedding, of course,' he replies with all the carelessness I'd expect of a prince. If I didn't know him. There's something beneath that answer. He smiles and clinks his glass against mine. I'm not convinced. It's a long way to come and he was on Cuore for a long time. And Cuore, it seems, has followed after him.

'Bel's right. You need watching.'

One eyebrow goes up in amusement. He leans in closer and I'm trapped by those hazel eyes. My breath gets caught somewhere in my throat.

'And you're still the one to watch me, are you?'

A dozen witty retorts drain away as all I can think about is his mouth and how close it is. The old magic hasn't gone anywhere. I'm just as much a fool as ever I was. But I know where this leads.

Nowhere good.

Before I have to say anything or make a move, there's a burst of excitement from the door to the audience chamber. Scandalised noises. We both turn to look, everyone does. You can't help it.

A small party enters, looking like something from the society and scandal media on Cuore. I've never seen anything like it. Old Anthaeus has its moments but this is so much more elaborate.

They're beautiful. Every single one of them, male and female. Their slender faces are ethereal and they wear jewellery that looks like spun glass. The gowns on the women cradle their bodies, enhancing and highlighting every feature. The men have tailored frock coats in peacock colours, trimmed with gold. Not one of them has hair in a natural shade. Rather it seems to change as they move, shimmering and glowing with hues like summer. They are birds of paradise surrounded by a flock of starlings.

In their midst is a man as different and as breathtakingly beautiful as can be.

His hair is a dark reddish brown, like polished mahogany, and it's cut short at the back while the front hangs longer, almost down to his high cheekbones, over large, almond-shaped eyes that tilt high at the corners and give him the look of some kind of cat. They gleam like silver. He's pale, and lustrous, as if he's made of ice. Unlike the others, his clothes are all black, trimmed with a hint of silver. He looks like a god among them, like the old tales of fae creatures and the one dark master of them all. It's as if the simpler his apparel, the more his beauty shines through.

I think my mouth may be hanging open. I close it hurriedly. I've never seen anyone like him. Never.

'Valentin,' Zander says, in a soft voice. It's almost the tone of a long lost lover.

'Sorry? What?' I don't even look at him. I can't. I'm transfixed as the party from Cuore sweeps through the now stunned and silent room and greet Con with a deep and profound respect I wouldn't have expected from them.

'Valentin Teel,' Zander says, a little more firmly now. 'Lord Teel, more properly.' He gives a brief and slightly bitter laugh. 'I wonder what he did this time.'

'What do you mean?'

It's Daria who answers. She moves up beside us, on silent feet. *She* hasn't been forced into a decorated travesty of a uniform. I'd like to see the fool who tried. She looks cool and efficient, the perfect soldier. I envy her so much right now. 'The Empress doesn't let him just wander around the galaxy at a whim, you know. She likes to keep him close. You can see why, can't you?'

It isn't actually a question. I *can* see why. If you had something so... *magical* to hand why would you ever release it?

'Where's he from?'

'Cuore,' Daria says, with a dismissive tone. 'He's lived all his life in the Imperial capital. You're looking at generations of the finest Imperial selective breeding and gene manipulation in person. The story is he was born on the Firstworld, but I doubt it. He likes to spin stories about himself, the bigger the better.'

'He's the perfect specimen of mankind, if you believe him,' Zander says.

Daria snorts in derision. 'Well *you* certainly did, your Highness. He's pretty, but he isn't exactly loyal. Has his pick of lovers, women and men, and goes through them faster than a Melian partygirl.'

Zander's laugh is strange. It doesn't even sound like his laugh, not the one I remember. Perhaps he learned it there. On Cuore. The Empress demanded his presence and it was a long time before he left. He was clearly enjoying all the Imperial capital had to offer. Perhaps with Teel.

I don't know how to feel about that. 'Jealous' is the first word that springs to mind, but I'm not sure who of.

'You know him?'

'Of course. Don't mind Daria. She's just overprotective.'

Daria doesn't look in any way overprotective. If anything she looks exasperated with him. Was she there the whole time on Cuore too? Looking after him? Trying to keep him in line? I'm about to say something to her but she turns away, looking for her troops who are manning the corners of the room and being eyed warily by my troops.

The formalities over, the royal niceties addressed, Con and Bel talk with the group from Cuore easily enough. It almost looks like a normal conversation now, at a completely normal party. Con is discussing the latest developments in solar tech with one of the women, the blue haired one. She's clinging to his every word.

I'm distracted for a moment and that's my fatal mistake. Before I know what's happening, Zander has slipped his arm in mine and is propelling me forward. 'Come on, I'll introduce you.'

Horrified, there's nothing I can do but go with him. Normally I wouldn't balk at making a scene, but right now it feels sacrilegious. I look back over my shoulder, seeking help. Daria stays where she is, shaking her head.

So there I am, with Zander – his prize or his pet, or I don't know what – about to be shown off to members of the Empress's own court. To the Empress's *favourite*. Con smiles and greets Zander courteously as he joins them. He's family – he can come and go as he pleases and protocol just has to deal with it. Bel, however, has a little crease of puzzlement marking the space above the bridge of her noise.

The woman with pale blue hair which falls all the way down her back in rich glossy waves looks at me as if Zander has produced some kind of farm animal. She covers her mouth to hide a snide smile and turns to her friend, ignoring us.

I know this is a mistake. I move to step back but Zander's hand on my elbow is like iron. I can't get away without making a scene and that's the last thing I want to do. I have enough eyes staring at me.

'Val,' Zander says in a familiar way that seems wildly out of place here. 'I'm surprised to see you away from the court.'

Valentin Teel tilts his head to one side, studying us. I can feel his gaze taking in everything.

'Lysander.' He positively purrs Zander's name. His voice is melodic, rippling through the air, strangely soothing. 'Where else would I be? This wedding is the event everyone is talking about. And your charming sister is quite the celebrity. After all you told me of her on Cuore, how could I resist?'

Bel laughs, a little self-consciously. She hates attention like this but honestly, after previous publicity stints as 'the Bloody Bride' and the 'the Saviour of Anthaeus' she can't avoid it. Sounds like Zander has been upping her reputation as well. And by extension his own, no doubt.

He hasn't let go of my arm either. I'm standing there like a really unattractive ornament no one has the nerve to point out. An interloper.

I shift on the balls of my feet and try to withdraw again. No such luck.

'Aren't you going to introduce Petra properly after you dragged her over here, Zander?' Bel asks pointedly. I'm really not sure if that helps or not. I'm better lingering in the background, watching the room, guarding. I am really not made for this sort of thing and it always ends with someone upset. If I'm lucky that's as far as it goes.

'Of course.' He snaps to attention as if suddenly remembering me. So flattering. Such a gentleman. It almost makes being pulled into the spotlight against my will worth it to see him embarrassed. Except for all the ways it completely doesn't. 'General Petra Kel, hero of Anthaeus, may I introduce Lord Valentin Teel—'

'—hero of absolutely nothing,' Teel finishes for him and he sweeps my hand into his, bowing low. Before I know what's happening or can calculate how to react, his lips press to my knuckles.

My skin shivers and at the same time my throat goes tight. I suppress a tremor of surprise, perhaps even desire, though I thought

I had smothered all sorts of childish fantasies like that long ago. They don't help a soldier. Ever. He looks up at me through the shadows of his hair and smiles wickedly. Just for a moment. Like he knows the effect he has on me, revels in it. Perhaps it's the effect he has on everyone. Judging by the adoring attendants, and the way Zander is floundering, perhaps it is.

'The honour is mine, General Kel.'

'Lord Teel,' I reply, and somehow my voice manages to sound cold and aloof, unimpressed. How that happens, I have no idea. It's not intentional, I just don't know how to respond to this. A glimmer of intrigue flickers across his face as he straightens, and his face is once more perfectly composed. You wouldn't imagine for a moment that his grin had ever been there.

'I heard stories about the occupation,' he says. 'Terrible stories, but also tales of great heroism and endurance. Her Imperial Majesty would have me report back on what really happened. And of course a royal wedding is always a cause for celebration and delight.'

'She doesn't believe us?' Con asks, a sliver of ice punctuating each word.

Teel spreads his hands wide in supplication. 'On the contrary, the words of the people of Anthaeus are the few she does believe. She mistrusts the media, journalists and so forth. She believes there is an agenda behind their words.'

I exchange a glance with Bel, but even as I do, I recall the sensationalist headlines and prurient reports which followed our liberation of the planet. The Empress might be wise.

But we've sent testimonies, we've sent reports and in the aftermath we were promised reparations. The Empire, the aligned planets, and all parties to the interstellar accords agreed to sanction Gravia. Nothing transpired. Not yet. There's always another hoop to leap through. This is just the latest. The words come out before I think twice about it.

'So are you here to check up on us then?' I ask. There's no point in letting him beat around the bush, after all.

I don't know if I startle or amuse him.

'I am her eyes and ears. Lysander, every word you said was true. I should never have doubted you.' He smiles at me and there's true pleasure in his eyes. 'You really are charmingly direct, General.'

I'm not sure when Zander released my elbow or if I pulled free without realising. I'm standing on my own now, and I'm irritated. What has Zander been saying about me now?

I give Teel an arch look. 'I'm known for it.'

Beyond him Jondar has turned as white as a snowfield. Bel is struggling not to laugh because she's fed up as well and we've always seen things the same way. The woman with the blue hair looks fit to strangle me. I'd like to see her try. Con… well, you can never tell with Con. He has a face that gives very little away.

We all know, it is not a good idea to insist I attend diplomatic events. How many times do I need to prove that?

And then a hand presses to the small of my back, an intimate and tender gesture. It's Zander's hand. I'd know his touch anywhere. It's unexpected, this gesture of support, and I can't say how grateful I am for it. Surprised. But grateful.

'Shall we go into dinner?' Bel asks lightly, as if nothing had happened. As if I really hadn't just said something that implied the favourite of the Empress was the spy everyone knows him to be. She links her arm with Con, the devoted fiancée, and effortlessly leads the guests towards the dining room adjoining the reception. Lord Teel moves at their forefront, the blue haired woman stiff and irritated beside him.

They go ahead of us, even though this was meant to be a dinner in Zander's honour.

Once they're out of sight, the usurped guest of honour laughs. 'You were perfection as always, Petra.'

I'm pretty sure that's sarcasm. I decide to ignore it.

'Who is that woman with the blue hair?'

'Lady Kaeda de Lorens, daughter of the Empress's third cousin, Head of Imperial Research and the would-be Lady Teel. Mind you, there are a lot of would-be Lady Teels around the place.'

I can see why. Power, position, looks, charm and humour. There's a lot to like. At least he seemed to take me seriously. Even if no one else does.

It's almost as if Zander reads my mind. His voice drops lower and a strange look of concern flickers over his carefree face. 'He's dangerous, Petra.'

Like I need the warning? From him? I bristle. Everything about Zander rubs me up the wrong way. He knows exactly what buttons to press. 'So am I.'

Zander just shakes his head and his voice is strange. Now he sounds like the Zander I used to know. 'Not like him, Pet.'

I freeze. No one has called me Pet in over two years. Before I can formulate a reply, he's gone, heading for the dining room after the others. I should follow. I'm going to make yet another scene arriving late. And I can't not arrive at all. But I can't seem to make myself move right now.

I knew this would be a disaster. I'm not keeping Zander in check. I'm making everything worse.

He has got himself into the bad graces of the Empress. We all know that. He was summoned to Cuore to answer for rash words said in public and then fought a war for Anthaeus rather than go. When he had no choice but to obey he was stuck there for months at her pleasure. And now, when he has finally come back to us – not even to his homeworld, mind you, but to his future brother-in-law's planet for his sister's wedding, a convention even the Empress wouldn't cross – he's followed by the most prominent member of the Imperial Court next to the Empress herself. Her favourite. Her eyes and ears. Her hand in the shadows, the one which wields a knife.

Bel thinks Zander is in trouble. I'm inclined to agree with her.

If Zander needs protecting, it's from Valentin Teel.

Chapter Four

Petra

There's a routine to the court, one which Jondar keeps running with a fanatical zeal. He's good at it, that's for sure. I know he's not the only one making everything go to plan, but he's been doing it all his adult life and knows the ins and outs of it like no one else. His is the sure hand on the tiller.

The next few afternoons and evenings are going to be a trial of dinners and entertainments, and I have no escape this time around. As a general reporting directly to Con and Bel, I have to be there.

Kaeda de Lorens is sitting between Con and Zander. She has eyes that are far too clever for my liking and she's alternating her attention between them. She questions Con about his work and flatters his intellect, I'm sure. But her hands stray to Zander too much. I bet he loves that. It won't be long before she's actually sitting in his lap.

The banqueting hall isn't the biggest of the remaining rooms in the palace. Once it was a minor receiving room and it was one of the few that survived the liberation. I had a lot to do with the explosions there so I feel a bit guilty about that. The ballroom for example, collapsed when Thom and I blew up the generator during a fight with the Gravians, and while that wasn't entirely our fault – a lot of the structural damage had happened in the invasion itself – it had been beautiful.

This room has arched doors down one side, all glazed with delicately shaded panes, which lead out onto the terrace. The vaulted ceiling is painted a deep blue with tiny golden stars picked out in delicate patterns. The window which dominates the far end is a circle overlooking the western hills and as the setting sun hits it, the room is bathed in gold. It's beautiful, making the most of ancient Anthaese architecture and the splendour of this world. It's designed to impress. I'm hoping it's doing the trick.

I pour myself another glass of sparkling water into the slender crystal wineglass and sip it. I'm sitting next to Thom, who leans back in his seat and laughs at something his other dinner companion says. It's so easy for him, isn't it? I just push some of the succulent pink fish around in its cream sauce and try to fade into the background. Maybe I should have accepted more wine instead. It just didn't seem like a good idea. Not with Zander and the Cuoreans here. I want my head clear. I had some earlier and it's enough.

'I'm sure General Kel could tell us all sorts of war stories,' Kaeda says from the other end of the table, loud enough for everyone to hear. At least she's stopped quizzing Con on his latest inventions. He's never going to tell her. Or at least I hope not. Maybe this is some kind of different tack. I don't care for it.

The table goes quiet, expectant, as I look up at her, and unavoidably, at Zander, right beside her. I wonder which she'd like – when Bel's lady-in-waiting was turned into a Mecha while still alive and sent to back to us as a spy and assassin? When Con was tortured to appease our enemies?

I catch Daria's eye, further up the table. If anything I'd say she looked as annoyed as I feel, but I couldn't be sure. I mean, she usually looks like that.

'Everyone here has war stories,' Con interrupts before I can say something terrible. 'Why not something else? There's an old story we recently translated from the ancient city far below us, carved in hieroglyphs, thousands of years old…'

I almost sigh. It's a mixture of relief and resignation. I know what's coming even if none of the visitors have figured it out yet. At least I don't have to speak.

'Uh oh, ready to sit here for another four hours?' Thom whispers to me under his breath. I glare at him and he just grins. Lucky I heard him and not his husband.

Con's stories sometimes need charts and a series of explanatory slides. He's not one of life's natural storytellers. I pour myself some more water and wonder again why I haven't switched back to wine.

'It tells of a goddess, or a being of great power – the word doesn't really translate specifically – who came to Anthaeus in a thunderstorm. She made her home beneath the earth, among the stones and the crystals, swimming in their currents as if in the sea. It's an interesting phrase isn't it? The crystals as the sea? We've found that the Anthaese crystals carry vibrations and energies in a way that is far superior to those found elsewhere, the same way water is a conductor—'

Bel smiles, nudges him a little. 'The goddess?'

'Oh yes, The Coparius. Or that's as near as I've been able to establish her name from conversations with the Rondet. The stories are far older than them. She was their goddess for a few thousand years. Her touch could bring the sweetest of dreams – a lovely phrase – and to know her was to adore her. She could divine any secret and grant her servants their hearts' desires. I should really arrange to show you the carvings, shouldn't I?'

There's a pause and Valentin Teel fills it with only the slightest delay. I'm pretty sure the enthusiasm is feigned.

'That would be an honour, your Majesty.'

'I'll speak to the archaeologist in charge, Professor Dain Fuccil. Do you know him? I believe he has lectured extensively on Cuore.'

Teel laughs gently. 'I'm not one for lectures, your Majesty. Unless the lecturer is particularly enchanting.' He winks at Con, actually winks at him. Is he – is he flirting with the Anthaem?

Or at least, trying to. Con is oblivious.

'Oh, you should try to hear him speak. He's wonderful. Anyway, where was I?'

'The Coparius,' Jondar supplies dutifully. 'The *Stoneheart*.'

Thom mouths the words 'suck up' at him. How Jondar keeps a straight face I don't know.

'Yes, the Stoneheart, well there was an uprising eventually, or they left behind their belief and moved on in science and engineering. And the Coparius became just a word. It's in their language. Look…'

He uses his knife to sketch out a symbol in the sauce on his plate and lifts it up.

There's something about the symbol. I can't explain it but it sets my teeth on edge.

'What does that mean?' Kaeda asks. She gazes at it, fascinated. 'How is it used now?'

'It means *heartless*,' he says. 'Not the most flattering end for a goddess, is it?'

Coparius. Bringer of dreams with a heart of stone. I haven't heard the story before. Not exactly a comforting bedtime tale.

*

After dinner, there's music, a quiet and delicate string quartet. I step out onto the terrace. It doesn't surprise me when Zander follows me.

He's never been able to leave well enough alone. I'm down the stairs to the lower terrace before he catches up with me and I can't get away.

'Hello, Petra,' he says gently.

I really don't want to talk to him. But I missed him. It's been too long. 'Escaping?'

'It seemed like a good idea. Kaeda de Lorens is very…'

'Handsy?'

He gives me an admonishing look. 'Enthusiastic.'

'Wonderful. Maybe you're the one who needs to be careful. You don't want to end up with a wife just yet, do you?'

He shrinks back at the thought and I grin. Unfair, maybe, but maybe not, given the reaction.

I left him, I remind myself. *I had to*. Still, I'm glad he doesn't appear quite so eager to find someone else.

'Perhaps she's more interested in Con,' he says absently.

'Better not let your sister hear that.'

He laughs, a short, almost broken noise. 'In his brain. In his inventions. She's a scientist too, you know?'

I snort, trying to picture her in a lab. Or in anything other than her flimsy gown. 'Her? What's she specialise in? Cosmetics?'

Zander shakes his head and smiles, and this time I can see the amusement is genuine.

'Never change, Petra. I should go back.' He leans in and kisses my cheek before I realise what he's doing. It's an easy gesture, something relaxed and comforting and… The scent of him is the same, the warmth coming from his skin, and it still sends little shivers of familiarity alight inside me. Even now.

'Wouldn't want to miss anything.' I just can't help myself. His face falls for a moment before he turns away and starts back up the steps.

I'll wait to make sure he's back inside, just in case.

Then I hear it, a tapping of metal on stone. It's not something that has a place here, not in the citadel. I listen intently and rap my fingertips on the coms. I don't sound an alarm yet. It's just a feeling. So far.

But I've learned to trust my gut.

Something slides through the shadows on the wall at the far end of the gallery ahead of me. I suck in a breath and pull a blaster from my belt. There's a figure there, dressed in black, tall and slim. And I have never seen anything move like that.

No, I lie. I have seen it. There's a gleam of metal against skin and I know what that means. Implants.

Mecha.

What the hell is a Mecha doing here? During the liberation we destroyed so many of those man-machines made from the dead, lethal and terrible, implanted with tech to control them and turn them into weaponry. I press the alarm on my coms but I don't dare say a word. I just watch it as it moves towards the wall and then looks towards the terrace outside the banqueting hall I've just left.

It's following Zander. It has to be. I thought we'd destroyed every last one left here during the Gravian withdrawal but this looks different. It moves to the arch and leaps. Metal spikes extend from its hands and feet, digging in to the old stone. Slowly, it starts to climb.

'Halt or I fire!' I yell at it. It twists around, ocular implants fixed on me. I hear the whirr of the mechanics as it focuses.

'Kel, Petra,' it intones in a bleak, emotionless voice. 'General. Vairian. Eliminate on sight with extreme prejudice.'

I don't hesitate a moment longer. I open fire, but the thing pushes off from the wall, leaping through the air straight at me. I dive aside, hit the ground and roll. It scrambles across the mosaic floor like a lizard and comes up again. The weapons fire glances off it. Shielded then. Damn. That means close quarters. We learned that during the invasion.

I reach for the long knife in my belt, and sink back as it advances. I watch it, looking for a weakness. It doesn't move like the Mechas I've faced before. There's something more animal about it. It's unnerving. Where are the backup? Security should be here by now.

It leaps forward again, quick as a cat, and I twist but I can't avoid it. There are long metal talons on its hands, the ones it was using to cling to the wall. They score through the yellow stone where my head just was, a shower of sparks lighting up its face. The mouth is wide and lupine, gleaming with teeth which appear to be metal hooks. I hear that whir again as it focuses on me once more.

I scramble back from it, but I'm too slow. It's on me this time, legs pinning mine down as I struggle. The metal claws sink into my shoulder and I can't help the noise of raw agony that comes out of me as it twists them. My other hand is still free though, the one with the knife.

I go for the jaw, stabbing up through the mouth and into the throat. Black fluid gushes out on me. There's blood there, but something else as well which burns like acid.

I hear guards arrive, hear the shots fired and the rebounds as they strike the shield. If I'm unlucky they'll hit me instead.

'General, can you get clear?' That sounds like Lorza, a corporal of the fourth royal guard. *No I can't get clear.* Neither can it. I hold on to it as it convulses on my knife, the blades in my flesh twisting and tearing.

'Petra!' Thom yells but someone else is there first. Zander rips the creature from me and the ceremonial sword he wore all evening, the one I thought was just for show, takes its head right off.

He stands over me, drops it and then looks down. He's trembling, though you'd have to be standing close to see it.

'Are you okay?'

'Sure,' I lie, breathless, blood gushing from my shoulder. 'Never better.'

I start to get up but he drops to his knees beside me and stops me. 'What was that?'

'A Mecha. It was heading up towards you lot. After you, I suspect. It was alone?'

'Scan the area,' Lorza snaps at her security team. 'Multi-spectrum. I want to know if there's another one of those things anywhere on this planet.'

Good woman, Lorza. One of the best we've trained. I found her in the forest when we formed Bel's guard. Neat, precise, a good leader. Needs to be faster, but I don't have to tell her that right now. Freeing myself of Zander, I pull myself painfully to my knees clutching my shoulder. Ancestors, it hurts.

'I've never seen one like that,' I say to Thom. 'Con's going to want to have a look at it.' I lean on him, mainly because he's the first one to me who I'm going to accept a hand from. Zander's just watching, his face pale and his lips in a tight line of anger. I remember that look. It means trouble. 'It knew who I was, Thom. It knew my name.'

Chapter Five

Bel

The arrivals from Cuore, coupled with the attack, have put the whole court on edge. Now we have to accommodate the eyes and ears of the Empress and all her minions while we investigate a new form of Mecha, the likes of which Con has never seen. No one has. I get Jondar to arrange for the party from Cuore to go on a tour of the rebuilding works with the chief architect. It's not often that a creative genius is supremely boring but Ultan manages it, especially when he gets on to the subject of matching columns and arches to the aesthetic of the native Anthaese architecture and how the discoveries below ground have added to our store of knowledge about their building techniques. That should be safe enough.

Valentin Teel is determined to be all charm to all of us, to winkle his way into our good graces, so he'll comply… but for how long? We don't have much time to put this in motion.

He needs watching. He needs close watching. And I have an idea.

And that's not all. Halie, the royal doctor, comes to us shortly before breakfast with a worrying report. There's some kind of illness spreading quite rapidly among the people near Montserratt. Just what we need. As populated areas of Anthaeus go it suffered the worst during the occupation. *A sleeping sickness*, she calls it. She doesn't have any more information than that, but she'll get to the bottom of it. She always does and the team she's built up are second to none.

'I was thinking of sending Liette up that way to source more crystals,' Con suggests. 'Can she help?'

Halie gives him a hard stare. 'She can accompany my team. But we need to consider how this might be spreading. We don't want a full blown epidemic on our hands.'

'How's Petra?' I ask her.

Halie rolls her eyes towards the ceiling. 'Fine. I've patched her together again. She's going to be tender for a while but the reGen patches have done their work.'

Petra is already back in her office when I go to find her, with Dwyer fussing about her not resting. She's ignoring him, but that's just normal for her. When he sees me, Dwyer goes entirely quiet and his eyes take up half his face. Normal for him. He does it every single time, even though I visit Petra all the time.

I'm used to it. Quite a few of the Anthaese have a similar reaction to me. Until they get to know me.

'Walk with me?' I ask Petra.

Dwyer makes an attempt to protest but Petra is already on her feet. 'I'll be fine,' she tells him, the long suffering tone a subtle warning.

'I'll look after her, Dwyer. I promise.'

My guard, Beq, trails behind us, carefully giving us space but close enough. The last time I wandered off alone he sulked so I let him stay. Petra looks tired, like she hardly slept last night at all. Stress, I suppose. Or pain. A night spent in the infirmary is hardly relaxing, although with Petra it might act as a break. If she's not training or overseeing troops, she's up to her neck in paperwork. I must persuade her to take a holiday soon, though it will be like trying to make an addict give up their drug of choice. Of course, it would be easier if I didn't keep finding impossible tasks for her to perform.

Like now.

She looks suspicious as we walk in silence. Her golden brown eyes study me and I'm sure she can see that I'm up to something. She reads me too well. But she doesn't argue. Her hair is tied back from her face, pulled tight into a pony tail so it's like a long black mass of curls down between her shoulder blades. She's in that sleek black body armour again which makes her look so deadly. Or, rather, as deadly as she is. Why she feels the need to wear armour as a daily outfit should probably tell me more about her worries than anything she'd actually admit.

Mind you, she wasn't wearing it last night, and look what happened. Perhaps she has a point.

I think of the way both Zander and Teel acted around her before dinner last night. Sometimes armour is figurative as well as practical. Which makes this harder. All of it.

'Where are we going?' Petra asks. I haven't spoken in about five minutes, just walked along, lost in my own thoughts. And she's just followed, ever loyal.

I have to be careful I'm not taking advantage of that. I have to give her the chance to back out. Not that she would take it. But still. I have to try.

'Con's study,' I tell her.

'Has he found anything out about the Mecha? Where it came from? What it was?'

'He's found many things. He'll explain.' I don't want to take a chance that what I have to tell her will be overheard by anyone. There's too much at stake.

'I'm sure I will. Bel, are you – are you all right?' She towers over me, always has done. But there's no one I'd feel safer with. No one still alive.

'Fine.'

'Fine isn't really an answer, Princess.'

'I'm worried about Zander,' I lie. Well, not actually a lie. I am always worried about Zander. More so now than I ever was when I thought he was just coming for the wedding.

'Zander.' His name comes out a bit flat. The way it had when I first asked her to keep an eye on him. Perhaps I shouldn't have. But I needed her invested right from the beginning.

I pick up my pace. She just follows, her long legs easily letting her match me. She's fully aware that I'm avoiding talking to her about something. But she's good at following orders. My orders anyway.

I still wonder if Zander has forgiven her. Or if he ever will.

He saved her life last night. I mean, to hear Thom and the corporal tell it she was most of the way there already, but my brother dealt the killing blow.

'Before we see the others, I have a request…' My words trail off. I'm not sure about this. It's not part of the plan.

'You mean an order, don't you?'

I can never get anything past her. She knows me too well. 'Teel has taken an interest in you. I was thinking—'

She turns on me, horrified. 'Bel, no!'

'I'm not saying you have to do anything. Just… just encourage him.'

Her flat look hides everything but I can sense she's less than impressed with my idea. '*Encourage* him…'

'He's just a man. Distract him.'

'I'm not *that* distracting.'

'I'm sure you can be.' She doesn't look like she believes me but she doesn't say another word the rest of the way. I think she guesses why I wanted to ask her on her own.

The moment we reach Con's study I hear someone clattering around in there. Poor Con is following my brother about, trying to stop him fiddling with everything in sight.

'What does this do?'

'That's a new type of gear. You see, it—'

'What about this?'

'That's an experimental blaster, variable settings. It's a bit unstable. Please, don't—'

As I enter, I see that Con has got it back and is deactivating it as quickly as he can. Zander hasn't stopped though. Zander never stops.

'This is pretty.' He picks up a small honeycomb of tiny polished crystals set in a panel of glass and bronze.

'A power cell. Solar. It's for—'

'It's really delicate.'

'Yes, it's—'

'If you break it, you'll have to pay for it, Zander,' I warn him. Petra closes the door behind her, eyeing him warily. Beq takes up position outside. Con smiles and I lean in to embrace him, just for a moment. I can't help myself. I just need to be near him sometimes. Times like this. 'Where's Thom?'

'On the way with Jondar.'

'Good.' I look at the way Zander and Petra are eyeing each other and sigh. Who would have thought last night's attack would have made them *more* awkward? Or is it what I've just asked her to do? Thom and Jondar can't get here quickly enough. 'Put that solar cell down, Zander.'

'You even *sound* like our mother, you know that?'

His attempts at insults have got worse. He must be out of practice.

He picks up one of the crystals instead, holding it up and trying to catch the light with it. 'Can I have this? Souvenir?'

I glance at Con, who just shrugs. It's just a crystal. He can have it. Zander grins at Petra, who ignores him studiously as he pockets it. He's like a magpie, attracted by shiny objects.

We wait, making small talk and avoiding the lingering shadow of Valentin Teel and the Empress, and more importantly of the reason why we're here. It's not fair to tell them ahead of Thom, and I don't want to have to repeat myself.

But Jondar is always efficient. Even when I only asked for his help half an hour ago. He arrives with his husband in tow. Thom looks irritated and I realise I've taken him away from his trainees this morning. But they'll have to wait.

I nod to Con, who closes the door and flicks a number of switches beside it. The door seals and a coms dampener hums into life. We're cut off from the rest of the world.

'There's a lot of mystery going on here, Bel,' my brother says.

'I had a communiqué from our father,' I tell Zander. 'Relations between Vairian and the Empire are foundering. The trade lobbies have been throwing their weight around and the council of aligned worlds is refusing to get involved. He told me to get a full and unexpurgated report from you. Clearance alpha-Yolande.'

Our mother's name, a code word, and a command. Share everything. No matter what. It started as a game when we were young, code words and clearance levels. We didn't even realise he was already training us. Though what for, I don't know. We were never meant to be a ruling family. Perhaps it was habit on his part, the way he had grown up.

'We need to tread carefully,' I go on. 'What happened on Cuore? You were there for months and then you left suddenly. With Teel arriving here so quickly after you—'

'You're worried about me.' He gives me a stern look. He's still my older brother, even if he does act like an idiot at times. 'And so is Father. I've spoken to him. He knows.'

'What really happened on Cuore, Zander?' asks Con. He heard the same rumours I have, saw the reports. About drunken nights, self-destructive tendencies and a number of incidents in various clubs, parties and brothels which could have destroyed the reputation of another noble. 'We need to know.'

My brother sighs and pulls up one of the stools to sit on. He kind of folds his legs beneath it, perching there. He looks tired all of a sudden. Vulnerable. And I'm more worried than ever. Zander has never looked vulnerable to me.

'A number of things,' he said. 'None of them good. There were continual delays in my departure, additional requirements and permits. All polite, of course. Security was cited a lot. No matter what I did, no matter how outrageous, she wouldn't let me leave. And seriously, I tried everything. I should have been exiled twenty times over for the things I did there. I tried everything, outrage after outrage, tipped off the press myself to make sure it was covered. Eventually I made it out, mostly with dumb luck. When I reported back to Vairian, Father sent me here instead. Out of her reach, as it were. Out of the aligned worlds.'

'But why, Zander?' Petra asks. 'Why was she so obsessed with keeping you there? Why are they so determined to have you back?'

'The Empress wants a consort.'

There's a long, stunned silence.

'You?' I blurt out the word too loudly.

He fixes me with a flat stare. 'Yes, me. Don't worry. There's nothing romantic about it. Not even an infatuation. I would be a means to control Vairian and on Father's death bring it firmly within the Empire. Which would then tie you – and Anthaeus – in as well.'

I consider it. She hasn't had a consort for as long as I've been alive. I can't imagine what sort of role it would be. From the expression on Zander's face, not one he'd relish. I'd worried once about being married to someone older than me, about not having any choice in the matter. I remember all too well what it felt like.

'But Vairian…'

'On Father's death it would lose all independence. As would I. She needs me to be… obedient I suppose. Compliant. Not so much a husband as a servant, or a hostage. If I behave, Vairian is safe. If Vairian behaves I'm safe. And she has a way of ensuring it. Mecha tech. Just a little, just enough.'

He pulls a small box from his pocket. It's plain and unadorned, eminently practical. He hands it to Con, who opens it. There's tech inside. An implant. Con studies it with a grim, focused expression. 'This isn't Gravian,' he says at last. 'It's a brain implant but it's…' He scans it, reading through the resulting data on his screen.

There's a long silence.

'Zander… That's awful,' Petra says finally on a breath. She's gone pale. Like me, she assumed he was acting out, that he was being his usual idiot self.

'They put it all in beautiful terms of course,' Zander continues. 'That she must ensure loyalty from a consort thanks to someone several hundreds of years ago trying to stage a revolt from within. And that it's the highest honour she can offer Vairian given our valiant defence of Anthaeus and the Empire. But when you get down to it…'

'You're insurance,' Con says without looking up from the screen. 'To keep your father, and by extension us here on Anthaeus, in line. And she's going to cut out part of your brain to make you compliant.'

'Yes. Exactly. Which is the second point, the other reason our father sent me here. I've been trying to track down information on the tech they're using… or planning to use.'

Gravians. But to do a such deal with a sworn enemy of the Empire is unheard of. I glance over at Con who clearly has the same thought. Father sent Zander here, after all. To Anthaeus. Not just for my wedding but for his own sake, not for a celebration but to save his life.

And last night… the Mecha that was so much more than a Gravian Mecha ever could be…

'Con?'

He's scrolling through data again, and with a flick of his fingers he transfers it onto the screen on the wall so we can all see. The images of the dead Mecha should be shocking, but I've seen too much over the last year to be shocked any more.

'It's not Gravian. It can't be.' Con pulls up various details but I turn away. 'The tech Zander brought is the same. Here, it matches exactly. Whoever made this Mecha grafted animal elements on to the human at the core, genetically manipulating it before the implants and the programming. Gravians wouldn't do that. They're obsessed with purity. They'd find the very idea repugnant. They would never have made it… well, like this.' He gestures towards the images of the dead and broken thing.

'To be fair,' Petra cuts in with a wave of bravado. 'I made it like that.'

Zander is the only one who laughs. I half expect him to argue for credit. Did she say it just to break the pall of misery and worry over us all? I wouldn't put it past her.

'Quite,' is all Con says in response with a small flicker of a smile. 'Before it was in pieces then. I found lupine and reptilian elements, some kind of bird as well, a raptor and... look, it's a mess of gene-grafting and it'll take weeks to untangle. I'd have to get an expert in and I'm not sure whether I should even share this. It could cause panic. It wasn't left behind when the Gravians fled. It's got tech that isn't common to the Mechas they made here. It's new. And highly advanced. And I think I know where it came from.'

I can see at once where he's going with this.

'Kelta.' But it doesn't seem possible. 'The moon is dead. They took everything of worth.' The Gravians invaded Kelta before they came to Anthaeus. They killed everyone there and strip-mined it, taking everything of value, especially the crystals which power half the galaxy. Dead doesn't begin to cover what was left in their wake.

'True, but we ran scans, picked up some anomalous traces. There was a meteor shower the other night. They could have used it to mask some sort of drop.' Con goes over to the monitor and quickly brings up some of the files, working directly on the main system. Jondar joins him, pointing out several connections as they work.

Thom is staring at Zander. 'And they just told you about this plan?' Thom asks, ever the man to dig a little deeper. 'Just like that?'

Zander shakes his head. 'I think that was going to be a fun, wedding night surprise. Actually, it was Teel who passed on the information and the tech.'

'Teel?' Petra interrupts. 'Why would Teel help you like that?'

Zander shrugs, but he doesn't meet her gaze. He does that when he's not sure how someone will react. And when he's not telling the whole truth. 'Why would Teel do anything? It has to benefit him in some way. Maybe he doesn't want the Empress marrying anyone. It might threaten his position.'

'A puppet prince wouldn't threaten him. And why would he then follow you here?'

'I imagine he was sent. I don't know everything, Petra.' He gives her an exasperated glare.

She just smiles back at him. It's one of her least pleasant smiles. 'There's a first.'

Con interrupts before a full blown war of words, or worse, can erupt between them. 'It's hard to tell because of the background radiation but there are identifiers which could indicate incursions into Anthaese space around Kelta, and from Kelta to here, all of which would violate our treaties. They've given no reason and asked no leave to land there. We only sent cursory expeditions after the liberation. Once we knew the moon was dead, and the Gravians had definitely gone, we left it while we dealt with more pressing matters here. If there's some kind of outpost up there now, even on a tactical level, it's very bad news for Anthaeus.'

'We have to go,' I say. 'We have to find out. And if they are there, we need to drive them off.' As calls to arm go, it's not exactly rallying. But that has never been my forte.

'We need a small group,' says Zander. 'Hand-picked and trusted. Thom, Petra and I, some of my crew, a few others, your best and most discreet. No one else can know. No one outside this room and those we take. And while we're gone, you're going to have to keep Teel busy. I mean swamp him with balls, exhibitions, tournaments, trips to the hidden city.'

'And the Rondet,' Con says suddenly.

Even Zander falls silent, looking at him in shock. After a moment I find a single word. 'What?'

'Let's take him to see the Rondet,' he goes on. 'It doesn't have to be here. We can make a ceremony of it. We're Anthaese. We can make a ceremony of anything. He wants to know about them. Couldn't stop asking me about them after dinner. Let's have Aeron or Favre look inside his mind and see what they can see. But... let's make it so he thinks he's working it out himself. Give him a secret to distract him.'

It's more devious than I would have guessed. But Con always has a way of surprising me. I glance at Petra. We're all making plans to distract Valentin Teel these days.

'Fine. If they agree. They may not want him to know more about them.'

'We have two days until the wedding,' Jondar says. 'The masked ball is tomorrow. You'll be missed if you go before then.'

'Then immediately after the wedding,' I say. 'We'll make a ship ready for your team. Find out what's happened on Kelta and get evidence. There may be more of those things. If it's Gravians they've made a huge leap forward and that's bad enough. If the Empire has forces stationed there, we need to know.'

Whatever happens, the Empress is not taking my brother to be some sort of mindless slave. She's not getting her talons into my homeworld or my adopted one. And if she's using Kelta somehow, or has got technology from there, we need to put a stop to that right away.

Con slips his hand into mine. Either he's read the expression on my face or some echo of my feelings filtered through the psychic bond we have through the Rondet.

'We need to tell them,' he says. 'They deserve to know what we're planning to do.' Talking to Teel is a risk to the Rondet as well, one they may not agree to. They have risked so much for us.

'Of course,' I reply.

Chapter Six

Petra

I have precious little free time but I desperately need to clear my head. Bel's idea of distracting Teel isn't going to work. How could it? Especially if I'm also to head off to Kelta with Zander. Distract him too much and he's going to want to know where I am. Doctor Halie has patched my arm back together, but I still feel stiff and I need some physio. I change into my running gear and set off around the gardens. I run along each terrace, down to the bottom and then back up again. I do it several times on any given day and once I'm finally breathing, my blood pumping with adrenaline, I start to feel human again. When Zander told us about the plans the Empress has for him, something inside me tightened to a knot, hard and painful. I couldn't explain it, couldn't shift it. I have to run it loose.

What will Zander make of it if I start flirting with Teel? Not that I care. And how am I meant to flirt? I don't flirt. It's not in my nature. I'm just going to make a fool of myself. He'll see right through me. Stupid bloody plan.

And there's still Zander…

I'm on my fifth circuit, fixed and focused, aware of everything around me but letting nothing distract me, when I sense rather than see someone coming up behind me. At speed.

I twist aside at the last minute, planting my feet, bringing one arm wide to block them and the other up hard to wind them. An old trick of Shae's.

'Damn it, Petra!' Zander gasps, barely stopping in time before I bring him to his knees. He grunts as he hits the ground in front of me.

I stare at him in horror.

'What do you think you're doing?' I ask. What the hell is he doing *here*? Shouldn't he be off being princely somewhere?

'Running. I thought I was running.'

I help him to his feet, mainly because I'm the one who put him on the ground.

'Running…' I say flatly.

'I saw you running and I thought I'd join you. Is that a crime now?'

'If you weren't invited, maybe it should be.' Ancestors, he takes so much for granted. 'Asking would have been nice.'

'You never slowed down enough to ask. I've been watching you tearing along and you never even noticed.'

He brushes himself off. He'd changed too, out of the more princely attire and into plain, service clothes. They look good on him. They always have. I deliberately turn away before I start thinking things I really should not be thinking. He's going to be king one day. I have to keep that in mind. He'll marry an off-world princess, rule Vairian, and found a dynasty. He doesn't do things by half.

Then I remember the Empress's plan and that knot is back. If he gets the chance, that is. If he doesn't get trapped in her machinations. I try to picture him without that spark of independence, without that devil-may-care attitude, without everything that makes him Zander. It hurts.

Besides which, if I'm going to distract Teel, I can't be distracted by Zander.

Where are his guards? Daria wouldn't let him go off on his own like this, would she? I wouldn't. Has he given them the slip? It's a Merryn family trait, one with which, thanks to Bel, I am all too familiar. He was with Con so they may have believed he was safe. But he's not with Con now and he should have at least one bodyguard. I can't just brush him off and leave him here. I promised Bel I'd look after him. Babysit. I've been promising Bel a lot of things and I'm not certain she knows what she wants.

'Come on then,' I say brusquely, before he can say anything else. 'Let's run.'

He runs the way I do, focused, silent, determined. There's no chatter, no nonsense. *For once*, I think, *it isn't so irritating being around him*. It isn't hard or awkward. He doesn't compete with me, not like other men often do, trying to prove themselves stronger or more resilient than me. Not that they ever manage that. He just matches me. It's refreshing.

At the base of the terraced gardens I pause, stretching out my muscles by one of the reflecting pools, surrounded by the flowers of a thousand colours. He's quiet. Too quiet.

When I look up, he's staring at me.

'What?' I say.

'Do you miss it?'

What is he talking about now? 'Miss what?'

'Home.'

I consider this for a moment. I hadn't really thought about it. I don't tend to reflect on Vairian and life there. I believe things are better. Marcus Merryn is a good king, fair minded and conscientious, who takes care of his people. And though he has inherited a vow of fealty to the Empress from his predecessor, he has a way of standing up to her as well. He walks a fine line. Things are improving all round. I'm here on a world light years from home. I have a job to do. Besides, life on Vairian always carried the shadows of the past, shadows cast by my father. Everywhere I went, there was always a question in others' eyes, always the same question. Life as a Kel is not exactly easy. He doesn't understand that. He never will.

'I miss the air. It's sharper than here. Less—' I wave my hand at the flowers and the foliage. Everything about Anthaeus is bright and scented, beautiful, but sometimes it's too much for me. I remember the pines above Elveden, the way you'd smell them on a crisp clear morning. Distinct but sharp. I miss that. I don't know how I'd ever explain that to him.

'You never applied to come back.'

'Of course not. I have a job here.'

'No I mean...' he shifts awkwardly. 'To the ship.'

Oh. *To him.* To his unit on board the Hawk. Years ago, when we were traipsing across the galaxy, fighting Imperial battles, when everything was an adventure. I almost miss my step. My legs wobble and I think I'll fall. That would be the worst, wouldn't it? I'd just collapse at his feet now and make an even worse fool of myself than I already have. Not even while running, just standing there.

'I thought it was probably best, Zander. It was all too complicated. The command staff hated me. And the others thought...' I still can't say it, not to him. It didn't matter to me what the others thought. I never cared. I was used to being the outsider. Kel's daughter. But *he* cared. And it would have destroyed him, eventually. He'd never put up with everything I heard said about me and my father on a daily basis. He's obsessed with honour. They all are. And after I left... well, words had a way of reaching me no matter how far away I went. Cruel words, spoken in haste and pain no doubt. But that didn't make them less painful to hear. Not when I knew they were his. 'No one was going to miss me. And then Higher Cape fell and all the other Vairian royals died, and I was assigned to Bel and—'

'And everything changed anyway.' He shrugs, as if casting off the thought. Or maybe just pushing it back as too much to deal with right now. 'We should go back.'

I can't have this conversation with him anyway. Bel wants me to play up to another man, someone with whom Zander has a history too. I saw that. It was written all over his face the moment he saw Teel.

And I can't… I can't stand here and talk to him, as if nothing has changed. As if I didn't break his heart and he didn't break mine.

'Things to do, your Highness?' I make my tone teasing. I don't know how else to ease the mood. Default defence mechanism. I know he hates it.

I hear the movement in the bushes before I even register what it is. Instinct slams into action, propelling me towards him. Zander's face looms up, shocked and startled, as I wrap my legs around his and bring him to the ground safely beneath me.

The creature shoots past us, crashing through the low hanging branches of a nearby tree. It skids in the soft mud, turning sharply as it does so. I push myself back, positioning myself between Zander and the Mecha. It's less stealthy than the first was, made for speed and violence. A shield glimmers around it. The blaster strapped to my leg won't have any effect on it until I'm up close and personal. I grab a broken branch from the debris in its trail. It's not much but it's something.

Why didn't I leave the body armour on? I mean, I know, I was only going running and it's meant to be safe here, and running in armour is punishing, but still… I slam my hand onto the coms unit on my wrist.

'Code one, code one, attack in progress. Units to this location, beacon activated. Code one. Immediate response.'

Impossibly fast, animalistic, it bears down on me again. There are blades instead of fingers, long metal claws. They slash towards my face and I dodge back. It jerks aside as a rock slams into the side of its head. Zander hefts another one, ready to throw it as hard as the first.

'Get out of here,' I tell him.

The Mecha shakes its head, growling, and drags itself back up to stand on two legs. That's about the only thing anthropomorphic about it. The shoulders are hunched and muscled like a bear, the legs seem to bend the wrong way and the face is a mesh of technology. There isn't even a mouth. I assume it doesn't need one.

Ancestors, they can make Mechas which look just like human beings so why do this? What sort of twisted mind would create such a thing?

'I'm not leaving,' Zander says, stubborn as ever. 'It went straight for you.'

'Just to get me out of the way, Zan. Just to—'

It leaps forward again and I lash out knowing as it hits that the branch will shatter. But that's just a distraction. I sweep its legs from under it and fall with it, grabbing the blaster and bringing it up, inside the shielding. Before it can respond, I fire into the face. Three times. I choke on fumes, coughing furiously and it sparks, fizzes and goes still, a melted mass of wires and circuitry.

It's only when I go to move that I realise a sharp pain stabs me, just below my arm, between the ribs. I'm bleeding. There are shallow wounds on my arms, but the one in my side goes deep. *Not again. Ancestors, not again.* I'm only just out of the bloody infirmary. Halie's only just put me back together again. She'll have a fit.

'Petra!' Panic in Zander's voice makes my heart lurch as I turn. Coils of some kind of metal twist around his body, almost up around his throat, another Mecha, tentacled and less human than the first. He's holding back a barbed tail with a stinger. A viscous drop of liquid drips from the end. And he's losing the fight. I can't shoot it. Not now, with my vision blurring and that thing engulfing him.

'Hang on, Zander.' My words grow thicker, slurring together. Ancestors this is not good. I can feel poison pumping through my body. The claws must have been treated too.

I fire down on the wrist of the thing I've just killed. Without the shielding there's no resistance. I grab the clawed hand that stabbed me. It comes free with surprising ease. Now I have knives. Several of them.

'Stay back! That's an order, Petra.' Zander's arms are shaking, his strength failing him. The tentacles wind across his torso, cocooning him in metal, crushing him. If it can sedate him, or even simply overpower him, it can just wrap him up and carry him off. I can already feel that I'm slowing down. Whatever sedative or poison was on those blades it's already in my system. I don't have time to hesitate or to be wrong.

And I don't take orders from him.

I hurl myself at Zander, my body against his, the bladed hand in mine. I plunge it up under the remaining Mecha's jaw and up into the brain. My skin burns and a surge of electricity ravages through me but I hold on. Zander's grip fails as the shock passes through him too and the stinger comes down, into my back.

The world twists around me and the ground hits hard.

'Petra? Can you hear me?' Zander says. His face is blurring. He shakes himself free as the wires go limp and gathers me in his arms. I can feel him shaking as his hand strokes my face. 'Petra please, don't… don't…'

There isn't time for this. Where there are two, there could be more.

'Weapon.' I feel him take the small blaster in strong and sure hands. 'Hold ground. They're on the way.'

Everything slips sideways, like rainwater on a window pane.

Chapter Seven

Bel

It isn't hard to summon the Rondet, but getting them to actually listen is the trick. Rhenna prefers to fly as far as she can. Con says that I've rubbed off on her that way. Aeron is usually around. He loves Con's inventions and the discoveries, both ancient and brand new. Limasyll is, and was long ago, his home. But quite often he's too caught up in whatever has captured his interest at the moment. A bit like Con. Favre – I don't know. He was always the most distant of them. Sometimes he appears when we call. Sometimes not. More usually not.

Once upon a time, we had to travel to them while they slept beneath the ground, sheltered by the great dome of multi-coloured glass. Now they can come to us. If they are willing.

Con and I stand on the remaining tower of Limasyll, above the eastern gate. It's perfectly round, the top terrace where scented plants grow riot. I don't know how it, or they, survived the devastation. To me it's a small miracle, every time I come up here, where the warm wind blows up from the valley below us, carrying the scent of forest and the salt water beyond it. In the evenings you can pick out the lights of the settlements below Montserratt in the far distance.

'Ready?' he asks.

We hold hands, which sometimes seems to amplify our call. I don't know if that's just the way it seems to us though. Communion with the Rondet was simple enough when they hibernated in the chamber beneath the great crystal which channelled their mental abilities. They could spread their consciousness across the whole planet using the network of crystal veins and outcrops. So much of that was broken – mined, destroyed, blasted away. The crystals on Kelta were renowned as an unparalleled power source. But the ones on Anthaeus were more powerful by far. And once the Gravians had strip-mined Kelta, they turned their attention here.

I shiver, despite the warm breeze and Con's grip on my hand tightens. He doesn't like thinking about it either.

Please, I hear him send out the request. *We need to speak to you. We have news.*

And we miss you, I add, without thinking about it.

Well, it's true. I miss them, I miss the easy alliance we had. I miss their presence in my mind.

But everyone deserves their freedom, even those we love. Especially those we love.

Con pulls me into an embrace, his free hand on my cheek, and he kisses me gently. It's easy to melt against him, to know that I fit there in his arms, that I belong with him. I wouldn't be anywhere else.

A rush of wind heralds their arrival. All three perch around us, their vast wings glittering in the sunlight as they fold them back against the sleek crystalline bodies. They are almost transparent, like looking through precious gems, each carrying a different shade. Rhenna is almost like amber, her long slender head tilted to one side so she can watch us closely. Favre is all smoky quartz, and Aeron like a moss agate. Their intricately facetted eyes glint with old knowledge and new-found love of life.

When they speak it is mind to mind, but I've noticed a soft, humming purr they often make at the same time, almost like a song. I think of it as a lullaby.

'*We have missed you too, little queen*,' Rhenna says. '*You have not brought your brother this time?*'

'Not this time,' I reply.

She gives one of her purrs. '*I may have been hasty in my judgement of him. I will no longer ask you to make him leave.*'

That's as good as an apology from Rhenna. I accept it immediately with a smile.

'*Rhenna should stop acting like a child*,' Favre growls. His purr is more deep throated and intimidating, a rumble. Rhenna doesn't care, however. She flicks her tail towards him as if she's making a rude sign. Maybe she is. Favre chooses not to notice. '*You have news for us, Anthaem.*'

'News and a request for help,' Con says. He reaches out and Aeron leans into his touch, rubbing his smooth cheek against Con's palm. It's a tender and intimate gesture of friendship and fraternity.

'*We will always help you, Anthaem*,' Aeron replies. '*You and your Queen gave us back our lives and woke us from our dreaming. You rescued our world from the scourge.*'

The scourge. That is always how they refer to the Gravians.

'You helped,' I add. 'We couldn't have done it without you.'

Favre's laugh sounds deep in my mind. '*As you were so insistent in telling us.*'

Rhenna flutters her wings. A shimmer of bronze ripples through her, darkening the amber. '*She is right.*' Her ferocity reverberates through me. She's bigger than I remember, and I've seen what those claws can do. Though Favre is still larger, and Aeron a storehouse of knowledge, Rhenna is closest to me, my friend.

There are about a dozen xenobiologists writing papers on the Rondet, on their social structure and their interactions. Favre and Rhenna have no time for them at all but Aeron seems fascinated. Perhaps he's running some studies of his own. The fervent-eyed scholars who arrive looking for permission to study them really don't get it. They must look like lab rats to him, a creature his age, with his wisdom and experience. Perhaps one day he'll find one he considers worth lecturing. Or dictate a paper of his own.

Con reaches for Aeron, pressing his hand to his flank, and leaning in to commune more closely, privately.

Aeron chuckles. Perhaps Con is passing on his own thoughts on my musings.

'*These new arrivals… they worry you.*' The native Anthaese creature responds.

'*Then we should kill them.*' Rhenna replies instantly. I can feel her satisfaction at the thought. '*That will get rid of them and discourage anyone else from coming. It is really very simple, little queen. I wonder that you didn't think of it yourself.*'

I swallow a laugh. If only it was that simple. Rhenna is a childish spirit at times and sees things very much in black and white. She's also incredibly dangerous.

'That's not as straightforward as it sounds, Maestra Rhenna,' Con replies. He glares at me when I'm still smirking. Yes, I know, I'm not helping. But I really don't care. I'd love to see what Rhenna could do to the group of pampered and preened creatures who gate-crashed last night. '*Aside* from the fact that we don't just kill people for no reason… The man in question is a favourite of the Empress who rules the worlds far from here. And imagine how you would feel if an… accident occurred to Bel, or myself, for example? The Empress protects her own.'

Rhenna snorts. There's no other word for the sound she produces, and she rears back, fanning her wings out behind her. '*She probably should not send them so far away then. I should like to meet her. I would demonstrate how to protect.*'

I can only imagine.

'Rhenna, please, you know we can't hurt these people. They will cause trouble. But we also need to keep on their good side. And this man, this Teel, we must know what he knows, or what he suspects. Or what he plans.'

'*You want us to spy on him,*' Favre says. '*To peer inside his mind.*'

'Yes.'

'*We would need to form a mental communion with him. We would be taking him within ourselves. This is not something to ask lightly.*' His confusion isn't feigned. He's genuinely bewildered by the request. As if it is rude. '*You have never asked this of us before, Con.*'

'There was never a need.'

'And it isn't so different from what you did in the war. Watching the scourge, reporting on troop movements and encampments,' I add helpfully. Or at least I hope it's helpful. The blank look he gives me says otherwise. But then, Favre has always been the most distant to me.

'*I'll do it,*' Rhenna tells me. '*And if I don't like what I find…*'

'Oh Ancestors, you can't *kill* him, Rhenna. Not yet anyway. We need to keep him busy, distracted, and away from Petra, Thom and Zander.'

'*Lysander?*' Streams of gold and turquoise ripple through her wings as she flutters them suddenly. '*What is he going to do to Lysander?*'

'He wants to… to steal him. To take him back to the Empress.'

She growls. Well, that's a quick turnaround. Whatever she saw in him when she met my brother, she's no longer so antagonistic. Not at all.

To my surprise, it's Aeron who answers.

'*That is not acceptable,*' he says. '*He is not meant for that. He is meant for your homeworld. For Vairian.*'

'I know.' The question is how does Aeron know that? I stare at him but he's inscrutable when he wants to be. We may, on occasion, share our thoughts but that only goes as far as they want it to. It's never been this frustrating before. 'So we need to find out Teel's plans and intentions. We need to find out how much he knows about the plans the Empress is hatching. And we need to counter them.'

There is a long pause while they consider matters. Whether they are conversing or not, Con and I are not privy to the words. Not this time. There are a series of sounds, low hums, the kind you feel in your sternum rather than hear, and high pitched clicks. And purrs.

'*Bring him to us,*' Favre says at last. '*We will tell you what we can.*'

Rhenna thrashes her tail around again, clearly unhappy about something. 'What's wrong?' I ask her.

'*Your brother...*'

Zander? Oh ancestors, what has he done now? Did they form some kind of link that no one told me about? Or is Rhenna just spying on him?

'Has he upset you, Maestra?' Con asks defaulting to her title in formality. 'He doesn't understand our ways. Please, I beg you to be patient.'

'*You have no need to beg me for anything, Anthaem.*' Her mind snaps the words at us nonetheless. '*No, it is not something he has done.*' The implied *not this time* is still there, however. '*He fears. Why would he feel such fear?*' She turns her head this way and that, as if trying to look at a problem in a different light. And I can understand, Zander is a problem. But fear? What would make Zander—? And then she stiffens, bristling as pulses of a dark bronze flashes through her body. '*Petra! Petra is hurt.*'

She swirls into the air, a scream of alarm coming from her. I don't even try to control the spear of terror that lances through me. Petra is in danger. Rhenna has never shown much awareness of Petra before but now she is clearly terrified that something has happened to her.

I lunge towards her. 'Wait! Rhenna, what happened? Where is she?'

She flinches in the air and spins towards me. '*Come, Belengaria.*'

She takes to the air, flying high and then plunging down into the valley at the heart of the palace. I follow her on the ground, running ahead of my husband who is already shouting into his coms. I keep my eyes on Rhenna as she flies over the gardens, and see the weapons' fire slice through the air beside her. She banks right, avoiding it with ease but my heart lurches inside me. What's happening?

My own com is vibrating against my wrist, but I'm almost at the bottom now and I see five guards thundering ahead of me. Daria shouts something and I dash by her. She's also running, the same direction as me, down into the gardens for the lakes but I know the way. Her outrage is clear as she yells at her squad to fan out.

'Princess!' Beq yells, as he draws level with me. 'Princess there's been an attack. Please, stand down. At least let me go first.' I ignore him. Of course I ignore him. I always do when they're trying to keep me safe. Hasn't he realised that by now?

I reach the bottom, the other end from the Memorial Wall, the lake spreading out like a mirror. In a glade on its edge, pinned down by the beating wings of the furious Rondet, a figure holds a weapon at them but they keep just out of range.

Zander yells at them, waving the blaster. He's not making a lot of sense. And if you don't know them you'd be sure they were attacking *him*.

'Your highness, please,' Beq tries again. He doesn't grab me or pull me back. He's not suicidal.

I don't care. Zander crouches low over something, a prone body, sprawled in the long grass. The scattered remains of two Mechas lie around him. He turns and I see something I have never seen before.

My brother is terrified.

'Zander? What are you doing?'

His skin is white, his eyes wide, and the blaster he holds almost shakes as he brings it up towards us. Just for a moment I'm looking down the sights of it, into certain death at his hands.

'Bel? Call them off. Just call them off!'

'Rhenna, please! Leave him alone.'

They must look like monsters to him and they're in a rage. He can't tell the difference.

'*He shot at me!*' I'm sure he never came near hitting her, let alone doing any damage but that's not the point.

I walk forward, my hands held high, desperately trying to reach them before something goes desperately wrong here. 'I know. But, please! Put the weapon down Zander.'

The three of them pull back further, wings still beating furiously as they hover above us. The wind from their wings batters the foliage around us, sends flowers and leaves skittering from the plants, and waves rippling across the lake.

He drops the blaster and gathers something in his arms, lifting it with the kind of care I've only ever seen him show to family. 'Get a medic. You've got to have a bloody medic around here, don't you?' And then I see what he's been guarding. *Who* he's been guarding and why the Rondet are so angry and afraid. She hangs in his arms, limp and lifeless.

Petra.

Chapter Eight

Petra

I'm still running. Running through the ancient forest that used to stand outside Limasyll but is now little more than blackened stumps and scorched earth. Running to catch up with the others because I should have been with them. I should never have been left behind. I'm running so fast my heart is hammering in my chest, slamming itself against the inside of my ribs as if it will punch its way through, but no matter how much effort I put in, the ground sucks at my feet, pulling me back. It's like running through treacle. Anthaeus won't let me go. I can't catch up with them. Shae looks back over his shoulder, one blue eye so very bright in the golden sunlight. He shakes his head.

He was my captain, and my friend. I would have followed him anywhere. He died saving Bel. I should have been there instead.

'You can't come with us, Petra,' he says. 'Not yet. You have your own mission. You know that.'

It's like being punched in the guts, like a force beyond me smacking me down to the earth harder than anything has ever hit me before.

'Come back,' *says another voice. It's not one I know, but at the same time I feel like I have always known it.* 'Come back, Petra Kel. Awaken. This is not your sleep. Awaken…'

*

The light stabs at my eyes, so painful that I crush my eyelids together, screwing up my face to hide from it. To deny it.

'*There*,' says the unknown-known voice again. '*I have done as you asked.*'

'Thank you, Maestre Aeron.' Bel's voice. I'd know her voice anywhere.

I struggle to put reality back together.

Aeron? I try to scramble up from the hospital bed, hampered by the crisp white sheets tucked in too tight around me. Someone grabs my shoulders, pushes me back down effortlessly.

I glare up at the face of Dr Halie, suddenly aware of how weak I am.

I'm in the infirmary. The long white curtains billow out from the high arched windows. Two other beds are occupied, right at the far end behind a flickering containment field. The patients are asleep and several monitors scroll through readings at their bedside.

'Easy now,' Halie says in that gentle voice. 'Easy. I've patched up the wounds but you were hit with a heavy dose of tranquiliser. Take it slowly.' She may be smaller than me – but she's in no mood for argument. I know she's a force to be reckoned with.

Tranq? I had been sure it was poison. Still, enough tranq can cause system-wide damage, especially if you were to – say – be given a dose meant for someone else. Someone much bigger than you. Twice. 'Where's Zander?'

'He's fine,' Bel assures me. 'A few cuts and bruises, mainly to his ego. He didn't realise the second one was there until it was too late.'

'Neither did I,' I confess. Bel just purses her lips.

'I think you had enough to deal with. And tranq in your system is nasty.'

'I can extract it from the blood samples, see if I can trace the origin,' Halie says. 'It won't be exact but it could give some clue as to where it came from.'

Bel accepts the offer with a nod. 'We were lucky you were there with coms and a weapon.'

I give Bel one of those looks. 'I always have coms and a weapon. Zander can't be too impressed.'

'Can't he? He's been frantic.'

'It worked out all right.'

Halie clears her throat loudly, more than making her point. 'Luckily no one else was hurt. It was a close thing though.'

They cast each other a look and I really don't like it. 'What happened?'

'Zander was… worried…' Bel's picking her words carefully. *Oh ancestors, what did Zander do?* 'He thought the Rondet were attacking him.'

This time I really do push myself up. My consciousness reels around inside my head and I fight the urge to throw up as I imagine a dozen versions of disaster. 'What did he do? Are they hurt? Is he?'

Halie shakes her head. 'Everyone's all right.'

'Not really,' says Bel. 'You almost died for the second time in two days.'

I roll my eyes and sink back on to the pillow. 'Come on, Bel, no one was after me. The first Mecha was heading for Zander before I interrupted it. And those things were working together to abduct him. Who would want Zander nice and malleable, under control? Who just arrived from Cuore and serves the woman who wants him permanently in that state? It could have killed him in the process.'

Bel looks perplexed. 'He was lucky to survive.'

'Zander would survive anything. Probably out of spite.' I've had enough of treading softly around the issue of Zander Merryn. I hurt everywhere and it's his fault. 'Have you at least confined them to quarters?'

'We can't. Not even Con can do that, but I've got people watching them. Especially Teel.' That at least was something. I allow myself to relax a little. 'Now, are you ready to see him?'

'Teel?'

She gives me the strangest look. She doesn't mean Teel. Of course she doesn't. That would be too ridiculous. Why did I say that?

'Zander,' she replies.

My head is still fuzzy. I must look a sight. I'm still in running clothes – what they haven't cut away to treat me – and my hair is mushed up all over my face. And... *when have I ever cared about things like that?*

'No?' I try. *It's worth a shot, isn't it?*

'I don't think he'll accept that.'

Neither do I. Of course he won't, especially not from his little sister, even if she is the queen.

'Can I at least get out of the bed?'

Halie examines me again, running a scanner over my head and checking the dilation of my eyes. Whatever she sees must be good enough.

'You can sit in one of the chairs. Don't get up without help, understand?' She points to one by the window. It's something and I need to grasp at any straw right now.

One of the nurses finds me a robe, which covers the numerous reGen patches decorating my torso. They both have to help me get there. My legs feel like rubber and the room spins sickeningly as I move. But I make it. As much through force of will as with their support. I glance at the other patients, still silent and unmoving, not even stirring in their sleep. They're like corpses, but for the deep, even breath.

'We need to flush out your entire system,' Halie helpfully informs me. *That sounds charming.* I make a face and she makes one right back at me. 'Well, you should stay out of my infirmary longer next time.'

'Can it wait half an hour?'

She smiles rather than laughs and slowly shakes her head as if I am the most exasperating patient ever. But I can't be. She's Bel's doctor too. 'I have some studies to read through. This sleeping sickness in the south isn't responding to normal treatments, Bel. I think we have some sort of unknown strain. I've sent out requests to a number of my colleagues on the other worlds. I'm going to have to insist on quarantine procedures. Have you heard anything about people going missing? I'm concerned they may have wandered off in the early stages and be lost somewhere, asleep and helpless.'

Bel glances around at the other patients, realisation dawning. Her expression turns grim. Slowly, she nods. 'We can arrange search parties. Send the information you have on to Thom. And in medical matters, you do whatever is necessary, Halie.' Then she looks at me. 'Ready?'

I can't put this off any longer, no matter how much I might want to. 'Let him in.'

I don't know what I expected. Gratitude perhaps? An expression of admiration at my bravery and skill? Even a question about my health and the prognosis for my recovery. But of course, this is Zander so I get nothing of the sort. He bursts into the room, leaving Bel and Halie standing at the door staring in appalled shock as he bears down on me like an enraged wolf.

'What did you think you were doing?' he roars. 'I gave you an order. You could have been killed, Petra.'

I look at him, thinking – *of course. Of course this is his reaction. Of course.* For a moment I thought there might be concern or even, ancestors forgive my optimism, simple thanks. Something. Anything. He's always reacted like this. If I took a bullet for him it would be my fault. And this is the same.

I let that thing stab me for him. I knew he couldn't hold on to it. Perhaps he thought he could? Well, try holding on to anything with a corrupted power source spilling electricity into your body. Doesn't he know that?

But it's something Zander can't control. Like me. So of course he takes it out on me. Just like always. His crazy ex, the one who wouldn't listen, couldn't obey an order, just like her father, wasn't that what he said?

I can't let my emotions get the better of me now. I bury it all down inside and keep my features fixed and unmoving. I'm hurt, I'm exhausted, and I've had enough. I won't give him the satisfaction. A perfect way to deal with an unreasonable superior. An age old military technique.

'I was just doing my job, your Highness.'

It's almost comical, the expression on his face.

'Your job?'

It's not entirely true. I mean, there are probably some people I would hesitate to throw myself in front of a weapon for, but not many.

Did he think it was personal?

Did I?

It used to be. But it can't be, not any more. It broke me to leave him, even though I knew I was protecting him. It broke me to pieces. And then I had to put myself together again. Scar tissue is the toughest of all. I should know. I'm covered in it.

'My job. Bel asked me to keep an eye on you while you're here. And it seems you need watching, your Highness.'

He freezes, horrified and then turns back to the door.

Bel has, conveniently, made a judicious exit. Clever girl. Halie is studying the readouts on her tablet. She doesn't even look up. She knows better.

He turns back to me, thoroughly confused. 'But why?'

Why? Because he gets himself in trouble faster than a toddler in an armoury. Because she's his sister and she loves him. Because I'm damned good at what I do. And because... because even now I couldn't bear the thought of him being hurt. Because I'd do anything for him. All those things that I can never say.

I grit my teeth.

'Pick a reason,' I tell him.

'Bel told you to act as my bodyguard while I'm here? Like I'm seven?'

'Of course not. You have bodyguards. But...' I heave out a sigh. I don't want to do this.

'But what?'

'Zander, we broke up a long time ago. It's ancient history. What do you want with me?'

'You left me, Petra.'

I did. It was the hardest thing I ever did. But there was no other choice. I wish I could tell him. I wish I could explain, but he'd never understand. How could he?

'You coming here doesn't change anything. We were always a mistake.'

Is that a flash of pain in his eyes? I can't bear seeing him hurt and yet I seem to do it every time. Just another reason why I was right to go. Just one more in a long list. Once again, he seems to scramble for words, for meaning. And fail.

Well not entirely. But not the right words either.

'I don't need you,' he says. 'You're not my bodyguard, my babysitter or anything else. Look at you. You still can't follow an order. You're the daughter of a coward. You're barely a Vairian.'

It's like a physical blow. I sit there, so shocked I can't reply. I just stare at him, probably with my mouth hanging open.

Doctor Halie clears her throat loudly. We both snap our attention to her and I can see the restrained fury in her. She's very pale, and her eyes are like gleaming points of light.

'Your Highness,' the tone of her voice is so much more scathing than mine could ever be. It's withering. 'I insist that you to leave immediately. I can't have you upsetting my patient.'

I don't think anyone has ever spoken to Zander like that before. He doesn't even say a word in reply, just turns on his heel and leaves. She all but slams the door behind him.

'Well,' I say, trying to make my voice light. I feel anything but light at the moment. I wish he hadn't come here. Not to see me. Not to Anthaeus. 'Remind me not to get on the wrong side of *you*.' It's a way of breaking the awkward silence.

She pinches her lips together. 'He should not talk to you like that. Perhaps he doesn't understand what you did for Anthaeus, or for him. But that's no excuse. And if you aren't Vairian enough for him, then this world is more than happy to make you ours instead.'

'Oh, he was just—'

'Just nothing. Just an embarrassed boy who doesn't want to admit you saved his life. Just an idiot.'

I decide not to argue. She's too terrifying.

'Maybe I should... get some rest?'

She smiles at me, the sternness gone. 'A good idea. I can give you a sedative while the purgative gets the rest of that tranq out of your system.'

It sounds awful. But like I said, I've decided not to argue with her. It's too late now and I want to get out of here soon.

Besides, what can she do to me that's worse than him?

Chapter Nine

Bel

Liette comes back from the expedition to Montserratt the following morning. She asks to see Con, and immediately begs an audience not just for herself but for a religious group that has come with her.

'They were so helpful,' she says. 'I'd never have found the crystal without them. It's a wonder. Really a wonder. I can't begin to describe it. You have to see for yourself. Con, it's just what we need.'

Con agrees to see them, scheduling it for later that day. He doesn't look too keen but Liette promises they've brought the crystal they need for the chip and he can hardly ignore the very thing he sent her there for. If it takes being polite to a few oddballs, he can manage that. He does it all the time with ambassadors and other delegations. I know there is less time than usual. It is the day before our wedding. Everything is in turmoil. And yet, still, court life doesn't stop.

The report Halie has from her team is bleak. Fifty-two cases of sleeping sickness in the greater Montserratt area, all ages, all walks of life, no discernible connection. Halie delivers the data they've brought with a grim expression.

'There are other people missing,' Con says, reading through the information himself. 'From Doon and Kir too. Do you think they're somewhere in the cave system? If they're asleep we might never find them.'

'I thought we could send out search parties,' I suggest gently. 'We have to try.'

He seems to freeze for a moment, staring at the names of the missing. 'Yes,' he says at last. 'Thom, will you see to that? As soon as possible, please. The timing of this…'

'The timing of what, Con?'

'This epidemic, these people with Liette… it's a strange coincidence.'

'And?' I know there's an *and*.

He shakes his head, as if trying to dismiss a thought that won't budge. 'I don't believe in coincidences.'

*

The delegation from Montserratt files in to the audience chamber, twenty of them. Liette is there too, eager and delighted. She speaks with a few of them, embraces them like brothers and sisters. I can see her encouraging them. I don't think I've ever seen her quite so alive. *Greymen*, they call themselves, and they look it. Not only are they dressed head to toe in grey robes, but their faces have that bleak hollowed-out look. There's no colour to them, no joy. The bombing of the caves there during the war claimed many lives. And now, the leader of the party is a man, perhaps thirty-five, with the fire of religious fervour in his eyes.

Religion is not unknown on Vairian, but we look to our ancestors for guidance, those who came before us, rather than an unknowable supernatural being. The Imperial planets of Melia and Camarth have a complex and intricate cosmology which involves hourly rituals and special prayers, fasts and celebrations. The Empire encourages it as it keeps them happy and profitable. But there has never really been an Anthaese religion, other than that story of a forgotten early goddess, set aside long ago. She's more of a folktale than a religion, not something the colonists ever embraced.

Sometimes I'm sure there are things the Rondet have forgotten over the course of their long sleep. Or perhaps they would have us believe that. It's a handy fiction.

But the colonists didn't bring a religion with them and though many think the Rondet are a religious group, there has never been such a thing recorded.

Until now.

'We are simply asking for an audience with the Rondet, Anthaem,' the leader says in a calm, conciliatory tone. He has blue eyes, bright and clear, almost the same colour as Shae's had been, although rounder and not as heavily lashed. He would be handsome if he didn't have the look of a zealot to him. It unnerves me.

'And I am happy to request it, Faestus—'

'*Prime* Faestus,' he interrupts. 'I am the chosen leader of my people, as you are Anthaem.'

I grit my teeth. He's setting himself up on the same level as Con and I don't like it. My childhood nurse Nerysse made me read extensively about the religious wars on the Firstworld and they always started with someone claiming they were chosen, or special in some way. Usually without any evidence to back them up. Now this Faestus was trying to get validation from the Rondet and from Con himself.

And I just don't like him. Or the way he looks at me.

It's a long time since anyone made me feel like an outsider on Anthaeus. These people do it right away without a word. Hostility rolls off them, each and every one.

I shudder. It makes me think of when I first arrived here, that sensation of eyes in the shadows watching me, hating me.

'But Prime Faestus shouldn't have to *request* an audience, Anthaem,' says Liette. She doesn't look well, if I'm honest. There's a sheen of sweat on her face and her blue eyes are wider and more intense. I wonder what's going on. I need to talk to Con, but there isn't a moment. Not now.

Con is a far more patient person than I am. 'And why is that?' he asks kindly, clearly bemused at this change in his assistant.

'Because the Stone's Heart itself has chosen him. The heart of Anthaeus. The Coparius—'

'The Coparius is a myth,' Jondar interrupts. 'A half remembered fairy tale from thousands of years ago.'

Faestus looks suddenly triumphant. 'Not so, Prince Jondar. The bombing which took so many lives opened up forgotten tunnels and passages. We followed them, lost in the darkness, starving, drinking the water the rocks themselves provided. And deep within the mountains, we found it. We found the Stone's Heart.'

Con has that contemplative look on his face now, no doubt thinking of the city we uncovered, and the archaeological finds there.

'Impossible,' Jondar says. Something has been sprung on him and he hates that. 'No one can find a myth. The Coparius does not exist.'

'Doesn't it?'

Two of Faestus's followers unveil a box, intricately and beautifully carved, no more than a foot square. It must have taken a master carver months to complete. It has been polished to a shine and inlaid with precious metals that gleam in the light of the audience chamber. Three guards start forward at a glance from Jondar. It could contain anything – weapons, a bomb, a poison…

The devout Greymen immediately stand, forming a shield around it, blocking it from sight.

'Only the Anthaem can look upon it,' Faestus announces loudly, with all the pomposity of righteousness. 'The Stone is not for other eyes. Those not worthy cannot hear her. And unrighteous souls are struck down.' He looks right at me. The antagonism is palpable.

When I first arrived, I knew there were factions who didn't want me here, but I never actually came across them. Now I'm looking right at them.

Con gets to his feet and the guards bristle even more.

'Either this artefact is offered freely to Anthaeus, or it is not. Nothing about our patrimony should be for my eyes alone. If this truly is the Coparius, it belongs to all of us.'

The Greymen all look to Faestus, who waits, his gaze locked with Con's for long moments before he nods. 'The Anthaem is wise. Come, look. It will show you your heart's desire.'

Con glances at me. 'I already know that,' he says softly. I blush but at the same time, an uneasiness settles on me.

The Greymen fall back, revealing the box once more, and slowly, Con walks towards it.

Prickles run up my spine. This feels wrong. Worse, it feels dangerous. I reach out blindly, seeking help, equilibrium.

Rhenna?

Con has reached the box and the Greymen are all watching him, as if they are starving and he is meat.

'Conleith... Anthaem...' Jondar sounds as worried as I feel. 'Con, this is unwise. Tests should be run. Security, the archaeologists...'

But Con just smiles. It's a mystery to him, a puzzle to be solved. I know him. He can't resist something like this. He's never looked more handsome as he opens the box and turns, bathed in a shifting golden light, like the sunlight of this world reflecting on moving water. His green eyes are brighter than ever, shining with inner fire.

I recall his story of the Coparius, the bringer of dreams. What had Faestus said? That unrighteous souls are struck down? You dream when you sleep, don't you? There has to be a connection. Con doesn't believe in coincidences and neither do I. How long have they had this thing? How long since the sickness started?

I get to my feet, almost tripping over the throne in my need to reach him. To stop him. I don't know why. It's blind panic, all my instincts screaming.

Favre suddenly bursts through the doors out onto the veranda, slamming himself down on the mosaic floor. He looks bigger than ever, the size of a prize bull. He roars, an unearthly, rage-filled scream. I know where the panic is coming from now. It's his. It's all three of them.

No, Conleith! Do not touch that thing!

Con doesn't move, neither to take the stone or to step away. He seems frozen there. As I reach him, my hands close on his arm and I'm startled by how cold he is, how hard the muscles feel under my fingers. He's staring at it, transfixed, its light dancing in his pupils. His lips part and he sighs, as if he's suddenly exhausted, drained of all strength.

'Con?' I hold on to him, clinging to him as if I can pull him back.

'Arrest them!' I hear Jondar yelling as guards surround the Greymen. 'Arrest them immediately.'

And then Con moves again, sucking in a breath so sharply it's almost a gasp.

'No,' he says and pulls away without sparing me a glance. 'No, they can go. It's all right, Jon. Don't panic. I'm fine. It's just a stone. Like the crystals.' He closes the box and the light goes out.

'You understand?' says Faestus. He's ecstatic. I can see it in his face and in his eyes.

'I'll need to study it.'

Something seems to pass between them. I don't know what but there's definitely something. And I don't like it. Liette smirks at me.

He sounds so strange. They've done something to him. I don't know how I know it but I do. What have they done to him?

My heart is hammering in my chest. I can feel Favre in my mind. But he isn't making sense. As I stand there, Rhenna and Aeron arrive too.

The Greymen drop to their knees, all of them in unison. Faestus raises his face to Favre, and smiles in delight. 'Greetings Rondet. The Coparius sends her regards and says the time has fallen due.'

Rhenna digs her claws into the stonework, snarling. Aeron shakes his great head, lashes his tail from side to side. Favre stands like stone, his eyes flashing in rage. Waves of horror roll off him.

Slowly the Greymen get to their feet and bow to Con. Just to Con. Then they leave.

The reaction is instantaneous, everyone in the room breaking into shocked and appalled chatter, outrage and disbelief, so many questions. All except for Con and me. The noise sweeps over us.

'Con?' I say again. My voice is shaking.

He turns then and smiles at me. His own smile. The one I know better than my own, the one that always makes my heart soar. He is so handsome, so sweet, the light of my life.

'I'm fine, my love,' he tells me and leans down to brush his lips against mine. But even his lips feel cold. 'We should get ready for the ball tonight, shouldn't we? And our wedding tomorrow?'

In the back of my mind Rhenna gives a terrible sob.

I can't hear him, Belengaria. I can't hear him any more.

Chapter Ten

Petra

It's afternoon in the infirmary and I'm still stuck here, useless and probably in the way. Halie sinks into the chair beside me and pulls off her IsoMask. She looks exhausted. Worse, she looks defeated.

'Lost him,' she says. 'It invaded the central nervous system and systematic organ failure was rapid.' I must look particularly dense. She tries again. 'Like his whole body drained of energy and shut down while he slept.'

'I'm… I'm sorry.'

I can understand losing a soldier in battle. But here, where everything around us is designed to save lives, it doesn't seem right. Another one of the sleepers just died. That makes two, the ones that were in here when I first came in. This one was a fisherman from the lower city. The other one was a squad leader from the seventh.

She pushes her hood back from her rich copper hair which curls against her scalp, sweat-dampened. The IsoMask and the suit protects her as well as the patient. 'There are three more on the way in; a girl from the first group and two more from one of the villages. Ready to go back to the real world, General?'

Of course I am. Besides, they need the bed. I should have been in my own quarters from the start.

Halie releases me – under strict orders, of course. Ones which, for now, I've promised to obey. She particularly doesn't want me over-exerting myself, but that just confirms that she doesn't know me as well as she thinks. And she has so much more to deal with than I do.

Dwyer is waiting for me outside my quarters. He has a sort of shifty worried look which can't bode well for me.

'Ma'am, I tried to explain, I tried to stop it.'

'Stop what?'

I push open the door. My room is full of flowers, blooms of every kind, every colour. The scent alone is overpowering.

'What…?' I say again, because I don't know what else to say in the face of this. No one has ever given me so much as a daisy before. And now… this?

'Lord Teel said—'

'Dwyer, did you let Lord Teel fill my room full of flowers?' He shifts from foot to foot, looking profoundly uncomfortable. I can picture the scene now. The poor boy didn't stand a chance. 'Why?'

He hangs his head. 'I didn't know how to stop him.'

'No, I mean, why did he do it?'

'He said… he said, that you were a hero and heroes deserve accolades. Then his people came in with all the flowers. And then… he asked leave to take you to the masked ball. There's a gown.'

Of course there's a gown.

I'm about to tell him what to do with it when it occurs to me that this is exactly what Bel wanted. That I'm distracting Teel, even if he thinks he's playing me in some way. If he's occupied with me he's leaving Zander alone. And just as satisfying, if anything is going to annoy Crown Prince bloody Zander bloody Merryn, it's going to a ball with Teel. The pain and humiliation of saving his life, only to be rejected like that – not only as a soldier, but as a Vairian – swamps me.

'Tell him, I accept,' I snap. 'And get the flowers out of here. The living ones to the gardens and the others to the infirmary. To that man's funeral. Or wherever. Somewhere useful.' There's got to be *somewhere* – maybe Bel needs some for the wedding.

Speaking of Bel, I head for her chambers next, since I can barely fit in my own room at the moment. I need to talk to her about the attack, and I'll probably have to tell her that Zander doesn't want me anywhere near him but that Teel does, so maybe we should go with that plan after all.

She's not getting ready for the ball though. She's pacing back and forth, waiting for me. Her maids look at their wits ends. But Bel looks worse.

One of them approaches and she waves the girl away. 'Not now, Della.'

She couldn't be having second thoughts? I suddenly wonder what could have happened. And why did nobody tell me?

'Oh thank the ancestors you're here!' she blurts out. She explains everything in one mad rush of words, all her fears, all that she saw, all that Rhenna said. The idea of Con being shut off from the Rondet is terrifying to her. The fact he doesn't seem to care is even worse.

'Did he talk to Jondar? To Thom?'

'Yes, he says he's fine. That everyone is panicking over nothing. He says it'll come back. That it always does. He thinks it's just like when the Rondet fly further away – he hears them less then.'

'Well, maybe it is. He'd know, wouldn't he?'

She shakes her head. 'So would *they*. They've been close, they've tried everything. And they are afraid, you understand?'

They've never talked to me except for yesterday, and Aeron has been silent ever since. They don't talk to everyone, something that Bel, Jondar and Thom often forget.

'Bel, I know you're scared but—'

'I'm not scared,' she lies, bald-faced lies, but I'm not going to call her on it. Not now. 'He could be ill – from that stone. Couldn't he?'

'Has anyone else studied this stone?'

'Security found nothing. It's a lump of rock. Sorrell is examining it first. Con would but… I asked him to leave it alone. For now anyway. There's a queue of them lining up, scientists and archaeologists. Liette has already done some tests, or so she says… but then, she fell in with the Greymen while visiting Montserratt. I don't know. She's… different. I mean, she was always a little odd. But now she seems… changed. Anyway, Con wants to run a series of scans and I don't know how long he'll wait… Petra, you didn't see him. The colour drained out of his face. I thought he'd collapse right there. And he's so… so tired. He says he's fine and they're all going along with that. You know how he can be. Halie checked him over, but she says he's just been over-exerting himself.'

I don't know what to say. I'm not good at comforting. I'm not a comforting person. But I know what it sounds like. I think of the sleepers in the infirmary again. It's not an image I want to dwell on, especially not when Con is concerned. But then, Halie knows too. Halie knows better than anyone.

Bel purses her lips and glances back at her waiting attendants. 'I have to get ready. Just… keep an eye on him for me tonight? On both of them.'

'I don't think your brother wants me anywhere near him.' That's putting it mildly.

'I don't care what he wants. Having Teel and his companions in the palace only makes it more important. I don't care what anyone else says, that tech Zander brought didn't come from Gravia. It's too high-grade, and that means Imperial. And those Mechas are like nothing I've ever seen. Be careful, Petra. Please.'

'And Teel? I've only got two eyes, Bel.'

'Don't underestimate yourself. His eyes are going to be on you.'

Chapter Eleven

Bel

The microblade shrieks as it slices into the gleaming surface of the crystal the Greymen think is the Coparius. Con barely looks up as I walk into the study. He didn't wait that long after all. He couldn't. Typical.

All his attention is focused entirely on the stone as he removes the sliver with tongs and places it carefully on the dish, which he seals. He reactivates the shielding array around the stone, but it just gleams malevolently at him.

'Don't touch it,' he tells Sorrell and, from the look on her face, it's not for the first time. 'We just want to analyse it as quickly as possible and then see if it will embed.'

'Do they know that you're cutting bits off their magic rock?' I ask him.

'No of course not. And if it hasn't told them it's not a very magic rock, is it? Watch this.'

He opens a container holding a number of standard crystals he and Sorrell have been testing. Selecting one, he lifts it out with the same tongs and carries it towards the Coparius. Before it even reaches the shielding, it begins to glow with a faint, warm light. As he gets nearer I hear a distinct hum. Except... that's not quite right either. I feel it.

'What's it doing?' I ask.

'Powering it, I think. The energy transfer rate is phenomenal. Isn't it amazing?'

It doesn't look amazing for the smaller crystal, the glow of which is flickering and fading.

'The Coparius is draining it?'

'Yes, at an exceptional rate.'

I can see his delight in the reaction, the need to solve a mystery. But the light reflecting up into his beautiful face is unnerving. He looks like one of Faestus's zealots, like Liette since she got back. And the humming sound is almost like chanting. It vibrates in the back of my brain, setting my nerves – and my teeth – on edge.

'You think you can use this for your chip?' I ask, dreading the answer.

'It makes sense, doesn't it? The way the thing networks is like neural pathways. I really think it will work. I just need to—'

'No testing it on yourself. You promised.'

He sets the dead crystal down on another workbench.

'Bel, the things we can do with this—'

I can imagine some pretty terrible applications actually. That's the problem.

'No, Con.'

'Bel, you have to understand—'

'No, I don't. Not in the slightest.'

'I can't ask someone else to be a guinea pig for me.'

'Why not? We ask soldiers to fight for us, guards to protect us, pilots to fly us—'

'It's perfectly safe!' he protests.

'That thing cut you off from the Rondet, Con. It just drained that crystal of power in seconds. There's nothing safe about it.'

'It's just a stone, Bel. It's made of a crystalline element – not the same as anything on Anthaeus or Kelta, but close enough. There are traces of it threading through the others, see?'

He waves some sort of readout at me on the tablet. I just see numbers. 'Like a virus?' I ask bluntly.

He pauses, considering that. 'Maybe? Actually, yes, it's not unlike that. Sorrell, will you make a note of that and credit my genius fiancée?' He smiles at me, radiant, as if I'm meant to be delighted at the praise. I'm not. I know he means well, but he's hardly listening, just caught up in the wonder of discovery. 'It absorbs and stores energy at an astonishing rate. I can retro-engineer that, use it to link into the chip and tap into it. I can power any number of things. But it's just a stone. It doesn't grant wishes or speak truth, it can't predict the future or change matter, or whatever else Faestus and his deluded followers believe. But it *can* help people who desperately need help. It can help me give them the time and strength to heal. That's all I want.'

I glance at it. I still get the feeling it's watching me. 'I'm not sure, Con. I still think it's risky.'

'All science is risky, my love.'

I leave them to it. I mean, it's not like I'm going to be a lot of help, and I'm not sure they're going to notice if I'm there. And I have other things to do. A whole day of meetings, and preparations for the ball this evening and the wedding tomorrow. Plus the Cuorean group to entertain. I wonder what my brother is doing. I was so angry with him when I heard about what he said to Petra that I didn't want to see him at all, honoured guest or not. He's still my brother and I reserve the right to completely ignore him if needs be. Or to tear strips off him if I catch him on his own. I'm pretty sure he knows it too and is avoiding me just as studiously.

Arianne is waiting for me outside.

'Your dress for this evening, your Highness…' she begins and my heart sinks. I haven't thought about it at all and I should have. The masked ball the night before a royal wedding is a time-honoured Anthaese tradition, one they all look forward to.

'I… um…' I try not to make eye contact with my chief lady-in-waiting and continue walking. Unperturbed, she matches me step for step. Damn, I'm not getting out of this discussion. 'Maybe a green one?'

'Might I suggest the emerald Amazzuti gown with the gold trim? With the rubies?'

Of course, Arianne has already picked out a dress for me for this evening, but she's too subtle to say that out loud. She's good, possibly even as good as my first lady-in-waiting – and eventual friend – Elara was. Arianne sees dressing me as a testament to her taste, so I always look incredible so long as I leave everything up to her. It suits us both to be honest. She has free rein and I don't have to sit through all the choosing. And it's a matter of pride to her that I, at all times, look like a queen.

She sometimes even lets me wear clothes that are a little bit comfortable. Usually there is a distinct nod to my heritage that I deeply appreciate. She manages to combine Vairian and Anthaese elements, which is the most diplomatically perfect answer to many of my courtly woes.

Elara was younger, and more of a political animal – at least on the surface. Arianne is forty, widowed with two teenage children, and carries herself with all the calm assurance of an admiral. Everything runs smoothly on her watch.

'I'll have everything ready for you by this afternoon. I know you have a packed schedule today but a little extra time for the hair stylist would be appreciated, your Highness,' she warns me in that way only she can before she takes herself off to wrangle a dozen maids, stylists, make-up artists and wrench some of the remaining crown jewels from Jondar and the royal treasury.

As I make my way along the gallery towards a meeting with a group from the rebuilding committee, I indulge myself for a moment, pausing to watch a flight of birds take off from the gardens below. Their wings flicker bright and dark as they reel around in a great shapeless mass, a murmuration that is bewitching to watch. They're jewel coloured and beautiful. Like everything here in my adopted home.

And then I hear the voices, quiet and cultured voices, raised on the edge of an argument.

'You might as well have hung up a signpost.' It's Lord Teel. He sounds irritated, which is at odds with his usual suave demeanour.

I can see them down there, on the terrace below me, Teel a tall slim shadow and Kaeda de Lorens, as colourful as the birds even now winging away from us. I'm hidden from view up here. People forget to look up in these gardens. 'What else am I supposed to do? I don't want him hooking up with some long lost love and ruining all my plans, do I?'

'I'm just saying you could be more subtle, Kaeda.'

She preens, throwing back her blue hair and smiling her dazzling smile. 'I don't do subtle, Valentin. You know that.'

He's unimpressed. I think perhaps nothing would impress him. 'Everything that happened between them hurt her too deeply. He hasn't forgiven her either. I've heard all his stories. You've seen how she treats him and how he treats her.'

'And you'd know that, would you?' She laughs. 'I bet he confessed everything to you. Which drunken night was that?' He starts to protest and she waves him aside. 'Fine. Don't gossip. What do you suggest?'

'She's a charming, strong and elegant woman. Let me take care of her. I've already set my plan in motion. Let it ride out and don't interfere any more. Leave her alone. You deal with your end of things, wait until after the wedding, and I'll deal with mine.'

Kaeda gives him a nasty, snide look and the jealousy is plain to both see and hear.

'You're an idiot, Teel. Don't underestimate her. It's a shame those attacks didn't put an end to her, or at least land her in the infirmary for longer. She's out of our way there.'

'Any further threat to either Lysander or Petra Kel will just disrupt matters now and jeopardise everything. We will not be treated kindly if we return empty-handed.'

They move off, still bickering and I don't have the heart to follow. *Empty-handed…* they mean without Zander.

I knew I needed Petra to watch over Zander, and that I needed her to distract Teel too. Now I know why. I just hope she knows that while she's playing him, he's playing her as well.

Chapter Twelve

Petra

The evening gown is beautiful. Perfect. So elegantly unlike anything I would ever wear. I don't even look like myself. Red velvet, the colour of blood, is embroidered with gold in delicate patterns. Tendrils of intricate needlework encircle my wrists and arms, embrace the bodice and arch up over the shoulders. It reminds me of royal gowns of the Vairian court, back in the old days before the first Gravian War. It's beautiful, reminiscent of a lost time, a lost place. I stare at the woman in the mirror, wondering where the soldier has gone.

'I can braid your hair,' Dwyer offers in his awkward way.

I can't help but laugh. 'Where did you learn to braid hair?'

'I had a little sister, once,' he replies and suddenly my frivolous mood is gone. He has no one now. No one but me. He looks tired. I really need to get him to take some time off.

He's fast and sure, and the finished product is somehow ethereal and delicate. A great length of my hair still falls down my back, but he's created a braided crown. He studies me like I'm a final exam and for once I let him. The mask that matches the dress is gold filigree and shaped like a series of stars falling across my face from the left to the right, getting smaller as they descend. I fit it on and somehow it makes the look complete. Dwyer slides little garnet pins into my hair.

'It's good,' I assure him. Dwyer blushes and sets off to tidy everything away.

I sit there, staring at the creature in the mirror looking back at me. Slender, graceful, my long black hair wound in intricate swirls. Delicate curls hang by my ears. It's not me. It can't be. My skin looks gilded and smooth, polished. And behind the mask of stars my eyes glitter like something alien and beautiful.

I rise carefully, afraid for a moment that I might disrupt the illusion but everything stays where it should be. It's a miracle.

A thud from the other side of the room makes me turn sharply, the spell broken by reality. The hairbrush is on the floor and Dwyer is leaning against the doorframe, his eyes closed. 'Are you all right?' I ask.

He blinks at me, his gaze unfocused. 'I'm sorry, General. I just... I...'

And he falls, almost slowly, to the ground, limp and unresponsive.

I run to his side and crouch down, cursing the fabric billowing around me as I do so. He's flushed, but he's cold to the touch. This isn't good. Not good at all. I think of the patients in the infirmary and my heart hammers away at the bottom of my throat.

'Kel to Halie,' I say as I key up my coms. 'I've a medical emergency in my quarters. Dwyer's unconscious.'

'I'm on my way,' Halie says. She sounds exhausted too. That's not good.

'I can bring him—'

'Negative, Petra. Don't... try not to touch him. We still don't know enough about contagion.'

Contagion... it's a bit late for that.

She's as good as her word. There's a knock on the door.

'It's open!' I call. Halie sweeps in with her medical team and a gurney. Everything is chaos as I step back and try to keep out of the way. I've got to let her work. I've got to let her help him. He's only a child. I know he thinks he's older but really, when you get down to it, he's just a child.

'Halie? Talk to me. What is it?'

'It looks like the same thing. The same sickness.' She examines the reaction of his pupils and runs a scanner over his head, frowning as the results scroll down on the handheld screen in front of her. 'I'm taking him back to the quarantine hub to run further tests.'

'I'm coming too.'

I don't know what I'm expecting to do when I get there, but I can't just let them cart him off without anyone else.

Halie arches an eyebrow at me. 'Don't you have a ball to go to?'

'It can wait.'

The move is chaotic and so very fast. We rush along the corridors up to the infirmary and before I know what's happening he's behind the containment field with five others. Medics swarm over him and I stand there, helpless and ridiculous in a golden party mask and ball gown.

I wait, pacing back and forth, all my thoughts on Dwyer. He doesn't have anyone else. Eventually, Halie comes back to me.

'He's stable and resting. I have him on fluids and I'm running a full battery of tests. But you alerted us right away. There's nothing else you can do here, Petra. And you have somewhere to be, remember?'

I shake my head. 'I can't.'

She smiles. There's a kindness to her I forget. That's why she does what she does. 'You can't stay here. You'll be in our way and you have a job to do as well, don't you?' The subtle emphasis in her voice reminds me that she always seems to know more than we realise. 'I'll update you if there's any change, I promise. Go on, you look beautiful. Don't waste it.'

I open the door to leave the infirmary and stop in surprise.

Lord Teel is sitting outside. What is he doing here, outside the infirmary?

Teel gets to his feet when I open the door and smiles. I have to admit, it is a devastating smile, right up there on the Zander scale of charm.

I'm meant to be distracting him. Not the other way around.

'General Kel,' he says, his voice strangely soft. 'How beautiful you look.'

I'm instantly defensive. In the scarlet and gold gown for the masked ball, I feel oddly vulnerable, not myself. Why I couldn't just go in my stupid formal uniform I don't know. That's what I did the last time they were getting married... of course the last time I was just a corporal and bodyguard. And I was working, not prancing about in this get up. I know he asked to escort me and I said yes because I promised Bel. I know he sent the gown and now I'm wondering how he got the size and style so perfect. I know he engineered this but still...

I've never been fêted as beautiful. I'm hard. A soldier, a fighter, a killer. Every part of me is honed to fight and I train every day. But I'm not beautiful.

'Lord Teel, are you... are you lost?'

He laughs as if I've cracked a hilarious joke and offers me his arm. Politeness dictates I should take it and walk with him, laugh in return and probably simper. I don't simper. I stare at his hand for a moment and then lift my gaze to meet his.

He looks back at me without faltering, his expression knowing, and the smile gentles.

Without missing a beat, he folds his arms back behind his back, the perfect courtier.

The Empress admires him, trusts him with her life. Some say she loves him. I could be looking at the next Imperial consort, except that I know she has other plans. Why would she choose Zander over Teel?

I could really screw up here. Not just for myself but for Bel, Con, Zander, Anthaeus, Vairian. For all of us.

'I came to meet you as your escort. As is the custom.'

It might be. I wouldn't know. I don't pay much attention to the various customs of the courts anywhere. It drives Jondar up the wall. Usually Thom and I find it hilarious. Not now though. Not this time.

'You're very kind, Lord Teel, but I—'

'Val,' he interrupts. 'Please. I can get all the Lord Teel I want on Cuore.'

He's not meant to say things like that. He's not what I expected, I'll give him that. I'm not normally turned by a handsome face. He makes me spin.

'Val, then.' I try to breathe evenly but I feel like a new recruit on parade. 'And thank you for the flowers.'

'They pleased you?'

'They're… there were lots of them, but… I know I agreed to have you escort me… but I… I don't need an escort.'

'Of course not. You're a general. And a firm fixture here. But…' he smiles again, looks down at his feet and then up at me, through dark whisper-fine strands of auburn hair, like a boy caught stealing apples. 'Perhaps I do?'

I almost trip over my own feet, which is impressive since I'm not moving. A lord of Cuore and the Imperial Court isn't meant to say things like that. He isn't meant to be this disarming. I know he's playing me somehow, but ancestors, he's good at it.

'I'm sorry, Val... I'm... my equerry was just taken ill and I—'

'I heard. Poor Dwyer. He's a fine assistant for you. I was most impressed.'

I give him a stern look. 'You bullied him about the flowers.'

'That's a very strong accusation,' he says. 'I merely encouraged him to let me spoil you a little. He cares a great deal about you. How is he? Is there anything I can do?'

Is there? Would I ask him if there was? Still, it's good of him to ask. I had imagined that like most of the Cuoreans I've ever met servants were meant to be invisible and never something to worry about. The kindness in his voice is disarming. 'He's stable. The doctor is keeping a close eye on him for me.'

'Well then,' Teel says softly. 'Come with me to the ball?'

He steps closer, right beside me and in my space. If it was anyone else I'd shove them away but all I can think right now is that he smells so good.

'I really think I should just...'

I imagine Dwyer's face if I don't go, after he finally managed to get me dressed up. I imagine how he'd feel if I didn't go because of him. I don't want to.

Teel hangs his head, looking down at me, his eyes searching mine.

'Please, don't run away, Petra. I understand that it's hard with Lysander being there. You have history together. And he's been quite... candid about your part in recent... events...'

Zander...

He's been gossiping. Of course he has. I'm sure his stories can entertain an entire room for hours. I suddenly feel as if all the confidence is being sucked back into me, as if a black hole of embarrassment has opened where my heart should be. Ancestors, how many people did he tell? What did he say?

The urge to escape shudders through me. I don't want to go to the ball. I don't want to see Lysander Merryn—

And just as quickly anger floods in to take the place of the mortification.

I'm not running away from Zander any more. That's the last thing I'm going to do. Ever. I can't have people thinking that. I reject the idea utterly.

And everyone says Dwyer will be fine. He's stable. He's not in danger. We got to him in time. Bel is expecting me. I'm her witness so I should be there. And I…

I want to go with Teel. It's not just about duty.

I'm not meant to be thinking things like this. Especially not about him. He's elegant and sinful, and just a bit feral. The stories I've heard don't really help. I did some searching on the interstellar net, found references in society pages and gossip feeds. His various affairs, the scandals, the fact that the Empress always forgives him and no one knows why… Zander isn't the only one to gossip, nor the only subject of it.

'Are they true? The rumours about you…' I blurt out and then stop before I can go any further and embarrass myself.

He grins, that wicked smile that makes something somersault inside me. *What am I doing?* He's using me and I know it. Because I'm doing the same thing to him. I'd have to be an idiot to be taken in by any of this.

But I think I am.

Both taken in, and an idiot.

'True? All of it, my dearest general.' He offers me his arm again. 'Shall we add to it? Imagine the shock if we walk in there together?'

Oh ancestors, it is so tempting. I imagine Zander's face. And Thom's. And Jondar's. Oh, poor Jondar would be scandalised.

Back when I was just plain old Petra Kel I never imagined I'd make captain, let alone general. Given my family history, I knew that was never going to happen. Who on all of Vairian was going to give me such a commission?

I remember Zander's comment – about having forgotten that I'm Vairian. I remember his face when he looked down at me and said 'that's a lot of medals', and when he yelled that he didn't need me. All the things he has said about me…

Damn him and everyone like him. I'm sick of it.

Why not? I'm wearing a mask. We're meant to be something else this evening, something different. That's what masks are for. Why should I do what I have always done?

'All right, Lord Teel. Let's do this.'

He puts on his own mask, a moon, made of a thin silver material, the same colours as his eyes.

I fall into step beside him. His touch on my arm is very gentle and it makes the nerves tingle. I haven't felt this close to anyone in years.

'Val, please. Petra?'

I smile, and I know it's radiant. 'All right, Val.'

We almost run towards the ballroom and enter it laughing. I stand there, my hand in his and he leads me directly to the dance floor, twirling me in front of him, like he's showing me off. And I know people are looking at me in a way they've never done before, even if they've known me for years.

I see a figure on the far side of the crowd of spiralling dancers, his hands by his side, staring at me. Not that I can see his eyes. But I can feel them on me. Zander tilts his head to the side, studying me as he raises his glass to his lips. But he doesn't drink. He's wearing a mask too, a golden sun, but I'd still know him anywhere. Just as he clearly recognises us. Zander smiles and says something to the blue-haired woman at his side. Kaeda, resplendent in a wisp of silk in rainbow colours and a mask like a hummingbird's face, throws back her head in laughter and winds her arms around him, far too intimately.

So that's how it is.

The amusement turns to ashes in the pit of my stomach.

I think of Dwyer again. I shouldn't have come. If only for that reason.

But Teel isn't put off by my hesitation. Not in the slightest. His fingers intertwine with mine and I remember my old sergeant telling me that when people hold hands you can tell their intentions. *Palm to palm*, he said, *is the clasp of a brother.* When you wind your fingers together, like we are now, you want to—

'Dance?' Teel asks, his tone teasing, his eyes sparkling. Like he's reading my mind and finds it enthralling, hilarious, and wonderful all at the same time. *I won't let you get away*, his eyes say. It's a dare, a challenge, and something else. *Prove to me you aren't a coward. Show me that you won't let them define you. Let them all see the Petra I see, what you are willing to do, what you will dare. Don't let me down, Petra.*

Still angry with Zander, I fit myself into his arms and we spin across the ballroom floor as if we were made to be together.

Perhaps it's a dream. Perhaps I'm a fool. But I'm damned if I'll stand by and let them laugh at me. At least I'll earn it. To hell with the consequences.

I don't know what I was expecting. To have Zander challenge Teel or fight for my honour? Hardly. People like him don't fight for people like me and my honour is my own affair. I'll fight for it if necessary. But as the ball goes on, as Teel pays me every attention, others begin to notice too. Before I know what's happening I have more potential dance partners than I know dances.

Part of me still isn't convinced that this isn't all a practical joke. Elaborate and complex, possibly involving everyone there. At midnight they'll all take off their masks and reveal what a fool I've been.

I long once again for my body armour and my weapons. I've got a knife strapped to my leg – I'm never without a weapon, as I told Zander – and one of those tiny pv2 blasters, tucked away out of sight. If all of this is a hoax I'm going to have to restrain myself from killing them all.

But right now, dancing with the most handsome, eligible man in the room, my head is whirling. Teel is a master – he even makes me look like I know what I'm doing.

The dance ends and Teel takes my hand, leading me from the dance floor. We step out into the evening air, the terraced gardens lit with tiny lights in the trees, and candles in lanterns on every level.

'Fresh air,' he sighs. 'There's nothing like it. When I moved to Cuore I never realised how much I'd miss it. It's beautiful here. This place, these gardens, magical.' He reaches for a flower, one of those weirdly coloured bright things, white, blue-purple and green, all jumbled together. With his elegant fingers he cups the bloom and lifts it towards me, but he doesn't pull it from the stem. I stare at it. He wants me to smell it or something. That's not the kind of thing I do. Teel just smiles and bends his face towards it instead. He closes his eyes as he inhales the scent

'Passionflowers. I don't know of many worlds where they grow as beautifully as this.'

'I thought you were born on Cuore.'

He releases the flower, and forgotten, it snaps back into the riot of growth beyond the balustrade. 'Oh no, I was born on the Firstworld.'

I stare at him, trying to work out if he's having me on. No one comes from the Firstworld. It's a broken planet. I don't even know where it is.

'Really? But I thought…'

Teel grins at me. 'That nothing lives there now? My parents were scientists. They were stationed there, retro-engineering the terrain. Pockets of it are idyllic. The rest…' He shrugs. 'Not so much.'

I can't help myself. 'Where is it?'

Teel tilts his head to one side. 'That's an Imperial secret,' he teases. 'Only the Empress and her court favourites know the location. I'm not sure my parents really knew. They would have been transported there when I was still in the womb.'

'Pregnant? Isn't that risky?'

'You never met my mother. She claims she didn't know. I suspect quite the opposite. But her work was everything to her.' He smiles with genuine pleasure. 'You probably would have liked her. She would have liked you.'

Embarrassed I stare up at the night's sky, looking at the spray of stars and wondering which one he was born in orbit of. And how far away it might be.

Teel leans in, his body warm and his scent wrapping itself around me. He points past me, up to the sky and I feel enveloped in him. It's not a bad feeling. Not at all.

'See that little light up there?' he says softly, as if whispering a lover's endearments to me. He points. 'That's where we're from. It's where we're all from. That's the sun of the Firstworld.'

I don't really know which one but I gaze along the length of his finger, out into the darkness, as the bright and the palest stars look back at us, flickering, spinning, like diamonds. I smile. I can't help myself.

'So far away,' I whisper and disentangle myself from him. I have to. The temptation to stay there is far too strong. *What am I doing?*

'May I fetch you a drink?' he asks. Alcohol, that's the last thing I need. But I also need him to be not so close to me for a moment or two so I can actually think. When I nod he gives me that same devastating smile. 'Stay there. Just there. You are so beautiful there.'

What else can I do? Besides, it's pleasant out here, away from the noise and heat of the ballroom. As he vanishes back inside, I realise I'm not the only one out here. A giggle comes from the bushes off to my left and as I turn sharply towards the sound, ready to draw the knives, finger on the coms at my wrist, a young couple burst out of the bushes. She's flushed and delighted while he's like a lovelorn fool. They see me, freeze and then rush off inside in a flurry of beautiful, dishevelled clothes and laughter.

I frown, and then catch myself. I've never felt so old.

And they aren't much younger than me. Perhaps I *am* old. If not in body then in heart. There's only been one time when I was like that – carefree, reckless and so in love. Or in lust, anyway.

It's like my stupid brain summons him.

Zander steps out into the night, the guards assigned to watch him tonight his shadows. When he sees me, he freezes momentarily. His guards stand to attention on either side of the door when they see me. I don't say a word, watching that they both keep alert, watching everything without being seen to do so. Daria trained them well. She's probably here somewhere, watching too. Judging.

'Petra,' he says and suddenly I can't think of anything else. There's something in his voice, something full of longing. Why do I have to remember how it was back then?

'Zander.'

He swallows hard. I can see his throat moving.

'I wanted to say...' His face gives that flicker of discomfort. I remember it well. 'I'm sorry.'

I'm not sure how to reply. The old Petra would have laughed and turned it into a joke. We would have gone on drinking with everyone else and that would have been that. She would have teased him mercilessly for months for being the first to back down.

That was a lifetime ago.

It means so much more now. I had to push him away. I still have to. But this... this means something to me. Something special.

'Thank you,' I tell him. And I mean it. Zander has never found apologies easy. Male pride, family pride, and probably about seven other varieties of pride get in his way.

'Ah, there you are,' says Val Teel as he emerges through the double doors, drinks in hands. The guards only just stop before they leap on him, but their training kicks in. They know who he is. They're fully briefed. Val pauses, waiting to be sure he's safe and then sweeps on as if nothing happened. 'My two favourite people. Come to steal her away from me, Zander? Doesn't she look beautiful tonight?'

I expect a flippant remark, or something cutting, but he just looks at me for a long moment.

'Petra is always beautiful, Val,' he replies. 'But as you get to know her, you'll realise that's the least of it. Excuse me. I should go back inside.'

If he had said something unkind and bitter it would have been easier. I stand there, frozen, reeling.

Teel leans back on the balustrade, his long legs stretched out in front of him. They're pointing right at Zander, as if they can fix him in place. He's slim and elegant next to Zander, a complete contrast to his broad shoulders and height.

His voice is very soft. 'Stay with us. We're the best company here.'

Zander frowns at him, but there's something else in his eyes now. He likes Teel. I can see that. Genuinely likes him. 'Don't let Kaeda hear you say that.'

Teel laughs. 'None of us will ever be good enough for Lady Kaeda. Stay, Zander. Let her machinate alone.'

He actually pats the balustrade beside him, his eyes twinkling wickedly. I want to go to him and I can see the same desire in Zander. Who wouldn't?

'I can't,' says the crown prince and it's as if he's refusing something far more. He still doesn't move though. Like he wants to go and at the same time he doesn't. Or doesn't want to leave us alone, perhaps. Whatever the reason, he can't draw the moment out for ever. 'Please,' he says and looks right at me, with an expression in his eyes that I don't understand. It spears through me and suddenly I'm afraid for him. *What is it?* 'Please, excuse me.'

He steps back as Kaeda herself comes sweeping through the door in a wild rush, clearly searching for him. Her eyes gleam as they alight on him.

'Oh, there you are, Zander darling!'

I'm not sure if she even sees Teel and me at first. She launches herself into Zander's arms and kisses him entirely too intimately.

I can't help but watch. There's no way to avoid it. I knock back nearly half of whatever fizzy, sweet alcoholic concoction Teel handed me. It roils in my stomach.

Who he kisses is none of my business. I made it none of my business years ago.

Teel's hand touches mine. Just a touch but it's a comfort I didn't expect. His skin is very smooth and warm. He does no more than that, just that gesture of support. I'm glad I still have the mask on. I'm glad no one can see my burning face.

'Oh!' she squeals. 'Oh, I didn't realise you were there too! Hello Valentin! Hello, oh… um… general, isn't it? General something?'

She sounds drunk but she isn't. She knows what she's saying. I'm certain of it. I don't so much smile as grit my teeth.

'General Kel,' Teel tells her. He doesn't look amused.

'Hello, General Kel,' she sing-songs and then throws back her head laughing. 'Zander, I want you to meet someone. Stop wandering off!'

She winds her arm through his and leads him helplessly away. Just as they vanish through the doorway and are swallowed up in the noise of the ball, I hear her voice.

'I thought you said she was pretty!'

I flinch. I can't help it. I feel like a fool, standing here in a gown designed by the finest dressmakers from the heart of the Empire. I should never have agreed to this. I should have just worn my uniform and done my job, and not even try to play their games. My face is burning and my eyes watering, stinging like I've laboured through an inferno.

I heave in a breath.

'Forgive me, Lord Teel. I ought to go. I shouldn't have come.' I pull off the star mask and drop it.

'Petra,' he says gently, half admonishment, half apology as he removes his own mask. It's worse when I can see his whole face. Even his pity is beautiful. 'De Lorens is a foolish snob with her eye on a throne.'

So dismissive… I think it's probably foolish to dismiss her. There's more to her than she would like people to think.

And that doesn't mean she's wrong about me. I have no place here, in this playground of the aristocracy. I want to get back and check in with Halie, see how Dwyer is doing. Even though my coms haven't made a single noise all evening.

'And Lysander is a fool too,' he murmurs.

I don't know why I say it. I'm hurt. I'm feeling utterly betrayed. Teel's empathy isn't helping. 'He always was. That was one thing we could rely on after a mission – we always knew he'd end up passed out in a brothel. It's just got a bit more high class, hasn't it?'

My voice shakes. Why does my voice shake?

Before I realise what's happening Teel steps closer to me, pressing his cool hands on either side of my burning face, holding me there with no force at all. He waits, for me to pull away or to fight him off, for something. I don't know what. But then he breathes my name again, and kisses me. I'm no expert. But he is.

I struggle for equilibrium as all the sensations wash over me, as my own body reacts and ignores all logic. I fit against his body, aware of the hidden strength there, the lithe muscles beneath his silken clothes, and the scent of him which bewitches me. His lips, his kiss, his touch on my face and everything I am. I long to give in, surrender and for this never to stop.

Somewhere far away I hear the bells chiming for midnight. The ball is ending, the masks are being removed, but mine is already gone and so is his, in more ways than one. I open my eyes to look at the silver slivers of his. They gleam with desire. True desire.

Any moment now the assembled party goers will pour out through the doors – just like that one behind him – and find us here, intertwined. I wish I could freeze the moment, hold it forever. I try to lock it into my memory, to keep every sensation with me. I can feel his heart beating against me, so loud, so desperate.

It isn't real. It can't be real. Both of us are playing a game. Both of us are acting. But it feels real. I pull free of him.

'I've got to go.' I say it in a surprisingly calm voice. I'm not sure where it came from. I don't wait for a reply. I turn and run, down into the darkness of the gardens, away from the lights and the music. The trees loom over me, an avenue of beeches which line the path, slender and ghostly in the moonlight. I run until I feel safe once more and can find my breath. My own breath. My own heartbeat. Just mine. Racing. I force it to calm.

Leaning back against the trunk of a tree I try to make myself believe that really just happened. When I trail my trembling fingertips over my lips, they are still tingling.

Chapter Thirteen

Bel

The morning of our wedding the whole of Anthaeus is a hive of activity. There are streamers and pennants and thousands of other silken flags and banners hanging from every possible place. Flowers abound – including a number of bouquets from Petra, oddly enough – lining the path from my chambers to the main reception rooms. It's beautiful. The birds are everywhere too, but most amazing of all are all the tiny clockwork wonders Con has created and hidden everywhere. When he had the time, I don't know, but he did. They play music and sing. When the wind catches them they dance. Little rabbits hop and birds flap their wings, bobbing up and down. The children of Limasyll laugh in delight and compete to find them, running through the gardens, up and down the terraces and in and out of the palace. Many of them are being cared for here until the orphanage is complete. Sometimes I think we should just transform the palace instead. They love it here and his inventions delight them.

That would have been why he created them.

The first time we tried to get married, I was filled with dread. There was nothing I could do, I had no choice. I'd broken my childhood sweetheart Shae's heart the night before and with it my own. I'll never forgive myself for that. This time – oh ancestors, this time, I'm uneasy for another reason.

The Rondet act like they're in mourning. Con behaves as if nothing has happened. I don't even know what to think as I put on a third silver wedding dress.

The sight of it against my skin makes me shiver. The first two I wore ended up soaked in blood, torn and destroyed from battle. This is not what the superstitious would call a lucky colour for me.

Arianne, and the maids, Cresti, and Della, fuss around me, happy and excited, seeing this as their chance to finally make me look like the queen I am supposed to be.

The ornate coms unit on my wrist keeps attracting my attention, as if it will trill out any second with a message or an incoming com. But it doesn't. In the end, I lift it and press the control.

'Bel? Is everything all right?' Con sounds scared. No, not scared. Not as extreme as that. Concerned perhaps. Or maybe I am just projecting my own thoughts on to him. I hope that's all.

'Con?'

'Yes.' There's a thud of something heavy falling and he swears. He's dropped something, or knocked something over, in his study. Of course he's in his study. He's happiest there. And that bloody stone is a mystery screaming out to him to be solved. 'Bel, what's wrong?'

'Nothing.' I hope I didn't pause too long before I answered. Yes, I'm annoyed. A bit. So long as he doesn't forget to meet me at the wedding. 'I just – I just wanted to hear your voice.'

I hear his sigh. I can almost feel it against my skin.

'I'm here,' he says softly. 'I'm always here.'

But he isn't. He's been in my mind, via the Rondet and I've been in his. We've entered their dreamstate together and flown over the planet. We've shared things more deeply than I would have thought possible.

That's gone now. I didn't know how close it made me feel to him until it was gone. Now, just when I'm about to finally marry him, something vital is missing.

'Bel? Is this about the stone?'

Yes. No. I don't know. 'It's about us.'

'We're getting married today.' He pauses as if something awful just occurred to him. 'We are, aren't we? We're *still* getting married today?'

The sudden rush of fear in his voice makes me smile. Not because I'm mean, but it reassures me that he cares.

'Yes.' For once I answer without thinking and hear him breathe another sigh of relief.

'Don't scare me like that, your Highness.' I can sense his smile. 'Do you need me? I'll come right—'

'Isn't that bad luck?' *The ancestors know, we don't need any more bad luck.*

'We don't need more bad luck.' He says the words like he has plucked them from my head and something in me gives a leap of excitement. 'But Bel, you know I love you, don't you? More than anything.'

He once gave up a world for me. Or tried to. The Gravian Ambassador who had led the occupation of Anthaeus had threatened to kill me if Con didn't sign away his kingship and turn Anthaeus over to the enemy. And Con would have done it.

'I love you too. Just…' I don't know how to say it, how to explain it.

'I won't get lost on the way. I swear. Just a few more hours, love. And a lot of fuss and nonsense, of course. But I'll be there. No one will stop me.'

The passion in his voice is undeniable. My fingers caress the coms unit, a slim and delicate piece of engineering that looks like jewellery, which he made for me and which I treasure. I wish he could feel my touch.

'Don't make me have to come and rescue you again, Con,' I murmur.

I hear him laugh softly, filled with affection that can't be disguised or faked. 'Not this time, love.'

The carriage is not as elaborate as the one which took me through the city the first time we tried to marry. We don't have to go as far anyway. The distant Rondet chamber – where royal weddings were blessed before the war – is an empty ruin. Favre and Aeron suggested we use the main chamber of the hidden city with its sparkling underground reflecting pools and ornate, beautiful carvings. So many people had a hand in the preparations for this day that in many ways it isn't simply our wedding. This ceremony belongs to all of Anthaeus.

Music starts as I enter the vast chamber. A dozen harps, bright and spritely, are joined by the choir. I can't ever remember hearing music quite so lovely. I know there are vid cams on me, but right now I can't think where they might be. So many figures turn to look at me in my silver gown, wearing a narrow, diamond crusted crown and silver filigree chains which drape like gossamer down my shoulders. They contrast with the heavy necklace which caresses my throat. My coms unit doesn't look out of place – so beautiful because Con made it for me. And everything he makes is beautiful.

How he has come to care for me I will never understand. But the one thing I know above everything else is that I love him.

At the far end of the chamber I see him watching me with the eyes of a man who has seen heaven.

I hardly notice the world around me as I make my way towards him. How can I think of anything else right now? If I didn't know Jondar and several others would have instant heart attacks and die, I would throw etiquette aside and run to him. Imagine having to explain that to Thom.

At the forefront of the onlookers, Petra grins at me. The witness dress is beautiful on her, almost as beautiful as the one she wore last night. She wears a simple pendant in the shape of a bird at her throat and her hair is braided in such an elegant style that I know Arianne must have got her hands on her this morning. My chief lady-in-waiting stands beside her and Jondar beside Con, looking like the crown prince of the Imperial court I once took him to be.

Of course now I've seen the true faces of the Imperial court. I give a slight nod of acknowledgement to Lord Teel and his party, as is expected, then put them out of my mind. If they're slighted, too bad. I didn't want them here. I'm not sure what he was playing at with Petra last night but if he hurts her I will find such ways to punish him for it, empire be damned. The thought of protecting Petra should sound laughable, but the rush of anger I felt when I found out she had left abruptly after whatever happened with Teel hasn't really faded.

I haven't had a chance to talk to her about it or about what I over-heard in the gardens yesterday. But I will. She's more than my general, and my bodyguard. She's my friend. I have to. I owe her that much.

As I join Con, as his hand touches mine, the sound of wings fills the chamber, louder than the music, the wind they whip up blowing all the perfectly coiffed hair and fine clothes back in disarray. Favre, Rhenna and Aeron set themselves down on the edge of the pool before us, their hides like diamonds, their colours those of joy and happiness.

'Rhenna,' I murmur, aware that she can hear me even as the music starts up again. 'You're making an entrance.'

Well, so did you, the native Anthaese mind inside my own laughs at the same time as the words form. My friend, closer than a sister. *We are here to witness your union, little queen. In the past we came as projections but now we come as ourselves. The change is good.*

I remember the strangely beautiful creatures – the attempts they made to simulate a human as far as they could see and understand them – and the curious tea ceremony during which they had interviewed me when I first arrived on this planet. They had been the colours of metal rather than flesh and they had been charming, so alien and so strange. But enchanting.

They are more fierce now, more alien, but not as strange to me.

I love them, I realise and as I think it or feel it, ripples of light run through Rhenna. She purrs and I hear Favre laugh. Only Aeron doesn't react. He is focused entirely on Con, trying to reach him still. His pain is palpable.

Con releases me for a moment and steps towards the crystalline being. He bends down as Aeron's head comes up and the two of them lean against each other, Con's hands on his cold, smooth hide, Con's forehead pressed to his.

'It's going to be all right, Aeron,' he whispers and his voice is strained. 'I'll figure it out.'

Aeron's reply comes moments later, to me alone, which tells me he tried to talk to Con first and it didn't work. The ache behind his words makes my eyes sting unexpectedly. '*Tell him… tell him we will solve this together. As we always have.*'

I nod and relay the message. Con smiles. 'Of course, my friend.'

'*But this is not a time for sorrow,*' Rhenna protests, irritated at the Maestre. '*This is a time for joy. Proceed with the ceremony. Make vows. Make promises.*'

Jondar officiates, and binds our hands together in scarlet silk. The blood of royal houses combined, the blood of warriors joined together. He recites words millennia old. They run together in a litany of ceremony as we circle the pool and the Rondet watch us, while

Anthaeus watches us. *If anyone has just cause to object... I, Belengaria, declare my willingness, I, Conleith, profess my love... We are one, where we were two, our houses are one where they were two... I accept Conleith as my eternal beloved, I accept Belengaria as my eternal beloved.* We exchange coins, our house insignia engraved on them, and then our rings, unadorned silver, and by these symbols, our souls are joined as one. *The Rondet bear witness and affirm this union.* And suddenly, we are husband and wife.

Just like that. Without a drop of blood spilled. No deaths, no explosions...

I find a sob on my lips and Con laughs at me, with me. He wraps his arms around me and kisses me while our people cheer.

It's a miracle. It has to be. Finally.

*

It all goes by in a blur, while at the same time it is endless. People to greet, congratulations and good wishes to accept. All the while I just want to sneak away with Con – partly to be with my now-husband and, I admit, partly to simply escape. But, even though it's the worst possible time, I also want to talk to him, to figure out what happened to his connection with the Rondet, what the stone actually is. I know he must be working on a solution. He's Con. Of course he is. But the whole thing scares me more than I can say.

At the reception I notice Petra standing alone by one of the reflecting pools and make my way towards her, but someone else gets there before me.

Lord Teel bows to her in a gesture both respectful and intimate. As I watch, my stalwart bodyguard blushes, a deep red blossoming from her cleavage to her hairline. She takes a step back, flustered and I wonder what he could have said to her. If someone had told me about this I would never have believed it. Petra is made of stone, like her name.

But Teel is beautiful and charming. And, it seems, determined. He smiles at her as he speaks, a genuine smile of appreciation. And Petra is floored. If I hadn't heard him in the garden I'd believe it too. I don't know how much of Petra's reaction is feigned. If she's acting she's incredibly convincing.

I admit I never thought much about Petra's love life. Mine has been complicated enough. I suppose it doesn't make me a very good friend. But after Zander she always seemed complete by herself, strong and independent, unstoppable, a force of nature who didn't need anyone else. She always seemed whole. The rock I could rely on.

She hides her smile and glances around. Her eyes meet mine for just a moment, Instantly she transforms, straightening, her shoulders squaring and her face impassive. She makes a polite excuse, turns to come my way, but Teel catches her hand. If it had been anyone else I think she would have laid him out on the ground seconds later. But she doesn't.

It's not that she unbends. But she stops. She goes completely still.

Teel gives her a small box, unadorned except for the covering of shimmering silk. No doubt it's a jewellery box and coming from him, whatever is inside probably rivals the Anthaese crown jewels, most of which I'm wearing right now.

She stares at it. I half expect her to give it back.

Instead she frowns, nods and a curious smile flickers over her lips. The wonder in her face is beautiful.

How can they both be acting? How can this possibly be fake?

'Bel?' Con joins me, his hand on my shoulder cool and welcome. 'What are you—?' He notices the direction of my gaze. 'Oh. That would… complicate matters.'

I wonder should I tell him what I heard, and what I asked Petra to do.

'Petra's a professional. Don't worry. She won't let him distract her from a mission.'

'I didn't mean the mission.'

He nods in the other direction. Zander stands by ornate carvings which decorate the entranceway, a glass of something far too strong in his hand. He's glaring at the two of them, Petra and Teel, his face stricken.

As I glance back to them, I see Teel has left her there and as he walks away, he salutes Zander. My brother's face goes stark white.

I breathe out slowly, centring myself. I never considered that. 'I should talk to them.'

I don't know which 'them' I mean. My brother? My friend? All three? I can't imagine the sort of nightmare that would be.

'It's our wedding day,' Con reminds me. 'I'll get Thom to do it.'

And he grins.

I whirl on him. 'Con, that isn't fair.'

'Who ever said I had to be fair?' he asks, his expression the perfect imitation of innocence. Con laughs, sweeps me up in his arms and whirls me around. His kiss steals my breath and makes my heart sing.

But I miss the closeness, the communion, the sensation of his mind entwined with mine.

Chapter Fourteen

Petra

I make my excuses and slip away, heading back to my quarters as discretely as I can. Thanks to Teel's attentions quite a number of people – friends and strangers – are gawping at me and I don't like it one bit. I don't court attention at any time. I hate it.

Back in my rooms, I close the door and breathe a sigh of relief. Once I get out of the dress with its corsetry and petticoats, once I uncoil the knot into which my hair was twisted, I shower and change back into my simple clothes, and sleek black, body armour. The weapons belt hugs my hips and I begin to feel like I'm approaching normality again.

The box sits on the desk, reminding me that nothing is normal. Valentin Teel, beloved of the empire and the Empress herself, seems intent on seducing me. If I'm lucky, that's all he wants. But I've never been what you might call lucky. So what exactly is he after? However charming he is, I'm not a fool to believe in love at first sight no matter what he might say.

We wanted this, Bel and I. I'm meant to distract him. Not the other way around. None of this is real. I have to keep telling myself that.

And yet… I open the box, expecting something showy and extravagant that I can laugh at and dismiss. Hoping for it, perhaps.

The pendant inside is small, subtle, perfect. It's a star with a diamond at its heart. I've never seen a piece of jewellery so perfectly crafted. It's like a real star in the sky has been captured in metal and that single precious stone.

Last night he held me, pointed into the night's sky until I could pick out a single, distant star.

See that little light up there? That's where we're from.

My body remembers the kiss. It confuses me, more than I can say. I couldn't sleep last night, thinking of him. And of Zander. Thinking of both of them.

With a snarl of frustration I close the box again with a snap. And then open it. And close it again.

An image leaps into my mind – Zander wandering off with Kaeda at the ball. Her voice. *I thought you said she was pretty.*

At least Teel makes me feel like I might be. Even if I'm sure he's wrong. I take the necklace out of the box, hold it up so it catches the light. It's beautiful.

There's a noise in the outer room, a rustle of movement.

'Dwyer?' It can't be. He's still in the infirmary. I checked with Halie this morning and there's no improvement. He hasn't got any worse. He's still sleeping. Stable, she said. But he's not showing any sign of waking up either.

I freeze, the necklace in my hand twisting around. I move slowly, slipping it around my neck so it's out of the way and upholstering the blaster at my side. I remember the Mecha, a blend of human and animal and machine, the terrible speed of it, the feeling of its claws in me. My shoulder aches with the memory.

I don't call out again. Even if it was Dwyer, he would have answered. Besides he hardly ever makes a sound and if he knew I was in here he would have made himself known right away. Anyone who should be here right now would have said something.

I press the silent alarm and slide into the shadows at the edge of the room, where the lamplight doesn't reach. The intruder doesn't hear me move. I shove the door open with my foot and fold back against the wall. It swings silently. Nothing I hate more than a squeaking hinge.

A slim figure is bending over one of the cabinets, rummaging through the papers in the drawer. My papers. I keep personal material in there, not state secrets or military information.

'You could have just asked,' I say calmly, my weapon levelled at the back of their head. I can't see if it's male or female. Slim, dressed in black, with some kind of mask on their face, that's it. The figure freezes, and I wait for a reply. Only polite, isn't it?

But this isn't the polite kind of thief.

Crossing the threshold, I hesitate. The room is empty except for the intruder. Or looks empty. I pause, listening, waiting. Listening.

I only hear a breath. A single breath.

The figure moves like a shadow, so fast I hardly see them. I shy back, twisting to avoid a weapon but there isn't one. They're heading for the door.

'Stop or I'll shoot.'

They don't. Hands on the door knob, and I fire off a single shot, over their shoulder. Jondar will kill me for the smoking hole in his precious palace, but I don't care.

'The guards will be here in a second and I'm not going anywhere. Neither are you. Turn around and take off the mask.'

The hand reaches up slowly as they comply and I don't know why I do it. Complacency perhaps. Stupidity. Cockiness.

I relax for a second.

He's on me, straight on me. A man – young, hard, highly trained. He dives at me, moving from stillness to action in a heartbeat. His hand strikes my wrist, sending the blaster spinning away. One punch sends me reeling back but I catch myself. Pain bounces through me and I use it. I feed on it, adrenaline like copper in my mouth, making me sharper, harder.

Just like it always does.

Hand to hand is the oldest skill, the first skill, the one we all learned in the rubble and the chaos of the war which almost destroyed Vairian. Fight or die, that was how it was.

And it isn't just hand to hand. It's feet and elbows, teeth and knees. He doesn't know that. I feel that instinctively. He grew up somewhere where this wasn't necessary. Oh, he's good. He's very good. But he isn't me.

Or… and the thought flits across my mind like the touch of a moth's wing… he doesn't want to hurt me.

I catch him in the solar plexus, and he staggers back, gasping for air, unable to catch it.

And then he says something. Something impossible.

'Damn it, Petra. You're meant to be partying.'

He tears off the mask, gasping for air, wheezing and I recognise him.

'*Art?* What the *hell* are you doing here?'

Bel and Zander's brother leans over, hands on his knees, winded but trying to recover and I can't move. 'I came for the wedding.'

He's older than I remembered. Of course he is – he's my own age, but we haven't seen each other in years. He's always been solemn, quiet, but he's probably the cleverest of them. If clever means devious.

'I don't believe you.'

'Well,' he straightens, shuffling his feet. 'Yeah, you'd probably be right.'

Running feet herald the guards who should have been here a few minutes ago. I've got to decide here and now what to do with him. He's a Merryn. I don't know what he wanted in my belongings but... damn it. How will we explain any of this?

'What do you want?'

His dark eyes twinkle, much darker than Zander's. Almost as dark as Bel's. But he glances at the door, nervously. 'Right now? I want to get the hell out of here, Petra.'

'General Kel?' someone shouts from outside. 'General? We're coming in.'

Stop him or let him go? He'll never get out of here now. Not without help. I growl under my breath. I don't know what he's up to, but he's Art Merryn. I can't let them arrest him. Imagine Bel's face. Imagine Zander's.

'Get in the wardrobe.'

I don't wait to see if he obeys. I know he will. I fling open the window and turn as the door slams back against the wall. Troops flood the room.

'General.' Corporal Lorza is first in. She secures the room around me and then salutes. 'The alarm sounded, shots fired.'

'He got away,' I say, nodding to the window. 'Search the grounds. Human, not Mecha. Take him alive, if you can.'

She frowns slightly, as if she doesn't quite believe me. But she's Anthaese. She doesn't like to argue. 'Ma'am,' she says and swiftly hands out orders to those accompanying her.

I wait, heart going a little too fast, trying not to look at the wardrobe door and give him away.

Just what I need. Another Merryn in my life.

'Will we search the room, ma'am?'

'No. There's no need. Nothing is gone. I disturbed him.'

'Him? Did you see him? Can you give a description? We'll get it out on the interstellars and tie in with the—'

'No.' If I sound sharp, I can't help it. I need to calm down. But the last thing I need is to give a description of Art, or anyone else. I just need this to be over. 'It was just an opportunist, some urchin from the city I'm sure. Took advantage of the wedding to sneak inside and thought… I don't know what. If he was looking for riches he picked the wrong room.'

I know he wasn't looking for riches. I need to find out what Art was after, why he was going through my belongings. But I don't need Lorza trying too hard to find out.

I'd half hoped she'd laugh at my attempted humour, but she remains stony-faced, unhappy.

'Ma'am,' she says, which I'm aware is not an answer at all, because I've used it myself more times than I care to remember right now.

A bang outside makes us both jump. The sky lights up, fireworks of every colour tearing through the night. The party is going on, and all of Anthaeus is celebrating.

I find my voice again.

'You're dismissed, Corporal.'

She leaves, still directing her troops, speaking low into her coms. Just like I trained her.

I wait until the noise of their footsteps outside fades away.

When I open the wardrobe door, Art is gone.

*

'What do you mean, Art was here?' Bel asks. The disbelief on her face makes me cringe inside. I didn't want to tell her. It's her wedding day.

I have problems enough with one of her brothers, let alone two. But I couldn't *not* tell her. Especially when he vanished again. I'm still not sure how he did that.

He always could get out of anything and everything – probably comes with the territory of having Zander and Luc as older brothers. I'd never imagined what use he'd put that particular skill to.

But breaking into and out of my chambers without leaving any trace?

Some men might be doing that sort of thing for one reason, but I can't imagine that of Art either. He was always the studious one, his nose buried in his books. He's respectful too. Always was.

'Art was in my rooms. I didn't know it was him or I wouldn't have sounded the alarm.'

'Artorius. *Our brother?* She looks at Zander. 'I thought he was on Vairian, with father. Do you know anything about this?'

He does. The moment I said it, his eyes shifted away from me.

'I… I knew he might be here. I didn't know when or how.'

Bel punches him in the arm, hard. Zander recoils from her, more in surprise than pain or fear. 'Tell me what is going on *right now.*'

'I don't know. I mean he's working for father, for Vairian, on a mission, deep cover. I saw him on Cuore, that's all. And I wasn't meant to say anything about it.'

'So your brother breaking into my rooms is perfectly all right with you?' I ask.

Zander rolls his eyes. 'I'm sure he had his reasons.'

'Well I don't care about his reasons – if he needed something from me why didn't he ask? What is he up to? What is this mission?'

Zander purses his lips. We aren't going to get anything out of him, then.

'He's very good at his job. I'm surprised you caught him.'

I widen my eyes and stare at him, which makes my disdain even more evident. 'Well, *I'm* very good at *my* job.'

'I didn't mean—'

'When you're quite finished insulting Petra again...' Bel growls at him. 'I want to know what Art is doing here. If you don't know, find out. This isn't Vairian and like it or not Zander, this is not your territory. This is Con's world. A Vairian can't act with impunity on Anthaese soil.'

'It's your world too now, isn't it?'

She seems to freeze for a moment and she frowns. I don't know if it has occurred to her before this moment. But Zander has clearly thought all this through. I see anger flicker over Bel's face.

'Tell father that I'm not his pawn, Zander.'

'What?'

It isn't even convincing to me.

'I'm married to Con and I serve Anthaeus. Not Vairian. If he wanted otherwise he shouldn't have sold me in the first place.'

He looks shocked. I don't suppose he ever thought of it as that. It was her duty to marry. It was for her world. Our world. But she gave up everything to do it. Her home. Her dreams. Shae. And even her status as a Vairian.

And I went with her. I remember what Zander said to me in the infirmary. That I wasn't even Vairian any more. I don't regret it for an instant.

She smooths down her silver dress and fixes her hair. 'I have a wedding to get back to. And don't you two have a mission of your own to get on with?'

She sweeps out of the room, pausing only to pointedly slam the door behind her. I stare after her. My little princess has finally become a queen.

'Bloody family!' Zander shouts.

I fold my arms, waiting until he realises I'm still there.

'Did you send him to search my rooms?' I ask at last.

'No. I didn't even know he'd come here. Not really – I have no idea what he was up to.'

'Find out.'

'We have our own problems,' he says. 'Kelta, remember?'

'Oh, I remember. I'm the one person who can keep their mind on the job, it seems.'

He laughs out loud, a sharp and violent – 'Ha!' Zander advances on me, his face dark with anger. 'You could have fooled me.'

'What's that meant to mean?'

'Teel? All over you?'

Oh, he's one to talk.

'De Lorens? All over *you*?'

He hesitates as if he wants to say something. I don't know what and I don't care what.

'You don't understand, Petra. He's dangerous.'

'So am I.'

'Not like him, Pet.'

I roll my eyes and turn away from him. 'Ancestors, that's all you say. Give me some credit, Zander. Just—'

His touch is so gentle I think maybe I'm imagining it. His hand on my arm, his fingers pulling me back. He turns me around to face him and his other hand cups my cheek, a cradle, warm and so gentle. For all his bluster, there's nothing rough about Zander. I pushed that memory away long ago because it was too painful, but it floods back now.

'Pet…' he whispers. All the anger seeps away. He stares down at me, his gaze roving over my features, lingering on my lips. 'I wish I could explain…'

I have to make him stop. I can't let him tear open the old wounds. It took too long to heal the first time. I've moved on. I had to move on. It was the only way to survive.

I make myself a statue. I have to. *I have to.* 'Don't call me Pet, Zander.'

He's *so* gentle. How could I have forgotten that? Something is lodged in my throat, all the words I want to say, all the things I can't.

'I just need—'

I bring my hands up to his chest, both of them, flat against his pectoral muscles. I mean to push him away but the moment I touch him I can't do it. I'm so confused. I don't even know how this happens, how he does this to me.

The heat beneath my hands should burn me. But I can't move.

Instead I turn to the one thing that a Vairian will never deny. Duty.

'We need to go,' I tell him. 'We have a mission. The others will be waiting.'

He drops his head, half in defeat, half as if he just needs to be closer. For a moment I think he'll try to kiss me and what will I do if he does? I can't think.

But Zander just rests his forehead against mine. It's so tender a gesture, familiar, perfect... there's more tenderness filtered through that movement than any kiss could convey.

'Don't,' he whispers.

'Zan...' I used to call him Zan in our quietest moments, the most intimate. 'We have a mission.'

'All right.' The sighed words are half a groan and he closes his eyes. Defeated. 'All right. But we will have to talk about this eventually, Petra.'

He releases me and I walk away. I don't even check to see if he's following me, although I know he will be. Eventually. There's a long time between now and eventually. Perhaps even enough time to work out what I'm going to say.

Perhaps even enough to work out what I'm going to do.

*

Thom is waiting for us at the shuttle. If he has any comments about the two of us arriving more or less at the same time he keeps them to himself. Which is fortunate for him.

The team we put together are already at work loading the equipment. There are five of them, making us eight in total. The pilot will remain with the ship at all times. I requested Ellish and there she is, already warming up the ship.

Harmon Lees is checking weaponry. He's a soldier through and through, part of the Anthaese military before the invasion, Keltan mining security, and he knows the place backwards. He was on furlough on Anthaeus when the Gravians invaded. It was lucky for us that he was. He's experienced, reliable, exactly what we need. We exchange a nod as I join Thom.

'You know Taren Beq,' Thom says.

'Bel's bodyguard?'

'Yes, she insisted he come with us, says she's fine with Con's guards.'

She trusts him implicitly and he's one of Thom's trainees originally, one of the Queen's Guard he put together, so it makes sense she'd want him along. But Thom isn't finished.

'We had to replace Mithine Sorin.' I give him a stony glare, my suspicion mounting. 'Corporal Dale Lorza is stepping in.'

Corporal Lorza? She's one of mine. She's based in the palace, not on active duty. She doesn't have training for special ops like this.

'What the hell?' Thom doesn't answer so I just yell instead. 'Lorza!'

She appears, somewhat sheepishly from the back of the shuttle and salutes a little too crisply.

'Ma'am.'

'What is the meaning of this?'

'I volunteered, ma'am. When I found out Sorin was ill.'

'Volunteered? Didn't I teach you anything?' She just stands there in the face of my disgust. 'Come here.' I grab her arm and pull her out of earshot of the others. 'This isn't some sort of diplomatic mission. This is dangerous.'

The look of indignation is a picture. I couldn't have managed better myself.

'I understand that, ma'am. I scored higher than anyone in marksmanship training. I've seen combat in the war. I want to serve the Anthaem and his queen. I want to be of service to my world.'

And if I turn her away now, I'll put her to shame in front of everyone else. And word will spread. She's a corporal too, one of my direct command. I appointed her and I'm responsible for her. That's why she's here.

I'm stuck with her. No way out of it. Sometimes I just wish I cared less about other people's feelings. Life would be so much easier.

'All right then. Stay close to me and keep out of trouble, do you understand?'

A wobbly grin spreads over her face. 'Yes, ma'am.'

'And get your body armour on.'

Thom gives me a nod as I march back towards him and this time I really want to punch him in that far too handsome face. 'She's good, Petra. Really good. I talked to her commanding officers and went through her training records as well. You need to trust your instincts.'

'My instincts say she's too bloody young and you know it.'

'We're all too bloody young,' Zander interrupts.

'Speak for yourself, old man.' Thom laughs at him. Thom's older than him and they're both older than me. If I feel a million years old, what must they feel like?

'When you're quite finished...' I say, in tones that tell them I'm bored and will shortly start shooting.

Bel and Con are still dancing at their reception, completely distracting everyone if this all goes according to plan. At midnight there will be even more fireworks to light up the night, designed by Con himself. Who's going to notice a shuttle taking off in that?

At least that's the idea.

But I can't stop worrying about Art Merryn being here without Bel or it seems Zander knowing about it. I can't stop thinking about Teel and the way he keeps pursuing me.

I can't stop thinking about Zander.

But I have to.

We load up, and I speak briefly to Ellish. She's as focused and practical as ever. I know I can rely on her. Sitting beside her in the cockpit, is Daria. She nods in my general direction as she notices me, but to be honest, all her attention is fixed on the little red-haired pilot, who returns the look with a kind of stunned wonder. I don't know what Daria has been up to the whole time she's been here, but I'm beginning to suspect. They work together, completely in sync, often without having to speak – I can't imagine understanding another human being so well as that. The shuttle is a working ship, one of the many which ply their way through the air to the ships orbiting the planet, transporting good and passengers. At least from the outside, that's what she looks like. In reality Sorrell, Ellish and Thom have gone over her, upgrading every system, fitting her with new engines and dampening fields and several other technological marvels I don't have a hope of understanding. I'm not even going to try.

Time's up. I'm counting down in my head anyway but the timer in the shuttle is keeping us on track. Thom makes the call.

Silently, we strap in. Lorza is quiet, thoughtful. Zander takes a seat opposite me and doesn't say a word. The rear hatch closes like the doors of a tomb. Far off, I can still hear the fireworks.

The ship leaps from the ground, punching its way through the atmosphere. It has been so long since I flew in anything designed to leave orbit that the thrill of acceleration is a rush of adrenaline. I find myself grinning and glance over at Thom to see a similarly stupid expression. Zander just looks bored, while Lorza is gazing out at the gorgeous view of Anthaeus growing smaller beneath us.

The engines settle and the world grows quiet as the eerie calm after the storm of ascension muffles us. This one small ship will take us all the way to Kelta in about fifty-six hours.

From the cockpit, Ellish repeats the standard safety protocols but only half of us are really listening. Old hands know it off by heart. Lorza's mouth moves, repeating it to commit it to memory.

Thom checks his wrist com and his expression softens.

'A love note?' I tease. His eyes meet mine, both amusement and affection making them warm and gentle.

'He worries.'

'Well, you have a habit of getting into trouble, General Rahleigh. He's right.'

Chapter Fifteen

Bel

The other side of the bed is empty. And for the first time, it shouldn't be.

'Con?'

I scramble up from the bed, throwing off the sheets and trying to reach the light controls. It is neither graceful nor elegant, and not in any way queenly.

'Bel?' His voice comes from the other side of the room and when I finally manage to switch on a light, I see him there, by the window, a shadow against the night. 'I'm here. It's okay.'

He doesn't sleep much. Since the war, the nightmares are too bad. He's told me about it, tried to talk. The medics say it's the best thing to do. But it isn't easy.

I was so exhausted after the celebrations I barely stayed awake while Della and Cresti helped me out of the gown and into a nightdress. They brushed my hair until it shone and felt like it was about to be torn out of my head. They ushered me off to the royal bridal chamber full of laughter and comments that they'd considered quite risqué. But they didn't grow up with the military.

Con and I were so exhausted we simply fell asleep in each other's arms.

'Any word from the ship?'

'Just status reports.'

I sink back closing my eyes and wishing it didn't make me feel like I was somehow failing them, abandoning them. Up there in the dark, in the night, heading for the unknown. Because, despite the reports from the preliminary survey teams we don't know what's up there. We don't know what the Gravians left.

None of which explains why Con is up, standing by the window.

I pad barefoot across the thick blue carpet until I reach him, and wrap my arms around his waist. He leans back, tilting his face up towards the ceiling, eyes closed as if just having me this close is a wonder and he must drink in every second. I know because that's how I feel.

'What are you doing?' I ask, pressing my cheek against his back.

'I'm just...' He sighs. 'I was trying to reach Aeron.'

The pang that goes through me isn't all my own. The Rondet are still hurting from this separation. Con has been trying to disguise his own loss from them, from me, from everyone. But he can't hide it now. He misses them, a vital part of himself which is now gone.

'Come back to bed.'

For a moment I think he'll agree, that we'll curl up together and lose ourselves in each other. His coms give a ping and he glances down.

My heart falls a little. It's always going to be like this, isn't it? Other duties, other demands on our time.

'Everything okay?'

He smiles, noticing my dismay. 'It's just an automated alarm. I need to check on something in my study. I have some tests running on that stone and—'

'I'll come with you.' I say without hesitation. This is my life, I've pledged myself to him. I might as well try to understand his wonderful inventions, catch a glimpse of the mind that I love so well at work.

I'll have to share him no matter what. I might as well share my time with him while I can.

'Are you sure?' he looks startled as he turns around to face me. There are many moments that I adore him, but when he gets flustered like this, I can't help myself. 'I mean – you don't have to. I want you to, of course. I mean, if you want to. If you really think—'

I kiss him to silence. 'Yes, I want to. Show me.'

His first wife, Matilde, never had time I suppose. And up until now I really haven't either. But I'm not going to make the mistake of letting him dwell on things and not share them with me.

His workroom is a far cry from the airy dome above the library which was destroyed in the attack. Which took Shae from me. The ruins of the tower are little more than burnt rubble and I don't think anyone has the heart to rebuild it. Con moved himself and his inventions in as close as possible though, into two functional rooms.

We climb the stairs, hand in hand. It almost feels like we're sneaking away. Which I suppose we are. Neither of us has summoned guards. It hardly feels like we need them now.

'I've been running a multi-diagnostic system of scans and I have it in a containment field. The basic readings haven't shown anything unusual, so for this round I set up a broad spectrum analysis.'

If he'd told me that magic imps were dancing on it that would make as much sense, I guess. But I let him talk. Mainly because I love the sound of his voice. I love the joy in it. I'd listen to him talk all night if he wanted. And I'm sure I will.

He swipes his coms unit against the door and it clicks open. The lights come on as he enters and I step inside after him, into an Aladdin's cave of trinkets, wonders and technology.

It's more like the tents he used when we were hiding from the Gravians during the war than the study he once had at the top of the tower, the one my bodyguard Shae blew up to save the two of us. If there is a method organising the jumble of work, he's probably the only person who can decipher it.

The stone is perched in a sort of cradle of metal on a workbench. He's attached about a dozen different sensors to it and trained on it are a number of scanners which all feed back to a single terminal. The screen is scrolling through data.

But Con stands suddenly very still. 'Someone's been here.'

I don't know what sheet of paper or piece of equipment is out of place but I trust him to know. This is his world, his space. My mind immediately goes to Art. What is my brother doing here? Is he still here? Petra was the only one to see him and while I don't doubt her for a moment, there's no other evidence.

I placed a call through to our father but there's been no reply as yet. Interstellar communications can be tricky. Solar flares and matching orbits, a single satellite out of action… but at the same time, he should have come back to me by now. I used the right language. *Clearance alpha-Yolande*. Nothing.

I don't like this at all.

There's a scuffle of movement in the corner. No one else should be in here. No one at all. Con moves suddenly, reaching for the new form of blaster he's been developing. It's an innovative design, more efficient, multiple settings. He was telling me about it ages ago. He turns around, trying to shield me and the Greymen step out of the shadows. Three of them, two men and Liette, and with them my maid, Della.

She looks helplessly at me, her eyes filled with apologies but no one is holding her there.

'Call security,' Con says.

'No, please...' Della says. 'We haven't done any harm.'

'Della? Come over here,' I say gently but she doesn't move.

Liette puts her hand on Della's shoulder. 'It's fine. No one is going to hurt you. We won't let them. You're with the Coparius now. You're one of us.'

'Liette, please... she's the queen...'

'She's not my queen.' She brings up her own weapon, also from the study, the sight fixed on me. I'm pretty sure she worked on that one herself. It has a nastier look than anything my husband would create. And she clearly knows how to use it. 'You'll lower the field and set the Coparius free,' she tells Con.

'I'll do nothing of the sort,' he replies, his aim never wavering.

Her weapon charges with a high-pitched whine. 'I've no love for your Vairian wife. That must be clear by now. Do what I say.'

'And if I shoot you first?'

She smiles. She actually smiles. 'You won't, Anthaem. You don't have it in you. I know you better than anyone.'

That's when he does. To my horror Della moves first, flinging herself right in front of Liette. Con cries out, his hand already dropping as he realises the horror of what is happening and before she hits the ground, the other Greymen are on him. They rip the blaster out of his hands.

Della doesn't move. She's slumped on the ground, lifeless. I give a sob of horror and Liette laughs. She actually laughs. I look up at her, ready to tear through her myself, but I can see the light of a zealot in her eyes.

'I was wrong. Maybe you do after all.'

What happened to her? What changed her? She wasn't like this before. I realise she might have hated me, but she wasn't cruel. Not like this.

I wrap my hand around my wrist and tap out the emergency code on my coms. It won't take long. It can't take long. We should have waited for our guards in the first place, I know that. I'll get one hell of a lecture from Petra and Thom when they get back. We've grown complacent since the war. We thought we were safe and nothing could touch us. We were wrong.

'Lower the containment field,' she tells him as her companions shove him roughly towards it. Con glares at her but she just walks towards me and presses the cold muzzle of the blaster against my neck.

Come on. This is taking too long.

Con's fingers fly over the controls and the soft hum quietens. The glow of the field fades.

'Why are you doing this?' I ask, keeping my voice calm and quiet. I don't want to agitate her any further, but I need to keep her distracted. I need to keep her away from Con. 'Faestus wanted Con to have the stone.'

'Faestus is a fool,' Liette says, without even looking at me. 'He thought the stone would speak to the Anthaem, but he's useless. And now he's just locked it away. Mutilating it.'

'I've been studying it,' Con growls. 'Liette, listen for a moment. It's astounding – you were right. It's a miracle, the answer to all our problems with the chip. I can show you.'

She shivers, as if struggling against reason, against his words. 'It is a miracle. *My* miracle. It showed me. I don't need you.'

'Liette,' he tries again, spreading his hands wide in supplication. 'Please listen. We can study it together. Just calm down and—'

'You aren't even bothering to study it, just spending time with your Vairian bitch.'

She doesn't hesitate, just slams the weapon against my head, sending me down onto my knees. Con shouts something and Liette shrieks at him while my world spins sickeningly. My head throbs and when I bring my hands up to feel for a wound, they come away covered in blood. Petra and Thom would have been here by now but we sent them away. Where are security? Where the hell…

'Pick it up,' the woman tells one of her cohorts. 'Bring it to me.'

He goes to grab it without hesitation and a shot takes him right in the stomach. He staggers back, his expression startled as he crashes against the workbench.

'Con, get down!' Jondar yells. Security flood the room.

Behind me, the whine of Liette's blaster is deafening. I move on instinct, spinning to one side and kick her legs out from under her with my own. The worktop beside my head explodes in pieces, a smoking hole where I should have been. I come up like a fury and fall on her, knocking the weapon away from her.

She dives away from me, scrambling across the floor in the chaos. Con's experimental blaster is within reach and if she gets it I'm finished. I leap after her and we roll across the floor, crashing into the base of the workbench with the stone on it. Before I know what's happening her hands are like claws in my hair and she slams my head against the floor again.

She grabs the stone, rips it out of the cradle and everything seems to stop.

She crouches there, holding it against her chest, her face a rictus grin of triumph.

'Put it down!' Con shouts.

But still, she doesn't move. She stares into the light of the stone and it throws the reflection up into her face, like sunlight, like fire. It flickers on her skin and in her flesh, lines of light licking along her veins like molten gold.

She turns towards me slowly, moving as if unfamiliar with her body. Light falls from her eyes like glowing tears and the grimace is still fixed, like an agonised smile.

'*Belengaria of Vairian,*' she intones, in a voice not her own. It can't be her. Everything about it is different, as if something else is using her voice, something that doesn't really understand how speech works. '*Queen of Anthaeus but not of Anthaeus, protector and defender, liberator... special... chosen... I can give you your heart's desire...*'

And slowly, she folds up, falling like old clothes on to the ground. I lurch forward to catch her, or catch the stone – I'm not sure which. I just move.

Con screams my name as my bloody hands close on the stone. It's cool to the touch. I don't know why I thought it would be hot, but I did. The light perhaps. As I grab it, I can hear voices, so many voices, but somehow they resolve into one. One composed of many, a chorus that sighs inside my mind, crying out, shrieking, lost souls. It's like the Rondet, but without individuality, without the personalities, the humour, the curiosity, without everything that makes them so dear to me. But it's powerful, the Coparius or whatever it is that dwells inside it. Slowly it resolves into one voice, overpowering the others. One voice, whispering my name.

'*Belengaria...*'

A rush of power, of energy floods through me, overwhelming me, a wave of strength and light. It is everything, all I ever dreamed of, swirling through me at once.

Con snatches the stone from my hands, his own hands wrapped with a cloth, and shoves it unceremoniously back into the cradle. He moves like someone possessed, reconnecting the containment, powering it up as fast as he safely can, locking it away. Then he seizes my shoulders, pulls me towards him, shakes me.

'Are you all right? Talk to me. Bel, say something! Who am I? Do you know where you are?'

Shaken, stunned, I stare into his intense green eyes. 'Con,' I whisper. 'You're Con. My husband.'

That seems to do the trick. He visibly relaxes, his relief rushing over both of us as he pulls me into an embrace so powerful I wouldn't have guessed he had it in him when first we met.

'Don't scare me like that again,' he says, his face pressed into my hair. I breathe in his scent, his warmth. Relief, so strong it almost sends me to my knees, flares through me like wildfire.

'Majesty,' one of the guards says. Con pulls back, glaring at him, waiting for the report. 'Two in custody, two dead.'

He breathes heavily, containing himself. 'I want them interrogated. I want to know what they were after.'

But I'm looking at Liette, her arms bound behind her back, held between two security guards. Her head hangs down, her features vacant and empty. I don't think they're going to be getting anything out of her. 'Round up their associates,' I add. 'Faestus and the rest.'

'Is that wise?' Jondar asks. 'They're a close religious group. If they cry persecution—'

'Then be polite about it!' Con has lost all semblance of patience. They expect him to be infinitely serene and wise, but he's like anyone else. There's only so much he can take. 'But get them all into custody and question them all. Bring all of them here, to the palace. I want to know what they hoped to achieve with this. I want to know how they got to her.'

He's staring at Della's body. He killed her. I know he didn't mean to but it's not something that Con could ever treat lightly. She's dead all the same. Whether she betrayed us or not... that really doesn't matter to him.

'I'll get on it right away,' Jondar tells him with a solemn nod.

'Come on,' says Con. 'Let's get you to Doctor Halie. Get that head wound looked at.'

I'd forgotten about it. My head is aching and blood is still trickling down the side of my face. I'm dizzy and I think I'm going to throw up. Concussion probably. That might be why I feel so strange and distant, like I'm watching things from outside.

I glance down at my hands as we walk towards the door. The blood on them is gone, completely gone, like it has been sucked away. And beneath my fingertips, there's a strange golden glow.

Chapter Sixteen

Petra

The dark is endless, silent. Beyond the nearest porthole, the planet becomes small, a jewel in the night and I hold my breath. Beside me, Thom has closed his eyes and has been softly snoring for some time. It's easier to sleep on a mission like this, to conserve energy and while away long empty hours. I wish I could do that, just switch off for the duration and relax. But even now, even after so many flights, I can't. The wonder of it, the awe at the sheer power needed to bring us out of the atmosphere, the engineering which makes it seamless – it defeats me every time.

I think about Bel, now married at last, so far below us, on a world that adores her. I hope she's happy, not worried about us and our mission, or about Con. She deserves some happiness at last. But I know her better than that. She will be worrying about everything.

Jondar is there. He's reliable. The Greymen and their wretched stone, Teel and the other Cuoreans, and that mystery illness are all factors on which he has been fully briefed. He has an array of information at his fingertips, everything we gathered and probably more. I've learned not to underestimate Jondar. Anthaeus, the royal court, but most of all Con means everything to him.

He has a good team around him. We picked them together, the three of us.

And then there's Art. And whatever he thinks he's doing there.

'Petra?' Zander is still sitting opposite me, just like he has so many times in the past. In this half-light he looks his handsome old self again – not a crown prince – just my old commander, and my love. Or at least he was, once upon a time.

The thought of Val Teel pops into my mind, that passionate kiss, and my traitor body heats all over.

'What?' I ask.

'You looked a million miles away.'

I half smile. That sounds more like him. 'Maybe I was.'

He reaches out for my hand and takes it partly because I'm too stunned to pull it back.

'I wish it was just like this, all the time.'

'What? Riding off to face the unknown on a dead planetoid?'

I mean it as a joke but he doesn't smile. Perhaps he means exactly that. 'It used to be simpler.'

I don't know what to say to that. *Yes, it did.* When we were no one in particular and liable to get killed at any moment.

My other hand lifts to the small pendant Val gave me. It rests against my skin, under my clothes, my armour. I know I shouldn't have worn it. I know no one else can see it. But no one ever gave me a gift like that before. Not even Zander.

I'm a terrible person. I pull my hand free from him and before I say anything stupid, the ship's coms break the uncomfortable silence.

'We're on our approach vector,' says Daria. 'ETA twenty hours. You can get to work, folks. That equipment won't prep itself.'

'You heard the lady,' Thom says, far too loudly. Clearly he wasn't anywhere near as asleep as I thought. 'Petra, with me.'

I've never been quite so grateful to him, or as annoyed at him, as I am in this moment.

I wonder if Zander will follow us, but he heads for the computer terminal instead and starts moving data around with sure and certain fingers. We'll scan the moon as we approach and everything we find will be relayed back to his ship and to Anthaeus. Or at least it had better be. If it's blocked somehow we'll need to find out why.

That's what worries me most. If it's blocked, someone is blocking it. Someone with technology and the money to buy the best.

The armoury is pretty much where we're most useful, Thom and I. Always have been. We prep the weapons silently, without discussion. I know we could order the others to do it. But then I wouldn't know it was done right. And that's something I cannot bear. Thom and I haven't discussed it but I'm pretty sure he feels the same way. He trains our troops, oversees all of them. He'd never send them anywhere unprepared.

We are not going in without weapons, even if the place is dead as a tomb. Nasty things can come back out of graves.

Some of the weapons are Con's – state of the art, light and easy to operate, packing a hell of a punch. When he demoed the adapted grenade launcher a few weeks ago he sat there studying the gaping hole it left in the target for hours, horrified. Bel says he hates making weapons. His mind bends more naturally to engines and aerodynamics, to equipment to create power, or purify water, to help people. Weapons, as I know better than anyone, aren't there to help. Just to hurt, to maim, to kill. Bel tried to explain to Con about defence, about deterrent. I didn't. I understand where he's coming from. I agree. It just doesn't bother me any more. The things he makes are just tools. People like me are the weapons.

'Do you want to talk about it?' Thom asks. For a moment I just stare at him, trying to fathom what on earth he's on about. 'You, Zander and Teel,' he repeats patiently. 'Do you want to talk about it?'

'No.' I mean, I know I probably should. And Thom is my friend. If I'm going to talk to anyone about it, he'd be the best choice. But I really don't want to talk about it. I don't even want to think about it. Not now.

'It's just that Bel asked—'

Oh ancestors, it just gets worse. 'I won't do anything to embarrass her.'

He smiles gently. 'Come on, she knows that. She's worried about you, and about them. And what Teel might want.'

There's a spark of anger in me that I hadn't expected. 'What Teel wants… because he couldn't *actually* be interested in me?'

Thom freezes, his hands still loading the blaster. 'That's not—'

'What you meant. I know. But it's what it sounds like when everyone says it. And everyone is saying it, aren't they?'

'They're worried about you. Bel, Con… and Zander too.'

I roll my eyes. I bet Zander had a lot to say. 'I can mind myself. And my relationships are my own business.'

'So there is a relationship?'

I shove a belt of power cells towards him. 'None of your business.'

'That's not a no. *Relationships*, you say. There's more than one, then?'

'One more question, Thom and I'm leaving. You can finish this alone.' It's an ultimatum and I know he's going to ignore it. I know him as well as he knows me.

'Do you love him?'

I slam down the pack I'm holding on the unit.

'What's love got to do with anything?'

I turn my back on him and stalk out of the armoury, hardly able to believe that this is a real conversation and that he went there. Of all places. I notice, with painful insight, that he doesn't specify which man.

I pass Zander in the narrow corridor and I don't make eye contact with him, even though he's staring at me. I can feel his gaze, his anger, his pain. My stomach twists. I don't have time for this, not for any of it. None of us do.

Behind me I hear Thom greet Zander, and I realise I can hear them as clearly as if I was standing in the room with them. Which means Zander heard every word I said.

The remaining long hours of this trip, trapped on board this shuttle with nowhere to hide, are going to be excruciating.

*

I don't know what I was expecting from Kelta. All my life I've thought of it, *when* I thought about it at all, as the place the crystals came from which powered so many inventions and marvels. I know, logically, that it was home to a mining industry and across the galaxy such places are not exactly famed for their beauty. Then again, it's an Anthaese mining facility so you'd never know what they might do with the architecture.

The Gravians took Kelta before moving on to invade Anthaeus. We knew they'd strip-mined it for the crystals, and that the people stationed here were never heard from again. I suspect most became the Mechas at the forefront of the invasion forces. During the liberation of Anthaeus they abandoned Kelta too, destroying everything behind them. Scorched earth is a favoured tactic of theirs.

What I never expected was the sense of devastation. Most of it is black rock, sand, debris, burnt areas seared beyond recognition. As we pass above it, the surface looks dead and empty, a wasteland. No one says anything. In the distance I see a light, a reflection off metal and I realise it must be the base, the mining HQ. So they didn't destroy everything.

Ellish brings us in to land seamlessly. She glances at Daria, their eyes locked together.

'You know the drill,' Thom tells her. 'Take off and get into high orbit. We'll signal for extraction.'

'I know. But I don't like it. Come back safe.'

Daria just grins at her, teeth very white against her dark skin. 'That's the idea.'

Ellish blushes. Thom gives that familiar long-suffering sigh and Zander grins at them both. He knows Daria better than any of us. She has that rep, a girl in every port. This time, I hope she's a bit more invested. I'd hate to see Ellish hurt.

We load up and count them off – Thom, Zander, Daria, Lorza, Beq, Sorrell, Lees and myself. One sorry little group, really, in a vast and empty space.

'Masks on, coms linked, weapons ready,' I tell them and no one argues. 'One.'

'Two,' Thom sounds off in my ear as the coms sync.

'Three,' Zander's voice is softer and I push away a shiver of recognition.

Beq and Lorza form up, Lees taking point for them which they accept without question. Sorrell flusters a little, checking equipment. But I know them, I trust them. Good Anthaese soldiers, forged during the invasion, survivors all. I just have to make sure they all survive this too.

I have to stop thinking like this. It isn't a routine excursion but still, there's nothing to suggest it should be particularly dangerous. Covert isn't the same thing as deadly. But everything feels off. Everything. I think of the Mechas that attacked me. Faster than anything I've ever seen before, deadly.

Back among Vairian troops I wasn't considered superstitious. Many were. Lucky charms, amulets, lighting candles and mouthing prayers to the ancestors before deployment… Gut feelings, instincts that saved lives, premonitions and warning apparitions, everyone had their stories.

I've never felt such an abject feeling of dread as I do now, walking off the shuttle onto the landing area outside the facility. The open sky is huge and dark overhead. Ellish seals the hatch behind me and the engines start up before we're fully out of range. Daria watches her go, shielding her eyes until Ellish clears the thin atmosphere. It's breathable but the oxygen levels are low. The masks give us enough to operate. Without them, unacclimatised to life here, we'd be at risk of hypoxia in no time.

The airlock hisses as we enter. All operational then. Everything is in working order and that concerns me. If it has been left alone for months, I'd expect more problems. That's why Sorrell is here. She's Con's pick, a gifted engineer. If he called her that, she must be something. The first door closes behind us and there's a rush of more oxygenated air. The readings are good so we remove our masks, conserving supplies for later. That's when the whole plan hits a snag. The entry code for the second door doesn't work. Thom glares at it and tries again. Nothing. We're stuck in a narrow chamber, sealed in on either side. My inner alarms threaten to go off the charts.

Sorrell pushes by Thom. She prizes off the panel and pokes at the wiring behind it.

'There's a short,' she says curtly, as if it has personally offended her. 'Hold this.'

She hands Beq the weapon and digs into the tool belt around her waist. The young man looks on, perplexed, juggling the two blasters and clearly uncomfortable with the situation. I guess willingly giving up a weapon isn't in his list of things to do. Not a lot of trust there.

Sorrell gives a grunt of approval and the door opens for her. I make a mental note. *Cool under stress, competent, but too trusting.* Maybe team her with Beq inside if necessary. He's been Bel's guard for most of the time she's been working with Con. They can rely on each other. I check on Lorza again but she's fine. Just as calm and secure as ever, all efficiency. She's watching everything. Good. Lees and Zander are manning the outer door.

'Inside,' Thom tells us. 'Two parties, left and right.' We fan out quickly. The lights are on, the whole place immaculate and clear. No one's been here for a while though. The air is stale and there's dust on the ground.

We make our way down the corridor, while Sorrell brings up schematics on a handheld tablet, but Lees knows the way already. I nod him forwards. There are elegant Anthaese carvings swirling along the walls at hip height, beautiful and complex but the work of human colonists rather than ancient. They stand out in burnt umber against the cream walls, discoloured now. Every so often there's a disturbing splash of dark brown or a splay of ash. We take the stairs rather than lifts. The central monitoring room is three floors down. The whole complex goes five floors deeper. And who knows what the Gravians did while they were here. The scans suggest a lot more levels.

As to what is down there… that's anyone's guess. Again, the image of those twisted Mecha faces looming over me rears up in my memory. Did they come from here?

We work through a floor at a time, securing each one until we reach three and head for the monitoring centre. Here the groups will split, leaving Sorrell, Daria and Beq there, and the rest of us continuing onwards.

The door slides back and Sorrell is inside the circular room before anyone else. A column juts from the smooth, shining floor, topped with three built-in screens in a triangular configuration. It's more modern than I expected. Far simpler than the terminals on Anthaeus, with the screens sunken in ornate frames, mirrors and table tops. This is functional, state of the art. The lights come up and I can hear the hum of something powering up, that dull whine under the skin. Thom shouts a warning but Sorrell doesn't listen. Her mind is already on the server in front of us, the screens which can tell us everything we need to know.

The moment she touches the nearest screen, she goes rigid, electrical power coursing through her body. Her cry is thin and stretched. Alarms shriek all around us, deafening and pitched to cause pain.

Booby trapped.

'Damn it all to—' I slam my shoulder into her side as hard as I can, knocking her aside and breaking the connection. Beq catches her as she falls, shivering convulsively. Daria drops to her knees beside them, checking her eyes, her breathing.

'She's okay. Give her a minute. Get me the medkit.' I barely hear her over the noise.

Lorza is the first with one. She doesn't flinch as she drops down to help. 'Burns?'

Sorrell tries to calm her breathing, flexes her hands. 'No, I'm okay. I think.'

'I'll be the judge of that,' Daria tells her, the voice of experience calming them all. 'Get to work the rest of you. Turn that blasted thing off before we all go deaf. I'll see to her.'

'What do we do?'

'Hard reboot?' suggests Lees. The girl shakes her head, clearly still in pain. As Daria injects painkillers into her arm, she relaxes somewhat. 'What then?'

'Override,' she says. 'Old-style system.' She struggles to sit up, but only manages it when Daria helps her. 'Stupid. I should have guessed it would be protected.'

'Not the problem now. What's the override?' I ask.

'There's a second console. Down at the bottom of the unit, behind a panel.'

Beq is first down there. He finds the panel almost at once and prizes it off. The tech beneath is clearly Anthaese, beautifully finished, delicate and still functioning. The keypad gleams with an inner light. 'What's the code?' he asks.

She reels off some numbers and letters. He doesn't hesitate, entering them on the keypad. The machine makes a series of tones in response, almost a song, and then the screen clears. The alarm goes silent, the echo of it still slicing through my brain.

Everyone stares at the blinking lights on the screen, no one exactly willing to test it.

'Oh, let me,' I say, intent on doing it myself but Zander gets there before me. 'Well, help yourself, your Highness,' I say sarcastically. His shoulders tighten but he doesn't say anything. A treacherous little voice in my mind says maybe I should ease up on him.

The terminal responds to him easily, and he brings up the camera feeds. Most of this equipment is new, far too new to be Anthaese. The Gravians have been busy. And some of them... some of them, like the screens and the terminal itself, look even newer...

'What's that?' I ask staring at the tiny square in the corner of the screen. There's movement where there shouldn't be movement. Blinking lights, machinery, and something else.

'There's someone down there,' he replies.

We all crane in around him, even Sorrell who drags herself up off the floor. There are figures there, in the darkness. I count three at first glance, standing in a row, staring ahead. I can see restraints holding them.

'Here, let me,' Sorrell reaches for the terminal and brings up the resolution, raising the brightness so we can see them more clearly.

'They're Anthaese,' Lorza whispers. 'There are survivors of the occupation. Or the staff here…'

Locked up, abandoned, left here to rot. But it's been months. No, they can't be survivors. Who would have fed them for a start? This is something else. I think of those people Con mentioned, missing from Kir and Doon. Maybe we've found them. But who brought them here? And what has been done to them?

One of them looks up to the camera and we can all see it.

'Not survivors,' say Beq. 'Mechas.'

'Not all of them.' I point to the back of the room, where I can see cages, and other figures. They aren't standing stiff and unmoving, but sprawled on the ground, listless and without hope. One of them moves, rolling over like a child caught in a nightmare. 'That's not a Mecha. We need to get down there. What's the fastest way?'

'Lifts, or stairwells. But…' Sorrell still looks confused. 'This equipment isn't Gravian tech. None of it.'

'What is it then?'

'Something else,' says Zander darkly. 'Something new.'

I want to punch him. I have actually never wanted to quite so much before, not in all the many *many* times I have wanted to punch him so hard I'd relieve him of his consciousness and probably some teeth. He stands there in front of me, so calm, so cold, and he knew this was a possibility. He knew when he came here. He knew when he killed the first Mecha.

'So this is a rescue mission now?' Lorza asks.

There's a long and painful pause.

'Yes,' I say at last. And that's the decision made. I'm not leaving them there. Not to be made into Mechas, their DNA twisted and distorted, their bodies grafted with metal and weapons. The question of who's doing it… well, that's what we need to find out. 'Sorrell, download as much data as you can. I want evidence of whatever has been going on here.'

She sets to work at once, digging into the filing system. Very little is encrypted, or if it is she blows through it like it's spider webs.

'Petra,' Thom interrupts me. 'This isn't a rescue mission.'

'We don't know half of what our mission is, do we?' I glare at Zander who gazes back at me impassively, as heartless as a Mecha himself. 'We aren't leaving them.'

'We can't save all of them. There isn't room on the ship.'

'Then we'll find another ship.'

'Petra. We *can't* bring Mechas back to Anthaeus.'

I stare at him. He's right, in a sense. But not all of them are Mechas. And I'm not leaving them here to be turned into those things. I lost too many people that way.

'Screw that.' I heft my blaster in my hands and head for the doors.

Chapter Seventeen

Bel

The airship takes us from Limasyll quite early in the morning but then we have a lot of ground to cover and not a lot to do once we're actually in the air. It's dressed up as a presentation to honour Teel as the Imperial ambassador, but really I just want to know what's going on inside that pretty head of his. I've become more used to the luxury of the airships now. It's strange that losing them during the invasion just made them seem all the more wonderful now. Most were destroyed, some were repurposed or hidden. Restoration took some time.

The Royal Zephyr is beautiful. She handles like a much smaller vessel and she's a palace in the air. I sit in the observation deck, on a bench upholstered in red velvet, the rich mahogany decorated with swirls of gold leaf. Beneath me the forest is dark and luscious. The scars on the landscape are starting to recover. Swathes of timber ripped from the ground are growing back and the replanting has been a determined effort. Con consulted with a team of terraformers from Melia, and apparently they had some techniques which made all the difference. The wood won't be mature yet, but the results are already staggering.

The river is a sliver of gold in the dawn's light and the distant mountains look like a bank of purple-grey clouds on the horizon.

'Your Majesty? You wanted to see me?' Teel stands in the doorway, gazing down at the glass panels in the floor as if the moment he steps on one it might crack and send him plummeting down in a shower of shards. Interesting. He doesn't like heights then. I didn't think there was anything he was afraid of. I file that information away for later.

'Lord Teel. Please, join me.'

It's not that I'm malicious. I don't trust him – not when it comes to Anthaeus, and especially not when it comes to Petra. I want to know what he thinks he's up to. But if I come straight out and ask him, he'll never tell me. The man lives and breathes secrets.

Still, I'm glad to see him squirm.

'It was a most delightful ceremony yesterday.'

'It was.'

'And an entertaining party.'

'Thank you.'

'And will we continue to talk around the subject instead of facing it?'

I look at him out of the corner of my eye. He's smirking. He manages to make it look elegant and graceful, but still, it's a smirk. I have three brothers. I know that look.

'*I can show you his secrets. I can make him yours, if you so desire.*'

I shiver. I know it isn't the voice of any of the Rondet. This feels different. It courses through my blood and surges with my breath. And I've heard this new voice since I touched the Coparius. It sends a shard of ice into my heart.

I don't know how to tell Con. I don't know how to tell anyone.

What can I say? Hearing disembodied voices is not a good sign. Not good at all.

It's not the same as the Rondet. It's not the same as Con.

I used to share everything with Con, my thoughts, my emotions, my joys. Now I feel the loss so keenly, and this other dark voice is no comfort. Maybe I should ask Teel to get him. If I could tell Con, if I could show him…

'Ma'am? Are you quite well? Will I fetch someone? You look pale.'

He's all concern, the perfect courtier. His hand doesn't quite touch mine as he bows, but he comes perilously close. If I were the Empress I'd cut it off, no doubt. Lucky for him I'm not.

I have to pull myself together.

'I'm fine. Thank you for your concern. But we should discuss your presence here. And whatever it is you think you're up to with my general.'

'General Kel is a remarkable woman. I have not made any unwanted advances, nor have I made her unhappy.'

Not an actual answer, not to my first question.

I would be a fool if I believed him.

My head throbs suddenly and my vision blurs. If I were standing I'd have to sit down. My hands are too warm, burning. I stare at them in horror.

'Majesty,' Teel says, visibly worried now. He starts back towards the door, calling for help.

'Wait,' I say. Or try to say. But the world doesn't cooperate. I close my eyes and when I open them again, Con is with me, crouched in front of me with his eyes full of concern.

'Breathe, Bel. Just breathe.'

'I'm… Con?'

Teel had been there and now… now it was Con. How had that happened? I'm so grateful to see him there instead that I throw my arms around his neck and pull him into an embrace. He strokes my hair, holds me close.

'You sort of zoned out there,' he says. 'Like you were asleep with your eyes open.'

I was? Teel is still watching from further down the observation deck. I suppose I should be glad he only got Con.

'I'm fine,' I assure him. 'Really. Just…'

I don't know what to say. There's nothing wrong with me. And yet… I'm not sure what happened, or how long I was absent. Teel is watching everything and I feel distinctly uncomfortable.

'Perhaps we should turn back,' Con says. 'Talk to Halie and see—'

I imagine the speculation, the stories, the panic.

'No, I'm fine. Really, love. We should go on.'

The whoosh of air heralds Rhenna, flying alongside our ship. *'Bel? You're here. I thought something had happened to you. But you're here.'*

I get up and stretch out my hand. I can't reach her, of course, but she purrs nonetheless.

'Come and land, come. The others are waiting.' Giddy as a child, she swings wide around us, looping and dipping, twirling through the air.

'Rhenna,' I laugh. 'Slow down. We aren't as quick as you.'

It doesn't make any difference but it lifts the whole atmosphere, taking the attention off me at last. More comfortable for me, but Con still lingers beside me, his hand on my hip, the other at my elbow. He's not convinced by my sudden recovery, and to be honest neither am I. Something happened. Something that freaked Teel out and drew Rhenna. Something that made Con worried.

Teel is staring at Rhenna with his mouth open. I suppose the first sight of her up close is bound to shock. He must have seen her at the wedding but from a distance and she wasn't dancing through the air like she is now, sunlight glinting off her and refracting through her body to create rainbows around her.

The Zephyr sets down seamlessly at the airfield and we disembark. The area is one that I know like my own home. It was once the location of the Rondet chamber and the place where we hid for so long from the Gravians. The bombing damage is barely visible now and the vegetation has roared back into life all over the planet, wiping out traces of the damage as if the world itself wants to help recovery. In that we are blessed. It also makes food stocks less of a worry. The terraforming helped of course, but the scientists involved said they'd never seen a world so eager to help their efforts. Con was delighted.

I think sometimes he looks at compliments towards his world as compliments for himself.

The Rondet dome has been left as the broken tangle of melted metal and glass. As I walk through it so many memories flood back. My former lady-in-waiting Elara died here, as a Mecha desperately trying to fight her own programming and save me. Con was captured here and taken away to be imprisoned and tortured. I thought I'd lost him.

I reach out my hand for him now and his fingers slide in between mine. I smile, unable to do otherwise. We made it through everything. We survived.

Rhenna and Favre appear first. Aeron is last, lingering in the air overhead. I feel him reach for Con, his mind stretching out. He's still pining for my husband's communion. They were always the closest, their minds a perfect blend of creativity and logic.

With the three of them together, the hive mind is stronger than ever. And this is their place, their home, the location of their long sleep over so many years. They circle around us, watching the Imperial representatives warily.

'They won't bite, you know?' I murmur below the hearing of anyone but Teel and Con. Con smiles. Teel tries.

Rhenna's head snaps around towards me. '*I will.*' But there is humour in her tone. We share that and much more, a friendship the like of which I never dreamed.

'Join us, Lord Teel,' says Con, oblivious to her reply, but clearly guessing the context given my smile.

I recall the first time I came here, a princess who didn't want to be a princess. And they interviewed me as if it was a job. Not the Rondet as they appear now. They were still sleeping and to greet me they projected images of themselves through the crystalline structure, avatars that moved and interacted almost like real people.

How strange it must be for Teel now to walk forward under gazes so intensely alien and animal. At least I thought they were human. Or I was supposed to. That was the illusion they chose to project when I first met them. Beautiful, elegant people, dressed in strange elaborate clothing who poured cups of sweet tea in an intricate ceremony and asked me a single question to determine my whole future.

If I'm honest, I never thought they were human. Not in my heart of hearts.

Teel may have seen them from afar, but up close they are much more alien.

Rhenna stalks towards him as Teel approaches, sniffing the air around him. She looks back at the others and bares her teeth. There are no purrs, no murmurs. They're hostile which can't bode well.

'This is *Maestre* Aeron.' I make formal introductions, emphasising their importance in case he hasn't grasped that yet. 'This is Maestre Favre. And this is Maestra Rhenna.'

Each of them watch him with the eyes of hungry owls, unblinking, almost like statues.

They're being purposely intimidating. They're very good at it.

Teel sinks into the deepest bow born out of wonder more than anything else. I shouldn't have worried about him grasping the importance of this interview. He understands.

'I am most honoured.' I believe it. He looks at Con and me, waiting for some indication of the next step in this strange dance.

'The first time I met them I feared I would not hear them at all,' Con tells him. 'Matilde... the former Anthaem... showed me how.'

'She was, by all accounts, a formidable and wise woman. Much like your new bride.'

I hide a smile. I wonder what Matilde would have said about him. I mean, he's not wrong but still—

That strange dizzy feeling wells up inside me again and Rhenna brushes her flank against me.

'*Bel?*' she whispers, just to me.

I'm fine, really, I think, knowing she can hear me all the same. *It's been a long couple of days, that's all.*

Out loud I say, 'Why don't we all sit?'

There's a trill of shock from Kaeda and the other Imperial representatives. Con takes my arm gently and we settle ourselves on the grass, while Rhenna and Aeron lounge on either side of us. Favre, I notice, is doing his aloof and intimidating act again. Teel swallows hard and then sinks down to join us, his long legs stretched out delicately to the side. *He really is a ridiculously attractive example of a human being*, I think.

'*Is he?*' Rhenna asks privately. At least I hope it's private. '*But your pulse doesn't quicken when you look upon him. It does when you are with Con.*'

Yes, I tell her on a thought. *But attraction isn't love. I love Con, so it's different.*

'*Interesting,*' she sighs. '*Teel's pulse quickens when he thinks of Petra.*'

It does? That's not what I expected. *You're already in his thoughts?*

'*Not too deeply. Just the edges, just the thoughts he lets out. Want to look?*'

I recoil at the thought. I forget sometimes that she isn't human. Her mind doesn't work the same way as me, not really. '*Not without permission.*'

'*Then why is he here?*'

I'm not arguing about consent with a telepathic crystalline dragonfly alien... especially not when she might have a point.

'Close your eyes,' Con is saying, oblivious to my conversation with Rhenna. 'Bel will guide you.'

I will? I suppose there's no one else to do it. If I'm stuck, Rhenna will be happy to help. She's having too much fun on the periphery of his mind already. I hold out my hands in invitation and, after a moment of apparent doubt, Teel slips his into them. The hesitation is interesting. Maybe I intimidate him more than I thought. Maybe the Empress would never have allowed this, or maybe it means something else with her. I suppress a shudder. I can't show weakness now. His touch is soft but there's strength beneath it. They aren't calloused like Con's, or even Jondar's. Not an engineer then, or a swordsman. Iron underneath silk. I wonder what his secrets are, what strengths he hides away.

When I look up, I see his silver grey eyes gazing at my face, studying me. He's afraid, but he's never going to show it. Now, that is impressive. I remember how scared I was. It seems like a lifetime ago.

'*You were special, little queen,*' Aeron tells me. '*Chosen. We knew right away. There was no effort to reach you. We were meant to commune.*'

His words echo what the Coparius said, using Liette as its mouth-piece. I push the thought aside. 'Close your eyes,' I tell him. 'Listen for them. Don't try. Just wait.'

It only takes a moment. I feel them behind me, pushing, as if we're easing a pin into a bubble. He tries to moves back for a moment, just a moment, and then he stills, hearing them for the first time, seeing the wonders they can show us unfold inside his mind.

'*Remarkable.*' I hear him in my mind now. '*Truly remarkable. Show me more. Please.*'

The request is almost perfunctory, but they don't appear to take umbrage.

Rhenna and Aeron don't waste any time distracting him for us. I know how it feels. It's like flying and the wonder never ceases to amaze me. I'm a distant observer, watching him explore, the childlike wonder that surges through him something of a surprise. I thought him jaded, but that's not the case. They bring him high overhead, showing him the world as they see it when they're flying, showing them the way the planet had been ravaged by the Gravians and the pain they'd felt as a result. They showed him the death of Matilde and the raw agony still bleeding through their collective consciousness, though they don't name her or reveal who she really was.

And all the while I am aware of Favre, picking through the undercurrents of his mind. Perhaps it's wrong to use them this way, even if they agree to it. Perhaps it's wrong to treat him this way, but we need to know what he's doing here. What he wants. And this is the only way. I'm certain of that.

The only way to know for sure. Because Lord Valentin Teel is bound about with lies, half-truths and deceptions so thick and tight that you can barely see the man underneath.

'*Enough,*' says Favre. '*That is enough.*'

'No, wait!' Teel exclaims out loud, breathless and moved.

But they've already drawn back from him. He sits there, holding my hands shakily and his eyes are sheened with unshed tears.

I almost feel sorry for him.

The other members of his cohort wait for him, concerned and determined to reclaim him, but they dare not come any closer. Slowly, Teel gets to his feet, and bows again, reclaiming some semblance of his grace.

'I must – I must think on this. My thanks, Maestres and Maestra. Your Majesties.' Rhenna stalks after him as he retreats, seeing him off, out of the Rondet chamber. She's not quite growling this time. She's still not sure of him yet then. She's always been a good judge of character. I will have to quiz her about him later on. I'm sure they all have much to tell us.

But it is Favre who answers.

'*He is not as you let us believe,*' he says abruptly. '*He is a soul who hides much, cares deeply. And... he is conflicted. This intrigues me.*'

I smile at him but as I glance at Con, I see the pain in him. He's bereft that a stranger has experienced the connection he has lost.

'*Wait,*' Aeron calls suddenly. His idea floods through my consciousness, the brainwave that might finally help. Con looks at me, bewildered, because he can't hear them now. That's the whole problem. *But maybe, just maybe... if Aeron is right...*

'Con... you said Matilde helped you the first time you communed with the Rondet?' I say carefully.

'Well... yes.'

'*Interesting,*' Favre muses. I feel him turning the idea over and over in his head. '*It is possible. If you can help Teel who you distrust, then how much can you do for Con, whom you love?*'

I hold my hands out to my husband, begging him to trust me. I keep my voice low, not wanting Teel or the others to hear. They're far enough away, I think, but still, I don't want them to know, not if it might make Con look weak. 'If I could help him, maybe I could help you. Con, let me try.'

Con frowns, confused, and possibly afraid to believe it's possible.

Teel and his companions hold back, waiting at the edge of the ruined dome. But they don't leave either. They want to see the next act in this drama, whatever it might be. They can't know. I wish they'd go away, but this needs to look like nothing particular is happening, like nothing is wrong. Rhenna flops down beside me again and rests her head in my lap. She's heavy but I don't really mind. I run my fingertips over the smooth glass-like surface of her head.

'Here we could perhaps break the block, where once we were strong. Where the crystals were most attuned to us.' Rhenna nuzzles me. *'Hold his hands, just as you did with Teel. Draw him to you. Reach out with us to the crystal network.'*

I do as instructed. Sitting opposite my husband, I reach out and pull him closer, resting my forehead against his and letting my mind flow out with theirs. I can feel them, wrapping their shared consciousness around mine and pushing out, towards him. The crystals were shattered, but fragments of them remain everywhere. They're buried in the ground, they're scattered in the newly regrown grass, they're all around us and I reach out to them as well, using them to lend strength to our effort.

Con's mind feels like a stone, dark and impenetrable, like the Coparius back in Limasyll in its dormant state. I focus on that and picture it opening, the light coming from within it. The same light that reflected up into his face, the same light that threatened to consume Liette. The light I last saw soaking into my fingertips.

'Con…' I feel the warmth of his skin against me, inhale his scent. I know him better than anyone else alive. I love him so completely it hurts to think of any alternative. I need him so.

Intertwined with my longing, I sense that of the Rondet as well. Inside him is a seed of something dark, dragging away at him, sucking his consciousness away. Draining him. I reach for it and it recoils. Determined I pursue it, catch up with it, grasp it and pull it away from him.

It swamps my senses and I almost panic. It's like the golden light within my fingertips, the light that came out of the stone and drowning in it is like those lost minutes when I was with Teel on the airship, and other lost moments I haven't really considered. I can see them now, strung out since I held the Coparius. It grabs me, rises in me and darkness comes with it. The light tears through something inside me and for a moment I panic. But this is for Con. This is for the Rondet. I can feel their need for him, stronger than anything else. They have known him so long, communed with him for so long and they pine for him.

I open myself, letting the block bleed out of him and into me. The gold rises up and devours it. I'm lost in the process, lost in Con, lost in the communion that sweeps over me again. And the golden light is swallowed back into the hollow inside me, into the darkness. It pulls at me, dragging me down with it, sucking away at my will, at my consciousness. I feel myself fading away, spiralling downwards. I'm tired, so very tired.

What have I done? This is wrong. I know that with a sudden clarity. I've done something terribly wrong.

'*Bel?*' It's him. All of a sudden I'm back and I feel him, feel him holding me, feel him speaking to me. It's him inside my mind, inside my soul.

My love, my life.

Rhenna, Aeron and Favre all feel the same surge of unparalleled joy. Their minds rise on wings made of love and ecstasy, their consciousness swirling like dragonflies on the wind, spiralling through me, through us. They cry out and Con sobs, his body convulsing against mine, his mind everywhere, all around me. Relief and joy make everything reel like I'm falling through the air. But before I hit the ground he's there with me, lifting me on wings I didn't know he had.

'Bel,' he says it out loud this time. 'Thank you.'

Tears are streaming down his face, mirroring those on mine, the ones I didn't know I had shed.

He kisses me and I feel them all swirling through my mind, our communion complete again. I wasn't even aware how much I had missed him there, how much it was incomplete without him.

And then Con looks at me, confused, concerned. 'Bel? Something's wrong. I saw it. There's something... something empty... inside your mind.'

Chapter Eighteen

Petra

I'm first down the corridor and right now I don't care if I'm on my own. Orders or not, I'm not leaving those people here to let whoever has imprisoned them do the unspeakable to them. I don't disobey orders, I know that. Except... except when I do. My mind is whirling and I'm furious. All I can think of are my friends, my comrades, resurrected and turned into killing machines by our enemies, used, treated as no more than spare parts. My blood is roaring in my ears like the ocean in a storm and I'm fixed, entirely focused on the corridor ahead, on the cold weight of the blaster in my hands, the knife belt around my hips and the grenades strung across my chest.

I reach the door to the stairwell and try to wrench it open. It doesn't move. They've locked it. Sorrell or Thom or Zander... someone.

'Petra!' Zander yells as he charges towards me. I don't have time for this. I don't have the patience either. I kick the door, three times before I give in and aim the blaster at the control panel and obliterate it with one blast. I kick the door again and this time it gives, slamming back against the wall on the far side. I don't hesitate, diving through and down the stairs. I've made it to the first turn when he catches up with me. His hand on my shoulder is like a trigger.

I spin around, shoving him back from me. 'I'm not leaving them!'

'I know. I'm with you. We all are. *We* aren't leaving them.'

Thom is right behind him. So are Lorza and Lees. Daria's voice comes through the earpiece. 'We'll hold ground here. Sorrell's working on backing up the data and tracing transmission paths. Beq and I will keep the way out clear. Make it quick, General.'

I try to even out my breath. I stare at Zander, unable to completely believe it. 'But you said... this isn't the mission.' My voice shakes.

'Missions change,' says Thom, who has never changed a mission in his life. I hazard a wary smile at him and he raises his eyes to the ceiling. 'If you can't change a mission when you're a general, what's the point of any of it?'

At the foot of the stairwell, we enter the floor we only saw on the monitors above. The lights are dim and everything is spotless. Not a trace of dust or debris, no sign of a rapid evacuation as there was at surface level. On the wall next to the door, a monitor is blinking a series of lights.

The whole place is empty. I look at Lee but he shakes his head.

'This is all new. Wasn't here before.' His voice sounds grim.

'Which way?' Thom asks into coms.

'Left, there's a door at the end of the corridor,' Daria says. 'That should take you into the monitored rooms. Be careful. Sorrell says there are some weird signals coming out of there.'

'What weird signals?' I cut in. 'Specifics would be good.'

Sorrell takes up the coms. 'There are several signals converging on your location, but we can't see anything. It's shielded in some way, something I can't penetrate. We're seeing the gaps in the signal, General. I don't know what's coming... just picking up the traces... the network...'

The coms dissolve in crackles and static. This can't be good. Every instinct I have is screaming inside me. The hair on the back of my neck is standing on end. The others are feeling it too. We close in together, circling, covering every angle. There's something coming.

It bursts out of nowhere, a ball of metal, teeth and rage, barrelling down the corridor, careering off the walls, floor and even the ceiling, at a terrifying speed. There's barely any time to react before it crashes into us, knocking Lees to the ground and leaving the rest of us scrambling to get out of the way and hold our ground.

I start firing, almost blind, just trying to follow it. But it's too fast and none of the sensors are picking it up. I catch a glimpse of a muzzle and barbed teeth that flash like silver. I hear it snarl as it turns again and bounds forward, slamming itself into Lorza.

She screams as it bites down and the plasma from Zander's blaster explodes on its side. Not shielded, thank the ancestors. I hit it moments later, driving it back. Thom's fire takes the legs out from under it, but it just skids along the floor and comes up again, this time throwing itself towards me.

I hold ground and fire, round after round, but nothing seems to slow it down. The next thing I know I'm on my back and the air is gone from my lungs.

Lees is yelling something incoherent, on his feet again, trying to block them, and Lorza's still screaming and there's blaster fire everywhere. There are more of them. Four or five at least.

And the one on top of me glares down at me, baring row after row of teeth, metal like the teeth of a saw. It was an animal once, some kind of wolf or dog, before it was taken apart and put back together, armoured in steel, and driven insane by agony and programming. At least I hope it was an animal… I grab the throat with my hands, trying to force it back from me, kicking at its underbelly. I can't get purchase, and it's so strong. Too strong. The jaws open and from inside another jaw detaches itself and shoots out towards my face.

Whoever is making these Mechas has some sort of sick sense of creativity.

The butt of a blaster cracks against it, wrenching the head to one side and away from me. Zander flips the weapon around in sure hands and fires point blank into its head. The explosion throws shards of metal out like knives, but I barely feel the impact. I shake the thing off me and grab my gun, only to see another three bearing down on us from the end of the corridor.

I don't think, just react, pulling a grenade from the belt and hurling it at the pack. It detonates beneath them and part of the roof comes down on them.

'Watch out!' Thom yells and too late, another hurls itself on Zander's back, scrabbling and tearing at him, jaws perilously close to his neck. He drops and rolls, his full weight pinning it down and I fire repeated shots at its head, hoping to all the ancestors that I don't hit him.

The last one takes it out and it goes down, a heap of metal and flesh. And suddenly, everything is quiet.

'What the hell were those things?' Thom snarls. 'Sound off, who's injured? Who needs a medic?'

Lorza groans as she tries to get to her feet. She's bleeding badly beneath the armour. I have to take it off her to apply a med patch. White faced and silent, she watches me, never complaining. As soon as she can, she's up again. None too steadily, but determined.

I'm scratched and bruised but blessedly unhurt. Lees and Thom are largely unscathed and Zander quickly shrugs off any inspection, saying he's fine. I don't believe him.

'We should push on,' is all he says.

'Record this,' Thom tells Lees. 'We've got to document it and send it back. This isn't Gravian work. This is something else.' Lees sets to work with the camera on his coms.

Something else. *Someone else.* Using Gravian tech but with an entirely new twisted imagination.

I force myself onwards, securing the way ahead. The coms are still down, some kind of jammer cutting us off from the others. I just hope they don't do anything rash. This is feeling more and more like an elaborate trap the further we go.

Then we reach the final door, which opens for us with a groan.

Five Mecha turn to face us and behind me every weapon charges. But the Mechas don't move.

They aren't armed, or if they are the built in weapons aren't active. The light and the movement has attracted them, nothing else. They aren't programmed, I realise. Not yet. They have implants and they're sealed in some kind of unit to charge or contain them. They're like dull-eyed automatons, staring at us without blinking.

I can imagine Con wanting to study them. Too bad. We are not bringing them back.

Zander approaches one, weapon at the ready. He reaches up to the back of its head and pulls at something. A chunk of machinery slides out with a slurping noise that makes my stomach twist and the Mecha collapses, like a puppet that's just had its wires cut. I recognise the piece of tech in his hand. It's the same as the implant he brought from Cuore. The same thing in the Mechas that attacked me and tried to kidnap him.

Imperial. It's all Imperial.

A cold certainty settles in my chest. I want to throw up, but I can't. Not now.

'Stay alert,' I murmur to the others. As if they need telling. Every nerve is on fire. 'Lorza, stay here and watch them. If they so much as move open fire at once.'

A sob comes from the far end of the room. A broken, empty sob. And that's where we find them, huddled and broken, covered in tattered clothing and their own faeces, half starved, caged. Seven of them, all young and originally healthy, no older than thirty. They're inarticulate with fear, mad from their trials here. The ancestors alone know what's happened to their DNA. Broken people, tortured, abused and used as guinea pigs. Left to die. Of course, they're only really useful when they're dead.

I try not to think. Not now.

'Check them over and then get them out of there,' Thom says in a low, dangerous voice. The containment unit opens in front of us and we have the survivors to coax out so we can get them to safety. None of them have the implant. There's that small mercy at least.

The coms suddenly splutter back to life. 'Incoming… the ship…' Daria sounds so far away. She's repeating the same thing over and over. 'Incoming message from the ship. Can you hear me? Respond.'

'We're here, Daria,' Zander replies. 'Coms re-established. Repeat message.'

'There's a vessel coming in, weapons hot. Ellish is making rapid evasive manoeuvres. We need to evac now.'

'You heard her,' Thom says. 'Get moving. Back up the stairs. Get those people going.' He turns to the survivors. 'We're here to help. We're getting you out of here.'

We leave the remaining Mechas. There isn't anything else we can do for them. They're dead, even if the circuitry keeps them going. The ship must belong to whoever has been manning this horror show and they are not going to be happy if they find us here.

We're half way up the stairwell when the first explosion hits. The whole place rocks. The prisoners scream and cower and it takes all we have in us to keep them going without terrifying them into shutting down completely. I hear Lees up at the top, yelling at us to hurry. Zander shepherds the prisoners past him, falling back beside me to bring up the rear and keep them moving. He's grim and firm, probably scaring them more than helping them, but right now we just need them to move.

As we make it to the airlock, Ellish is coming in to land as close as possible. I take up a defensive position, Lees on the other side from me, and we herd the others through. Zander's last, of course. Couldn't possibly risk anyone else ahead of himself, crown prince or not. Really, he's going to have to get his head around this. He isn't just a soldier any more. The coms are finally operational again, and I can hear Ellish yelling at us to get on board. We're almost there. Almost. There won't be enough places to strap in but we'll deal with that later. Daria hauls Lorza and Sorrell in after her. There's just Lees, Zander and I left. We run for it.

The explosion rocks the whole building. The airlock rips away from the main complex, sending the three of us crashing into the ground and each other, rolling over and over. I land clear, on my back, staring up at the stars with my head pounding and vision swirling. I try to breathe but there isn't enough air. My vision blurs. The other ship swoops overhead, weapons blazing. It's a hole in the sky, heavily shielded and streamlined. I've never seen anything like the way it moves. State of the art, beyond state of the art. It's a next-generation ship. I hope Lees is still recording. A terrible whine cuts through my hearing. I can't hear anything, not the roar of the shuttle engines or the pursing stealth ship. I see it open fire and the shuttle bucks in the sky overhead. But it holds true. Damaged perhaps but still going. I shake my head, trying to clear it and I will them onwards and away.

Ellish lurches our shuttle up and out of the line of fire, into the blackness of the sky. She's gone in seconds. I'm alone, staring up at nothing.

She won't have fuel to come back. I know that, we all know that. We're stuck here. We're on our own. I retreat back out of the debris and realise it isn't we. I'm the only one up and moving.

The other ship, black and covered in non-reflective surfaces, swoops low again, surveying the damage and looking for survivors to pick off. Blast canons on the lower surface fire into the last remaining buildings and the mining headquarters is a momentary fireball. I duck down as it goes up and with the pathetic amount of oxygen in the atmosphere, the conflagration is mercifully brief. The devastation, however, is complete.

But Ellish is away. That's all that matters. I hunker down in the gaping hole left where the side of the building fell, hoping I'm hidden enough, and secure my mask. I've oxygen for now. I'll think about that when I need to.

The stealth ship sweeps low one more time. Imperial, I'm sure of it, but like nothing I've ever seen before. The shape is right, but the way it moves, the firepower and the way it merges into the night's sky… beyond the tech I know. It makes the thin air tremble, and then it's gone.

The remains of the airlock are only a few yards ahead of me. Once the black ship has passed by I make a dash for it, searching for the other two. I find Lees first and one glance tells me it's too late. His neck is twisted, and his eyes stare off into the distance, at the endless stars. Reaching down, I close his eyelids. I don't know why. To avoid his stare, perhaps. One of my people, lost. Another one. Almost on autopilot, I pull his coms off. The recordings should have uploaded but just in case… just in case…

Something horrible and cold clamps itself around my insides again. *Zander... he's got to be okay. He's got to be here.*

Movement alerts me, on the far side of the wreckage with half of the airlock door on top of him, but thank the ancestors, he's there, he's moving which has to mean he's alive. The reduced gravity works in my favour as I heave the debris off him. Zander looks up at me, dazed and probably concussed. He gasps for air but he can't reach his equipment.

I help him up and get his mask on. Relief floods his handsome features and he reaches out to me, touches my face. And then slumps down again.

I know I shouldn't move him. In ideal circumstances there'd be a med team with us in moments. They'd secure him and treat him for spinal injuries and concussion. No time for that. The ship could be back any second. I grab him by shoulders and pull him back towards the complex. It's venting oxygen now but there has to be shielding in there somewhere. If we can get inside we can get more air. A temporary solution because whoever shot at us might come down here and check what we've done. And if they find us they'll finish the job.

But there has to be equipment in there we can use. Perhaps even a ship. There isn't any choice here. There has to be a way off this rock. And fast.

'Come on, Zander. Wake up. You've got to help me here. Or we aren't going anywhere.'

But Zander can't answer.

Chapter Nineteen

Bel

Con doesn't move from my side the whole way back to Limasyll. It isn't that long a flight but it seems to take an eternity. Teel is watching too, taking in everything. I just know it. So is Kaeda de Lorens. Her gaze is less sympathetic than Teel's but then, why would she care if everyone suddenly thinks there's something wrong with me? Mostly the concern seems to be that I too have contracted the sleeping sickness. Con's been telling everyone I was only feeling faint, just the sun or something I ate. I expect there's already a rumour flying around that I'm pregnant. I'm fit to strangle someone. Possibly my new husband.

The Rondet soar alongside us, magnificent in their flight, wings widespread, reflecting the sunlight and their myriad colours shimmering through their bodies. They are the one saving grace as most people are watching them instead of us. There's a vidcrew from one of the Interstellar networks and they have probably got hours of footage by now. But they keep filming.

'*A once in a lifetime opportunity,*' I hear one of them saying. The other keeps mentioning various film awards.

Better they're focused on them than speculative gossip about me.

I'm sure it won't take long, though. I remember who gave me the name *The Bloody Bride* from the first time Con and I tried this marriage thing.

Back at Limasyll I'm straight into Dr Halie's surgery to be poked and prodded. I'm not alone. Half a dozen people lie on the low, temporary cots, deeply asleep, their vitals being monitored by an array of machines. The sleeping sickness is spreading faster. I ought to ask her for a full report but all the fuss is about me. Con goes straight up to his study to check on the stone and to pore over the readings to see if he can work out whatever he thinks has happened to me.

*

… And then I'm there too, listening to his voice without a single clue how I got there or what he had been saying a moment before.

I blink at him, and his voice trails off. 'Bel? Are you feeling okay?'

I draw in a shaky breath. 'I… I was with Halie.'

'I know,' he replies. 'She's already sent up her report. A clean bill of health. You told me when you got here.'

My stomach sinks inside me. I feel sick. *There's something wrong. Something terribly wrong. I know it now, even if I doubted it before.*

'Do you want me to get her?' he asks when I don't reply.

'I came up here myself? I spoke to you? What did I say, Con?'

'You don't remember?' He sounds incredulous. I give him a warning glare. He knows it well. Even so I feel a dark rage rising up inside me, which isn't entirely me. 'Okay, okay, don't panic. I'll get Halie and we'll—'

'No,' I tell him. 'Liette, we need to talk to her. She knows what's going on. She has to. When she held the stone, she spoke to me and it was like… it was someone else.'

He takes my hands in his, tenderly smoothing the skin of my wrists with his thumbs. 'She's dangerous, love. She tried to kill you.'

'But she didn't. Please, Con, we have to try. I think I'm losing my mind, or losing my memory and there's no physiological reason for it… it has to be connected to the stone. Faestus and Liette… one of them has to know.'

Whether I want it or not I am carted straight back to the infirmary and Halie will not let me out of her sight. Con won't let me anywhere near Liette or the other followers of the Coparius. They're here, all of them, inside the citadel, not so far away but the might as well be on the other side of the world.

*

I'm sitting by a window, staring out of the window and wishing I knew what on earth was happening. I wish my brother, Petra or Thom were here, someone I could talk to just as me, as Bel and not as Belengaria of Anthaeus. Not as a suddenly ailing queen.

When Jondar appears I'm unexpectedly delighted. That is before I take a look at his expression, deeply troubled, and Con appears behind him.

'This isn't a good idea,' my husband says. 'She's unwell. Jon, please…'

I've never seen Jondar disobey Con so directly before. But this is more than an urgent communication then. Something has gone wrong. Something has gone terribly wrong.

'Thom reported back – they found survivors on Kelta, and a Mecha processing unit.'

It's impossible. 'Survivors? After so long?'

'It's not… it doesn't appear to be Gravian. I mean, it was, in origin but someone continued it. And these people weren't from Kelta. Bel…'

The people who went missing. I should have known. I should have guessed. Between sickness and those who went underground, we missed them.

I sway on my feet. Con grabs my arm, steadying me. 'Jondar, not now.'

'She needs to know,' Jondar snaps. 'She'd want to know.'

'Know what?'

My stomach is twisting in on itself and that terrible void is sucking all that I am away inside me. I cling to myself, to what I know of myself. Because something is wrong.

'There was an attack, an unmarked ship of Imperial origins. The shuttle took some damage. Ellish got most of them out, but—'

The world spins around me. '*Most of them...*'

Con tries again. 'Bel, please, just sit down for a moment.'

'Your brother, Petra, and Harmon Lees are unaccounted for.'

I can't move. I can't feel my legs and something in my mind is screaming, but I can't make the noise come out. I sink down, back into the chair and everything goes dark.

*

The bed is soft and warm, and when I wake for a moment I don't remember anything. Until I open my eyes. Then it all floods back. I don't even know what day it is. Just that my brother and my best friend are missing. And that there are people on Kelta being changed into a new and more terrible form of Mecha.

I find my coms, the bracelet lying on the bedside table, and contact Jondar. 'Any news on the ship?' I ask.

'Your Majesty, the ship is clear of the moon and on its way back here.'

'Zander, Petra and – Lees, wasn't it?'

'Yes, Harmon Lees. There's no word as yet. Bel, Con has asked that I restrict information passed to you. I can't tell you any more.'

What? Why? I push myself up in the bed. I'm not in our chambers. I'm in the infirmary. In a room on my own, behind a locked door, with an observation window beside it... This isn't good. This can't be good.

I cut off Jondar and contact Con. 'What am I doing in here? Where are you?'

'I'll be there. You were asleep. Just a minute.'

Asleep? Sedated more like. There's a patch on my arm that wasn't there before. I pull it off and my mind spasms inside my skull.

*

Suddenly I'm freezing cold. I'm standing, barefoot, on a hard surface and I don't immediately know where I am. I twist around, looking for something I recognise. Anything. What I get is not comforting.

'Tell me again,' Liette says. She drops to her knees in front of me and seizes my hands. Turning them over she kisses them and I drag myself free of her.

'Where am I?'

I see the loathing stain through her features again. Her mouth twists to a sneer. 'You again. If only for a moment. It'll be over soon, Princess. Look.'

My hands are glowing, that golden throbbing light beneath my skin, tracing its way through my veins. I lift them up to study them, as if I can see a way to stop it.

Pain spears through me, pain and confusion. I'm losing myself. I can feel it now, the void rushing up to swallow me up, to devour me. There's nothing I can do. I cling to a thought of Con. A single thought—

*

'Bel, please, please listen to me. I know you're there.'

I open my eyes to find myself somewhere else again. I'm in the study, Con's study. And he's on the ground, blood running down the side of his face. There are bruises all over his golden skin, and he has a black eye, the white inside already red with blood. His hand reaches out to me and he's pleading. His voice breaks in pain.

The stone is right in front of me, under my hand. I just have to reach out and touch it, take it.

It sings to me, a siren song I can't resist. I want it more than anything I've ever desired. More than Shae, more than Con. And it's mine. I just have to take it...

'*Do not do this, Bel.*' It's Rhenna. '*You have to stop.*' She's faint and far away, like an echo of something I've lost. It's like she's a million miles away from me. I close my eyes so tightly that black and white spots dance in front of them.

'Bel—' Con whispers my name like a prayer and I look at him again. None of this makes sense. There's no thread to follow, no sense of how long I've been here, how long since our wedding, how many days and nights. Nothing makes sense any more. The thoughts, the needs, the desires... they're not my own.

His blood is rich and glossy, and there's a gash across his cheekbone. I flex my hands and feel it aching, contusions on the knuckles telling me more than I need to know.

Did I do that?

Did I hurt Con? Why would I do that? I love him.

'Con?' My throat stings like I've been screaming. My eyes ache as if something is trying to push its way out from behind.

As I start towards him, he flinches back, shielding himself with his arm.

What have I done?

'*The not-you hurt him,*' Aeron's voice snarls in my mind. '*The parasite, the thing from the Coparius. You have to fight it, Belengaria. It cannot prevail.*'

'What do you mean? Con, talk to me. What is he talking about?' I'm scared now, really terrified. I don't know how much time has passed, where I've been or what I've done. I don't understand. 'Rhenna, get help...'

I try to speak but the words seem to clog up in my mind before I can finish the plea. Fog creeps in all around me. The emptiness is seeping up through my veins, the darkness that devours me and steals my consciousness. I struggle against it, trying to cling to myself, to him, to everything I know and love.

Everything... my brother is gone. Shae is gone. And Petra...

'She can't help you,' Liette says. I don't know where she was but she appears from the other side of the study, holding some of Con's tech, playing with it, and when she can't make it work she tosses it aside like junk metal. It crashes loudly to the ground, breaking to pieces. 'Turn off the shielding on the Coparius, Anthaem, or your wife will start breaking your fingers until you do.'

That smacks me back into my senses for a moment. 'No, I won't!'

She smiles, a slow and vicious smile. 'Give it another minute.'

It surges inside me, like she's called it up. I can't stop it this time. I can't fight it. I'm like a piece of driftwood caught in a tsunami. I drop to my knees in front of Con, trying to reach him, my hands clawing at his. My fingers glow, under my skin, light trails up my arms, winds its way around my heart, my throat, my face... He calls my name – I see his lips form it – but I don't hear it.

I'm gone.

Chapter Twenty

Petra

Zander stirs and groans, blinking with drained eyes at the debris-strewn ruins of the complex where I found shelter. It's not much, one small outbuilding with a failing life support unit meant to be replenished from the central controls. The attack ship left the main complex devastated and has not returned. I'm just grateful the others got away.

Except for poor Harmon Lees.

There's no sign of anyone else, no landing party, none of the remaining unprogrammed Mechas. The main building where they were is a smoking hole. Whoever it was, they've destroyed all trace they were here and they either don't think there were any survivors or know that we won't last long. I've secured the section where we shelter. That's all I can do for the moment. That and watch over Zander.

He can't seem to focus, not even on me. Could be the blow to the head. Could be worse. *Oh, ancestors, don't let it be worse.*

I open a bottle of water from my pack and help him sit up.

'It's probably concussion,' I tell him. 'How's your vision?'

'I'm… okay. I think. Just… *ancestors*… my head aches.'

I give him the water and he drinks it carefully. He knows as well as I do not to rush it. It'll make him throw up.

'Yeah, you hit it pretty hard.'

'The *building* hit it pretty hard.'

I smile. If he's making jokes it's a good sign. It's just that there's nothing else good about our situation and I don't want to have to tell him that. Not yet.

'You're bleeding,' he says. 'Do you have your medkit? We should patch each other up.'

I purse my lips to keep from asking what for. So we can die a bit more slowly? Instead I rummage in my pack and get the medkit out. He examines his mask.

'Oxygen is low.'

I know. That's another problem that I don't want to think about.

'We had to use it to get to shelter. The oxygen here is failing too. They hit the main life support system when they bombed the place. Auxiliary power is failing. The situation… isn't good.'

'Well, that's an understatement.' Zander strips off his chest armour and peels back the shirt underneath it. It's soaked in blood and sweat, clinging to his skin and the wounds scattered across his body. I stare at him and for a moment I can't think of a single thing to say. My mouth goes dry and I really want that water now. Or something. I want something. I can't take my eyes off him.

Zander Merryn has always been my greatest weakness.

Even now, at the end of it all. Why did I ever think that could have changed? That I'd got over him? I'm an idiot.

'Petra?'

Yes. The medkit. I'm holding the medkit.

'They knew we were here,' I say as I help to patch him up, disinfecting wounds that should have been dealt with hours ago. His back is the worst. Those cyborg animals almost tore him apart through his armour. I try my best not to linger, not to make it worse. 'They were waiting for us. How?'

He shakes his head. 'I don't know. How much air do we have?'

'Probably best not to think about that. We've some. The atmosphere is breathable but thin. Like being on top of Mount Arden at home. People climb up there every year.' In situations like that you need to keep your hopes up, but Zander has never seen it that way.

'People *die* on the top of Mount Arden every year.'

'I know.'

Maybe it's the firmness in my tone. Maybe he just doesn't want to waste valuable oxygen arguing. He changes the subject.

'Are you going to let me see to you?' he asks. He turns around and my vision blurs, everything swimming around. Part of me wants to laugh. It's almost like the old days. If it was the old days those last words would be turned in to an off colour joke by one of the others on our team and we'd all fall around laughing. 'Petra,' he says, his voice sharpened by concern. 'Are you okay?'

Nothing is okay any more. We're stuck on a dead moon, in a ruined building. If we break cover, if that ship is still around, it'll kill us. If it isn't we'll die from lack of oxygen anyway. That's if there aren't any more of those wolf-mechas or their nastier relations stalking around looking for us.

I start to laugh. I can't help it. I know it isn't funny. And somewhere in the middle the laughter turns to wheezing, and the wheezing turns to sobs.

Zander moves so slowly, as carefully as he would with a panicked animal. He pulls me against him, strokes my hair and face like he used to long ago. And gently, so gently, he places the oxygen mask over my face. I breathe deeply and my head clears. Just a little. My aching chest eases up and a wave of sorrow floods through me.

This isn't real. I know this isn't real. But I don't care.

I push the mask aside and I kiss him.

The euphoria isn't just the hypoxia. His lips on mine, his hands on me. I bury my fingers in his hair and drag him against me. He's everything. He always was. He's the one I always loved, the one I could never have. He's my prince and he's the love I lost. The one I walked away from. Because I *had* to. For his sake. And it was the hardest thing I ever did in my life. I made myself cruel to him, made myself antagonistic and never told him why.

'Pet,' he whispers against my lips. 'We have to stop. We have to—'

He's breathless too and I can feel his heart racing beneath his chest. Under my lips when I kiss him. He closes his eyes in surrender.

But I have to stop. He's right. I pick up the oxygen mask and press it to his face as well. He breathes it in, precious life-giving air. And he opens his eyes again. They are dark with flecks of gold and amber with that touch of green at the edge. They are more beautiful than anything has a right to be. Like him.

'We're almost out of air,' Zander says, his voice muffled. 'We need to conserve what we have.'

I nod and rest my head against him. I'm so tired. My head whirls and I don't know how to stop it. Everything is out of control, but my strength is fading fast.

It won't be long. But at least I'm here with him at the very end. Even if it means nothing. At least we're here, in each other's arms. I'll never get to tell him. I can't find the breath, even if I could find the words.

I don't even hear the footsteps behind us. I just hear the voice.

'Oh, so it's like that, is it? You two can't be trusted alone for a hot second. What would Father say if he found you?' Art Merryn heaves a pack off his shoulder and pulls out fresh tanks with the masks already fitted. 'So do you want to stay here and make out or are you ready to go home?'

I stare at him, dumbfounded but Zander is already on his feet, lifting me with him. He's unstable, unsure, as he squints at his brother.

'*Artorius?* What are you doing here?'

'Rescuing you, it seems? Come here…' He's all business, holding out one of the oxygen masks. Zander hands it to me and I fit it on without arguing. How could I argue? I don't have the breath for it. Zander takes the second one but he doesn't use it right away.

He's good at arguing. Especially with his brothers. He always has to have the last word.

'How did you find us?'

Art takes his hand and presses the mask to his face. I suspect Zander doesn't have the strength to fight him. Even so, he glares, waiting for an answer. We breathe in, sweet, fresh oxygen clearing my head at last. Zander's grip on me relaxes a little, as if he's suddenly aware how close he's holding me.

His brother just tightens his lips. It isn't a smile, or a grimace, but an expression of resignation, that he knows he has to tell Zander something that will not make his brother happy.

'You'll have to thank Valentin Teel for that.'

'What do you mean?' I ask. He understands me despite the muffling of my voice from the mask.

He points at me, at my chest. 'He planted a tracker on you, Petra. He's known where you are all along.'

My hand flies up to the necklace and I rip it free, holding it in the palm of my hand and staring at it in horror. The little star gleams in the half light, laughing at me.

*

The ship is small and cramped. I'd say it was no more than short range but once we're inside I can see it's been souped-up beyond recognition. As Art slips into the pilot's seat, with that practiced Merryn ease, Zander and I strap in behind him. It's barely bigger than a Dragonfly or a Wasp and about as comfortable. Not that comfort is important now. It's getting us off this rock and that's all that matters.

'Thom and the others?' Zander asks.

'They're on their way back. All safe.'

'And the ship that attacked us?'

Art sucks in a breath from the side of his mouth. 'That's… something we'll have to talk about.'

'Imperial?'

'If it is, it's black ops. You won't get any data on that from the official records. And I'm not saying that it is.'

Black ops. Secret Imperial troops that report to the Empress and precious few others. But they could report to someone like Lord Valentin Teel. The man who had me ringed like some kind of prized pigeon so he could track me wherever I went. And I fell for it. He dangled a pretty bauble in front of me and I, like the very fool who was never given anything beautiful in my life, treasured it, wore it, even on a secret mission where no one was meant to be able to follow me.

If I hadn't, we'd be dead, Zander and I. But I still feel like a fool. More than a fool.

It's in a shielded box now. I wanted to leave it behind, hurl it into the rubble and walk away from it, but Art just took it from me and popped it into the little case which he slid into a sealed compartment under the pilot seat.

'Better this way, Petra. It's evidence.'

Evidence of what though? My stupidity? That's just wonderful. I can't wait to share that with… whoever he's going to tell. Bel? Their father? Ancestors, the humiliation will be complete.

'What are you doing here, Art?' I ask again. 'Why were you on Anthaeus to begin with?'

He pauses in the pre-flight check and leans his head back. 'I'm undercover. Or I would be if I wasn't pulling you two out of the shit. Now, can I just get on with it?'

'Undercover for who?' Zander asks, ignoring him in the way only an older brother can.

'It's *for whom*, actually,' Art tells him, the perfect living embodiment of a bratty little sibling. This is going to go on for the whole journey. I can tell. I might as well close my eyes and try to ignore them. Even in this ship, it's going to be a long journey back. 'For father, of course.'

'You're a child.'

Art makes an obscene gesture. 'I'm damn good at what I do, Zander. I always have been. Now will you let me concentrate and fly?'

He takes off effortlessly. You have to admire the Merryns and their ability to fly these machines. I mean, I'm good, I know that, but it's something I learned. This is something they were born to do. It's in their blood. They live and breathe it.

I don't know the make of the ship. Perhaps it's one of a kind. That wouldn't surprise me either. It's fitted out with everything necessary for long flights and I don't know what power system it's using but I've never felt anything move like it. I'd ask, but I expect he'd just tell me I didn't need to know.

Zander, however, is another matter.

'That's a phase regulator. Where did you get a phase regulator?'

'Don't touch it, Zander.'

'What do you even *need* with a phase regulator?'

He hasn't changed. He'll never change. If he sees something interesting he has to pick it up. If he can't pick it up he has to poke at it. He's always full of questions.

'I just do,' his brother replies. 'Just sit back and relax, while I fly the ship. There are supplies, medkits and you could probably do with some sleep.'

'I have questions,' he says.

'Yeah, too many.' He couldn't sound more like a surly teen if he tried.

Well, I have questions of my own.

'So, when you broke into my quarters—?' I leave it hanging, letting him know that I expect an answer. I'm not his family and I have the security of a planet to consider.

He sighs, something mixed with a groan. 'I was looking for the tracker.'

'And why didn't you warn me about it?'

'Because I didn't want you to *know* about it. Obviously. You weren't meant to be there. I was trying to do you a favour.'

'And how did you know about it?'

'I know Valentin Teel. Know his moves. This isn't a new one.'

I could slap him. But he'd have to line up behind Teel because I definitely want to slap him first. Diplomatic immunity be damned. He might be a favourite of the Empress but that's not going to save him from me.

'Art, tell her the truth,' Zander growls. 'Who are you working for and what is your mission?'

'My mission is to protect you. And I'm working for Father. As I always do. He sent me to Cuore, and then here. To look out for you, and Bel, and Petra too. Even Thom. You're Vairians. Okay? I can't tell you much more than that. If I want to carry out my mission, I'm not going to be able to play happy families. I'm taking a risk even being here now.' He glances back, apology written all over his face and his voice softens. 'Not that I wouldn't have come. What with you almost dying and everything.'

'Yes, yes, you're very good, little brother,' Zander mutters. He reaches out his hand for mine and surprisingly I let him take it.

'I am. You always forget that, Zander. I'm the smartest of us all. Certainly smart enough *not* to get romantically entangled with Valentin Teel.'

Zander snatches his hand back. That's when I realise that both of us are bright red with mortification.

I stare at him and it takes a moment or two to realise that my mouth is hanging open.

'I just…' he begins, and trails off.

I close my mouth, fold my arms and shut him out. 'It's your own business. Not mine.'

'Well, it's *kind* of your business too,' Art chimes in what I presume is meant to be a helpful way. In that it isn't in any way shape or form helpful. And he's grinning. Loving every minute of this.

'Shut up, Art,' I snap at him.

'I'm just trying to help. Zander, tell her.'

'There's nothing to tell. You've never been on Cuore, Petra. You don't know what the place is like. And, you see, Val…' He breathes in as his words trail off.

Oh, I see all right.

'Then why does he want me?'

Zander gives me a look of pity. 'He doesn't. He's using you.'

It's cold and it's bitter. And I'm completely convinced that it's the truth. It doesn't make it hurt any less. Especially not when I hear it from Zander.

'To make *you* jealous?'

He grins, an expression completely devoid of humour. 'I think that's just an entertaining side effect. He's done a remarkable job of keeping you away from me.'

'So have you,' I snap.

Great. Val Teel is using me. I'd thought that all along, but I didn't need it confirmed. Especially not by Zander. And I was meant to be distracting him…

I'm such an idiot.

Trust Zander to point it out so brutally.

'Maybe to make both of you jealous,' Art adds helpfully. 'Maybe for his own entertainment.'

'Shut up,' the crown prince growls at his brother and Art laughs.

'You really are a moron, Zander. He's using both of you. Keeping you apart. And biding his time until he and Kaeda are ready to bring you back to the Empress.'

I close my eyes and try to ignore everyone and everything else for the whole flight back to Anthaeus. Even in a ship this fast, it's going to take more than a day. Hours and hours stuck in here with Zander and Art. The Merryn brothers don't speak any more and that's just as well. I don't want to hear either of their voices. I just need to be still and quiet and focus on smothering the inner pain. If I open them, if I try to do anything other than breathe, I'm going to break apart.

Chapter Twenty-One

Petra

I sleep for a lot of the flight, exhausted, hurting and wrung out. I'm pretty sure Zander incorporated some sedatives in the reGen patches he gave me too because I never normally sleep that deeply. Hours and hours of unbroken, deep healing sleep. But this time, with Zander beside me, I do.

Art brings us down in an isolated farm on the outskirts of Limasyll. The ship has comprehensive shielding and the ability to deflect most forms of scans. You'd basically have to accidentally walk into the damn thing to find it. We still aren't speaking, not more than the occasional instructions, grunts and monosyllables. I slept through the landing too. I woke up and Zander was looking at me, chewing on his lower lip. But the moment I opened my eyes, he looked away.

So that's going well.

I have no right to be angry with him, even after what happened between us on Kelta. I think Teel has a case to answer for both of us though. And I fully plan to make him answer. Just him. I don't very much want to hear Zander's version of events.

There's a small house behind the landing site, a simple cottage built from local stone blocks and roofed with curved red tiles, and Art makes his way there without hesitation. Zander follows and I should do the same.

But first I send a coms hail through to Thom.

'Petra?' He yells in delight and it's a rush of relief inside me. 'Petra, are you all right?'

'We're fine. We had some help.' I don't mention Art. Not over coms.

'Where are you?'

And then I realise that isn't delight in his voice. It's worry. More than worry. Fear.

'I'm…' I'm concerned now. I don't want to say where we are but I'm not sure why. There's something wrong. Zander reappears in the doorway, like some instinct has called him. He's listening intently.

'Thom,' he cuts in. 'We can't give location right at this moment. Confirm?'

'Confirm,' Thom replies. 'I… I understand. Just… stay away from the palace. Do you understand?'

The palace? I give Zander a worried glance. 'Where are you, Thom?'

'I can't…' His voice is quieter now. 'We're all okay for now. We had warning and diverted. We're not—'

'Where's Bel?' I ask urgently. 'What the hell is happening in the palace?'

'Bel?' He almost laughs, but it's a choked sound, broken. 'Bel is fine. No, not fine, but… Bel is… Stay away. Please. And look out for the Greymen. We'll find you. Get undercover and stay put. Remember your mission and keep Zander out of—'

The coms cut out. He's gone.

Zander and I exchange a look, a desperate and worried look. Concern goes beyond our problems. His sister, our friend… I don't know what to do.

The Greymen? That weird religious sect? What do they have to do with anything?

And then I remember the stone and that scene when they presented it to Con. The way it closed him off from the Rondet. What have they done now? And what has happened to Bel?

The spike of my fear sharpens. I stare into nothingness, lost.

'Petra?' Zander calls me back, his voice calming, as if coaxing a child. 'We will find out what's going on.'

I couldn't agree more. I traipse inside with him. There's a table, some ratty looking chairs, a chaise and not much more. In the back room there's a bed, or something like a bed. No one has lived here in a very long time.

Art is already working away on a thin tablet, pacing back and forth as he searches for information. 'Nothing on the Interstellar. Nothing on local channels either. Wait… the Anthaem has been taken ill, struck down by the same sleeping sickness that has felled so many, confined to his bed. They're asking everyone to pray for him. Bel's ordered quarantine measures be put in place. All Anthaeus is in lockdown. Especially Limasyll.'

'Pray?' I ask. That can't be right. They don't pray here. Not in the way others do. They don't beseech the ancestors or distant gods for help. It isn't in the nature of the Anthaese. Something isn't right. 'Where did Thom and the others land?'

He reads the tablet again, his fingers deft on the screen. 'They diverted from the flight plan. Bel's issued a request for information about their whereabouts. Not so much a request as a bribe and a threat combined. That isn't like her.'

It wasn't like her. But Art doesn't know her now. It's been a long time since she was Belengaria Merryn, his little sister.

If Jondar thought something was wrong, he would have warned Thom. But about what? What is going on?

I don't know what to do.

'Sit down, Pet.' Zander steps in against me, his hand on my elbow, warm and strong. It's what I need. I don't want to wilt against him but part of me does. Part of me wants to turn to him and never let go.

But I can't.

'General Kel,' he says, more firmly now. Old instincts kick in and I stand to attention. I can't help myself. I hate it. But I do it anyway.

'Your Highness.'

'We will get to the bottom of this.'

I meet his eyes, and I feel a brief flicker of hope. He's the rock I could cling to, if I were the type to cling.

'Why would he warn us away from the palace if Bel is in charge?' I ask in a hushed voice. 'What happened to Con?'

'I don't know,' Art replies. 'But I can find out. You should wait here.'

'I'll go with you,' Zander offers and Art all but laughs in his face.

'You? Forgive me, brother, but you stand out far too much.'

'And you don't, you little runt?'

Art's shoulders drop, and he bows his head. His whole demeanour transforms. 'Begging your pardon, my lord. I don't mean to offend, sir.' The pitch of the voice is perfect, his body losing a few inches in height and his face twisting in such a way that you'd never for a moment recognise him as the tall, confident young man he is.

'You always were a mimic I suppose,' Zander says, impressed but trying not to show it. Art is his little brother after all. 'Very well then, go and see what you can discover.'

Art shrugs. 'Like I need your permission, Zander.'

'And find Thom,' I tell him. 'We need to regroup.'

'General,' he says, with a courtly bow, changing again like the wind. 'On my word.'

And he's gone. Just like that.

What can we do? I don't want to be alone with Zander right now. Not after what's been said... and done... I don't want to think about him and Teel, probably no more than he wants to think about Teel and me. And yet here we are.

Here we are.

Sitting in silence, trying not to look at each other, listening to every breath, every rustle of movement, every heartbeat.

Oh ancestors, what am I going to do?

*

Art doesn't come back that night. I let the various restoratives in his fairly impressive medkit do their work. Far better than the stuff we had. These patches and vials are like a kick to the system.

'Special ops grade,' Zander tells me. He doesn't say much more. I think he's terrified of what this might mean for his little brother. What he's missed in the last year.

Whatever it is, the child we knew is long gone. I don't exactly know the man who has taken his place. Neither does Zander, though he probably thought he did. And I can tell that disturbs him.

I sleep in the bedroom and Zander stretches out in the main living area on the long chaise facing the door. In the morning, I go through the packs and assemble two kits with everything we could potentially need in a number of situations. Then I go outside in the morning sunlight to run through a series of training exercises in the yard, to focus my mind, to feed the need to be doing something. Anything. Zander comes out too and I wonder if he'll join me, but he doesn't. He just watches.

If it was anyone else, I'd imagine he wanted to talk about it. The great looming *it* of Valentin Teel. And the fact he made an utter fool of me. Perhaps of both of us. Now at least I know how the Imperial ship and those Mecha creations found us, I suppose. Teel must have sent it. He must have used me to find us. I've tried to think my way around it – that maybe it wasn't true, that the base alarms had alerted the ship, that the Mechas we encountered sent a signal. I've tried to convince myself that it wasn't Teel.

And whether it was or it wasn't, that doesn't really matter, does it? It was how Art found Zander and me. It saved our lives.

I ignore Zander. Focus on movement, on breath, on working out all the iterations of my frustrations with the world in general.

'Petra,' Zander says, but I ignore him, going faster now, punching thin air as if it was a body, a face. 'Petra!'

I spin to face him. 'What?'

'Bel's in trouble. I'm not staying here.'

Thank the ancestors. I've been waiting all morning for this. I don't know when Art's coming back and I can't wait any longer. He's right, Bel's in trouble. Art could be too. 'Packs are by the door,' I tell him. 'Weapons, armour, food, meds. Pick them up, your Highness and we'll be off.'

He obeys, much to my surprise. Although he promptly launches one of them straight at me.

I snatch it out of the air. 'We're going to need some transport,' I tell him.

He just grins at me. 'Have you looked in the shed?' he asks with that infuriating smile on his lips.

There's a shimmer-skimmer inside, a swift, one person transport that will take two if we squeeze, and carry us more easily across the countryside and into the city. They aren't actually called shimmer-skimmers of course. A457 transport cruisers or something utilitarian like that. It's the way they move, and the iridescent light of the power cells that give them the name. They're sleek and polished, beautiful bits of machinery. Not Anthaese because if it was it would be made of wood and brass and covered in elaborate decoration. It'd probably be twice as fast too, although I know this model isn't exactly lacking there. I check it over. It's in good working order, the powercells charged. Art's, I'm sure of it. It's state-of-the-art tech.

Where is he anyway? And why didn't he take this? I wonder briefly what else he's got tucked away that I haven't already found. And how he got it all here.

Zander slings his leg over the skimmer, and powers it up. 'Ready?'

'Like I'm letting you drive,' I tell him and fold my arms.

'I'm the pilot, remember?'

I shove my way in front of him, forcing him back and taking control of the shimmer-skimmer. He's pressed intimately against me, and it's more comforting than it ought to be, but I need to ignore that.

'First lesson, Zander. This is not a flyer. It hugs the ground. Goggles,' I tell him as I put my own on. He doesn't argue for once. A miracle.

The landscape flashes by and the skimmer hums beneath me. I try to ignore the feeling of Zander's body pressed against my back, all but wrapped around me. I'm focused on the route, the speed with which we can reach Limasyll, rather than what might lie ahead. But as we reach the outskirts and slow, I wish I'd thought this through a little more.

There's no one on the streets. The city is almost empty. Or at least, no one is outside. The doors and windows are shuttered and quiet.

I pull up in the main square. 'What is it?' Zander asks.

'Something's wrong. Can't you sense it?'

'You know this place better than me. But… it's quiet.'

'It shouldn't be. The people here stay up all night given half a chance. They're forever throwing parties.'

'Quarantine?'

Maybe. This is as bad as it was during the occupation. 'Just… stay alert.'

We progress more slowly, aware that there is nothing to blend in with, nothing to stop us from standing out on the empty streets. It isn't even late. Early evening and Limasyll should be full of life. But there's nothing. Maybe he's right. Art said the city was in lockdown.

The troops are unexpected, the checkpoint even more so. They're alert and on edge. I wouldn't say keen. I'd say nervous.

I dismount and walk towards them, carefully unthreatening. Zander hangs back. If this goes sideways I hope he'll make a break for it. He might even get away. I don't even know why I'm thinking like this. These are my troops. But something is terribly wrong here. And I don't know what it is.

I'm about to find out though. If it kills me.

The girl nearest the front recognises me as I get closer. I see her lower her weapon and someone barks at her in reprimand.

'But… sir, it's the general.'

And suddenly there's consternation. 'General Kel? Call in to the palace. It's General Kel. She's back. She's safe.'

I smile. But the relief is short-lived.

'What are you doing out here? Sergeant Videt, isn't it?' I look to their commanding officer. He's barely older than I am. None of them are. There are few old men and women left on Anthaeus. The Gravian massacres, the Mechas, all the nightmares they wrought stole so many lives. Only those young and fit enough survived, and not all of them.

'There's a curfew, ma'am. We're under strict orders. We'll have to bring you to the palace, I'm afraid. And your companion too. Is that—?'

I glance back at Zander, who is making his way casually towards us. 'His Highness, the crown prince of Vairian. The queen's brother.'

The poor man goes pale. He looks like he might throw up. 'I... um... I'm to bring anyone found out in the city after dark to...'

'What's going on?' I peer at him and Videt looks away, staring at his boots like some kind of cadet. 'There's a curfew? Why? Report, man.'

'Some sort of problem at the palace. When you didn't come back... the Anthaem was taken ill, they say.' *They say.* I'm not so sure about anything that gets the addendum, *they say.* 'That sleeping sickness. But there's rumours. Rumours of poison and treachery. The queen declared martial law and—'

Shaken, that's the only word for it. He's shaken. They all are.

'And what?'

His voice drops to a whisper. 'Forgive me, ma'am. People acting strange. There's that new religion. They were everywhere in a couple of days. The Anthaem ordered them brought to the citadel and then, when he fell ill, the queen gave them free rein. And people changing... in moments, ma'am, finding religion and such... like they're someone else in the same body... If they're not just dropping down asleep. Sorry, ma'am. It's not my place to say.'

He stares at his boots. I glance back at Zander who watches as closely as possible. He's no fool. I see him bring up his coms and I wonder who he's talking to. His guards, I hope, checking in with them. Or his ship, perhaps. Ancestors, I hope he's made contact with Daria.

'Just as well we want to go to the palace then,' I reply before he actually has some kind of seizure. 'Come on, your Royal Highness, let's not keep people waiting.'

The sergeant doesn't move.

For a moment I think he's going to demand our weapons. Given I vastly outrank him and Zander probably has diplomatic immunity, it would be a poor decision. Thankfully, he realises that and seems content to just accompany us. Appearances are what matters here. He's doing his job. I'm his boss. And he hasn't been told what to do if he finds us so he's defaulting back to protocol. Lucky we came across him really. From the sound of it, it could have been worse.

We get back on the skimmer and move sedately along behind the transport, leaving the rest of his command behind us at their checkpoint.

Thom would never have sent such a warning without reason. I'm not sure I want to go to the palace at all but what choice do we have? It's where we need to be if we're going to find out what's happened.

I need to know what's happened to Con that has made her react this badly. Because that must be it. What else could it be?

Chapter Twenty-Two

Petra

The palace is as subdued as the city. Everywhere we go there are guards, even outside my chambers. I go there first, to wash and change. It's strangely quiet without Dwyer fussing around. I wonder where he is. I hope he's all right, in the infirmary with Dr Halie or one of her assistants.

I really need to speak to Thom.

I try the coms again, but he's not answering. The signal never connects. I try Lorza, but no luck there either. I don't have a chance to do much more. A knock on the door makes me jump.

'General Kel, the queen requires your presence now.'

It's not a voice I know, which ought to concern me. 'Just a moment.' I pull on my uniform jacket and button it up. It conceals my weapons effectively and right now I don't want to go unarmed. I can't say why.

Everything feels wrong. Like there's something in a corner of my mind whispering warnings, trying to make me listen. Trying to get me to hear.

The polite knock turns to a rapid bang. 'General Kel, I must insist.'

Must he? I try the coms one last time. 'Zander?'

'I'm here. Are you okay?'

'Yes.' I swallow down further words. I don't know what to say. 'I'm going to see Bel now.'

'Wait for me,' he says and the coms cut out.

'General Kel!'

The door is jerked open sharply. So much for that lock. There are men and women in grey out there, not guards at all. Greymen. Thom had said to watch out for the Greymen.

It's clear they've been watching me. Waiting for me.

'You will accompany us now,' says one of the boys, his hollowed out eyes starved as he studies me. 'The queen demands your presence. You will be examined before the Coparius where nothing can be hidden.'

'Examined? What nonsense is this?'

Not the right approach. I should have known. Their expressions are all bleak and miserable, filled with hate.

'Piety is not a matter of jest, *General.*'

It's the way he says the title, like he means something else. Something a lot less honourable. He nods to two of the others who start forward, but I hold my ground.

'Lay hands on me and you'll regret it. Broken bones don't heal any faster for you than for anyone else. And I'd like to see you explain to the queen what happened.'

'I'd like to see them explain it to me,' Zander says from the other end of the corridor. He has four of his guards with him. No sign of Daria – she's with Thom, wherever that might be – but seeing them there resplendent in Vairian dress uniforms, comes as an unexpected relief. 'As far as I recall she's still one of my people. And since my guard were confined to quarters, I have some questions about their treatment.'

The Greymen fall back, unsure what to do about him. He's the crown prince of another world, and they're not sure how to handle that. Not to mention that four Vairian warriors now reunited with their commander are not to be argued with. There are lines they're still afraid to cross. Thank the ancestors.

'Your Highness,' the boy tries to face him down for a moment and then bows awkwardly. 'Your royal sister—'

'—must be wondering what on earth happened to me, you're right. I'd better come with you.'

The Greyman gives him a helpless look.

Zander strides forward. His guards follow suit and the Greymen draw back, not quite scattering but hardly standing their ground. They don't go far though, like a pack of lap dogs turned rabid.

Zander's changed too, impressive in royal garb, all black velvet and silk, heavy leather and a cloak. He's actually wearing a cloak. He looks like a king, although I'd never tell him that.

'General? Shall we?'

I have a thousand questions but I can't ask them. It all feels strange, dangerous, like a shadow has fallen over the whole place. Limasyll is never this quiet. This dead.

The closer we get to the throne room the more uneasy I become. Bel is perched on her throne. Beside her, Con's seat is empty, but that hardly seems to matter. Something about Bel just draws the eyes. She is beautiful, but of course she has always been beautiful. Now she is resplendent. The gown is the darkest blue, traced with delicate crystals in patterns like frost on a window pane. Her hair is piled up on top of her head and she wears a crown which glitters in the light. It is covered in crystals too, the precious Anthaese crystals which are the rarest and most powerful in the galaxy.

But the eyes that gaze impassively down on us – those eyes aren't hers. Gone are the gentle brown, the warmth and good humour. Her eyes are black and cold, like polished stones.

'His Royal Highness, Crown Prince Lysander of Vairian and the Vairian delegation, your majesty,' the herald proclaims. Even his voice sounds shaky.

Her face flickers to a smile, just for a moment. It's not attractive. There's something cold and unnatural about it.

'Brother, forgive me. I have pressing matters with the general.'

It doesn't even sound like Bel, so formal and so cold. Where's Con? Where's Jondar? Or any of her regular guards, the ones I trained and picked. The Greymen are dotted everywhere and the courtiers eye them nervously. Those that don't have the same blank, dark eyes as Bel.

Zander nods his head. 'But of course. Since she's lately saved my life again, I wanted to commend her to you.'

'My thanks.' She doesn't sound like she means it. Something inside me is frozen. To anyone else it would be a dismissal, but she can't just throw him out. The diplomatic scandal would be unheard of. And so Zander and his guards stay put, watching, at my back.

It's my turn now. It can't be avoided any longer. 'Your Majesty, you sent for me?'

'Yes, General Kel.' She barely looks at me, certainly not to make eye contact. It's like she's talking to a stranger. A disgraced stranger. I have a terrible feeling about this. 'Certain matters have come to light while you were...' Her gaze flicks to Zander and her lips curve again. '... absent. We have received evidence of collusion between yourself and the delegation from Cuore, most inappropriate to your station.'

Cuore? She means Teel. And then I realise I haven't seen them either. Not one of the Imperial delegation is present. Ancestors, what has she done to them? The wrath of the Empress will fall on Anthaeus if anyone has harmed her favourite. I try not to look around for them. I don't dare take my eyes off Bel.

'Your Majesty—' I begin but I don't get far.

'Silence! I don't need to hear your confession. We have all the proof we need. You are hereby stripped of rank and relieved of your duties until a full investigation can be carried out. You will present yourself to Prime Faestus for interrogation. Turn in your weapons and get out of my sight.'

I stand there, reeling. It's like a nightmare, that sickening recurring nightmare that dogged me all the way through training. It's everything I've ever feared and now... now I'm facing it. There's nothing I can do. I'm frozen, trapped as if I'm turned to stone. And I'm lost. I'm standing there in this nightmare and I'm lost. Was this what it was like for him? For my father? Was this what it felt like when he lost everything that made him who he was?

I take it all back, every time I've called him a fool or a coward, every time I've railed against his memory.

When I don't move, a dozen royal guards step forward, all around me, their weapons at the ready. I can feel the bulk of my blaster against my side but I can't get to it. There's a knife belt at my waist but that isn't going to be much use in the circumstances. Draw any sort of weapon and they're going to think I'm attacking her, confirming my apparent treachery. I can't believe this. I can't believe this is happening. And these are guards I've trained, fought alongside, thought of as friends and they're now looking at me with disgust and hatred in their eyes.

Because Bel has called me traitor.

'Bel...' I whisper.

She surges out of the throne, takes two strides and strikes me hard across the face. A gasp of horror ripples around the room, but no one moves to help me.

'Get out of my sight, traitor. Your lover may have fled rather than face arrest – him and all his duplicitous hangers on – but you will pay for the attack on the Anthaem. And I will find Valentin Teel too. You can be sure of that.'

The attack on the Anthaem? What has happened to him?

'I didn't do anything to Con! I'd never – where is he? Where's Prince Jondar? What's going on here?'

But she's finished with me. 'Get her out of my sight.'

The Greymen move faster than the guards, ready to take me away but suddenly they stop.

Zander's guards fall in around me, blocking those who would arrest me. Soldiers since birth, with reputations across the galaxy, terrifying and efficient killers, perfectly trained. Everything I always wanted to be.

Zander's voice is low but crystal clear. Every syllable is a rebuke to his sister. No one could doubt it.

'Though she has served you loyally at every turn, even going so far as to defy me, Petra Kel is a Vairian by birth.'

Bel bristles. 'She is my sworn subject.'

'Yours? Don't you mean the *Anthaem's* sworn subject?' Zander stares her down, daring her to go too far. Especially in the middle of Con's court. And in earshot of whoever else might be listening. If she claims power now, they might take it for a coup. Con is still the ruler of this world, not his wife. 'No. Petra was mine from the day she first drew breath and will be until the very last. I will not allow you to convict her without even a shred of evidence.'

Bel freezes for a moment, her face pale with rage, but then she turns her back on him. 'Very well, if that's all you desire. Take her with you, Prince Lysander and, in the name of the Anthaem, get off this planet.'

'Belengaria,' he says, but she doesn't even flinch. She stands still as a stone. He narrows his eyes. 'What do you want me to tell our father?'

She spins around, her features golden and glowing, her eyes blazing darkness. I don't know her. Neither does Zander.

'Tell him Anthaeus does not belong to *him* either. Go!'

Zander takes my arm, which is just as well because I'm not sure I could negotiate turning and walking. I'm not sure how I'm still standing. He ushers me out, his head held high, more dignified than I would have given him credit for.

'Ships coms,' he says in a low, controlled voice. There's anger underneath it. I can hear it clearly. 'Send a shuttle for us immediately.'

'We can't leave!' I tell him. 'What about the others?'

'We have to leave. While we still can. Right now we need to get you out of here before you're quietly vanished, or worse turned into some kind of zealot like those creatures back there.'

I can't believe he's leaving. I can't believe it. 'But Zander, your sister—'

'*That...*' the crown prince says in a voice like eternal ice from a planet thrown as far away from its sun as it is possible to be. He chokes and takes a deep breath before starting again. '*That* is not my sister.'

Chapter Twenty-Three

Petra

I sit in the shuttle, staring at the featureless ceiling, trying desperately to find some way to turn back time and undo every single disaster since the wedding. So far, no joy. I'm on iteration number 4,017 or so when Zander comes back from the cockpit where he's been watching the pilot too closely. If it was me I'd have ordered him out.

'We're almost at the Valiant,' he tells me without preamble. 'Should I give you a moment?' There's no need. I get up instantly, raking a hand over my face to clear my bleary eyes. If I catch a glance of concern from Zander, I forcefully ignore it. There isn't time.

There's another shuttle already in the hanger when we get there – Anthaese rather than Vairian – the same old battered one which took us to Kelta and got some of us back safely. Well, almost back, almost safe. Thom's here. I glance at Zander and he grins. 'I didn't want to tell you down there. But they're safe. They're here.'

Thom's waiting for us as we disembark. He looks worse than I do.

I wait for him to salute Zander. I want to run at him and throw my arms around his neck but I can't do that to him. I can't do that to anyone. Instead, I stand there like a rock, staring at him and trying to speak. The words dry up in my mouth. I'm so relieved to see him. My friend. My best friend besides Bel. He's like my brother.

Instead, he pulls me into his embrace. I freeze for a moment, and then melt against him.

'Any word?' I ask. I don't need to inquire further. I can only mean about his husband.

'Nothing yet.' His tone is bleak, and the lines of his face hard and relentless. He has dark circles under his eyes. The laughter is gone. He hardly looks like Thom at all.

'Come to the briefing room and give your report,' Zander says.

'With all due respect, your Highness, we have wounded in the infirmary. General Kel—'

'I'm not a—' my voice cracks and I try to turn it into a cough. 'Just Petra.'

Thom frowns and I know I'll have to explain it eventually, even though I don't want to. 'Petra, you need to see Lorza.'

'Then we'll go there,' Zander says and I want to hug him. With all his command watching us, I can't. But still.

The infirmary on the Valiant is stark and clinical, not like Halie's halls with their billowing curtains. This is a warship, after all. Thom fills us in quickly.

Lorza's still in a bad way from the attack on Kelta. Sorrell's hands need attention and Daria got shot, although she'd probably say it was just a scratch. Ellish is still with her, refusing to leave.

Daria nods to me when she sees me with Zander. 'Thank you, Kel.'

'For what?'

'For getting him back here. I owe you.'

She doesn't, but I don't have a chance to explain before she's gone. I feel like such an imposter.

Beq took a hell of a knock during their escape but he's still limping on. The people they rescued from the moon are in dire medical need. Three of them didn't survive. The rest are in a quarantine unit, to be safe.

Lorza reaches out her hand to me as I approach her bed. I link my fingers with hers. Her skin is boiling hot to the touch. Infection makes her eyes very bright. This isn't good. Even I know that.

'Good to see you, General,' she says, her voice thin.

'Just Petra, Lorza. I don't have a rank now. You've done good, kid. Just a little longer and the medics here will set you all right again.'

She nods and closes her eyes. I try to convince myself she'll be fine.

'We did what we could for her,' Thom assures me. 'We had to hide out in a high orbit until we could rendezvous and we only had the medical supplies on board.'

'I'm sure you did everything possible.' I say the right things, but they're empty platitudes. Thom knows it as well as I do. She needed a hospital, specialists, far sooner than she got them, and the shuttle didn't have the range to reach anywhere but Anthaeus, and the Valiant, once it's orbit brought it in range. It could be too late now.

'What happened?' Thom asks.

'I could ask the same question.'

He sighs and I see the weight of it in the droop of his shoulders.

'I wish I knew where to begin. The world's gone mad.'

'Or my sister has.' Zander grips his shoulder with a reassuring hand. 'Come on, let's talk in private. The others will be cared for. I promise.'

It's hard not to believe him when he takes that tone. Like he can fix anything, make everything all right again. So long as you just let go and trust him. We follow him to his command room.

Thom sits down, his head in his hands and we give him the time he needs. He's been holding everything in, holding it together for everyone else. I know it straight away. I know him so well.

'Jondar got the message through when we re-established contact. Only by a few minutes. He'd barricaded himself in the situation room. I heard them break down the door and take him. He said... the Greymen had taken over, that Bel was under their control. When Con ordered them rounded up and brought to the citadel, it must have been what they wanted all along. They were just... just waiting.'

'Where's Con?'

'That... I don't know. No one does. No sign of him, no sign of Jondar.'

'The Cuoreans?' I ask. I have to. She wouldn't have done something to them. She told me they fled but we don't know that. They could be dead in a ditch somewhere. *No. She wouldn't dare. Would she?*

Thom shrugs. 'We don't know. Missing.'

'And Art?'

Zander shakes his head. 'Not a word. Not to me.'

'We have to find him.'

'And Val.' Zander's voice is strangely calm. I glare at him but he just looks back, unrepentant. 'If he's inside the palace he could have information. We need to get him off Anthaeus and fast.'

'He set us up, Zander. He planted that tracker on me. The ship found us because of him—'

'We don't know that,' Zander insists. 'If he's killed on Anthaeus... if any of them are killed, but especially him... do you know what the Empress will do? It's just the pretext she needs.'

I look at the two of them. He's right. An invasion of Anthaeus? That might just be the beginning of it.

'I'll go.'

Zander's response is instantaneous. 'No, absolutely not.'

'It has to be me.'

'It's too dangerous.'

'Why? You can't go. It could trigger a diplomatic incident. Thom can't. He's too emotionally involved.'

His outrage lifts Thom to his feet, makes him alive again for a second. 'How am I——?'

'Tell me you wouldn't drop everything to rescue Jondar, no matter what? And get yourself captured if it came to a choice of that or leaving him behind?'

He stalls, as if I've just sucker punched him and drops back down to the seat. He's also exhausted. Broken. Lost. But I can't say any of that to him. It isn't fair.

But Zander isn't so easily quelled. 'At least let me make contact with Art.'

'Your little brother—'

'You can't go alone. I won't let you. We need a plan. I'll lock you up if I have to, so no more arguments.'

I square off against him. 'You'll *try* to lock me up.'

It's like facing a boulder but it doesn't matter. My head only comes up to his far too broad shoulders but I know his weak spots. I can take him down in seconds. 'Pet—'

I swing before he can finish. He dodges expertly, but doesn't count on the kick to his shins which follows. I don't stop. The next punch he deflects with his hand.

He grunts as my left connects with his stomach.

'I'm not fighting you.'

He really isn't.

'I can see that.' God, the joy of it surges through me. I've wanted to do this for years.

And then Thom seizes me from behind. He knows me better than Zander, knows what twists I'll try, dodges me easily. Traitor.

'Calm down,' he says. 'This isn't going to help.'

Zander bends double, catching his breath.

'You can make contact with Art?' I ask.

But I know he can. I'd bet my salary on it. If I still had a salary. Well, why should he tell me? I'm not part of his family. I'm not royalty. I don't serve them. I've no reason to know their plans, the Merryns. And if he can't – well, we all know someone who can.

Zander swallows. He recognises the expression on my face then. He knows what I want him to do. Good. At least we still have that. I'd hate for him to believe for a moment that I had gone soft.

'I'm going, Zan, whether you like it or not. Put me in touch with him now.'

*

From high orbit, the planet looks peaceful, beautiful. We don't have much to do. Or at least, I don't. When Zander puts the call through to Vairian, I'm surprised I'm included, even though I do little more than sit behind him. Waiting.

I don't know what else to do though. I'm on board a foreign vessel, effectively court-martialled, stripped of rank, banished from the court and the planet. From everything I have worked so hard to protect.

I have a mission… *had* a mission.

And I'm not sure what is left to me now. Except to find out what has happened to her. What has changed her? I know who I need to ask, the Rondet, but when have they ever spoken to me. Only that once.

Come back, Petra Kel. Awaken. This is not your sleep. Awaken—

I can still hear the voice, like a ghost in my mind.

The signal finally connects. The channel is secure on several levels. Zander is cycling it through several substations on outer planets, each one kicking in a few moments after the other, and it's got some sort of new encryption which he spoke about in detail for a full ten minutes.

I wasn't actually listening. I was catastrophising instead.

King Marcus doesn't appear at first. There's a minor functionary who looks vaguely familiar. I'm not sure if I've seen him, or seen some relative of his, or even if they just all have the same face. What does it matter? I'm not there to talk to him. I'm just here to sit behind Zander and listen, to report when he tells me to report.

I feel broken inside.

'Please stand by for his Majesty.'

In front of me Zander's shoulders tighten. It's almost as if he's preparing himself, drawing himself to attention. It's a strange relationship, son and subject, father and king. Military commander and ever faithful soldier. And at the back of it all, the knowledge that when his father dies, he'll take his place.

Unless the Empress has her way.

We haven't had a chance to discuss that. Or the fact that someone tried to kidnap him. Instead we just fought and he insulted me and I ran away with his... whatever Teel is to him... Something else we haven't discussed.

I can't talk to him.

I only wish I could. But we never could talk. We could drink, we could kiss, we could dance and fight and do a thousand other things. But not talk, not Zander and I. And we still can't.

Zander checks the scrambling algorithm again. I've never seen anything so complex. And then, finally, King Marcus appears on the small screen.

He's still a handsome man. I can see where his son gets his looks. Bel is more like their mother but looking at Marcus, I see the man Zander will become. There's steel in him, not just in the grey hair at his temples. It's in his eyes, in his mouth, in the lines of his jaw.

Zander reports quickly, succinctly – what we found on Kelta, the attacks, Valentin Teel's appearance and Bel's strange behaviour. The King of Vairian listens. He doesn't interrupt or ask questions. He just listens and I'm certain he is taking in absolutely everything. The wheels of his mind are whirling and when his son eventually falls silent, Marcus looks past him, right at me.

'Petra Kel, it's good to see you.'

'Your Majesty is too kind.'

He smiles. Actually smiles. 'I see they've made a courtier of you at last.'

'Not really,' Zander replies before I can think of anything to say, helpful as ever.

'Ignore him. He still has no manners.'

And yet he saved me from whatever the Greymen had in store for me. I ought to defend him, even from his own father. But the king goes on before I can say anything more. 'Report, if you please, Petra.'

I draw myself up to attention more out of familiarity that anything else. I'm as concise as Zander was, careful to cover the complex nature of the new mechas, both the ones that attacked us and the ones we found in process on Kelta. Then I move on to the way Bel seemed like another person. He nods as he takes in what I say.

'You need to find the Rondet,' he says at last. 'They are the most likely to have information about the stone and whatever has happened to my daughter. She's refused communications with us, and I believe with the Empire as well. As for Teel's party... she would be ill-advised to do anything to them. That doesn't mean an accident can't happen. Tread carefully, you two. Share this with no one else.'

'And Art?' I ask. 'Why is he here?'

'He's doing his job, Petra. As I'm sure he told you. I'm not in a position to disclose what that is.'

'But it's to do with Zander and Teel.' I say it almost without thought. Bel and Con are so open about all things. I've forgotten that Marcus Merryn is not the same as them. 'Has he contacted you? We need his help.'

He laughs, a dark and unexpected laugh. 'Art is safe. He sent word less than an hour ago. I'll have him liaise with you on this mission. I always said you were too clever for your own good. Just like your father.' I hide the urge to flinch. I hate mention of my family. He knows that. 'Careful Petra. The Empress is playing a game on many fronts and we cannot afford to be complacent.'

'She wants your son.'

'She wants my world. My son is an additional enticement. I expect you to make sure that does not happen, as you promised my daughter.'

So he knows about that. Who am I kidding? He knows about everything. The Empress is not the only devious player in this game.

What else can I do? As he says, I've already promised Bel anyway. And even if I had not, I'm never going to let something like that happen to Zander. Never.

'I promise, your Majesty.'

He leans forward. 'On your honour and your fealty.'

'My fealty?' I frown. 'But, your Majesty. I am sworn to Anthaeus, and to your daughter.'

'Of course you are, but Belengaria just rejected you, I believe. She cast you out. And if Zander had not been there, you would probably be standing there blank-eyed beside her. So, as far as I can see that makes you a free agent. And your first loyalty was to us. By birth, Petra. By blood.'

It was. But… I'm not so sure I can just accept Bel's rejection of me so easily.

'Loyalty is not tied to a string, your Majesty. I… I can't just…'

'Give up?' he suggests. Whether it's the words I wanted to say or what he wants me to do, I don't know.

I stare at the screen, swallowing the words I want to say. I focus on the wall behind his head. It's the house in Elveden. It still looks the same. I thought, perhaps, since it's the palace now it would look different.

Zander's voice surprises me. 'Petra never gives up, sir.'

'Of course, she doesn't. I'd expect no less from the daughter of Levander Kel.'

My father the hero. The dead hero. My father whose reputation I've spent my life trying to play down and forget. Not because it's good… I mean, it was, up to a point. The point when he got the previous king's second son killed. Because he retreated. Because he gave up. Because he wasn't a hero any more.

The current king, whose son I'm currently meant to be protecting, leans forward and cuts the coms. There's an awkward silence and then Zander exhales, a long slow sigh.

'Well, that could have gone better.'

Chapter Twenty-Four

Petra

I'm not a patient person. I never have been. Even as a child, especially as a child. I learned to wait. But that didn't make me patient. Just able to wait.

It's not the same thing.

When I have to wait, I prepare. I train. I make sure everything is covered. The crew of the Valiant cluster my periphery, watching. I think, sometimes, that they don't want to get too close. I don't know if they see me as his, or as a threat to him. Or as someone who left Vairian for another world, followed the princess and never came back. Or as the daughter of the notorious Levander Kel. Doesn't really matter which one, does it?

Sweat drips down my face, and I blink it out of my eyes.

'You want a break?' Thom asks. We've been sparring for hours, ever since the word came through to me that Lorza died. There was nothing that could be done. It was too late. Beq and Sorrell have been drinking in the rec room. I think Daria and Ellish may be with them. Or possibly just with each other. I don't have the luxury of doing anything like that to stave off the feelings. Training is better.

'No. Let's go again.'

He doesn't go easy on me. Never has, never will. I can count on Thom for that. We've gathered an audience but I barely see them. They're just faces, just the crew members off duty, or supposed to be training themselves.

Well, hopefully they're learning something.

That's when Zander arrives with all the kit I could ever need.

New body armour is never an easy wear. It constricts, it chafes, it doesn't have flexibility. Sometimes it's even hard to breathe in it. That's the rule. Every soldier knows that. Whatever stuff Zander has just presented me with has to be a brand new system, because I've never felt anything fit so well or let me move as if I'm wearing nothing at all.

Of course, with Zander watching, that is not something I should be thinking about.

'It's good,' I tell him.

He just purses his lips. 'Of course it's good. It's the best Vairian has to offer.'

I give him a reckless grin. 'Well so am I, so we're a fit.'

The crown prince just shakes his head to hide his smile. 'If you don't come back—'

'You can bill me for it.'

His hands close on my upper arms, holding me still, as if he can hold me there forever. 'I was going to say, I'll come for you. I'll find you.'

The intensity with which he says it, the way he looks at me, steals the next flippant remark from my mouth.

'You mustn't,' I tell him, knowing that he won't listen to me anyway.

'Are you ready for the drop? I'll fly you there myself.'

Another risk. He shouldn't do that either. But I don't want to argue with him. Not now. 'Okay.'

His voice drops very low. 'We should... we should talk...'

'About? You and Teel?'

He hesitates, glancing around to see if anyone is close enough to overhear. They aren't though. They're making themselves scarce. 'If… if you want.'

It's like a barb in my heart. Just pull it out. It's for the best. Get it over as quickly as possible. 'You had a relationship?'

'I wouldn't… I wouldn't call it that. We had a…' He searches for a word and fails, his face getting redder by the second. His eyes flicker around my face, as if looking for an escape.

'A what, Zan?'

'I don't know. Cuore isn't the sort of place for relationships. It's hard to trust anyone there, but… I trusted him, Petra. And he got me out of there. I don't know if he truly had feelings for me but I…' The words fail him again, or are just too painful to say.

'Do you love him?' I whisper. It's cruel to ask, cruel to both of us. I don't want to know. And yet I can't bear not knowing. Were they together? No more than friends? Did they part on good terms or bad? Did they part at all?

But Zander doesn't answer. Not really.

'Do you?'

Yes, this is a terrible conversation. This is a mistake. I look away but Zander doesn't let me go. I breathe in his scent, so close to me. I feel his warmth. I want to wrap myself in him and never leave.

'He used me, Zander. He planted a tracker on me. If I see him again, I'm liable to break every bone in his body, diplomatic immunity or not.'

A smile quirks at the corner of his beautiful mouth, just for a second as I glance back. 'Yes. He has that effect on people.'

'You too?'

He whispers. 'Me too.' I pull away from him and this time he lets me go, as if he doesn't have the strength to hold me any more.

'You'll have to tell me eventually,' I say. 'Promise.'

'I promise.'

And, ancestors help me, I believe him.

*

The Wasp isn't the beat-up old-style wood and canvas ones they flew at home. It's a state of the art drop ship and the equipment is strangely familiar. I've seen a lot of it over the last while. This thing has Con's fingerprints all over it. I wonder if he's been working with Vairian on military projects or if they've just stolen his work. I'll have to ask.

If I get the chance to ask him.

I strap in to the jump seat and fix the mask over my face. I won't need the air for long. It's the chute that could give me away so I'll need to leave it as late as possible. A suicide drop, that's what they call it. Is it any wonder I didn't want to bring anyone else?

Zander climbs into the cockpit and runs through his pre-flight. There are any number of people who could do this. Good, experienced, competent pilots. They all tried to talk him out of it. And failed. He'll have an escort. He'll only drop down into the atmosphere for a few minutes at most.

'All set?' he asks.

I nod and the next thing I know he's in the body of the Wasp in front of me. He pushes back the mask and kisses me. It's a thorough kiss, distracting and maddening. Unexpected. His lips on mine drive all sense from my mind. He places the mask back before I can say a word and then he climbs back into the cockpit.

We swoop out of the Valiant, flanked by his Wing, and we dive towards the planet. This is all calculated, I tell myself, a precision exercise, down and down, until I can make out landmarks, lost cities in the forests, great pits of darkness where the Gravians mined, the vast arable fields to the south of Limasyll, the ocean bright and glittering in the starlight. There's no moon tonight, not on this side of the planet. And then I see it, Arinsall lake, where we've set the rendezvous.

Zander counts down in my ear, and I count with him. The hatch opens smoothly and the wind whips at me, ready to suck me out the moment I unclip myself. We're almost there, almost. Just a few more seconds and...

Five, four, three...

'Come back to me, Pet,' he whispers in my ear.

And I jump.

The wind tears at me, buffeting my body as if it could push me back up and out of the atmosphere. But I fall like a stone. Spreading myself wide, I let the noise rush by me, embracing it, working with air currents, all my attention fixed on the lake, the waterfalls, the forest around it. The beach is the best landing place for miles and the land around here is empty of people. The town that was once here burned in the initial invasion and no one came back. Perhaps they never will. A ghost town.

It doesn't matter now. It's the location Art gave, or so Zander told me, our rendezvous point and I've got to take him at his word. I keep counting, trusting my instincts to know when to pull the chute. Not yet, not yet. It has to be as late as possible. I can't risk detection, not even in the dark. Almost there. Almost...

Something huge and dark surges up beneath me and snatches me from the air. It's cold and hard, like metal bands slamming into my chest and legs. I cry out, unable to help myself as the air is forced from my lungs.

Be calm, Petra Kel. No harm will come to you.

The voice echoes inside my head, dripping with irritability and disdain.

Aeron. It has to be Aeron.

My heart thunders in my chest and my brain aches with the voice inside it. This can't be happening. How is this happening? They never talk to me. Well, just that once.

We can. That has to be Rhenna. Who else could it be? But she sounds tired. So very tired. *We just chose not to. You did not belong to us. Now we have need of you. So you do.*

'I do not. I don't belong to anyone.'

Someone laughs. I hear him. Not one of them but I know that sound. I know it far too well. I just should not be hearing him inside my mind. That's too disconcerting by far.

'*I told you,*' he says, amusement thick on every word.

Aeron sets me down in an enormous cavern in the side of the mountain. Crystals twine their way through the rock face, like elaborate vines carved by ancient hands. Or claws. I glance at Aeron. He flexes his forepaws, rakes them on the ground. I had no idea he was the feisty one.

Besides, he's the least of my worries.

I pull the mask off my face and breathe in the clear, scented air of Anthaeus again. I missed it. I guess almost running out of air altogether makes you reassess things. It's heady, makes my head spin for a moment, and I come back to my senses. I look for him as I slowly unsheathe the knives strapped to my thigh.

'Hello, Lord Teel. I'd like to discuss a certain tracking device.'

Chapter Twenty-Five

Petra

Favre steps out of the darkness behind Teel, larger than I remember, darker and far more intimidating. Aeron remains at my side, a strangely reassuring presence. And I just glare at the man who used me, who played me for a fool.

He doesn't even have the good grace to look sorry about it.

And he's beautiful. Even on the run, living in a cave and clearly having seen better days, he's beautiful.

'Ah Petra Kel,' he says with an elaborate bow. 'We have all done things we should not have done, and here we are. How is dear Lysander? Has he shared our history with you?'

I press my lips together. I don't put the weapons away.

'Not yet then,' he goes on. 'Maybe one day. Come, come, you have to see this.'

'I don't have to do anything with you. Where's…' and I hesitate. Because I don't want to let him know about Art. Even if he already knows. 'Where's Rhenna?' It's a weak finish but that doesn't seem to matter.

'*Come,*' she breathes the words in the back of my mind. '*You may approach.*'

Bel never described her as so imperious before. She spoke of her as her friend. She gave the impression of a mischievous and playful creature. A chill creeps over me.

If Bel has changed – and ancestors know that Bel has changed – has something happened to Rhenna too? Could it have affected her when Bel… transformed?

This isn't something for someone like me. Okay, Thom might argue, but I know the truth. This is for kings and rulers, heroes and the great and good of the land. The Rondet are viewed as the spiritual heart of this world, and until recently were a jealously guarded secret. Why are they talking to me?

The others fall back as I walk forward. I see other people sheltering here, the other members of the group which came from Cuore with Teel. And a few Anthaese as well. Not many. Outcasts all. A number of them are sick, I can tell that instantly. Their skin is glossy with sweat and they're sleeping on the cold hard rock, stirring fitfully.

No sign of Jondar, Con, or Art.

Kaeda de Lorens sits by the fire, her blue hair piled high, framing her perfect face. She watches me carefully, missing nothing. Teel's circle is still with him then. And about a dozen others. I recognise some of Bel's maids, a couple of courtiers, Con's valet. People close to the two of them, trusted.

And now exiled. In hiding.

I push on. I need to see Rhenna. I need to find out what she knows and what is wrong with her. Because I am sure there is something wrong with her too.

There's a gap in the wall, a dark mouth into nothing. She must have squeezed herself inside. Is she hiding? Is she trapped?

Aeron stops by the entrance and behind me I hear Teel and Favre come to a halt as well. I face it alone. I face her alone.

Suddenly I realise I've never felt so afraid in my life. I've never been afraid. Not like this. I'm a soldier, a fighter. I face my troubles head on, I always have done. And now, for the first time, I don't want to.

There's a monster in the darkness. There's a creature in this cave, an alien.

Except she's not the alien. She belongs here, and I don't.

Breathe. Breathe, Petra. Get a grip. It's Rhenna. It's just Rhenna. And she's Bel's friend.

'*Come in,*' she tells me. Commands me. Once again I think she sounds tired. Exhausted. I feel another surge of alarm. And my feet move almost of their own accord.

It's like walking into the heart of a geode. The crystals are everywhere, under our feet and over our heads, a million colours flickering with light and life. Rhenna is curled up in the heart of it, her crystal skin glittering, reflecting everything. She's purring to herself, adjusting the tone and pitch every so often so that it reverberates back through the stones, makes the crystals vibrate with power. She's like a cat, her body wrapped around itself, the wings forming a silken cocoon.

And she's watching me. Her eyes are bright and glow with life, with intelligence.

'Hello, Rhenna,' I make myself say. *Manners*, my mother used to say, *are everything.* A lot of use that did her when the bombs fell on our house in the last days of the war. But still. Some things stick with you.

'*I was so tired. Bel won't come here and I'm too tired to go to her. I asked her and asked her, but she was busy. And then she went quiet. I've lost her.*'

'Is this where you've been hiding? It's… it's beautiful.'

'*It's powerful. And special. It gives me peace. I need that.*'

There's heat emanating from her. She's warm, far too warm. I think she's sick too. 'How long have you been this tired, Rhenna?'

'*Since I came here. Since I lost Bel.*' She sounds miserable, so horribly alone. And she shouldn't be. Something in me quakes and I reach out a tentative hand. When I don't instantly lose it to those sharp teeth, I move further forward and press it to her forehead. She pushes against me, desperate for contact and I throw my arms around her neck and hold her. '*I need her back. Get her for me. Please, Petra Kel. Rescue her for me. I know of no one else who can.*'

'Tell me what happened?'

'*She touched the Coparius and it drank her down, tasted her blood and chose her. Now it walks in her skin, speaks with her tongue. It is drinking us all down. Everyone will sleep again. Human and the Rondet.*'

'I don't understand. What is the Coparius?'

Rhenna falls silent, like she's waiting for someone else to explain.

'*The ancient goddess, that which we put down,*' it's Favre's voice this time. '*We should have been honest. We should have told Conleith and Belengaria. But we were… we defeated it so long ago. We had no choice if we were to survive. And we were ashamed of what we did…*'

I rub Rhenna's forehead again, trying to comfort her, wondering if he can feel it too. I know shame. What did they do? Why are they so afraid of telling us what happened so long ago?

I know shame. I remember shame. It has strange effects on people. Maybe I should share my shame with them. The shame I felt when Bel stripped me of rank and dismissed me isn't the worst of it. It's just an echo.

I sit down, leaning back against Rhenna because I don't want to leave her alone. I cross my legs in front of me, surrounded by crystals and close my eyes just so I can get the words out. If I can do this, if

I can make them see they are not alone, that I know shame just as intimately… maybe they'll confide in me, maybe they'll help me find something to help Bel. Anything. Because I know all about shame.

'My father was a hero of Vairian. But he died in defeat, not in glory. His name was struck off the rolls of honour. He disobeyed a direct order that would have seen his men slaughtered in an ambush. Saved countless lives really. Not everyone agreed though and a small group of his men went ahead and they died. They died badly, cut to pieces by weapons' fire that he predicted. I mean, they were so badly disfigured that the Gravians couldn't even use them to make Mechas. A small blessing. But one of them was the younger son of King Veron. The rather talented, war-hero younger son, the hope of Vairian at the time. My father was stripped of his rank and sent to the front line, in the middle of the war. He survived, none the less. Six months after the war, eight months after my mother and siblings died in a bombing raid, he shoved his blaster in his mouth. If you want to talk about shame… try being the child of a warrior race when your father did all that and died that way.'

There's a long silence. My pain at the memory lingers with my words, seeping through the mental communion with them. It's not just words I share. It's everything. The agony, the misery, the ignominy.

'Does Zander know?' I hear another voice in the darkness. Not a voice in my mind, one which speaks out loud and sounds so shocked, so appalled. So human.

Teel! Oh ancestors, I forgot about Teel. My eyes snap open in panic. I didn't want him to know. I was trying to comfort them, not him.

How did he hear us? How does he know?

'*He formed a link with us,*' Aeron admits, trying to calm the panic rushing through me. '*Such a link works both ways. And here, there is comfort in his presence… in our loss…*'

Great, Aeron, I'm delighted for you.

'Petra?' Teel's voice is tentative now.

'Why are you *even* still here?' I blurt out loud. My voice echoes around the chamber, conflicting with the harmonies of the crystals and Rhenna growls at me. I'm upsetting her. Quickly I reach out my hand to her, to reassure her and apologise. She closes her eyes again and purrs.

Teel slides in through the gap and settles down beside me.

'I didn't like to leave them. They were agitated. Upset. Especially when the queen started to behave erratically. We were on the way from Limasyll to the Rondet's dome when I first noticed. And once she had helped me connect with them... well, it was easy. But soon after that, when we returned to the palace, that was when she changed. And they were so... scared.'

There's a kindness in his voice. A kindness in him that doesn't gel with what I know about him.

I chew on my lower lip.

'That was good of you, to stay with them.' It's all I can offer him at the moment.

'Does Zander know? About your father?'

I laugh, a soft, embittered sound. 'Oh Teel, *everyone* knows. All the Vairians anyway. Some of them don't care, but they're few – Bel, Thom, our former squad mates. That's about it. I worked to make people forget, to purge myself of his legacy and I almost did it. Almost. I made my own name, but when you get down to it, I'm still a Kel. I always will be.'

'So that's why—'

He stops speaking but the thought goes on. It's inescapable. *That's why Zander and I couldn't be together. That's why I left. That's why...*

'That's why.'

I might as well confirm it for him. He knows anyway. He knows everything. That's why I left Zander when he told me he loved me. Because more than anything else I knew I could not bring that shame on him. I still can't. Not really. Anything else is a naïve daydream.

His hand takes mine and he lifts it to his lips, turning my wrist up so he can kiss the most sensitive part. It's easy to let him, easy to forget what he did and enjoy it. But then I think of Zander's kiss, and rip my hand free of his.

'Why did you plant the tracker on me? Why disguise it as a gift?'

'I needed to know where you were? I wanted to know you were safe?' He spreads his hands wide and phrases it like a question even though it isn't. *An excuse maybe?* He looks so impossibly innocent that I know he's lying.

'What? Should I pick the answer? Do I get to add my own options?'

'You're too clever for me, Petra Kel.'

I really doubt he thinks that. I don't think Valentin Teel thinks there's anyone in the galaxy who is too clever for Valentin Teel.

'The truth, Teel.'

'I needed to know where you were.' It's deceptively simple as answers go. I long to ask *why? Why did he need to know?* But I don't want to know the answer. Or rather, I already know. I just don't want to hear it.

'Did you send the ship?'

But he just frowns. Perhaps he's pretending. Perhaps… perhaps he isn't. 'What ship?'

I don't know what to say to him in reply. There's no point in arguing.

I thought, when I confronted him, there would be violence, possibly tears and a lot of begging. But the unbearable sadness of this is too much for me.

You want shame, Favre? I think. I don't know if he'll hear me or not but I suspect they hear far more than they let on. *How is that for shame?* My father, my family, every aspect of my life has been coloured by that shame.

Even my love… Zander told me he loved me. He whispered it as he fell asleep and I couldn't close my eyes. I knew what would be coming, even though he was just a minor noble at the time. The whispers, the gossip, the sly looks and snide remarks. Levander Kel's daughter, social climbing, sleeping her way back to respectability, or dragging him down with her. Lysander Merryn, just like his father, slumming it.

First Lieutenant Penn Arbon was the first one to say something out loud. Not to Zander of course. Just to me. With the added implication that if I didn't want trouble and the world laughing at Zander, I'd let him do whatever he wanted.

And Zander would have been so appalled and angry. He'd want to fight for me. I couldn't let him ruin his whole career for me. So I did it instead. I punched Arbon unconscious and applied for reassignment. Not because of Zander, not entirely. But I had to do it. I left Zander behind, and Arbon never even dared to file charges. I don't know what happened to him. To be honest I don't care. Maybe part of me blamed Zander too. For being oblivious. For being foolish enough to dream that we could ever be together. Maybe that's why I'd always pushed him away, and said the terrible things I've said to him. Hurt him. I never told him. None of it. I couldn't.

I know all about shame.

Suddenly, something seizes hold of me, something huge and endless, something that I can't hope to resist, even if I had any warning in which to do so. The light surges up around me, blinding me and I feel Teel's hands on my shoulders, pulling me against him, but my mind is torn away. It's more than I ever imaged, far more than Bel or Thom ever described. I can't see, I can't speak, I can't hear. Wind rushes by me and my body wants to scream but there's no way to do that. Panic makes me nauseous and I struggle, but there's nothing to struggle against. In the light, in the brightness, I open my eyes.

And see everything.

I float high above the planet, but it's not Anthaeus as I so recently saw it. This is an Anthaeus untouched by the Gravian invasion. There's no sign of landing strips or the human infrastructure either. It's lush and wild, the ancient Anthaese buildings rising from the tangle of vegetation, rising from the waters of the southern ocean which has long since swallowed them up, and spilling down the mountainsides, pristine, unspoiled and shockingly beautiful. I can't quite get my head around it for a moment. Anthaeus as it should be. Anthaeus as it was.

'*This was our home. We have never shown it to a human before,*' Favre says in a strangely lilting, gentle voice. '*This was Anthaeus as we knew it, before our long sleep.*'

'*It's beautiful.*'

'*More than beautiful. But it was our folly. Our shame.*'

We dive down together. The forest rushes up towards us and just when I think it will be too late, we pass through it, through one of those great gates to the underground cities. We fly along through the caverns and they're alive again. Not with humans now, but with the ancient Anthaese. Their crystal bodies glow with light and they are everywhere, so many of them, bright wonders everywhere. They nest in chambers lining the cavern walls and make their homes in between the miracles they've made. The crystals glow all around them, dancing with life, their power and communication network.

There's music everywhere. It ripples through the air, through the rocks but most of all through the crystals.

And then we drop down again, through the lower tunnels, into the deeper levels, down to the roots of the world. The light grows fainter and the song fades away. There's just a thin thread of light filtering through the rock now. But at the depths, in the heart of the world, there is the stone. It sucks away at the world, at the life that inhabits it, slowly sucking away a little at a time. I can feel it stirring as we approach, feel its interest in us. In the darkness, it's waking up and it's sentient.

It's hungry.

Someone pushes past us, and I remember we're not really there. And it isn't Favre and myself it's reacting to. It's whoever has burrowed their way down here.

'*So pretty,*' the voice whispers. '*I heard your song, pretty.*'

I know it's not speaking my language, or any language I understand. But this young Anthaese is not making a lot of sense either.

He was an outcast, left to wander the lower levels of the city, left to dig and delve deep in the stones. He was forgotten. But he did not forget, and when he found the Stoneheart, the Coparius, it realised it had a way to gain so much more than the drip-feed of life it had survived on for so long. He was hurt and it tasted his blood. It wanted so much more.

Favre's voice is hesitant.

This is your shame? I ask.

This is my grandsire, he replied. *Natuel, the ancient. This is my family's shame. This monster.*

He doesn't seem like a monster. There's an air of tragedy about him, and about the way Favre reacts to the sight. He doesn't want to be here. He doesn't want to tell me. And I get that. I sympathise. But

I'm not going anywhere until I see what is happening because how else will I find out how to save Bel.

If Bel can be saved.

Natuel reaches out for the stone with a clawed forepaw. It swallows the blood on his skin from where he tore his way through the rocks and the light in it bleeds into him. It swirls through his body, billowing through him like a host of fireflies in the night. I can see the light replacing the fading colours, eating away at them, devouring him before us.

He lived, Favre answers my unasked question. *After a fashion. I think... I want to think... Natuel was gone from the start. By the time he emerged from the darkness with the stone, he was... other.*

As he speaks I see it happening. Natuel stalking out of the tunnels and up to the city. And when he shows the stone to his people, some of them turn away. But others seem infected with the same light, the same draining, drawing light that devours them from the inside and makes them his. Or rather the Coparius's.

And more of them, so many of them, fall into a deep, sickly slumber. The Coparius drinks down their energy, drains them until they become stone.

Bring me the Anthaem, he tells them.

And that was how the war started.

I thought I'd seen war. I was wrong. It raged for centuries. Longer. There was no way to tell the time that passed. The sun and the moons rose and set, the seasons cycled past, and the Anthaese, whose lives were so much longer than ours, died and died and died.

They tore each other apart. They ripped each other from the sky. They tortured and shattered each other's bodies, some trying to free their enslaved family and friends, some trying to make them serve.

If they didn't die in battle, they died in endless sleep.

The Coparius was relentless, pitiless. It drove its subjects on and the world began to crumble. The cities were destroyed, the forests burned, the mountains cracked.

And in the end, just a few were left. The Coparius commanded them all, and thought itself victorious.

And then I see Favre. Not Favre as he is with me. Favre is young and untried, half the size he is now. The lights inside him are a clear bright blue and he is just a child, playing in the ruins and the rubble, his wings fluttering, his tail like a kitten's.

But he is trusted. He is Natuel's family, his descendent, and the Coparius thinks it is only a matter of time. Soon, it reasons, soon, the child will fall under its sway, just as every other member of his tribe has.

It was our weakness, Favre tells me. *It was our shame.*

What did you do?

He flinches back from me, and suddenly this terrifying creature, this warrior from thousands of years ago, is a child again.

It was pretty. It stood alone, unguarded. It was always there, all my life and I knew it was evil. I knew the way I knew how to breathe or how to fly. So I took it. I took it and I buried it back in the earth.

Natuel, or the creature living in his body, went wild with rage. It slaughtered as it tore its way through the remains of Limasyll, killing everything in its way, whether friend or foe. And there were still foes. As the loss of the Coparius became apparent, they rose up, those enslaved, those thought broken and no longer a threat.

And they killed him. They broke him into pieces.

For a while all was well. Life returned. The planet thrived. Years passed and the stone was not so much forgotten but the memory of it was put away.

And deep in the earth where Favre had buried it, the stone reached out through the crystals which ran through the earth and stones that made up Anthaeus itself and it began to drink again. Hungrier than ever, no longer content with a little, with a dripfeed. It thirsted for vengeance, for life. And slowly, surely, the remaining Anthaese began to go to sleep.

They died, all but four of them and they too would have died if not for us.

As I come back to myself, I feel Teel's embrace around me. I'm lying in his arms, my face pressed against his chest. His shirt is wet and too late I realise that I'm weeping.

I never cry. I cried too much when I was just a child. I thought I had no tears left in me.

I wish Zander was here. Just for a moment. All I want is Zander.

'I know,' Teel whispers so softly I can feel his voice through his chest rather than hear it. 'But I'll have to do for now.'

Chapter Twenty-Six

Petra

The Rondet only succeeded in trapping the Coparius back in the earth because they killed Natuel. I mull that over in my mind. It's not a pleasant thought, and not an option I can entertain. Bel is my friend. We are not going there.

But Favre stole the stone and that weakened its hold on his grandfather. So perhaps that is the way to look at it. Get the stone away from her, stop it reinforcing its hold on her. And then...

And then what?

Natuel went insane with rage and started slaughtering everyone until he was killed.

There has got to be a way to reach her. I refuse to give up.

But... but... if anyone is good at killing... Maybe that's why they chose me. Because they know. I could make it quick. I could make it clean. I could make sure she didn't feel anything at all.

I can't think that way. There's nothing comforting in it at all. I ought to radio through to Zander and the Valiant, but that would mean telling him that there is no sign of Art yet. And that I'm here with Teel. And that it appears that the only way to free his sister is to kill her.

Not a conversation I want to have right now.

I walk to the front of the cavern where the sunlight streams down on to the stone, and gaze out over the lake and the treetops. It's beautiful. This whole world is beautiful. I'd never have believed I could be somewhere like this.

Then I remember what I've seen. The past, what the Gravians did, what the Coparius did and would do again.

'Kel, I want a word with you. Where is Lysander? What have you done with him?'

Kaeda de Lorens sweeps towards me, perfectly immaculate, as ever. She's managing then, living in a cave. Probably getting some other poor sod to do everything for her.

'I beg your pardon,' I say. Not because I didn't hear her. But because I don't like the tone. Or her.

'I said, *where* is Lysander?'

She's not going to go away. The entitled never do.

'He's safe, Kaeda. Back on the Valiant.'

She sighs as if it's the most irritating news she's had all day. Maybe it is, Zander being so far out of her reach. Good. I'm delighted.

'I told Lord Teel we should leave, summon our ship and fly away from this ridiculous world, but he will not hear of it. I have research to complete, you know.'

Charming as ever. I wish they had gone. It would solve one of my problems.

But they don't have a ship of course. They'd have to summon one and I doubt Bel would let it collect them. Or that Teel wants to reveal the Imperial stealth ship and the activity on Kelta. That said, they need to get off Anthaeus as soon as possible, back to their world of parties and politics. Back to civilisation.

'That's an excellent idea, Lady de Lorens. Why don't you do that?'

She laughs, a hard and bitter laugh which doesn't quite fit with her ethereal image. 'You try making him leave. He won't even let me get close enough to examine them. I can't imagine what I'd have to do if I wanted a genetic sample.'

'You'd need all sorts of equipment that isn't easily found in a cave. And their permission, I imagine.'

She gives me a look that brands me a fool. 'They're animals.'

Something tightens inside me and then hardens. 'No, they aren't.'

A most unladylike snort of frustration escapes her. 'You're all obsessed with those... those *things*.'

Those things. Lovely.

But I just hear a chuckle in the back of my mind. Favre. He finds her amusing. Like a fly buzzing around him. *I wish I could be more like him.*

'*You are. She is not. Aeron says she has a fine analytical mind, but lacks any form of ethics.*'

Thank you, I think.

She sweeps off, obviously bored with me now, or disgusted, or she's decide that I'm just not worth her precious time any more.

'Where's Con, Favre?' I ask.

Why he has chosen to speak to me, I don't know. The same way Rhenna prefers Bel and Aeron prefers Con, I suppose.

'*He is still in Limasyll. We cannot reach him.*'

That doesn't sound promising. 'What about Jondar?'

'*Aeron says he is imprisoned. He does not know where. He is in despair.*'

'Does Thom know?'

'*We thought it preferable not to share that information with him.*'

Probably a good idea. I can imagine him now going all gung ho and getting himself killed trying to rescue his beloved husband. I know Thom. He does a good impression of being the tactician, but he isn't.

Besides, he's up on the Valiant with Zander. He's safe for now and that's one thing I can count on.

I settle down on the floor, legs crossed and I run through my options, what I know, what I don't know. I can't do it alone but I'd counted on Art and his sneaky ways to get me inside. Now I've got the Rondet instead. And Teel, who can't show his face there.

Or can he?

He's here in embassy from the Empress. He ought to be able to just walk right in.

'Ma'am, have you eaten?'

Art Merryn is standing beside me, holding a tray with a mug of fragrant soup and some dry bread on it. I try not to react or draw attention to him. But by the ancestors, seeing him is a relief.

'About time you got here.' I get to my feet.

'You were meant to meet me somewhere else.'

'Well, the Rondet had other ideas.' I grab the soup and drink it. It's hot but the flavour is magnificent. 'Where did you get this?'

'I didn't make it, don't worry. Teel travels with his own chef. And chef is treating this as a challenge of his skills.'

'He's not doing so badly.' I dunk the bread in and let the combination of flavours explode in my mouth. I'm hungrier than I thought. Ravenous. 'So you're hiding out with the servants then?'

He tilts his head slightly. 'I quite like the servants.'

I smile. 'Don't let your father hear you saying that, your Highness. How are they?'

'Miserable. They didn't sign on for this. There's something of a mutiny fermenting. Kaeda de Lorens is making everyone wretched, those who aren't already sick. She keeps bossing them around and calling them lazy. So understanding.'

'Art, do we have a plan?'

'I'm working on it.'

'I'm faster. Teel can get us in, you know.'

'Where is Teel?' he asks.

Of course he'd want to know. He's meant to be spying on Teel after all, but something in his expression is a little too... hungry. I shake my head. I feel weird, foggy. Maybe I'm just tired. Maybe.

'What have you done, Art?' I ask warily.

'We need to get to Bel,' he says, not in answer to me, not really.

'Bel's not the sister you knew. Favre showed me what the Coparius does. It'll destroy this world. And then it'll move on to the next, and the next. And Bel... Bel isn't Bel any more. She's the embodiment of the Coparius now. We have to stop her.'

He smiles, that strange, distant smile, staring off into the distance, across the valley and the water below us, the beautiful vista of Anthaeus. 'I wish you had stayed where I told you to, Petra. You and Zander. It would have been so much easier.'

'Easier?' Something is wrong. My instincts are like a bee, buzzing away in the back of my mind.

Art moves faster than I would have imagined possible, not just that fluid, highly trained dexterity I saw from him before. This is unnatural. Then I realise it's not that he's fast. I'm slow. So slow. The tray slams into my stomach and I double over, air driven out of my lungs as he twists it around and brings it crashing down on my head.

'*Favre!*' I lash out with my mind in a panic as the world spins around me. '*Get out of here.*'

But I already know that Rhenna won't leave. She doesn't have the energy. And Favre and Aeron won't leave her. Where is Teel? What happened to him?

Something is screaming, a high pitched whine that borders on agony to hear and I fall to my knees. Art is standing over me, barking orders into a coms unit as Anthaese troops swarm up over the edge of the cliff and into the cavern. One of them is 'Find Teel' but that doesn't seem to be happening. I close my eyes and pray that he can hide, that he can get away.

My troops. My people. I try to draw in a breath but everything hurts. Has he broken one of my ribs? If I could just breathe, maybe I could get them to listen. But they see me as a traitor. Bel stripped me of rank and while they might obey and respect me, they worship her. This thing that has taken her place is counting on it. I grab Art's leg and my grip is too weak. I cling to him, trying to drag myself upright. I fail.

It comes as no surprise when he looks down at me and I see the cold black stones that are his eyes. *Like hers*, I think. He's gone, just like she is. I'm looking into something completely in thrall to the Coparius.

'Zander will come for me.' My voice sounds breathy, broken.

A cold smile spreads over his face. 'We're counting on that, Petra. This family, this bloodline... oh they are useful. And Zander has an in with the Empress. Can you imagine how useful that would be?'

And I can. Oh yes, I can. Imagine. The Coparius at the heart of the Empire...

He kicks himself free of me and I pass out.

Chapter Twenty-Seven

Petra

I almost come to during extraction. I'm not aware of exactly where I am or what's happening, but before I can shake off the muggy sensation smothering my mind and body, there's a sharp pain in my arm and the cloying mist rises up around me again. *Sedation*, I realise. I know the feeling. I hate it and there's nothing I can do about it.

I wake again, hands and feet bound and a black hood over my head. The ground beneath me rocks gently, steadily. Still on a transport, then. I listen carefully, counting breaths around me, making note of heartbeats.

'*Petra Kel? Can you hear me?*'

'*Favre. I hear you. The others?*'

'*Do not touch the stone. Whatever you do. Do not listen to its lies. Do not accept anything it offers.*'

'*Is Rhenna safe? Aeron and the others?*'

'*We are safe.*'

I hardly dare ask. '*Teel?*'

'*We are safe.*'

Great. No more information than that. Safe. At least someone is.

'*Can you get word to Thom?*'

'*He is too far, but I will try. Petra Kel… do not touch the stone.*'

'*Keep Rhenna safe. She's not well. I think… I think she's sick. The crystals are draining her. Look after her.*'

'*I will, on my honour. But… we are trapped here. Under the ground.*'

'*What?*'

'*They drove us back, collapsed the cave mouth. Teel and some others managed to hold the way to the inner caves. So they detonated explosives at the entrance. Petra Kel… we have little time. The air turns.*'

The air turns. What does that mean?

And then I realise – they're running out of air. They're trapped and they're running out of air. Was Teel hurt? Is he okay?

But I can't ask. Not now. I need to be strong. They left him behind which is strange. I know they wanted me, probably as no more than a lure for Zander, but still. If they want to get to the Empress, surely Teel would be a better bet. Unless he's just too much trouble.

Yes, maybe that's it. He is trouble. Right down to his bones.

'*Get word to Thom, understand?*'

My connection to him falters. Which tells me something I really didn't want to know. We're within range of the Coparius. We've reached Limasyll.

The transport engines rev as they switch to descent, and we come into land, the ship abruptly falling still and quiet. The troops don't talk. They simply lift me bodily and carry me out. They aren't rough, not as such, but they aren't kind either. They move me like so much baggage and my body, wrung out and drugged, is too weak to fight them.

Before I know what's happening I'm pressed back against something hard and unyielding. Straps secure my arms and legs and the final one fits across my throat, almost choking me. I can't move. I can't even struggle.

Someone rips the hood off my head. I'm looking at Art, but I'm not seeing him. I'm seeing something else.

Then Liette steps between us. Her too-pretty face has a cruel cast to it. One that has always been there, but now it's more pronounced. She's had time to indulge herself.

'General Kel. Oh, but we've missed you.'

'Don't play with her,' Bel says from behind her and Liette scowls for a moment before she deliberately smooths her expression and steps back, bowing to the queen.

'As you will, Majesty.'

And Bel… that's not Bel.

She's holding the stone against her chest, stroking it like a child, her face turned down to look into it. At first it's like she has forgotten that I'm there at all.

But then she speaks and I know that she remembers. There's nothing she doesn't miss.

'You should never have come back to Limasyll.'

I force my voice out, make myself make it as strong as I can, swallow down the fear inside me and hide it from her. Because I refuse to let her see it.

'It wasn't exactly consensual, Bel. You shouldn't have sent him after me.'

She laughs. I didn't expect that. A monster with a sense of humour. Or an appreciation of my sarcasm. Or, more realistically, an understanding of how helpless I actually am right now.

The door behind me opens and someone bustles in. 'I'm sorry, your Majesty. I was delayed with matters of the brethren.'

Faestus drops to his knees in front of her, his hands spread wide in supplication.

'Do the brethren matter more than our mistress?' Liette snarls at him.

The look of outrage on his face would be comical if it wasn't for my position right now. 'You go too far. I am Prime of the Coparius. Majesty, are you going to allow this chit to speak to me that way?'

'Are *you*?' Bel asks, in bored tones.

It's not the response he expected. 'Me, your Majesty?'

'You, if I remember correctly, thought the queen unfit to look upon the stone. You never saw her potential. Only Liette did.' Liette beams and almost dances up on her toes with joy. 'It's not my place to sort out your squabbles. You're both servants. Which one serves me best, Artorius?'

He shrugs. It doesn't really matter to him, I can see that. But Liette and Faestus have the fire of fanatics in their eyes. And they hate each other. Maybe I can use that.

'I'm bored with them, Artorius,' she says. 'If one of them can serve me best, then they can prove it.'

Art tosses a knife out into middle of the floor. It clatters to a stop between them. Faestus turns to plead with the Coparius, his goddess. Liette, ever the pragmatist, pounces on the knife and leaps on him, gutting him in seconds. She looks up from the floor, panting hard, covered in blood as he spasms and bleeds out beside her. It's over so quickly he hardly makes a noise. Liette shuffles forward on her knees, holding the knife out before her for blessing. Her mouth is split in a wide, toothy grin of wonder and relief.

'Am I Prime now? Majesty?'

Bel ignores her, stepping around her and drifts across the floor to me. The blood follows her, like a river, and when the stone passes over it, it vanishes. Light glitters in its wake.

Too shocked to say anything, I struggle against my bonds.

'Are you prepared to serve?' Bel asks. 'Not that you have a choice in the matter.'

She moves like grace itself, like a dancer, a delicate and beautiful thing to watch. Panic seizes me, a panic such as I have never known. I've spent my whole life facing fear, pushing it down, defying it.

But when you bury things, when they finally get out, they are stronger than ever.

My voice comes out in a yell. 'You keep that thing away from me!'

I struggle against the bonds holding me. It's like one of the machines they make Mechas with, the same frame, but not connected to anything. At least I hope it isn't connected to anything. Looking at that baleful glow in Bel's hands, I know it doesn't need anything else. It's just here to hold me.

'It will only hurt a little,' Liette says. Bel doesn't pause in her approach. It's slow and steady, menacing. She's playing with me. 'Well, actually, that's not true. It will hurt. It will hurt a lot.'

I've got to get out of this thing. I've got to get away. I want to wrench myself free, to tear my way out and get away, but I can't. My heart races, thundering in my chest, perhaps trying to break its way out through my ribs all by itself. I gasp for breath.

'We had to introduce the frame, for those not willing,' Liette says. It's like an afterthought, an interesting comment on affairs. Bel says nothing. Not Bel, that's not Bel, I have to remember that. She strokes the stone.

'It's easier really. All that running and screaming. But you… I'd like to see you running. And screaming. If we had time. Can't we, Majesty?' she asks, like an eager child begging for a puppy. 'Please?'

She's insane. Actually insane.

Bel – *not Bel, dear ancestors I have to keep hold of that understanding, this is not Bel* – pauses and looks enquiringly at her brother.

'Majesty, that would be unwise.' *Thank you Art, I think. But if I were free maybe I could fight back. Maybe I could escape. And maybe… maybe I could reach her.*

Bel sighs like it's the most irritating thing in existence, that she can't play with me. A petulant child with the powers of a god.

Not Bel. It's not Bel. It's not Art. I don't know about Liette. It's the Coparius and it's lurking in each of them. It's feeding on them and it will feed on me.

'Bel, listen to me. You have to fight it. You have to listen to me. Bel, please.'

Bel stops in front of me, staring into my face now, and the light from below makes her face infernal. She's studying me and she's as alien to me as anything I have ever seen. I've been on countless worlds, and I've faced down countless enemies.

'We're the same, you and I,' she whispers. 'Made of stone. With a stone heart. Bel can't hear you, Petra. No one can. No one but me.'

My voice hiccoughs in my throat. 'Please. Don't.'

I know I sound pathetic. I know. I don't care any more. I just need her to stop.

'Shhh,' she whispers. 'It hurts, like the girl said, but only for a little while. Then you won't feel anything. Trust me.'

And she pushes the stone against my chest. I suck in air and it blisters my lungs. I want to cry out again but I can't hear my own voice. Light pours out of the stone, wrapping itself around me. It seethes along my skin, burrows under it and surges up inside me, through me, burning in my veins.

And suddenly my voice is free again. I don't just scream. I howl.

*

Darkness encircles me. I'm lost in the shadows, in a cave, far below the ground, far from natural light. The crystals in the rock face glow only faintly, a sickly green colour which stains the world. As I try to get my bearings, I can't seem to find my way. The rock feels warm, far too warm. And I feel it too, like I'm feverish, like I'm burning up.

I stumble forward, feeling my way along the passage. It's cloyingly warm, the air humid and sickening. Sweat prickles on my skin.

The same panic I felt when Bel came towards me with the stone rises again.

I know this place. I've seen it before. Here in the deep darkness, in the deepest part of Anthaeus… it's not where the stone comes from in the first place. But it's where Natuel found it.

My stomach twists. The nausea is sudden and shocking. I know where I am. And I know what I'll see.

I squeeze through the gap at the end of the tunnel, the tiny cell at the heart of the world where that thing was hidden.

She's there, a pathetic heap curled up in the far end, her black hair spilling over her face, her hands buried in it, her eyes closed.

'Bel?'

My voice echoes strangely, twisting in the hollow. She looks up, her eyes wild and desperate. And I hear her.

'Petra? You can see me?'

The world spasms around us and she reaches out. I try to grab her hand but as we're about to touch, something rips her from me. She flies backwards, her scream deafening me, or maybe I'm torn away from her. And it's my scream. I can't tell.

I'm thrown against the restraints holding me, my head slammed back, and the band of metal crushes against my throat.

I gasp for air, open my acid drenched eyes and see her there, the stone still in her hands.

She doesn't look angry. Angry would be easier. She looks almost disappointed.

My voice is hoarse and broken. I try to breathe but I can only sob. But as I hang there, helpless, she presses her fingertips against my cheek. Her touch is cool and soothing, but alien. There's nothing comforting about it. It's not my friend. It's not even human. I know that now.

'We'll try again. We'll get there in the end, Petra. No matter how long we need. You're special. I want you to be mine. We're the same.'

The stone touches me again and I arch in agony beneath it.

At some point I pass out again and it's a blessed release.

*

I'm lying on cold, hard ground, somewhere underground. For a moment I think I'm still in the cave, either the one where the Rondet were hiding or the one in the nightmare, but there's no fresh air. It's stale and foul. And I hurt all over. I move, and I groan and even that hurts.

'Petra? Petra, are you okay?'

Someone stoops over me and I try to open my eyes, but it's hard to focus.

'Jondar?'

'Yes. Thank the ancients, can you sit up? Are you... Talk to us, Petra. Please.'

There are others, gathered in the corners, trying to make some small semblance of comfort in this dark, dank place. Not many. Far too few.

He looks terrible, gaunt and pale, bruises and contusions all over his face. He's unkempt. I've never seen him like that.

'I'm fine. I'm—' I'm not fine. My head is throbbing, my body aching and I've failed.

'Be careful,' Jondar tells me. 'Take it slowly.' He helps me sit up. Gingerly I lift my hand to the side of my head. It's swollen all down the side. I probably have a black eye as well. And a concussion. I'm lucky nothing appears to be broken. He looks like I feel.

'What happened?' I whisper.

But I know the answer to that. Bel and her bloody hypno-rock.

Jondar must recognise the struggle on my face. 'The Coparius.' He takes my hands and sits down beside me.

It floods back to me. Bel, but not Bel, holding that thing against me. The pain of it boiling through my veins, destroying my defences and casting me into that dark nightmare.

'She tried—'

Jondar shushes me, his hand gently rubbing between my shoulder blades. He's never struck me as a comforting person. But, ancestors, I need this human contact now. Impossibly, I relax against his touch, grateful for it beyond my ability to express.

'I know. It doesn't work on everyone. I'm a case in point too. It either does nothing but hurt or… or it changes us. And anyone else… it's causing the sleep, I think. Everywhere. And it's just getting stronger. The more people it controls, the more it drains. It's never sated.'

'And it's getting stronger… she said, eventually, she'll break me.'

Jondar nods again and his mouth tightens. 'And it'll keep trying to do that.'

I ignore the barely suppressed shudder that runs through him and I wonder how often she's tried to break him. 'But you're immune.'

'So far. Me and everyone here. That's why they've locked us up, so they can keep trying. And so, it seems, are you, but that doesn't mean we'll stay that way.'

I glance around at the other prisoners. Jondar is by far the highest profile, so I bet she's focused primarily on him. He looks the worst, the cracks running deep across that immaculate surface. But he's held firm and I can too. There is some kind of immunity. There has to be some way to use that.

Jondar stares at me, moves his lips but for a moment he can't quite ask what he needs to ask.

'Petra, is Thom… is he safe? Was he with you?'

'He's on board the Valiant with Zander, safe and sound among his own people. I came back for…' I groan and bury my head in my hands. 'I came back to meet Art because we were going to try to rescue you and Con.'

Jondar studies my face, his eyes keen and desperate. I know what he's thinking. He knows Thom as well as I do. He realises that his husband won't sit in safety on board the Valiant while we're down here in prison. And they don't know about Art.

I have a mission. I still have a mission. I have to focus on that. Not betrayal. Not my abject defeat and the disaster that everything has turned into. I'm inside the palace. I'm here, right now.

'Where are they keeping Con?' I ask.

'I don't know. He collapsed not long after they came back, not long after she… changed. Halie's treating him for the sleeping sickness. Or at least… that's what they've said.'

'What can we do?'

He looks lost. Jondar, who always had a plan, always had a routine and a tradition for everything, is lost.

'I don't know, Petra. I don't know.'

I close my eyes, and I can't think any more. I had a plan, but that plan depended on Art. And Art is no use to me now. I need to think. I'm here, I'm alive. Parts of me might protest that, but by their very protestations I know I'm alive. I'm just so tired. And I can't think straight. My mind is numb with pain and misery. If I just close my eyes for a few moments, maybe if I open them I can make this all turn out differently. Maybe... if I wish hard enough... maybe...

Yes, I'm a fool. But I can't fight any longer. Maybe later. Not now.

Chapter Twenty-Eight

Bel

In the darkness there is no sound. I'm broken in the darkness, crushed inside the rocks and crystals. But the crystals are my only source of light, of heat, of sustenance. I can't break free and I couldn't if I tried. In the darkness, I'm safe. Because everywhere else… everywhere else…

I remember the pain. I remember the fear. The terror. The darkness sweeping up from inside me and swallowing me whole. I am lost. I don't know how long I've been here, how much time has passed or where I am.

But I'm here, in the darkness. I'm lost.

I want Con. I'm so scared for him, but when I try to reach him, when I think of him, I see his face full of fear and pain. I know I put that expression there. I shy back from it and it blurs and seeps away. Back into the shadows, where I retreat.

When I try to reach Rhenna or the other members of the Rondet, I encounter only static and pain. Everything resolves in pain.

In the darkness I'm safe. I can't move against the rocks, and maybe that's for the best.

Then suddenly light blinds me, terrifies me. Not the baleful light of the crystals, of the Coparius itself which has stolen my life away and trapped me here. It's golden, like honey, like the sun of Anthaeus itself. It's warm and it's all enveloping. And it's beautiful. It's the only hope I've had in the eternity in which I've been here.

'*Bel?*'

The voice is shaky and it might as well have been the voice of an angel. It wakes me up, stirs something inside me that I thought was as cold and dead as the rocks surrounding me, eating into me, turning my flesh to stone. I look up and there's Petra, bathed in light. She's golden and glowing, the colour of amber and gemstones, her hair pooling like ink in water behind her head. My hands shake as I push the mess of my own hair out of my face.

'Petra? You can see me?'

No one can see me. Not down here. I'm lost, hidden away and no one sees me here. No one else has come looking for me. Not even Rhenna. Not even Con.

Con wouldn't, of course. Con can't. Because of what I did to him.

'*Bel!*' Petra calls again and she stretches out her hand to me. I try to take it, try to reach her, but she's an entire world away. I know it. I know I'll never reach her.

'Petra, please…' I don't know what I'm begging for. That she stay? That she try harder?

The world freezes, just for a moment. I try to reach her, I try to make myself stretch up to her, and I long for the feel of her hand in mine. A human touch. One brush of her fingers against mine.

And then the darkness seizes her and hurls her away, back through the rocks, back into nothingness. It closes over me, like an obsidian cage slamming itself shut.

I scream.

I scream over and over again with no one to hear me and no air for the sound to carry and nowhere for it to carry to.

Eventually I have to stop. There's nothing to be gained by it. I saw her. I saw her for a second. She knows I'm here and if there is one thing I am certain of beyond everything else it's that Petra will not give up until she finds me.

I force myself to calm down, to consider that. I have no idea how long I've been here, no idea where I am. But for the first time in what seems like an age, someone knows that I'm still here, I'm not dead.

It's the first spark of hope I've had. And if she can get in, maybe I can get out. Somehow.

I touch the crystals and they sing. I've never heard them sing like this, not even when I helped Jondar and Thom with the reconstruction of Con's communications device. It was a lifetime ago. Their song is quiet at first, a faint hum, but when I press my phantom fingers against their surface – their warm, smooth surface – it reverberates through me. I'm so grateful that I feel tears on my face. Not real tears of course, because I realise now I don't have a real body. Not any more. The Coparius has it.

The more I press against the crystals, the more they sing and I don't want to let them go now. They're the only comfort I have. They are the veins of Anthaeus, the living stuff of it and now I am locked away at its heart, they are my only companions.

I lean closer and hear a whisper in the singing. A voice so familiar it makes me jerk my hand back, instantly cutting off the contact.

But I heard it. I heard it more clearly than I have ever heard anything.

Con. It was Con. Calling out to Aeron.

With my breath trapped in my throat, with my heart aching for him, I slam my hand back against the crystals, not calmly, not carefully, not even gently.

Suddenly, suddenly, I'm not in the hidden heart chamber any more. I'm flowing through the crystals, I'm part of Anthaeus, and I'm everywhere, all at once. I see the ruins, the towers, the forests, I see the oceans and their depths. I see... I see... everything. It's not like flying with the Rondet, not like being in the hive mind. This is more like being underwater, swimming, drowning.

It's too much. In an instant I am everywhere. I hear voices, so many of them, people all over Anthaeus, but I can't focus on all of them at once. They are too many and they swamp all my senses. I shy back, trying to claw my way back into the darkness but I'm in the crystal network now and I can't find my way out. I'm dragged apart, torn to pieces, shattered to smithereens. I try to focus, to pull myself together.

'*Bel.*' I sense him. I feel his touch, his fingertips pressing against me. '*Bel, is that you? Please hear me. Please.*'

'Con?'

I fix all my awareness on his voice, on that strange sensation of his touch when there is no way he can touch me. I try to picture him in my mind. He looks tired, dishevelled, as if he has just woken from sleep.

'*Bel, please... am I still dreaming?*'

His voice shakes and he drops to his knees, staring into a piece of polished crystal. I know it. He used it to test the Coparius and it pulled every last scrap of energy from it. Did it form some kind of connection? Or is this Con and me? Is this some kind of miracle?

'I love you,' I tell him. 'I'm sorry. I'm so sorry.'

And then the energies in the crystal network sweep me away. I tumble with them, my consciousness buffeted against the rocks and stones that make up the world. I pour through the roots of ancient trees and well up in springs.

I delve deep into rocks. And I reach out for those I know, for those I love. As I try to find Con again, I find someone else.

Rhenna is surrounded by crystals, shaded in rose and purple, blue and indigo and those colours seep into her as well. *'Belengaria? Little queen, is that you?'*

Her surprise is palpable.

'Rhenna? Where are you? Is Petra with you?'

'Petra was here but Artorius took her prisoner, when he trapped us here.'

Wait, what? I struggle to focus, the figure out what she means. But there's no way to misunderstand what she just said. Petra has been captured by Art... but...

'What happened to Art?'

'He was hollow, emptied out like you. He was other, Bel.'

Like I was... am... She has him. She has taken my brother and made him her servant, her slave, her puppet. The pain that spears me would drive me to my knees if I was still able to stand. Rhenna reaches out to me, trying to comfort me, to help me. And that's when I realise that I could lose her too. I could lose all of them. I have to pull myself together.

'Rhenna, are you safe? Are you—'

'We are trapped. Your brother sealed the cave mouth. And the other humans, the ones from the other world, stand with us. But they will not last. We can sleep. They will sleep. But not hibernate. They... they will die.'

They? Who are they? 'I don't know who you mean?'

'Valentin Teel. He is... not as we thought. He helped us. He tried to defend us, and he will pay a price.'

Valentin Teel is there with her? Trapped. Dying. I don't understand. But if the Cuorean delegation dies on Anthaeus because of something my brother did… the Empress will destroy us all. It's just the excuse she needs to take Vairian and Anthaeus, with or without Zander.

'I will get help. I promise. I will find someone.'

She laughs. A sad, musical sound which I have missed. I've heard it so often in the last year, that it is part of me.

'*There is a way,*' she replies. '*You have already discovered it, have you not? You are using the crystals, the veins of this world, its life force. You are travelling with the blood of Anthaeus. But it is dangerous. You could be lost.*'

'I'm already lost, Rhenna. Show me.'

She does and it is genius. Suicidal, but genius. I would smile if I could and I think she feels that. It's what Con calls my recklessness.

'We have to try,' I assure her. 'Can you keep hold of me?'

'*I can, but… Bel… remember what we are. Remember what you are. You must not stray too far.*'

Remember what I am? I'm trying. I'm really trying. But I'm spread out so far now. I could lose myself in here, I realise. I could vanish in the network and never find my way back.

One more gamble though, I have to try it.

This has to work. And it is so far away. But there is one crystal, one more, which might save us all.

And if I am lost reaching it, so be it. It might save the others and that is what matters.

'Try to hold on to me, Rhenna, as long you can.'

I reach out, far above the planet, nestled in the stars and I see it like a far off supernova. It glows for me, drawing me to it.

My brother took an Anthaese crystal, polished and beautiful but small, so small. I reach out for it now, so far away from the world and the network. It's on board the Valiant, and through it I see his command room. It's on his desk. He's probably using it as a paperweight, knowing

Zander. But that doesn't matter. I pour my consciousness into it. I won't last long. But I have to. Just long enough.

And then I hear him, I sense him coming closer. I can feel my grip fading, the tenuous thread holding me to Rhenna beginning to fray. But I cling to it, try to reach out to him, to call him to me.

Zander enters the room, his expression troubled. The confusion is swirling through the air all around him and I sense that too. Did he hear me? Or sense me? We're family. He has to.

He checks his coms and curses. That's when Thom appears at the door. *'Any word?'*

'Nothing. Petra should have checked in by now. Or Art should have reported.' He heaves out a sigh.

'They can't,' I try to project my thoughts to them and my brother stiffens. He whirls around, and then I realise he can hear me. Somehow. 'They can't report in. She's been captured, Art has been compromised the same way I have. Do you hear me, you two? Please hear me.'

'Bel?' Thom drops to his knees in front of the desk, staring at the crystal. *'Where did you get this, Zander?'*

'In Con's study. I think they were trying to fob me off at the time.'

Thom picks up the stone, and I feel his hands, his strength, his reliability. My friend. My trusted friend.

'How are you doing this? Bel?'

'Bel? My sister, Bel?' Zander is staring into the rock and I wonder if they can see me. Please dear ancestors, let them see me.

'The Rondet and the Cuoreans are trapped. They're going to run out of air. They're in a cavern above the lake and Art collapsed the mouth. You have to get to them, understand? Rhenna told me.'

They're both looking at me like I'm some kind of alien lifeform never seen before. And maybe I am. I don't know.

'*How do we know it's really you, that this isn't a trick?*' Zander asked.

Really? I don't have time for this. My grip is slipping and Rhenna is trying to draw me back, for my own safety I'm sure, but any moment now that thread of connection will snap. I don't know what will happen to me then. I could be trapped here. I could spin off into the void. I can feel her trying to reach me, her warnings, her legitimate fear.

'Do you really want me to tell Thom about the fact you wouldn't sleep without a cuddly toy until you were ten, Zander? Or about that time you ate so many sweetcakes you hurled all over the prototype Wasp father was trialling? Or the time—'

'*All right! All right!*' he exclaims. There's rush of joy in his voice, in spite of the childhood embarrassments I'm sharing. '*But Bel… how is this possible?*'

'It doesn't matter. Get Con out of his study and we'll ask him. But first… first you have to find the others. Please.'

He presses the stone against his body, and it feels strangely as if he is hugging me. It's the best comfort I could have asked for. More than I dreamed of feeling again.

'*Where's Petra?*' He sounds so desperate, so scared. I *knew* he cared about her. I knew it even when they both had themselves fooled.

'She's in the palace. They captured her. She woke me, Zander. She found me in the darkness.'

My grip is loosening. I want to stay with my brother, and our friend, but I've exhausted all my strength. Rhenna is pulling me back and I can't fight it any more. But I have to warn him.

'Teel and the others… they're dying… The Empress will… retaliate…'

They have to understand. They have to. I send the location of the cave to my brother, try to tell them everything even as I fade back from the crystal, falling towards the network below. I hope he understands. But there's no way to know. No way to keep going. I'm too weak. I won't make it back. I can feel Rhenna trying to help, but her grip is slipping.

I wilt and I feel the crystal network reach out to swallow me up.

This one last thing, this sacrifice… it's all I can do. I hope it was enough.

Chapter Twenty-Nine

Petra

I don't know how long I'm asleep. I dream of Bel, dream of her swimming in crystalline waters, through the deep waters and the secret waters in the heart of the planet. I dream of Zander and Thom. I dream of Rhenna. I dream of Teel. I weep and my tears are like rain on my face.

And I'm afraid.

When I wake up, it's evening. Not that you can tell much from down here. The moonlight does reach in as far as our cage. I know where I am now, in the deepest parts of the cellars in the citadel at Limasyll.

I've had enough of this. I know they're going to come for me again. She more or less told me as much. She's going to keep torturing me with the Coparius until I buckle. I'd ask Jondar how he's withstood it so far but something in me is afraid to do so. Afraid of the answer. There's a haunted look in his eyes. He was always so neat and precise and now it's as if a wild man shares a cell with me. Are the cracks in his appearance reflecting cracks in his mind? I owe it to Thom to keep him safe, to get him out of here. If I can't help anyone else, at least I can do that. Can't I?

The worst part of it is that I'm not sure any more. Once upon a time I would have been certain. I could fight anyone, overcome any obstacle, break through any cage. Now? This place sucks the will from you. Or maybe that's an after effect of the stone. I've no idea. All I can say for sure is that the urge to lie down in a corner and wait for the end is so powerful I'm not sure I'll resist if for long.

Is this the sleeping sickness? Has it finally caught up with me too? I'm so tired. My body is heavy, broken, and all I want to do is put my head down and give up. Like the others.

I can't give up. I just can't.

So I watch, and I bide my time.

The guards are shoddy. That's the first thing I notice. They're not my guards, not the ones I trained. That gives me a surge of hope. Then I realise they aren't actually trained guards. They're Greymen, sent down here to make sure we stay put. Half the time they aren't even watching us. They talk among themselves, or they pray. They take breaks at the same time. They wander out of sight.

I couldn't have asked for more.

Assessing what we have to aid us inside the cage is not so easy. There are only eight of us. Jondar and myself I have the measure of. If I can get him a sword somewhere there is no one better to fight at my side. The others… a cook's assistant, a chamber maid, the royal librarian… not promising. The three gardeners are actually more hopeful. They're physically strong, even if they are miserable and depressed. Give them hope, give them direction and we may have something. I have done it before, during the occupation. I made farmers into warriors. I also got a lot of them killed and I don't want to think about that.

Slowly, carefully, I formulate my plan.

The food they deliver is basically slop. It's designed to keep us alive but that's all. They deliver it in the same way every time. They unlock the door, bustle inside, beating back anyone nearby, and then drop it on the ground before turning and walking out again. It's basic stupidity and I mean to capitalise on that as much as I possibly can.

Jondar is with me, of course. The others take more convincing. Having a general, even a disgraced one, and a prince tell you that you can do it must carry some weight though. They form up the way I want them to, taking positions as directed, and they even manage to look like they believe this will work.

I can't let them down. My body is still reeling from the effects of the Coparius, the beating Art gave me and the drugs with which he sedated me. I'm trying not to show it but I feel like throwing up and the shivering that comes over me at inopportune moments is a dead giveaway. As I mull it all over, as I prepare the final stages, I clench my fists so my nails bite into the palms of my hands and double over, trying to quell the panic.

If I get this wrong… if I get this wrong…

A hand on my back rubs gently, easing out the kinks and soothing the tension.

'Breathe,' Jondar tells me. 'Just calm yourself and breathe.'

He's my best friend's husband and although I've thought of him as an ally, I've never really imagined that he too is my friend. I've sold him short. He's an unexpected comfort. I understand now what Thom sees in him.

'I'm okay,' I lie.

'Of course you are, General.' And he smiles that wickedly knowing smile that Thom talks about. The one that makes him weak at the knees. I envy them for a moment. In all the mess of my feelings for Zander and Val, I wish for the simplicity they have.

'Get them out when the time comes,' I remind him. 'Keep together. If we're the only ones immune to the Coparius, we need to find out why.'

He just nods. His hair falls into his eyes and for a moment he looks like a child who wants me to tell him what to do. That crushing weight of responsibility comes back all at once.

'The person to find out something like that is Doctor Halie or Con,' he says. 'I'm not certain if the good doctor is still free. She could have been working with them through practical duty but I fear not. And Con... Con is as trapped as we are.'

That's one problem I plan to deal with first. 'Not for long,' I remind him. 'They should be on the way.'

'Right.' He stares at me for a long moment and I know he's trying to gauge if I am up to this or not. I'm not. I could tell him that if I was feeling like being honest. Which I'm not. I don't think I have to anyway. He knows. But what choice do we have? In the distance, we hear footsteps. 'They're coming.'

I straighten myself up and he helps me to my feet. I nod to the others who take their positions as planned. It's not the greatest plan in the world but it will work. It has to work.

I slide into the shadows against the wall. As they enter one of the gardeners shoulders his way to the front of the others.

'Give it to me. These fools will just waste it.'

The guards stop, confused. 'No, you each get a share,' the blank eyed man says. 'Get back.'

'You can't just give it to him,' the chambermaid sobs loudly. She glances at me and for a moment I fear she'll give us away, but she rallies. 'We all need to eat.'

'We... we're not.' The guards close together around the pale of slop. 'No one is getting extra. That is not the way. Her Majesty decreed it.'

'Are you crazy? Look at them.' He gestures wildly and his hand slams against the bucket, sending it flying.

I launch myself forward, out of hiding, and throw my arms around the neck of the nearest guard, bringing him down in a heap of limbs and curses. The other turns on me, tugging at a weapon from his belt, and Jondar slips between us, snatching it out of his hand with a dexterity no one else could manage. I tighten my grip on the airways of my victim, the noose of my arm robbing him of oxygen and consciousness.

He slides away from me.

The others rush to secure the open doorway. I turn to the remaining guard, now held at knifepoint by a furious prince.

'Where is the Anthaem? Where are you keeping them?'

He presses the knife forwards, the tip biting in to the skin of his throat. The guard tries to pull back, but Jondar grabs a fistful of his hair and holds him in place.

'The… the… the Coparius will protect me. The lady will rescue me. The Prime will redeem me. The Majesty—'

The knife digs in and he gasps.

'I'd answer him,' I say. 'He's been here a while. He's testy.'

The kid's eyes go wide, focusing on me and the pupils shrink to pin points. 'You're the one she warned us about.'

A warning? How wonderful. He really should have listened. I smile a thin smile and narrow my eyes. If I'm the stuff of nightmares I might as well live up to it. 'You can bet on that. Where's Con?'

'His study. She wanted him out of the way.'

Who? Bel? Liette?

Before I can ask, Jondar slams his head against the wall and he's out like a light.

I stare at him, the smug satisfied look on his face. 'Why did you do that?'

'He wasn't going to tell us anything else useful.'

To be honest, he's probably right. But I would have liked to try.

'Right,' I tell him. 'The study. You get them out of here.'

'Not on your life,' he says in a voice that is not going to be argued with. 'I'm coming with you.'

'But the others…'

'Carey can look after them, can't you?' The gardener nods. Hell, he probably knows a dozen more ways out through the gardens and the caves below than either of us do. But I wanted to get Prince Jondar out of the way as well. Thom would want him safe. No such luck. His husband is as stubborn as he is.

'Well then…' I search the other guard and relieve him of another knife and a blaster of some kind. It's point and shoot, effective but easy to use. I toss it to Carey. 'You know how to use that?' He studies it and in seconds I can see he knows enough to do some damage with it. We've all been soldiers, those of us still alive. He gives a curt nod. 'Good. Get them out of here, then.'

The palace is quiet. Far too quiet. I'm used to it buzzing with life, people everywhere. Now, it's silent as a tomb. It's as if no one dares to move around, or talk above a whisper.

I take the lead at first, but as we trace our way from the cellars I realise that I'm heading for the main concourse and the gardens. We're bound to encounter someone who will give us away. This isn't going to do at all.

'Let me,' Jondar says in hushed tones, and he slips by me, changing direction down a narrow passage I've never noticed. Of course – he's lived here most of his life. But even this route seems more disreputable than a prince should have more than a passing familiarity with. 'I grew up here. When Matilde became Anthaem I was just her little brother. Sometimes I needed to go unnoticed.'

I wasn't expecting that. But it makes sense. No wonder no one could get anything past him as Master of the Court.

We make our way up to the kitchens and skirt around them until we reach the servants' stairs. Even here, there's barely any movement at all, no staff, no one cooking or cleaning. When we hear footsteps we huddle into an alcove. Three Greymen pass us, heads lowered and lips muttering prayer after prayer I can't even make out. Who they're praying to, I don't know, but I can guess.

She's not even listening to them. She isn't going to answer even if she does hear. She's no goddess but a hungry entity feeding on their energies, and otherwise she doesn't give a—

'They're going to be guarding the upper floors,' Jondar tells me.

'I know. Not a problem.'

'It's more a matter of who is doing the guarding. It could be people we know.'

'Of course it will be. She—'

'*It.*'

He says it without even looking back at me. Like he doesn't want to risk eye contact.

'It?'

'*It* isn't Bel. Don't call it *she*. Please.'

There's genuine pain in his tone, just for a moment and I regret my harsh words. He cares about her as much as I do.

'Fine. *It.*' And he's right. That isn't Bel and I should not give it power by referring to it as a person, as She.

It is a monster. Like the Mechas that attacked me and tried to take Zander. Like those wolf-creatures on Kelta. The fact that it wasn't created by Gravian or Imperial hands doesn't really matter to me. The fact that I don't understand how it happened doesn't matter either. I don't understand half the tech I use. I just know that it works and trust in that. I've never had time for supernatural belief. It's a monster and I know what to do with them.

We reach the top floor. Con likes to be up high, near the air, near the wide open spaces. Because he had spent too long imprisoned and tortured underground during his captivity. He wouldn't have survived in the cell with Jondar and the others. Not for long.

And there are people up here. Greymen, guards, and a number of servants. There's laughter and celebration from the upper gallery of the ballroom. Music plays, a dance reel which seems so strangely out of place. Jondar flinches back, reversing into me for a moment and then he turns away from it, leading me the other way, down through the reconstructed portrait gallery which is empty.

There's a narrow spiral staircase up to the tower at the far end and we take that. At the top, there's a door and it leads to Con's study. I know that much. And it will be guarded.

Jondar slows and hefts the knife in his hand again. I press my hand his back and he stops, glancing over his shoulder at me. I slide by him. If we're taking on anyone, I'm going in first. I'm not explaining to Thom later that I let him get injured. Or worse.

I stop at the final bend, listening. The carpet on the stairs has hushed our footsteps so there's that. I can hear someone shuffling and clearing their throat. Bored guards. Worst kind.

Or the best, considering our circumstances.

I nod to Jondar and then break into a run. I come at them in a rush and I catch a glimpse of a startled and unprepared face as I punch it hard. He slams back against the wall and slumps down. His weapon skitters on the stone.

'General! It's us!' the other one yells. He's holding a weapon on me, and his hands are shaking. But he doesn't waver.

Kelvin Tran, looking fit to piss himself, stands between me and the door. And he doesn't seem to be under the influence of anything. And the one on the steps, out cold, is Dax Cobourne. Jondar steps over him delicately, scooping up the blaster as he does so.

I stretch out my neck and hear it crack. Kelvin winces. You wouldn't think he was the one with the gun and I've just got a knife. Admittedly, if he shoots me, Jondar shoots him and this stairway gets very messy indeed.

'Ma'am, please, just listen to us. It's all gone so…' Then he sees Jondar and tries to bow, half his instincts screaming at him to do so while the rest scream at him not to take his eyes off me. Perhaps there's hope for him yet.

'Tran?' Jondar sounds cool and functional. 'Report. Quietly and quickly, if you will.'

I make sure he can still see my knife too. 'We locked him in to keep them out. He was so tired. We all are. The whole citadel… But we… we haven't… we take it in turns to sleep, just for an hour or two, because otherwise we were worried we wouldn't wake up… Mostly they leave him alone. I mean, Liette comes and she shouts a lot. She wants him to make things, work on things, the stuff they were making before.'

'Why not you?'

'Sir?'

'Why aren't you changed? Why not imprison you?'

Dax begins to come around, groaning. Kelvin looks down at him, then back at us, swallowing hard. He tightens his grip on the blaster. 'I think... I think they forgot about us. Or thought... thought we weren't important enough.'

Fear comes off him in waves, but that isn't stopping him from holding his ground. I knew I picked him for a reason.

'Good man,' I say more gently. 'Is he safe?'

'He's hurt. She... she really... I thought she might kill him. And then he slept for so long... But we got him up here and ...'

'Her Majesty is not herself,' Jondar says in the tones of the ultimate diplomat.

'Well no shit,' the guard exclaims, then seems to catch what he just said and who he said it to. 'I mean... I... Sorry, your Highness. I just...'

'You're just saying what's true,' I tell him. 'Can you lower the weapon? I think we're still on the same side. We need to see Con, Kelvin. We need to get him the hell out of here.'

He wilts in front of me. The blaster lowers, but he doesn't holster it.

It's good to know the guards I chose aren't completely stupid.

Kelvin knocks on the door. 'It's safe, Anthaem. It's the prince and the general.'

A heavy bolt grates back and Con opens the door. 'It's about time,' he says. He's black and blue with bruises, and he looks exhausted, as if in spite of what we've been told he hasn't been able to sleep in weeks, his cheeks hollow, his eyes sunken. He's ill and overwrought. His clothes and hair are a mess. But there's a light in his eyes. 'Come inside, quickly.' He glances at Dex. 'All of you. We've very little time.'

Chapter Thirty

Bel

I'm floating, just as I remember floating long ago, when we snuck away to the shores of the Derringer sea and swam out under the starlight, into the stars reflected there. I turned on my back and I floated, staring up at the sky, surrounded by stars.

'Belengaria, come back to me. Talk to me, little queen. Please, don't be gone. I need you. Please.'

Shae had kept watch over us, my brothers and me. And while the boys splashed and laughed and generally acted as boys always do, he kept his gaze on me.

I felt something in the deep darkness beneath me, not living, but sentient. A greater darkness. In the shadows of my mind and in the depths of the water.

I close my eyes and listen to the water lap against me. The current is strong underneath me, and it pulls at me. It sings a song, a siren melody, that calls me to join it. I let myself sink, let the water flow over me. Under the surface, everything is quiet and muffled, everything is peaceful. The music is clearer. I want to follow it, want to let it flow over me. I can sink down into the darkness and forget.

But something draws me back to the surface, and I open my eyes. Shae is calling my name, wading out into the waves, trying to reach me. He shouts my name and I don't want to leave the safety of the water, but I know I have to.

'Belengaria, please, wake up. Don't let it take you. Don't be swept away.'

He never called me Belengaria. Just Bel.

Until he called me princess as well. Until we came to Anthaeus.

Anthaeus… I'm not on Vairian. I'm nowhere near the Derringer Sea. I'm on Anthaeus. Or I was.

His hands pull me from the water, his arms pulling me into his embrace. His mouth fits against mine and for a moment, just for a moment I want to forget what I know. I want to forget everything that happened.

But the kiss makes me think of Con.

I tear myself away.

I'll always love him, even though I love Con as well. There's a tiny part of me that will always belong to a ghost.

'Bel…'

I know the voice now. It isn't Shae. It isn't Con. But it sounds strange. Not the voice in my head that I know so well. This is something else.

'I'm here, Rhenna,' I tell her. And I'm still lost, but when I open my eyes this time, I see crystals everywhere. They cling to the roof over my head and to the walls around me. They are purple and blue, shades of rose and sapphire.

And that's when I realise, they aren't my eyes.

'Rhenna? What have you done?'

She doesn't answer at first but I can feel her nervousness. It vibrates around me. Tentatively I reach out and feel more of my surroundings. I open my mouth and feel too many teeth with a long, dexterous tongue. When I stretch… I feel her tail uncoil. Her wings spread.

'Rhenna—' I don't know what to say. I am... I'm in Rhenna. Somehow. I'm part of her.

'I had no choice,' she says at last. 'I could not let you be lost. Conleith would never recover. And we... we would be lessened.'

'The Rondet?'

'You are part of us, Belengaria. Do you not realise that yet?'

I try to still the rising panic inside me. This can't be happening. It just can't be. I'm not part of an alien hive mind. I've not living inside of an alien body. I am me. I have to be.

'It is worse than slipping into the void?' she asks and there is desolation in her voice. It swamps me in misery. Here, where I have no walls against her powerful emotions, it's hard to bear. Her emotions are also my emotions. We're one.

'No,' I tell her, sorry to have hurt her so much. I know she means well but this is all too much. Of course I don't want to die but neither do I want... this!

The desire to curl back into a ball and hide is so strong. Tears sting my eyes and something swells in my throat. Except – they aren't my eyes. The lump is not in my throat. A high, tragic keening echoes around the chamber and I realise I – or rather – we are making it.

'I'm sorry,' Rhenna whispers, over and over again. 'I'm sorry, but you would have been gone. I had to. I *had* to.'

'Is this what happened with Matilde and Berine?'

'Yes. But Berine was old and almost gone in our dreaming, fading into the void and the crystal sea as you would have. Matilde was dying.'

They merged, that was what I'd been told when I first discovered the secret. Rather than abandon her husband Con, the dying former Anthaem Matilde had chosen to live on as one of the Rondet. During the war she gave her life to save us both.

Have I inadvertently done the same thing? Although, without a choice. Has Rhenna, so afraid of losing another friend, trapped me here?

Panic again… it's like having the heart of a bird – high and fast, fluttering instead of beating, a constant trill of the need to flee, to hide. I can't seem to catch my breath.

What'll Con say? What will Con think? Ancestors… what are we going to do?

And then I sense him, miles away. But he reaches out and I feel the touch of his mind on mine like a caress.

'*What are we going to do about what, Rhenna?*'

I hiccough in surprise and desperation. He hears me. But he does so as Rhenna.

'Don't tell him!' It sounds like an order. I've never been able to get away with ordering one of the Rondet, but it comes out that way anyway.

'*Con,*' Aeron cuts in before Rhenna or I can reply. '*Thank the stars. We could not reach you?*'

'*I'm still in Limasyll. I'm using the crystals I have here to amplify my contact with you … I thought I saw Bel, or heard her, in the largest one. But that's… it's not possible… is it?*'

Oh Con – my heart surges. It had been real, that moment, that brief contact. I don't know how or why. Petra woke something in me and now I can almost reach him again. And he's there, trying to use that magnificent intellect to fight the Coparius, to reach the Rondet again. My husband, my love, is everything to me.

His mental gasp of surprise is almost palpable, like a rush of air on my skin. If I still had skin.

'*Bel?*'

He knows. Somehow, he knows.

'Con,' I whisper, afraid to make my presence felt. 'Con, I'm here.'

The wave of love and relief that crashes through the mental bond we share should sweep me off my feet.

'*Rhenna…*' Favre does not sound pleased. '*What have you done?*'

Rhenna shies back inside her skin, recoiling with alarm, but I'm here with her, supporting her and standing up for her. She rallies, lifts her head, preens a little and then her defiance is inspiring. 'What I had to do.'

'*Wait—*' Con withdraws a little, distracted. '*There's something outside, someone—*'

He's gone, like a star blinking out in the night's sky.

'What is it? What is happening?'

Aeron answers, sounding more like a governess than ever. '*It appears to be the proximity to the crystals allowing communications. Something has formed a psychic link between them. Just as we found when building the communications machine. It has become part of our bond. Through Bel's consciousness. We must study this.*'

'I reached Zander. He had one on his ship. He took it from Con's study. Can we contact him as well?'

'*It was a mighty feat, little queen. And I believe that helped reform, or reconstruct many of the links broken when the Coparius was reactivated. Your sacrifice made the network rebuild itself. Even now I can feel new pathways forming. It is intriguing, most intriguing. But it is too far as yet to reach your brother again. We are… still tied to the rocks and soil of Anthaeus.*'

It's possibly the most he's said to me since we first met. Like I'm one of them.

The thought of what that means sets me reeling.

'Calm,' Rhenna coos at me. 'We will find a way. We will make this right. You will see.'

She sounds so sure, so certain. Like Rhenna has made up her mind and the world will come to order. It should be reassuring. Once it would have been. But now?

'*Make what right?*' Con asks. '*Bel? What's going on? Where are you?*'

Don't tell him, I think frantically into the hive mind. *Please don't tell him.*

Two other minds join us. I feel them as if I've tasting colours. Petra – glittering and bright, citrus. Jondar – smoky and complex, a swirl of complications. They're holding Con's piece of crystal and barely able to contain their amazement.

'*Bel?*' Petra's voice spikes with fear and shock. I've never heard her afraid before and it sends an icy shard through me. She's afraid. Of me.

'*It's me,*' I try to reassure her. '*Really. I promise. I-I can't explain now, but – it really is me.*'

'*This we vouch,*' Rhenna finishes for me. '*She is with us. She is safe.*'

'*But she's in the palace. I've seen her. She's—*'

'*That's not Bel.*' Con's voice is implacable. '*This is. I know it.*'

I could cry.

'*Art is under her power. And is – is Teel still there?*' Petra's voice is unexpectedly tentative.

'*He is,*' Favre answers her in kindlier terms than I would have thought. I sense his affinity with Petra, fraternal and fond. '*Will I bid him join us?*'

'*No.*' She says it too sharply, too firmly. '*We need to get out of here. We need to get Con to safety and then we have to find some way of stopping her.*'

I've never heard Petra sound so determined about anything.

The rock walls of the cavern shake and rock. Someone screams, and there's the sound of panic as something rattles the side of the mountain. I move with Rhenna, out of the crystal encrusted cavern where she's nesting and into the larger one. She roars, the noise reverberating through the caves. Aeron and Favre join in, their deeper tones harmonising with hers.

The vibrations subside and the sound of falling rubble continues for a moment or two.

'What is it? What's happening?' I ask.

'*Someone turns weapons upon us.*' Aeron says. He moves like a caged animal.

Teel comes forward, hands raised as if in supplication. Others follow him, dishevelled and hesitant. Not him though. He's masterful. A born leader really. I can see that light in him, with Rhenna's eyes. Not that he wants it. No, not Teel. He wants nothing more than his freedom. Interesting.

'They aren't attacking us,' he says. 'We're trapped in here. They're trying to get us out.'

'Or finish the job they started when they took Kel,' his blue-haired companion says, her eyes flashing with disgust. Her gaze skirts across Rhenna and I, dismissing us. Kaeda, I remember. Kaeda de Lorens.

Petra was here. Art was with her. And he betrayed her.

Another crash from outside shakes us. The humans stagger and draw back again but we hold firm. Aeron and Favre fall in beside Rhenna and me, and we shield them from whatever is coming.

The rocks fall, light streaming in on us. I hear voices, human voices. And then something fires again. Weapons fire. I can hear it now, clear as anything. And I know the sound, I know its music and its subtle tones. It's Vairian. It's a Vairian Falcon.

It hovers outside the broken mouth of the cavern.

'Clear!' someone shouts. 'It's clear.' And I know his voice. Zander. My brother.

The Falcon pulls back, the engines turning the air iridescent. A practiced, elegant flip, a turn in the air, and I know that pilot too, Daria. It has to be her. I've never seen anyone else pull off that move so gracefully. I tried so many times to emulate it but never came close. The ship comes in to land just beyond the landslide it created, sets down neatly.

Figures are climbing up the surface, led by Zander. He doesn't hesitate, doesn't pause or let anyone else go first. Why would he? His safety has never mattered to him, not even when it matters to everyone else. He's a force of nature, my brother.

'Zander!' I shout, forgetting myself as he reaches the cave mouth.

He hesitates, stares at me… no, at Rhenna. He doesn't know I'm here. And he can't know. He hesitates, and bows his head. 'Maestra Rhenna,' he says.

But then someone else shouts his name and runs past us. Teel throws his arms around my brother and hugs him, hands slapping his back.

'I might have known you'd survive,' Zander laughs, holding him close.

'You can always bet on me, my friend. I was born lucky. But Petra… they took her with them.'

Zander's shoulders tighten. 'And Art?'

'Your younger brother, I believe.' He shakes his head, laughing as he turns away. 'You didn't have to send him in to spy on me, Zander. I would have told you whatever you wanted. Don't you know that?'

It even sounds like he means it.

Thom makes his way straight to Aeron, already communing with him, passing all their information on to him and receiving all Aeron can tell him.

'Where's Bel?' Zander demands suddenly, dragging my attention back to him. He's standing right in front of me, Teel right beside him. 'I spoke to her. Through this crystal.' He digs it out of the pocket of his jacket. It looks painfully small.

Should I tell him? Should I speak? How am I to explain any of this?

'*She is safe,*' Rhenna tells Thom solemnly. '*Her body is still held by the creature called the Coparius, but Bel herself is safe.*' Thom passes on the information to Zander, giving Rhenna an odd look. They're not ready to link themselves to my brother, it seems. And that's probably for the best.

'Where?' Anger sizzles in his dark eyes.

'*It is impossible to explain to him,*' Favre says. '*He will not understand.*'

I *think* that's not a comment on his intelligence.

'*We don't have time for this,*' I whisper to Rhenna, hoping Thom will not hear me. Though he frowns, he doesn't seem to notice. '*We have to help Con. We need to go to Limasyll. Con, Jondar and Petra are trying to escape. The least we can do is help them.*'

Thom turns as if mentioning Jondar's name sets off an alarm bell. He stares at Rhenna and I wonder if he heard me. I almost think he could. I'd put very little past Thom, especially when it comes to his husband.

'Maestre Aeron,' he says. 'We fly for Limasyll. If we go in on a Vairian ship, we risk a diplomatic disaster. But the Rondet can come and go with no difficulty. In fact, to drive you off would be tantamount to announcing an insurrection. The Anthaem is the ruler by your grace. We need you, all of you.'

Zander reaches out to touch Rhenna's face. She lets him, or perhaps I do. He's my brother. I'd trust him with my life. And now, so does she.

'Please. I need to find Petra.'

A jolt of energy passes through Rhenna's body and the exhaustion dogging her fades. I can sense it still lurking in the distance. It's not entirely gone. I wonder if she too has the sleeping sickness. But for now, just for now, she feels more like herself. She nuzzles against his hand. A sense of life, of energy comes from him.

'*He is special like you,*' Rhenna says softly. '*And as full of love.*'

Teel joins him, standing so close to my brother that I can see the trust between them. They became friends on Cuore. I don't know how, but I can see it woven together, their lives. And something else. It flows like a web, a light which is echoed in each of them. I blink, or rather Rhenna does and I see it more clearly.

'*It is love of the same person,*' she tells me. '*Of Petra.*'

Both of them? But I know that. It's the way I feel about Con, the way I felt about Shae. It is everything and it drives each of them in a way I could never have predicted.

'*Oh yes. She is difficult, and headstrong. But who among us does not love Petra Kel?*'

Thom smiles at her. 'Then you'll come. All of you?'

'*We will,*' Rhenna and I say, together.

She spreads her wings and leaps into the air. And suddenly, in a wonder I never dreamed possible, though it was always my dream, I am flying. Actually flying.

Chapter Thirty-One

Petra

We move through the palace like ghosts again. Down from Con's study through the narrow passages and servants stairs, into cellars and out into the lower levels of the gardens, below the terraces and the lights and music of Limasyll.

'She's holding a ball,' Jondar says, his voice bleak.

Con doesn't look up or pause. Head down, he just keeps going. 'The more people she has there, the more to expose to the stone, I fear.'

'But why?' I ask him. 'What does she need more followers for?'

'I think she... *it* feeds on them. It's stronger than ever.' And he stops. Of course he stops. They're his people. 'We can't leave. We can't abandon them all to her. We can't abandon Bel. She wouldn't leave us.'

His guards pause, torn between obeying him and protecting him. I've never thought of how hard it might be for them.

He's right. I know that. But it isn't a helpful thought. Not now. It's emotion talking, not logic. Not strategy.

'We aren't abandoning them, Con. We're regrouping.'

There's a struggle written all over his handsome features. But eventually I see him come to a conclusion.

'Yes,' he says, his hands balling into fists at his side. 'We need to find the Rondet. She said she was with them. But… how can she be there and here?'

I don't have an answer for that.

We make our way back down the narrow stairs, towards the cellars and, I hope, the way out. If we can get to the lower gardens and then across them into the ancient tunnels… It's the quickest and quietest way out. It should be deserted.

But it isn't.

The Greymen are waiting for us. Twenty of them fan out, robed in the colours of smoke and all of them wearing that flat-eyed expression of disdain.

Jondar stops in his tracks, pushing Con in behind him as Liette steps out in front of her followers.

'Anthaem,' she says, that same sneering tone I remember too well. 'Let us take you home. To your wife.'

'Not on your life,' Jondar mutters, his blaster held before him never wavering from her.

Liette rolls her eyes. 'You really aren't important to us, you know? Just him. I might even be inclined to let you go. Neither of you are of any use to us if you can't serve the Coparius as you should. But the Anthaem is the heart of Anthaeus. The planet will follow him. The people will follow him. When he loves her as he should, we will be able to control them all.'

'I'll never love her. She's not Bel.'

'You'd be surprised what you can be persuaded to do, Anthaem. With the right encouragement.'

They surge forward, faster than I would have given them credit. I get a few shots off, Jondar does too, but then we're grappling hand to hand. The guards take the worst of it, but they're good and they're determined. It's over painfully quickly and Liette stands there alone, staring in shock. Her strategy, such as it was, should not have failed. Problem was she underestimated us. She sucks in breath after breath, shaking as she surveys the rubble of her masterplan.

'Let's get out of here,' Jondar tells us, ignoring her. He ushers Con ahead of him.

'You can't. You can't just leave!' she shrieks. 'You're the Anthaem and she is your queen. She is the Coparius.'

Something in Con snaps. He swivels around and stalks back towards his former assistant, the girl he had trusted, who betrayed him. I can't remember seeing Con quite so full of rage before.

'That thing couldn't control me, even though it tried. It cut me off from the Rondet and has stolen my wife's body. I am never going to cooperate with it.'

She leaps at him, pulling him to her, her hands going around his throat. I should have shot her the moment I saw her. Con twists and lands an elbow in her stomach and then... then he just stops.

Breathing hard, doubled over, he doesn't move. His eyes are wide and desperate. It's as if he's somehow frozen. Liette disentangles herself and buries her hand in his hair, pulling him back upright. Con obeys like a jerky puppet, his weapon trained on us. Liette lingers behind him. If we fire, we'll hit him, not her.

'Like I said, there are ways you can be *made* to cooperate. And you are not the only one who has been working on our wondrous inventions.'

'What have you done to him?' Jondar asks in that cold, quiet voice that heralds violence. I say nothing, waiting, watching for my opening.

'Applied a little pressure.' She laughs at her own joke. 'Now, like I said, I'll let you two go. I've no interest in you. But he comes with me. I need this precious brain to finish my work. And she needs him at her side if this world is going to comply.'

'It's not going to happen,' Jondar snarls at her.

'Shoot them, Con,' she says, as if telling someone to do no more than pass her something.

The struggle on his face is clear. He strains to disobey, but somehow he can't. The blaster trains on me. He's shaking, the tendons in his arm standing out as he tries to resist.

And Jondar shoots him, full in the chest.

Con drops like a stone. Liette screams in frustration, seconds before I fire on her and the sound cuts off in a groan as she falls. I don't even watch but turn on the prince.

'What did you do?'

'Stun settings,' Jondar says. 'Remember? The weapons. They're stunners.'

I glance down at the gun. I'm not entirely sure I did. I just really wanted to shoot her. I'm glad he remembered though and in time to take Con out of the equation.

'What did she do to him?' I crouch down over him, checking his pulse. It's strong and even. That's when I see it, a small metal disk embedded in the skin. 'What is this?'

Jondar joins me, frowning as he studies it. 'That looks like his work. The chip they were working on using the crystals. It was supposed to combat PTSD. He said…' Suddenly he pauses and then swears. 'She changed it. She used it against him.'

'Can you take it off?'

He pulls it from Con's neck. It tears at his skin, leaving a circle like a ragged bite mark.

'There.' Jondar takes out a handkerchief. Only he would have a handkerchief despite being imprisoned for days. He drops the chip into it, as if loathe to touch it any further.

'I know he was hoping to create a medical device, but not... *that*.' I think of him tinkering away, disgusted by weapons and more interested in power cells than anything else. 'Why would Con invent something like *that*?'

Jondar pulls him up, beckoning the guards to help him. 'I don't think he did. I mean, not intentionally. Someone else has been at this as well. Her, I presume.' He turns it over in his hands. 'He'd never leave the back so unfinished as this. Damn it, Con.'

He wraps the chip up in the handkerchief, folding it over and over to protect the evidence, and then he slides it into his inside pocket.

'Who was working with him?'

'Just Liette and Sorrell.' I glance up at the guards – they were there too but I don't want to say that out loud. 'Con would know though. He'd recognise the work, I'm sure of it.'

'We're going to have to wait until he wakes up then. Come on, let's get moving.' I give Dex and Kelvin a pointed look and they take his weight between them both. They were listening to us, of course they were. They must guess my suspicions. But they don't hesitate. Given Con's build there isn't much for the two of them to carry but all the same, they don't look happy. 'I'll take point, Jondar the rear. We need to move fast. If you two start tiring let me know, and we'll switch. Let's go.'

'And her?' Jondar asks, nodding down at Liette.

Instinct tells me to stick a knife in her throat. Leave no enemy behind you. Once upon a time I would have. Now though? I sigh. Maybe Anthaeus really is rubbing off on me. But I don't have time to argue with them right now. Con would refuse. I don't know about his guards and the prince.

'Tie her up?' he suggests.

'All right. Get on it.' If that's as far as he'll go, that's fine. 'They've got some shackles they were going to use on us. That's almost poetic.'

Like a milder form of using Con's emotional control chip to control his body. Poetic.

As we reach the gardens, I keep getting the sense of being watched. The hair on the back of my neck prickles and I don't want to say anything but I am pretty sure we're lost. When we stop to rest, the boys lie Con down and he stirs. The fresh air helps, I think, or the scents of the plants all around us. He opens his eyes and winces.

'Head hurt?' I ask.

'Everything hurts.'

'Well, you invented the stun-guns.'

'What?'

'Jondar had to shoot you with one. You were being Liette's puppet at the time. You've got to consider the uses of some of your inventions, Con.'

'Jondar shot me?'

He looks so bewildered, the poor thing. It's like kicking a puppy.

'I'm sorry,' Jondar says and he looks it. 'I really had no choice. Whatever she had done to the inhibiter chip—'

'She had the chip? Where did she get the chip?'

'She's clearly been playing in your toybox, Con.' I try to make it light because the last thing I want him to think about it the full implications of her having access to some of his technological wonders.

'It's a coup, isn't it? They're using Bel as the figurehead but…'

Something like that. Who's in charge… well, that's another question. 'I'm not sure the Coparius sees it like that. She's picking and choosing whoever she wants or whoever she can control and draining the others of life. Without any regard for the Greymen.'

He pushes himself up, groans as he does so and doesn't move again for a moment or two. Jondar hovers beside him like a mother hen. 'Part of the original stone was in the chip. It had better connectivity than the others.' Con looks around him, his expression bleak. 'Where are we?'

'We're still in the palace, in the gardens, right at the bottom.' I try to make it sound less desperate than I fear it is.

'Let's get going. The further we are from Limasyll the better.'

'On all counts.' I get to my feet, check the weapons and the two guards follow my lead. I take charge. 'Right, you two, you don't have to carry his Majesty any more so you can make yourselves useful and take point.'

They chorus 'Ma'am' at me and Con makes a face. He never was one for formalities.

'And you two,' I address the Anthaem and the prince with my most stern glare. 'You're going to slot in between us and not give me any trouble at all. Understand?' They nod in unison and for once I think they're actually going to listen. I'm probably kidding myself but I think I'm going to allow myself that for now. We've got to make our way out of here. At the other end, there's Zander and Teel…

Whether that's good or bad, we'll have to see.

Jondar directs us effortlessly, or at least it seems that way. He knows these gardens. He's so certain that we don't argue with him. My own doubts aside, I make sure to memorise the way we've come out of habit more than anything else. You never know when it will come in handy. At the same time I'm listening, the way Shae taught me to listen when I was first assigned to his team. The way he taught all of us.

Go still inside yourself. Focus outside, stretching your senses beyond. Listen. Listen as if your life depends on it. Because it probably does.

Part of me wonders again about his final moments and his resurrection as a Mecha. I can't get it out of my head. *Did he know? Did he really know? Ancestors, I hope not. I can't imagine anything worse.*

We pass the memorial wall, enter the cave system and I feel a sudden sense of wild relief.

And then I hear it. A tapping, far off, but steady and deliberate. Feet. Marching feet. They're coming the way we're heading. And something else. Like a wind, moving the air, a rushing sound like waves on a distant ocean.

I'm about to signal the others to stop, to get down and hide, when Con lets out a cry, pure joy echoing through the tunnels, and he breaks into a sprint. We rush after him, but can't keep up. Not now. Even though he's hurt, even though he's exhausted, nothing could hold him back.

I'm past Jondar, Dex and Kelvin before Con goes out of sight around a bend and I pelt after him, blaster already charging. I skid on loose gravel and come to a halt just in time to see Rhenna coming in to land in front of him, her wings still widespread and glittering.

She bends her head to him and Con stops, his hands wide. But he's confused, I can see that. It's written in every detail of his stance. Something's wrong. He doesn't touch her. He doesn't move.

'I don't understand,' he whispers. 'Bel?'

Rhenna purrs and sighs, trying to nudge him with her sleek muzzle.

I reach out for her myself, asking her to explain, but I'm rebuffed, gently enough. She doesn't want to talk to me, just Con.

'*Let them talk,*' Favre says and a moment later he and Aeron arrive, alighting with the same grace and elegance at Rhenna. '*They need to... come to terms. Others are looking for you, Petra Kel. And you, my lord Prince.*'

'Jondar?' Thom yells as he appears from the far end of the tunnel and all formality forgotten, the two of them run to each other, embracing like they never thought to see the other again. It's the kind of love I recognise, the love that shows itself all the more strongly in times of distress.

Like Con and Bel.

'Petra, thank the ancestors you're okay.' Zander doesn't run to me. Neither does the man beside him. Teel just smiles. They glance at each other for just a moment and I want to slap them. I'm tired of feeling like the brunt of some unspoken joke between them, tired of their secrets and their meaningful glances.

'Of course I'm okay, Zander,' I tell him with all the bravado I can muster. 'It would take more than that to take me out. Or had you forgotten? Anyone got food and water?' There's a moment of strained silence. *Yes, he was showing concern. No, I can't allow that, ingrate that I am.* I holster the blaster and push by them.

'Told you so,' Teel says, so softly that only Zander and I could possibly hear.

Chapter Thirty-Two

Bel

Rhenna senses him at the same moment I do, or perhaps it's my senses at work, amplified by hers. I can't help myself. Every instinct in me cries out his name.

'*Con!*'

And the answer comes back at once. 'Bel!'

I hear it, bouncing off the walls, reverberating through the cave system and through me. We sweep down through the tunnel, wings outspread and heart singing. I'm so desperate to see him, to know that he's safe, to be with him again that I forget. For a wild, insane moment, I forget everything that's happened.

Con comes to a halt as we land, confused, his eyes wide as he realises it's Rhenna. Not me. Or at least not me alone. Rhenna spreads her wings out wide, mantling us, and bends her head towards him. But he doesn't touch her.

'*Conleith, beloved Anthaem,*' Rhenna says. '*Hold and listen. We are here, both of us. She is safe, as I promised you. Safe with me.*'

He's frozen, staring at us.

'I don't understand,' he whispers. 'Bel?'

'*Talk to him, Bel,*' Rhenna tells me. '*You have to talk to him.*'

But I don't want to. I don't want to see the look I know is going to come over him. I don't want to break his heart. But I've no choice...

'Please... please listen to us, to me,' I say. *'I don't understand it either. I was lost in the stone's power. And then I was lost in the crystals. I talked to you, remember?'*

And there it is. His mouth opens to an 'o' of dismay and his eyes go wide. He nods slowly and his hands come up to Rhenna's face. He presses his fingertips against the smooth surface of her hide.

'This... this isn't possible. Not... not again.' Tears well up in his eyes and he closes them, tries to force them away, presses his forehead in between his hands, hard against her crystalline skin. 'Bel, *please...*'

Rhenna wraps her forearms around him and spreads her wings, arching them forward, mantling him, but it isn't the same as me holding him, or him holding me.

It hurts. I never imagined anything would hurt as much as this. Everything I've been through, every torture and every misery, is nothing to this. His pain, my pain, the loss reverberating through us.

He thinks he's lost me. Even though I'm still here, I'm gone. And I'm not sure he's wrong. I can feel it all, every agony, every misery. Everything he feels.

Arguments are no use to anyone. Con and I argue anyway. Shut away in Rhenna's mind it's hard to remember why. We share emotions, sensations and reactions – things that we would normally shield one another from. Here, that isn't an option. He sees my doubts, I sense his feelings of betrayal, and his self-loathing because he knows I didn't betray him and he feels guilty for that thought. And fear. We can sense each other's fear.

His fear of me. Of the memory of what I put him through.

Fear that we can't fix this.

That's the greatest fear of all. I know he spoke with the Rondet for a long time after Matilde's second death, trying to discover why she did what she did, how it was done, but I don't believe he ever got anywhere. Now he's facing it again. Just when we had everything.

And as for me, I see what he went through, the shock of me turning on him, or at least what he thought was me. My hands turned against him in violence. I see her trying to turn him with that wretched stone. I feel his pain, echoes of all that the Gravians put him through. All the things he withstood for my sake turned against him. He believed, all the time, that I was still in there somewhere, that while he called my name and begged – *begged* me for help – I stood by and did nothing to help him.

'At first you would reappear.' His hands are still pressed to Rhenna's side, as if he can reach through her and touch me. He gazes into her solemn, multifaceted eyes, as if he can see me in them. 'I lived for those moments. When she gave up, she ordered me locked away. I was tired… so tired… and I dreamed of you. Dex and Kelvin managed to get me to my study instead of the cells. They told the Greymen it was more secure.'

'*Clever.*' I should thank them. I owe them so much. They looked after him when I could not.

He closes his eyes and I feel his tears leak from the corners.

'Bel? What are we going to do?'

I make myself cold and hard. I have to. For one of us. I have to be strong. '*There has to be a way to drive her out. I don't know what it might be. She banished me to that dark place. There must be a way to do the same to her.*'

He pulls himself together, a problem giving him the excuse to focus on something else. A problem, that's what he needs, something to solve, to fix. '*Favre? Please, I need you to talk to me, to tell me what to do. How do I fix this?*'

Favre doesn't answer though. Trying to reach him is like trying to talk to the stone walls of the caverns and tunnels around us.

'*He's afraid,*' Rhenna interjects. '*They killed Natuel, the first host of the Coparius. His grandsire… He blames himself. And… and… He doesn't want the same thing to happen to you.*'

If I could still breathe, I would sigh.

'*Maybe that's the best thing,*' I tell them at last.

'Don't you dare say that,' Con chides me instantly. 'Not you. You never give up, Bel. That's one thing you taught me.'

He seems to glow as he speaks. Looking at him with Rhenna's eyes I can see his love more clearly, his trust, his faith in me. I can't let him down. I just… don't know what to do.

It's himself he doubts.

And I'm not worthy of his faith.

'We need to move out!' Petra calls. She's been assessing the route ahead, and forming up those with us into teams, falling into her perfect military partnership with Thom. 'This area isn't secure and they could be in pursuit. We're still too close.' *They.* Our own people. Turned against us either through lies or coercion. All the Coparius has to say is that Con has been kidnapped and the Anthaese will turn over every stone on this planet to find him. Because they think she's me.

The tunnels give us some cover, but it won't last. They aren't the secret that once they were.

'*Where to?*' I ask.

Petra flinches a little. She can't get her head around this any more than I can. 'Somewhere safe? The old Rondet chamber. It's not far and it's home ground.' The thought of moving again sends a wave of dismay through me. I know the others feel it too. I'm tired… exhausted… or maybe that's just Rhenna. Perhaps we're blending together faster than she thought.

'*I need to sleep, Bel. I'm so tired.*'

Rhenna slumps down on the hard ground and closes her eyes. There's nothing I can do.

'I guess that means we're not moving for now.' Petra swallows hard, waves of discomfort coming off her. 'Bel?'

'*Yes, Petra.*'

'I saw you in the Coparius. I… I tried to reach you.'

'*You did. I think you woke me. I would have been lost in there forever, without you Petra. I owe you everything.*'

She grimaces. 'Tell me that when we get you out of there. No offence, Rhenna.'

'*None taken,*' Rhenna says drowsily. '*I like her, Bel.*'

Well, they're very alike, the two of them. My friends. There's a tightness in my throat. Rhenna's consciousness coils protectively around me as she drifts off to sleep.

But there's someone else still waiting to speak to me. My brother. It's a conversation I'm not ready to have. When he approaches, I hide from him in the depths of Rhenna's mind. She decides it's time to play dumb too.

'You can't hide forever, squirt,' he says.

'Leave her be,' Petra tells him, as protective of me as Rhenna and Con. 'They're exhausted. We're all exhausted. We can rest here for a little while. Bel has been through enough without you reading her the riot act.'

Zander raises his eyebrows at her. 'Who says I was talking to my sister?'

*

The noise that wakes me isn't human. It's a hum, deep and resounding. It's just at the lowest edge of hearing and it's terrible. It hits the Rondet first. Aeron gives a cry, a mewling whimper as he tries to rise and his legs go out from under him. His wings splay themselves wide with disjointed clumsiness. Favre tries to reach him, faring little better. The swipe of his tail sends four guards to the floor. He shakes his head violently, trying to clear it. Failing.

'*She's coming,*' he tells us. '*She's coming.*'

And Rhenna, my Rhenna, my friend and saviour, pitches forward in agony. I'm rattling around inside her mind, lost, as she tries to fight against something she can't touch. Like a wasp loose in her head tormenting her. But not me, not this time.

Con's consciousness joins me, trying to calm her, trying to reach her. We join together, strengthening each other until she manages to regain a semblance of equilibrium.

Abruptly it stops.

And that's when I realise we're surrounded.

We should have kept going. We should never have stopped.

Rhenna spreads her wings wide and roars at those who have drawn weapons on us. I recognise many of the faces. Guards, servants, friends – even Halie is there, but her expression is blank and uncaring, so different from the face she usually wears. And Art. Oh my ancestors, my brother is there too. We have weapons but not enough stunners. It's a lose-lose situation. If we kill her followers we're killing our friends.

Con stands in front of Rhenna and me. I watch him take in each face and feel something inside him fail just a little when he realises who they are, his people. Turned against him. Against us.

The Coparius walks forward slowly, Art and Liette at either side of her. I can't take my eyes off my brother, not the clever, laughing boy I knew. Zander gives a snarl of anger and dismay, but Petra puts up a hand, holding him back, preventing him from doing anything foolish. At least I can rely on her to protect him, even from himself.

The anger inside me grows to boiling point. I've hated before now. I've fought and killed and raged against others. But she has taken *everything* from me. Everything. I won't let her take Con.

'Don't,' Con whispers, and I know he's talking to me. Trying to calm me down. Trying to work his way through this without a disaster.

'Come quietly, Anthaem,' she says. 'This is for your own safety. Those creatures are not your friends.'

He shakes his head. 'They are more true to me than any other.'

'Even your wife?' She smiles, artful heartbreak in the corners of her mouth. 'Come, Con. Please. We both know that they have changed from what they once were. They are dangerous to us. Alien. Just look at them.'

Someone has to be filming this, I realise. Broadcasting it already perhaps, or else they're recording so they can edit it together as they will later on. It's evidence for her coup. One false move and she'll show the world, and the galaxy, that the Rondet are monsters. The interstellar media would love that. They're never going to accept them. They're too different. Too powerful. Most of Anthaeus has seen nothing of them until recently, and their influence on this world, while powerful has been subtle.

They can be terrifying. If you only saw them in battle, destroying the Gravians, tearing their ships apart in the air, or as a far off distant creature, like something from barely remembered legends or from nightmares… what would anyone think? Spread rumours of missing people, dead livestock, a claim or two of them carrying off a child…

Liette smirks. She's won. Her campaign of rumour and hatred has won. She's at the right hand of the de facto ruler of Anthaeus. She can remake this world however she wants so long as she keeps her mistress happy.

And with the Coparius that just means keeping her satiated.

Not all these people are under her spell. Some of them, too many of them, must believe that the Rondet are dangerous.

That's when Teel steps forward. He bows with all the grace and elegance he has in him, the Empire personified.

'Your majesty,' he says. 'Perhaps I can be the broker in this. My Imperial mistress wants only peace and cooperation with Anthaeus. No one else here needs to be hurt. Conleith need not be concerned.'

What is he trying to do? What is he thinking? Just defusing the situation, or is he trying to distract her from Con? It won't work. I know it won't work.

She tilts her head to one side, as if trying to figure him out, to see inside his head and decide what to do with him.

'Lord Teel,' she replies. 'You may approach.'

He walks forward slowly, carefully and I notice Kaeda de Lorens start forward as well, as eager to be involved in this peace brokerage as he is, eager for the credit that would go with it.

'Your Majesty should be aware that Lord Teel is less in favour than others.'

'Kaeda,' he growls, and it is indeed a growl. I've never heard such a dark tone in his voice. 'Not now.'

Liette leans in to the Coparius and whispers something. As she pulls back her smile is doubly cruel.

'Lady Kaeda may also approach.' The Coparius stretches out her free hand. In the other, the stone glows a little brighter.

Kaeda flutters forward, curtseying low, her head bowed. 'Allow us to serve, Majesty, and bring your requests to the ear of the Empress herself,' she twitters.

'Liette has vouched for you, Lady Kaeda. A fellow seeker of scientific truth. Rise. Lord Teel, your offer?'

He hesitates. 'My... offer?'

'Lady Kaeda has offered to serve.' She stretches out her hand to Kaeda who takes it, delighted with herself. She throws a glance at Teel, filled with triumph and one-upmanship. Abruptly, the Coparius drags her forward. Off balance, she falls to her knees and the thing in my body shoves the stone against her forehead.

Light blazes from it and after sucking in one frantic breath, then another, Kaeda screams. It's a terrible, broken sound, wrenched out of her.

'Stop it!' Teel shouts. 'Please. Let her go!' The Coparius looks up, her mouth – my mouth – twisted with delight, and then she drops Kaeda. The woman slumps onto the ground, blue hair spilling everywhere, her chest moving fitfully as she sobs quietly. But when she looks up, she tries to smile, a rictus grin.

'What have you done?' Teel asks, horrified.

The Coparius takes a step towards him and he flinches back. Before he can bolt two of her guards seize him. There's nothing we can do to help. Nothing.

'No!' Petra cries out and this time there's pure desperation in her voice. 'No, you can't.'

'Of course I can, Petra Kel,' the Coparius says. 'You know that better than anyone else. Kaeda will recover. And she'll be mine. True and loyal. Your friend didn't last very long, Lord Teel. But then, she's not really your friend, is she?'

He struggles against his captors, but it's more a show of defiance than an actual attempt to escape. I wonder for a moment if he could. 'What do you want of us?'

'Service. And life.' She steps in close against him, inhaling deeply, like an animal breathing in his scent. He shivers as she does so and I wonder if that's the first time he's ever shown fear. 'You are so full of life, Lord Teel. You'll serve me, and obey me, and bring me to the Empress herself so I can make her mine as well.'

'No.' He goes so still, so painfully still and now I see what Petra sees in him. And what Zander sees in him too. He isn't the feckless lord he likes to portray to the world. He's so much more.

'You don't get a choice. Except in this. Take it. Take the stone. Accept all I offer and let it make you strong. It will hurt less if you accept it.'

He glances at Kaeda's slumped form.

'It didn't hurt *her* less.'

She smiles again, a brief flash of humour before the malicious nature of her leaks out again.

'Clever boy. Now, shall we see your heart's desire?'

And she pushes the stone against him.

Petra screams and Zander seizes her, barely containing her but somehow holding her back. Teel arches in agony, his spine like a stretched bow, his teeth clenched together, his hands in fists. The guards' grips dig into his upper arms as they hold him in place while his legs go from under him. Tears stream from his eyes and he shudders as its power courses through him like electricity. His mouth opens wide, stretching into a scream he can't find the air to voice.

'Let him go!' Petra cries out. 'Let him go! Please! Don't do this to him.'

And when the Coparius finally releases him, he falls instantly, broken and hardly moving. This time there's no sign of life. He tumbles down like a rag doll, still and silent.

All I can hear is Petra sobbing, and Zander trying to comfort her, his words so soft, so desperate. He wraps her in his arms and holds her wrung out body. Pain comes off them both in waves, bleak and blue-grey. It makes me ache, the misery of it.

'Some of them die, Petra Kel,' the Coparius tells her in the sudden quiet. 'It can't be helped. And now, Anthaem Conleith, it's time to come home. To join me.'

The stone, in her hand, is incandescent. Power rolls off her in waves. You can feel the air sizzling.

The Coparius stretches out her hand, as if drawing Con to her and Aeron, fearful for his friend, lumbers forward to help him.

'*You're so predictable,*' I hear her voice – my voice – as I hear them. Inside my mind.

Con flinches. He hears it too. I can picture the footage, the faithful wife, trying to rescue Con from the treachery of the Empire, and the monsters who have beguiled him.

She closes her hand into a fist, closes her eyes and something deep inside me lurches. Rhenna shies back, wings spread as she rears away. Strength drains out of her, out of me, all energy, all ability to move. The instinct to flee is a high whine of panic but it's already too late. Favre screams, but Aeron just falls like a stone.

Rhenna goes down next, her heart slowing, her mind seizing up. I know what's happening. I remember the tests Con and Sorrell ran on the crystals in the study, the way the Coparius stone connected to them and drained them of their energy. That's how she survived all these years, draining the life out of Anthaeus, out of the ancient

Anthaese and out of the world. A thriving world reborn, repopulated. She's the reason the Rondet slept in the first place. She's the reason for the sleeping sickness and the missing people.

She's doing it now, draining all life from the Rondet, but faster and with far more malice. She'll kill them outright. I know she's going to kill them.

'Stop it!' Con shouts, desperate. 'Stop. I'll do what you want. I'll go back with you. Just… let them go.'

She hesitates. It is, after all, everything she demanded. But not what she wants, not now.

She's hungry.

'Get up, Rhenna.' I push against her from the inside. I try to get her to move, to wake her. I manage to get her onto her feet, shakily, open her eyes, and I look through them. The colours are brighter. She sees things I can't, flows of energy, power fields.

The Coparius is a nexus of energy and light, golden and fluid, moving all the time. It's draining everything now, everything in Anthaeus. She came from a dead world, but she was the one who destroyed it.

'*Con, don't,*' I tell him. '*Don't do what she wants.*'

Her eyes come to rest on me and she smiles again. I hope my face doesn't look as cruel as that when I smile, when it's mine.

She has the stone in one hand, a knife in the other. Faestus's knife. The one Liette gutted him with.

'You. Why do you keep fighting? Where do you find the strength, little queen? Let's see what happens when you can't reach your friends, will we?'

The full force of her turns on me. I recoil as the stone blazes and that power seizes me this time. It wraps around me like barbs, digging into my consciousness and pulling me away from Rhenna. Several voices cry out – Petra, Zander, but most of all Con.

'Stop it!' Con yells at her. 'I said I'd do whatever you want. Let her go.'

'Let her go? A wise idea, Anthaem. She should not be tethered here. No one should.'

And the link I formed to Rhenna, whatever she did to save me from the void, shatters. I'm swept away from her, power raking through me, as she falls like a toy discarded by a fickle child. I scrabble for purchase as the void looms up again. I grab at anything, anyone.

Con reaches out for me on instinct. I know he can't see me but he can still sense me.

'Bel, please. Bel!'

The light – something different in his hand, a ring of ice like shards of luminescence – draws me in, centres me for a moment. I taste copper, like blood in the back of my throat. I feel wires tightening around me, locking me in to some kind of structure.

Con launches himself at the Coparius. Before she, or her followers, can react, he throws his arms around her. She swings around, off balance and enraged. And she acts on instinct, pure instinct. She wants to live. That's all that matters to her. Nothing else. Maybe she panics. Maybe. The knife flashes as I scream a warning, but he doesn't pause, doesn't hesitate. She slams the blade into Con's stomach, right up to the hilt.

But the disk in his hand bites into her neck, the thing he created latches onto flesh and burrows into her – my – body. And so do I.

Despite their weakness each one of the Rondet howls, the sound of panic, rage and terror rising to a crescendo. I haven't heard such a noise since Matilde died and it almost killed me then. To be part of it now, to make part of it with my own voice, it almost shakes

me apart. The Coparius throws back her head, and screeches. Half
the humans present double over, hands over their ears in agony. But
Petra, Thom and the guards still free are already moving, cutting
through her followers. Zander shoots the stunner with pinpoint
accuracy, taking down her followers but it doesn't matter. None of
it matters.

Con is wounded. Con is falling, sliding down onto his knees, the
shock of it making him colder than any stone.

My Con. My love. My life.

I want to rip myself free of her. His blood is thick and hot, it's
covering my hands. I can see him again, through my own eyes. His
face is white. His body going into shock. He can't move. He can't stop
falling, he can't even catch a breath for the all-encompassing pain.

The Coparius, the not-me which has stolen my face and my life,
doesn't move. She stares down at him with my eyes, and she's frozen.
And so am I.

The single disk on her skin, Con's chip, like a tiny maze, edged
with part of the stone she still holds, the stone which is now blazing
with her rage. She's frozen there, trapped in my form. I can see rage
in her eyes just for a moment before something dark as night engulfs
me and pulls me down with it.

*

We grapple in the shadows. In a world of fire and stone, plummeting
through the atmosphere and smashing into the earth, crushed beneath
rock and plunged into endless crystal water. She almost drowns me in
herself, and I almost escape her. I move like Rhenna, spreading wings
and soaring up, but she winds molten lava around me and brings me
crashing back down. We stand in bleak desolation, facing each other at

last and I think if nothing else, at least I can keep her here. If nothing else I can stop her from hurting anyone else. I can…

'I can save him,' she says, the voice insidious, cajoling. 'He's dying right now, right at this moment. That's your heart's desire, isn't it? Just give up, Belengaria, let me out of here and together we can save his life.'

Eyes open – my eyes, the eyes I haven't been able to use – and it's as if suddenly there is light pouring in on this side of the darkness. I can see him. Jondar's on his knees, trying to help him, yelling for a medic, for Halie. And we are frozen, trapped there, watching.

And she says she can save him. But only if I share my body with her. Or worse, give it up to her forever. I don't trust her. I can't risk it. But neither can I lose Con.

'Well?' she asks. 'Are you going to let your beloved die?'

My choice is stark and she knows it. Impossible and yet barely a choice at all. She knows that too. She has me. Everything in my life revolves around him. Everything on this world.

'You can't let him die,' I tell her. 'You'll lose Anthaeus if you do.'

'I *am* Anthaeus.'

'No you aren't. You're a parasite. You came from somewhere else and you burrowed into this world like a tick. You lived off it. You almost destroyed the ancient Anthaese, and I won't let you do that again.'

She sneers – my own face sneers at me. Like I'm looking in a twisted mirror. And I hear my voice. *Con, my love, my life…*

'Then he dies, Bel. And it will be by your hand.'

Chapter Thirty-Three

Petra

The shockwave ripples out from the Coparius as she freezes. Weapons drop from suddenly limp hands, and those still fighting fall back in surprise. Like a bubble bursting, the coup is over, her spell is broken.

And Bel's body stands like a statue, gazing on impassively as Con bleeds out before her. Halie is the first to recover, shaking her head and then her gaze fixes on the devastation before her. Perhaps her vocation is stronger than anything else. I don't know. But she recovers first and immediately knows what to do. She runs to Con, her hands already trying to stem the flow from his wound.

She doesn't even look at Teel. I hate her for that. I understand, but I hate her. I wrench myself out of Zander's grip, even as he calls after me, follows me, and I run to Teel. My hands touch him and he's cold. He's so cold. His skin is pale and drained of life. What was he thinking? Trying to protect Con or me or whatever? Trying to work an angle?

'Petra,' Con gasps through clenched teeth. His is the one voice which might be able to reach me right now. And it's not so much his voice. It's what he says. 'You've got to help Bel. Please, help her.'

Me? How will I be able to help her?

'She trusts you,' Zander says. 'Talk to her.'

'You're her brother.'

I don't want to leave him. Not now. I don't want to let Teel go.

And then – suddenly – he sucks in a breath. In my arms, he starts to breathe again, like the spell on him is broken too, or there's just too much life in him to give in to death just yet.

I say his name, whisper it. 'Val…'

'I'll mind him,' Zander says. 'I swear it on my honour. Please, Petra.'

Like I've ever been able to deny him. I press a kiss to Teel's forehead. When I look up, Zander is watching me and his eyes glisten with pain.

'*I can guide you,*' Rhenna tells me. '*And Zander will never fail you. You know that. Bel has gone back in there, and in the stone itself. She is fighting even now. She needs your support. You are her warrior, her champion. Trust me.*'

Trust me. Trust the alien creature with mind melding powers. Because aliens stealing bodies and messing with minds has got us here. Except she is right. And she isn't the alien here. I am. We are. And that thing – that creature which has been living like a parasite off the life of the whole planet for millennia is *definitely* alien.

What choice do I have? I promised Shae I'd protect her. I promised her.

'Okay, I'll do it. Show me how.'

She doesn't. Not really. Rhenna doesn't have the patience for that. She just reaches out for me, wraps her mind around mine and I fall.

I plummet through endless dark, lost in the void. I'm so cold. I can feel nothing at all, nothing but endless space, and all the stars are far too far away, their patterns strange to me. And then I see it, Anthaeus hanging like a jewel in the endless night.

'*Find her,*' Rhenna commands. '*Find her now.*'

Bel. Yes, I have to find Bel. This is all about her. My assignment, my mission, the girl I left my homeworld to protect at all costs even though I was barely older than her myself. The girl who became my friend.

I plunge down, caught in the gravitational pull of the planet. As I enter the atmosphere I burn, I scream. The agony ignites inside me, the fiery descent burning away all semblance of what I was, of the cold and unfeeling thing I became. And in that fire I am reborn. And the hunger in me is terrible. Below me is a world, verdant and thriving. There is so much innate life in it, flowing through the crystal veins inside its rocks, blossoming forth on its surface, swimming through its oceans.

Life everywhere. And I am so very hungry.

Not me, I realise. It's not me. These are her feelings. *Its* feelings. Its memories. The Coparius fell from the frozen, endless heavens. It burned its way back to life and then…

The impact is horrific. The stone slams into the earth like a nuclear weapon, sending a shockwave out over an area of a thousand miles. It tears up the earth, knocks down trees like skittles and incinerates them. It plunges deep under the ground, deeper and deeper until there is no light left, nothing but dark rocks and the crystals in their veins. It has gone too far, delved too deep.

It is trapped again in the darkness and it is angry. So angry. I can feel the rage building, impotent and terrible. It chews on that anger for millennia, but there is no escape. It'll die here if it doesn't do something.

But it doesn't die. Somehow.

Even in the depths of the planet, there is still life. It flows through the crystals, drips down like water and it is lifesaving. Tethering itself to the crystal network of Anthaeus is the only thing that saves it. And it waits.

I try to breathe. Try to bring myself back to myself. It's trying to make me belong to it, to see the world, to see existence through its eyes.

It wants sympathy.

I recall the waves of pain as it tried to control me, the entitled, arrogance that would never take no for an answer. It's asking the wrong person.

In the darkness, I open my eyes. Bel is down. She's on her knees in front of a being made of borrowed light, stolen life and pure malignant hatred.

'Bel,' I say. I don't even have to raise my voice. 'Bel, don't listen to it.'

'I will save him,' the Coparius repeats its lies. Bel shudders and looks up. She's desperate, I can see that. And I know what blade it's twisting in her heart. Con. It's promising to save Con.

'It lies.'

The Coparius shakes its golden head. 'No. I have never lied. I am pure truth. I am all things. I am the life at the heart of this world.'

'Tell that to all the life forms you've destroyed with your greed, to all those who sleep until they die. To the countless Anthaese who you drained of life. Con told you to let her go.'

It glares at me. 'And you're going to save her? You? Who can't even decide between the two men you love?' It laughs then, probably at the expression on my face. 'You're one to speak of greed, Petra Kel. Why not have both? Your heart's desire. All you could want. I can give you that. Can you imagine it? Lysander Merryn and Valentin Teel as your most ardent slaves… you'd love it.'

The image springs in my mind, conjured by her, designed to beguile me. The two of them, devoted to me and me alone, mine forever. But it's a lie. I know it's a lie. That's all the Coparius is.

Love isn't about slavery or servitude, no matter what the poets say. We're all about truth here if that thing is to be believed. And it is not. It wants to use me, and to do so it's offering to control them. The very thing the Empress plans to do to Zander. I could never do that to him. Or to Teel. Not to anyone.

'No.'

'I can see inside you, Petra. I know what you really want.'

I calm my breath. I can't fight this thing with my strength and my skills. All I have is truth. It can see inside me, it knows what I want... perhaps. But it isn't very good at interpreting. We can want things we will never have. It's part of being human, knowing the difference.

'Not that way.'

Suddenly it's leaning right in, its glowing face, a swirl of light and shadow, right up against mine. 'Why won't you just obey? You were created to take orders. It's the only thing you're good at!'

Not the only thing. I used to think that. But it isn't true. I hold my head up high. 'Let her go.'

'Your precious Anthaem will die. He'll die screaming for help. He'll bleed out at your feet.'

'Let her go.'

It lashes out, the fist like solid rock as it strikes my face, snapping my head to one side. I taste blood but I just spit it out. I don't hit back, as much as I want to.

'You don't belong here.'

I stand firm, cautious, ready for another attack, but it doesn't come. We three are here at the end, in the dark, in the heart of the world and Anthaeus is all around us. There is no need for violence. That doesn't mean there isn't a battle to be won.

I am her champion. More than that, I am her friend.

'None of us belong here,' I say. 'That's part of the problem, isn't it? At least Anthaeus has accepted her as one of its own.'

I reach out my hand and rest on Bel's shoulder. She looks up at me, her face etched with tears.

'But… Con…'

I shake my head. 'She has no power over Con. Halie's already treating him. Everyone is okay, Bel. Everyone but you. I'll stay here if I have to. I can wait forever. I promised to look after you. I promised Con. I promised Shae.'

Her hand reaches for mine and our fingers lock together.

'No,' the creature snarls. 'You can't do this.'

I look up into that glowing face that isn't really a face. It doesn't even look human any more, certainly not like Bel. It's a shifting mass of light and energy and even as I stare at it, study it, it's growing weaker.

'You won't last in here, will you? You'll go back into hibernation or… or whatever it is. I can wait for that too.' It snarls at me, the sound ripping through me made of malevolence and violence. Bel flinches back against me, but I stand firm. I'm not impressed. I'm not even scared of it any more. I know what it is. 'Ever heard of the patience of a stone?' I ask. 'Try the stubbornness of a Vairian. We are stone.'

The Coparius sinks to its knees in front of Bel, losing its humanoid form now, dissolving down into a vague shape.

I don't want to die.

Who does? Not one soul I've ever encountered wanted or was ready to die. It didn't make any difference.

'Too bad,' I tell it. I want it to die. I want to watch.

But Bel isn't the same as me. Not really. Where I'm hard, she has empathy. Far too much. I think it's been growing in her since we got here, like a disease. I blame Con.

She struggles to her feet beside me, still holding my hand. 'We can't just…'

'Yes we can. That *thing* was willing to leave you here to shrivel up and die. You weren't meant to be able to get out in the first place. It was going to leave you here, just like it did with Natuel, and it was going to drain all life out of Anthaeus before moving on to another world. It would have been easy now. Just get on a ship. Go to Vairian, go to Cuore. That's all it does. It moves from world to world and it devours them. It destroys them.'

I need to feed. I need to live. Don't leave me in the dark.

Imprisoned, starved, kept in the darkness… no wonder it was terrified. And insane.

'Petra…' Bel's bleeding heart is at it again.

I almost scream in frustration. 'That thing stabbed your husband. And maybe he isn't okay. Maybe I just said it to give you hope.'

Her eyes go huge. 'Did you?'

For the love of all our ancestors. 'No. Halie was there, the spell was broken. We're close enough to the infirmary I guess.'

'I don't need guesses. Get us out of here.'

The steel is back in her. Threaten Con and she's going to go nuclear. It's a wonder no one else seems to have figured that out by now.

'Not in my power, your Majesty.' I nod at the glowing rock at our feet. It's so small now. You could pick it up and hurl it into the deepest darkest hole imaginable. Weak, helpless, but it's still got the two of us in here, in this weird dreamlike hell.

She bends down before I can stop her, and scoops it up.

'Get us out of here,' she says. 'And I won't leave you here alone.'

'Bel!'

She glances at me. 'Trust me, Petra. Just once. Trust me.'

The stone in her hand glows and the darkness slides away like paint down a drain.

*

I heave in a breath, an actual breath. I'm on my knees in front of Bel and the rock in her hand is glowing, pulsing with a rhythm like a heartbeat. I struggle to get up and my stomach heaves.

'Take it easy,' Zander says. He's at my side, helping me up.

Teel is standing now, still wearing a dazed expression, but he's on his feet. He almost falls trying to reach me.

'Take the disk off,' Con wheezes. He speaks through clenched teeth and blood. 'Let her go.'

Yes, I lied to Bel too. He's not in a good way. Halie is swearing under her breath, working as fast as she can. She tries to shush him. The stretcher has just arrived. Other medics are helping now.

He won't be silenced. 'If Bel is safe, take the disk off. The chip. Off her neck.'

Teel is the one to do it, standing closest and not doing anything else. His touch is so gentle it barely leaves a mark. Bel collapses in his arms and almost takes him with her. She blinks, steadying herself and him.

'Petra,' she holds the stone out to me, the Coparius, the source of all our problems. 'Quickly, while it's weak. I can't hold it for long or it'll try again, take control or feed off me.'

But it can't touch me. It can hurt like hell but I've got that weird immunity. I snatch it away from her before we can lose the little we've won.

'Take it to Con's study. Get it back under the shielding. Now!'

And like that I'm forgotten. So is the stone. She drops down beside her husband, tries to smooth back his hair from his sweat drenched face until Halie yells at her to get out of the way.

The stone sizzles and burns in my hand. I can feel the hatred rolling off it. She promised not to let it die alone. I didn't.

I run. I don't think of anything else. I can't. I've got to get this parasitic lifeform under control for once and for all.

At the foot of the stairs, she comes at me out of nowhere. Liette gives a strangled sob as she lurches at the stone in my hand. I don't know how she got here. She must have slipped away when she realised Bel was free.

'Give it to me. I must take it to the Empress. It belongs with her. At the heart of everything. It is the heart of all things. Give it to me!' She rambles on, the words just spilling out of her, wild and uncontrollable.

I jerk back to avoid her and she hurls herself at me. Ducking to one side, I evade her but she isn't going to give up. I launch myself up the stairs, and she's right behind me. The steep climb barely slows her down. She's like an addict, obsessed with the Coparius. It gives her power, it gives her purpose, it gives her everything she's ever wanted. And she can't have it.

I reach the door ahead of her and try to slam it shut, but she wedges her foot in the gap at the last moment. The crunch is stomach churning. She must have broken every bone, but it doesn't stop her.

I don't have time for this. Get the stone into the cradle, turn on the shielding array and then I can deal with her.

And I'm looking forward to dealing with her.

'Stop, you have to stop!' she screams at me, but I ignore her, intent on that one workbench. I shove the stone into the net of golden wires and grab the controls, just as she tackles me, taking my legs out from underneath me. I try to kick free as I fall but I'm off balance. I crash into the ground, my head taking a glancing blow off the leg of the workbench. Her hands close on my throat. She's surprisingly strong. I reach up, blindly trying to punch the controls. I just have to turn the grid on, after all. How bloody hard is that? Easier without a psychopath at your throat though. Her grip tightens and I see spots in front of my eyes.

The contraption whines into life and Liette snarls at me. She drags me back and slams my head against the workbench again. I slide down and her hands crush my windpipe, her grip grinding me into the floor. I can't breathe, I can't fight her. Everything is spinning and sickly, everything hurts and there's no air. Blackness seeps from the edges of my vision.

The shot catches her in the head, blood splattering all over me as she's thrown aside. I gasp for air and blink through red gore.

Zander is on me in seconds, gathering me up in his arms as I wheeze and cough. My throat burns, and I'm desperately trying to clear my vision. Everything hurts. Everything.

'Zander... thanks...'

'Wasn't me. Are you okay? Don't try to talk. Just breathe.'

Not him? I look over his shoulder.

Val Teel has the blaster in his hands. He's leaning against the door, barely able to stand, still focused on the two of us as he slowly lowers his aim. It's some distance. He's a crack shot, even though he might pretend otherwise. There's no way you'd make that from the doorway with luck alone on your side. Especially not as weak and drained as he is.

Liette was dead before she hit the ground. No, she was dead the moment she attacked. Zander had run to aid me. Teel had just shot her the moment he could. He might have hit me. He might have hit Zander. He did neither.

'Is it safe?' I ask. 'Is the containment field on again?'

'Yes,' Zander assures me, trying to wipe blood off my face. 'Yes, you did it.'

Chapter Thirty-Four

Bel

Maybe I should just move my quarters into Halie's infirmary and have done with it. She operated on Con herself, letting some of her assistants run the million or more scans she deemed fit to be run on me. Psychological scans, physiological scans, blood tests and any number of things. Too many to count and certainly too many to keep track of what any of them is meant to show. Petra spends a lot of time at my side, a spectacular array of bruises decorating her neck. Jondar comes in and out. I don't really follow their conversation.

They told me about Liette. I can't say I'm sorry.

They won't let me see Con. They won't tell me how it's going. So I just have to wait. It takes hours and it feels like a lifetime.

When Halie finally reappears, she's still in her scrubs and there's blood everywhere.

I surge up from the cot, ready to kill or be killed to reach him. She raises her hands and I can see it in her face, the exhaustion, the strain in her face. 'He's out of immediate danger. And awake. You can see him – briefly!' She says it like a dire warning. Petra helps me up and walks in behind me. She isn't letting me out of her sight, which isn't comforting. I don't know if she's protecting me from everyone else or everyone else from me. She's watching me like a hawk.

Con looks very pale. He's lying in the bed, with an array of machinery around him. He's never looked so helpless. His eyes are closed and his chest moves in staccato breaths.

'Con?'

He looks at me then. His green eyes focus on me and to my everlasting relief, he smiles. 'Bel.' His voice is breathy and weak, but it's his voice. 'I missed you.'

I run to his side and my eyes burn with tears as I bend over him. But the moment I reach him I'm afraid to touch him. *What if I hurt him again? What if he can't forgive me for the things I've done? What if—?*

He pushes himself up – even though he shouldn't move at all – and presses his lips to mine.

It doesn't last long but it's the most wonderful kiss I've ever experienced. He lets himself down onto the bed again. 'Sorry,' he says. 'Sorry, I'm not… I just…'

'You should be resting,' I tell him. 'The doctor said—'

'Oh, she says a lot of things,' he whispers. 'I love you. I always knew it wasn't you, Bel. Right from the first moment she appeared. I swear. I knew it wasn't you.'

Something breaks inside me and I sob, a great retching, completely unqueenly sob, followed by another and another. Con just wraps his arms around me and holds me against him. Is weeping on a desperately wounded man something that a doctor frowns on?

'Petra?' he says at length. *Ancestors, I'd forgotten that she was there.*

'Your Majesty?'

'Ask the princes Lysander and Artorius to join us, will you?'

I struggle to get myself under control again. I've made a fool of myself many times in front of Petra, too many times. But I can't show weakness in front of my brothers. I'd never hear the end of it.

I pull myself together, wipe my face and sit on the chair beside him. Con just watches me. 'I want to make a plan. I want that thing off our world. I can't rest easy with it here.'

He shouldn't have to deal with this already. He should be resting. But there's no way he'll do that until he has control of the situation.

'Of course. Whatever you want.'

He makes a face. 'Maybe they'd better check you over again. That doesn't sound like my wife.'

I laugh, in spite of myself. And then I kiss him again, because there's nothing in this world I want to do as much as that. I kiss him for a very long time. And Con just lets me. There's not much more he can do.

'Oh ancestors, get an actual room, you two,' says Zander. 'I don't need to walk in on you doing that. And what about poor Art? You'll corrupt him. Again.'

Art shuffles in behind him, scarlet faced. My own cheeks heat and I glare at my brother, my mood quelled.

'Not fair, Zander,' I tell him. 'Art and I didn't have a choice. We weren't—'

'In your right minds?' Petra finishes dryly.

'I'm sorry, Petra,' Art mumbles. I take it that their interactions since he snuck onto Anthaeus and was brainwashed by the Coparius have not been of the good variety.

She folds her arms, raises her eyebrows and says nothing. He'll need to grovel a lot more than that. So will I. Zander just grins like a bloody idiot. I hate that expression. I want to slap him.

'The stone?' Con asks, dragging the conversation back to the subject in hand. He sounds so tired. Broken. But he doesn't give up.

Petra stands to attention. 'It's secure for now. Sorrell says no change at all. The field is holding and shows no fluctuations.'

'Good.' Con winces as he tries to shift to a more comfortable position and fails. 'But I don't like keeping it here. It came from the depths of space, according to your report, Petra.'

'That's my understanding, your Majesty.'

When had she made a report? When had Con read it? I look from one to the other feeling weirdly betrayed. 'Her report?'

'Jondar took it while you were asleep.' I don't even remember being asleep, but I remember Jondar being in the room with us. And then not. It's eerily like those first days when the Coparius was interfering with my consciousness. 'He passed it on to me immediately after the surgery, while Halie was getting you.'

He was recovering from emergency surgery, waking up from anaesthesia and yet he still managed to take in the details of a report and make plans. He amazes me daily.

'What do you want us to do?' I ask.

'We need to get it away from here. Back into the depths of space where it can't hurt anyone again. Sorrell can make the calculations. I'll give her the parameters. We need some shielded casing to enclose it and we send it off on as distant a trajectory as possible.'

Zander frowns. 'But if it encounters another world—'

'We'll attach a warning beacon. And believe me, my trajectory is going to take it into the emptiest places possible. But I want this done soon. I want it done fast. And I don't want anyone to know about it. People like our guests from Cuore might have a lot of questions about the Coparius and I don't believe they can be trusted with the answers.

Artorius, I believe you have a ship which is fast and barely detectable? Given that you're on my planet without my knowledge or my leave…'

I've never actually seen Art squirm before. I didn't think it was possible. But there he is, standing in front of Con's emerald gaze like a chastened schoolboy.

'Yes, your Majesty. It is at your disposal. I'll fly it myself.'

'No.' There is no arguing with that tone in his voice. 'You and Bel cannot be anywhere near the thing. It had too strong a hold on you. Until it's gone I want the two of you under constant guard. For your own safety. No arguments.' He turns that gaze on me and I nod. I can't argue with him right now. In the future, well, things will be different. But in this, he's right.

'I'll take it,' Petra says. 'It hasn't had any effect on me.'

But Art looks horrified. 'Your Majesty, the ship is a top secret Vairian—'

'I'm a Vairian,' she says darkly.

'You are…' but he doesn't sound convinced. He doesn't trust her. Not implicitly. Not the way I do. Because she has always sided with me. There's more. I don't know what. He looks helplessly to Zander. Who is, of course, no help to him at all.

'Then *I'll* fly the ship,' Zander chimes it. 'It's Vairian. I'm the crown prince. It should be me. Or do you want me to send a message through to our father asking him what to do? I'll have to tell him that you—'

'No! Zander, you can't!'

Trust my brothers to know what buttons to push on each other.

'So that's sorted then. Now, Con needs to rest. Dismissed,' I tell them. And like that, they're gone. I watch until the door closes. Who knew that would work on my brothers? I wish I'd tried it before. 'Did you get everything you want out of that?'

'Well, I couldn't exactly order them, could I?'

'You're a criminal mastermind, Con.'

'Can an Anthaem be a criminal? I don't think that's ever been cleared up. I mean if you make the laws, can you break them? Would you not just change them to suit you?'

'You're delirious. It must be the medication. I'll fetch Halie.'

'No, she'll make you leave. And I never want you to leave me again, Bel.'

I thread my fingers through his and squeeze gently. He needs to sleep. He needs more painkillers. I know that. And I'll make sure he gets them. 'Then I won't, my love. Never.'

Chapter Thirty-Five

Petra

I really didn't think this through. I mean, I volunteered because other than hurting me more than anything other than Zander Merryn, the Coparius didn't affect me at all. The fact that I'm now trapped in a very small spacecraft with the man I loved so much I gave him up to protect him for hours on end while we carry out Con's plan to dispose of the Coparius was not part of the original arrangement.

We take off without incident, the stone contained in a small heavily shielded pod with a beacon attached giving all the details of the contents and a warning from Con himself as to the nature of the Coparius. It's tagged as an extreme bio-hazard, dangerous to all life.

I sit behind Zander's pilot seat, staring at the pod. It's completely sealed and heavily shielded. Sorrell made sure of that and I trust her work. There is no way that thing is able to reach out and interfere with anyone. Zander never got near enough to be influenced, but as it wormed it's way into the minds and body of his siblings, I'm not taking any chances. I warned him – the moment he starts acting in any way out of the ordinary I'm shooting him with the stunner Con invented and flying the rest of the mission myself.

It's worrying that he doesn't argue. He ought to argue. Arguing is what we do.

We reach the coordinates Sorrell gave us without incident. He really is a good pilot, far better than me. He makes it look effortless, like he's hardly paying attention at all when really he's aware of every part of the ship, everything around us. I load the pod into the jettison tube and flush it out of the ship exactly as instructed. The Coparius shoots off into uninhabited space, one of Con's cells providing all the power it will ever need, the beacon warning away anyone who might find it.

I remember the thing telling me it didn't want to die alone, in the cold and in the dark and for a moment I regret that this is the only solution. But it would have said anything to keep on feeding on a world as rich and vibrant as Anthaeus. And it would never have stopped.

All the same, I ask my ancestors to watch over it and bring it peace. I don't know why.

A hand on my shoulder makes me turn sharply. There's only one person it could be, of course.

'Are you okay?' Zander asks.

'Yes. Just – ready to go home.'

His smile is fleeting. 'Which home?'

I study his eyes. They really are the deepest, most beautiful and complex mix of browns, golds and greens I've ever seen. His lashes are so dark and thick they cast shadows on his high cheekbones.

'For now?' I sigh. 'For now it's Anthaeus. It's the only home I have. Someone told me I'm not a Vairian.'

'I'm sorry, Pet,' he says, a little shamefaced. 'That was cruel. I should never have said it. I just – I didn't want you to be as comfortable as you seemed there. I wanted you to miss me. A bit.'

It's the most vulnerability I've ever heard from him. I'm shocked. I could make a joke or tease him. I could laugh. Once upon a time I would have laughed. But now I can't.

'I did, Zander. I always did. When I first got myself reassigned all I wanted to do was to go straight back to you. But it would never have worked.'

He holds his breath. I press my hands to his chest so I can feel the tension there. He bites his lower lip before he speaks. 'And now?'

I don't want to answer. I just don't want to. But I owe him this, at least.

'No? We live on different planets. Even if we didn't, who's going to accept you with the daughter of Levander Kel?'

He strokes my face. I lean into his touch. Ancestors, I never want him to stop.

'You think about your father's legacy far too much.'

'And you don't think about yours at all, Crown Prince.'

He flinches. Because he honestly *hasn't* thought about that, has he?

'What'll we do then?' he asks.

I'm saved from giving an answer I don't want to voice by an alarm from the computer. Something unknown is coming up on us fast. Zander dives for the controls, cursing as he throws the ship into evasive manoeuvres but whatever it is, it matches us effortlessly.

I know what it is. I just know. I drag the viewer up and the ship coming up on us is instantaneously familiar. It's got so close because of the stealth tech so similar to ours which we didn't bother to turn on. It's faster than Art's shuttle. It's faster than anything I've ever seen.

Except I have seen this before. I'll never forget that silhouette blocking out the stars.

It's the Imperial stealth ship from Kelta.

Zander swears in colourful terms as the docking beam locks on to us and something overrides our manual controls. The computer system suddenly stops issuing warning after warning and goes ominously silent.

He looks over his shoulder at me. His face is stark. 'There's nothing I can do.'

The cold certainty of it settles over me. It's rage rather than fear. I've got to do something, anything. I've got to protect him. But in this situation I'm eminently disposable. One wrong move and I'm dead and who is going to rescue him then?

I reach under the seat to the little box Art stashed there. Thank the ancestors he didn't get a chance to dispose of it. It's still there. I pull out the necklace Teel gave me.

'Put this on,' I tell him. He looks at me like I'm insane. He's still trying to get the computer back online and tries to wave me off. I sling it over his head myself. 'That's an Imperial ship and it's going to take you to the Empress on Cuore whether you like it or not. We're out of Anthaese space in an unregistered ship. They can do whatever they want and no one will know. Tuck it in under your clothes, hide it and maybe, just maybe I can find you again.'

If I make it out of this. I don't say that to him.

He stops arguing and lets me slide it under his collar so it's hidden. Our little ship jolts, throwing us against each other one last time and the terrible clanking noise tells me we're being dragged into a hanger. I pull out my blaster as well as the stunner Con designed. Any weapon that might give us an edge. Zander draws his too. To start a firefight here is going to be suicidal. But I may die anyway. What does it matter? I'd rather go out fighting.

The override opens the hatch. The design of the shuttle means we're instantly exposed.

'Petra,' Zander says suddenly, his voice so calm it's frightening. 'I love you. Always. Remember that.'

Now? He tells me now?

I swallow hard, taking in the troops arrayed before us, all in the standard black of Imperial special ops. All armed. All around the ship.

I turn my head towards him to say it back and suddenly they're shouting and I can't. I firm up my stance, both weapons unwavering in front of me, my body shielding him as much as I can. A host of red targeting dots swarm like angry bees over us. Mainly over me.

'Drop your weapons,' announces a voice that I know. This is hopeless. All I can do is keep him alive. Maybe myself too. They might take me prisoner. Maybe. I comply. Zander doesn't.

Kaeda de Lorens stands just behind the first line of marksmen. She's in black too, but the uniform has gold epaulettes and five golden stars on her collar. General. High command. The Empress's own. We're on her ship then. She almost killed us on Kelta. I should have known. I made the same mistake everyone always made with me and I dismissed her as harmless.

'It was you,' I say, stupidly.

She preens, shaking back her blue hair from her perfect face. 'I was bitterly disappointed in you, General Kel. I'd expected so much more. Oh, *are* you a general again? I assume they reinstated you. I mean, I wouldn't have but they're – what's the word? – *sentimental* on Anthaeus.'

But I'm barely listening any more. I've seen someone else behind her, moving forward like a disembodied spirit through the troops and my heart sinks. Valentin Teel, dressed once more in his austere, expensive black and silver, gives nothing away. Why I'd ever thought I could trust him, I don't know. I'm a fool for a handsome face it seems. Who knew?

'Drop the weapon, your Highness,' Kaeda tells Zander. 'You know how this is going to play out by now.'

He shifts his footing behind me, and he seems to get bigger. I know that stance, dread it. Stubbornness. I glance back just in time to see him lift the muzzle of his blaster to his tight jaw.

'Zander, don't be stupid,' I whisper, horrified.

'What are my options, Pet? Give up and let them slice and dice my brain until I'm an obedient concubine? I don't think so.'

The red dots converge on me. Tight on my chest and head. I knew they would. I could have told him. There is no way out of this. Not together.

'Your choice, your Highness,' Kaeda singsongs. Then her voice turns bitter with cruelty. 'I tried to make it easy on you. But you just were never interested in me, were you? Not really. I should have killed her from the start to get her out of the way. Believe me I tried twice. Teel thought he could do better, but here we are. So shoot yourself. We can fix you later. But you won't go alone. That's how kings of old went out, wasn't it? With their most beloved servants buried alongside them? Except you won't be buried. You'll be up and about in no time. Don't worry, you won't feel the grief. Mechas don't cry.'

'You promised she wouldn't be hurt,' Teel interrupts. He even manages to look genuinely concerned. Better actor than I gave him credit for.

Kaeda growls at him. 'God and goddess, enough of your games, Teel. I called off the assassins when you asked. You said you could handle her. You had your fun with her, led her on, tormented both of them until they weren't thinking straight. We all laughed. Now get over it.'

Teel pushes by her, coming closer through the line of marksmen. 'Zander, please.' He sounds truly desperate. 'Just put the weapons down and I can save her. Like in the Passionflower on Cuore, remember? I promise. I swear to you, I'll get her off the ship. Just… please, my friend.'

I feel Zander falter. He wants to believe Teel. In spite of all we both now know about him. There is love there, friendship, more. Zander wants to trust him. Part of me does as well. The rest is screaming internally.

'Promise,' Zander says, his voice thick with unvoiced emotions.

'I promise. Just drop the weapons and come here. Come to me.'

He's close now, right beside my own discarded weaponry. Not in the ship but right beside the hatch. From where he stands his body shields me from the sights of the blasters. The red dots have vanished behind him. He holds Zander's gaze with his and tries to give a reassuring smile. I almost believe it. Almost.

Zander wilts. He won't let them hurt me, but if he dies he surrenders. And she's right. They have the technology now. We saw it on the moon. They'll just bring him back, mindless and without his own will. He can't protect me now. But Teel can.

He drops the blaster and kicks it aside.

'I meant it,' the Crown Prince of Vairian says to me. 'Every word.'

'I know, Zan. I know.'

I swallow hard and painfully as I watch him step out of the ship and join Teel. I can see it playing out like a nightmare. There's nothing I can do. Absolutely nothing.

Valentin Teel, may the ancestors curse him forever, knows it too.

He pulls Zander into an embrace, watching me the whole time over his shoulder, never breaking eye contact with me, as he places the little disk he stole from Con on my beloved's neck.

Zander stiffens with the shock of betrayal, and then with the effects of the inhibitor chip.

'There,' Teel says in a low calm voice. 'Now, listen to my voice and my voice alone, Lysander. Turn around.' Zander obeys. He has to. He no longer has a choice. His face is devoid of expression but his eyes are screaming. 'Pick up her weapon. The nearest one will do. Aim at her.'

I watch in abject horror as Zander does it. *He knows.* Oh ancestors, he knows everything. The chip makes him malleable, but not stupid. All those promises, every word Teel ever said, they were all lies.

Zander scoops up my weapon. It fits in his hand like it belongs there.

Kaeda lets out a squeal of laughter. 'Perfect. Oh Valentin, how did I ever doubt you? This is what that stupid child Liette wanted to sell us, isn't it? He's perfect. She will love this. We'll reverse engineer it and she'll give us anything we want.'

Teel doesn't break eye contact with me. He smiles a cold, hard smile. I want to kill him more than I've ever wanted to kill anyone. 'I promised, Lady de Lorens, and I always deliver.'

'Oh you've made some promises, all right,' I say. I can't help myself. I can't believe I misjudged him so badly. I trusted him. I may have even loved him. I'd agonised over wanting both of them, felt like a traitor and a fool. And now I'm a fool indeed. I'm losing one, betrayed by the other.

'Sorry, Petra,' Teel says. 'It just wasn't meant to be. Not you and I. Or you and Zander here. You would never have been his queen in any circumstances. Let's face it, we both know what he's like. He doesn't have the ability to be faithful. What was it you said? He was always bound to wind up in a brothel somewhere, drunk as a lord. Or a prince. And I was never one to keep my word.' He smiles again, a softer expression now, almost gentle, almost real. If I believed anything was real any more. 'I might have tried for you. Zander, shoot her.'

And Zander shoots me. He doesn't even seem to struggle against it. He just pulls the trigger.

It doesn't hurt. That's the most frightening part. Not physically anyway. The impact throws me back into the shuttle and before I know what's happening or have a chance to register pain or assess the injury, darkness wells up around me and swallows me whole.

Chapter Thirty-Six

Bel

The reports from the medical team are good. All over Anthaeus those stricken down with the sleeping sickness are waking up. Con sits up in bed, moved from the infirmary to our own chambers now, reading through various data while I lie beside him, listening, reading, just happy to be there with him.

Jondar's latest report is one of the best yet. The Greymen have disbanded. Without Faestus and Liette, it seems there was little to keep them together. The influence of the Coparius is draining away and Anthaeus seems to be getting back to normal.

Of course there is no word yet from Petra and Zander so I'm not quite able to relax and shed the feeling that another disaster is just around the corner.

Perhaps this is my life now. It certainly seems to be the way.

When Art comes to see us, I'm not surprised. He's awkward and unsure. Which means he doesn't know how to explain the many *many* things he needs to explain right now.

Zander would shout at him, give him the dressing down of his life. It wouldn't be the first time.

I lead him to the gardens, the private one behind the Anthaem's chambers, which are covered in jasmine and roses. It reminds me of our mother and I hope it will do the same for him.

I know he would do anything for our father. He probably has.

'I'm sorry, Bel,' he says and sits down heavily on the stone bench carved with images of the Rondet. 'I'm so sorry. For everything.'

'For spying on us?' I sit myself beside him and smooth down the sleek skirt of my Vairian-style gown.

'I wasn't spying on you. I was spying on Teel. He was so close to Zander that we thought he might be a risk. Where is he anyway?'

The Imperial party left this morning, heading back to Cuore. There wasn't much notice but I suppose at this stage they just wanted to get off Anthaeus and back to their luxuries. A few days in a cave, sleeping sickness and all the other horrors they've seen and they probably summoned the first ship in hailing distance. I thought Teel would have at least wanted to say goodbye to Petra, but he didn't. Or maybe they did that already.

'They left.'

'Just like that?'

'I guess. We haven't exactly had a lot of time for diplomacy and all the parties they're used to. And Kaeda de Lorens probably needs to see her hairdresser.'

'Only if she was planning to run some rather horrific experiments on them.'

'What?'

'That's what she does. Head of Research for special ops. She was running the lab on Kelta. They haven't gone back there, by the way. There wasn't anything to go back to. I checked.'

I remember her quizzing Con, trying to get invited to his study. I thought it was just flirtation but now it takes on a darker shadow. Head of Research... ancestors, the laboratory on Kelta was her. All those people, those Mechas... it was her. She tried to kill Petra, kidnap Zander...

I recall the moment I overheard the two of them talking. '*You might as well have hung up a signpost.*' That's what he said.

I was so fixed on what he said about Petra that I never understood the rest of their conversation.

'*I don't do subtle,*' she replied.

And I just dismissed her. Underestimated her. I know I've missed something. Something terrible.

It's her technology, her monstrous Mechas, her stealth ship. We were all looking at Teel. And it was her.

*

Still no word from Petra or Zander. It's been too long. I'm sure of that now. I spend as much time as I can with Con, because there's nowhere else I want to be. When I need to, I carry out the various duties he can't yet do. Mostly I'm keeping an eye on him because we all know that the moment he thinks he's ready to get up, he will, whether he's actually fit or not. Halie is circling as much as she can. The number of sleepers is right down now. Only the earliest have any after effects still remaining. When Dwyer woke up the first thing I wanted to do is tell Petra. But I can't. The poor boy is so embarrassed, even though he had no control over an illness. When I speak to him, assure him that he's still got a job and that he can take all the time he needs to recover, he just asks to go right back to work. Petra would laugh and tell him to have a holiday, especially when a queen tells him to. But Petra isn't here.

It's easy to believe it's actually going to be all right. But I can't take a moment to believe that.

The first warning I have is when both Favre and Aeron appear over the city and they don't look happy.

Con is sleeping – finally – so I walk out onto the terrace and reach out to them. The two ancient Anthaese land in a flurry of wings and concern, instantly bombarding me with their thoughts. I've never seen them so scared. Furious, enraged, grief-stricken and a thousand shades in between but not like this.

'Rhenna is being completely irrational. There's no logic. She will not listen to reason. You must come and talk to her. You are the one person she might hear.'

'What's happened?'

Favre answers me with a series of growls and his tail swishing furiously from side to side. He's afraid, I realise. *'She has gone into hiding. She's taken herself back to the cave where she hid herself away when it seemed that she would start to hibernate again, when the sleeping sickness seemed to be conquering even her. And she won't come out.'*

'I can't leave Con,' I tell them. 'He still has not recovered.'

'And neither has Rhenna,' Favre tells me. *'There is something terribly wrong. You must come.'*

'I'll have to summon a flyer and—'

Aeron roars in frustration. *'No time. There is no time. You must come now, Belengaria.'*

Bemused, I reach out to touch him, trying to comfort him but the surge of emotions is so strong I snatch my hand back.

'Unless you're planning to carry me, Aeron—'

He snatches me up in his arms and takes flight. I scream, more from shock than actual fear of Aeron. Favre is right behind us and the city, the palace and the gardens are suddenly very small beneath us.

I can hear alarms ringing and my guards are shouting. But they don't fire on the Rondet, thank the ancestors.

'*Con, Jondar?*' I reach out for them. '*I'm okay. I'm just – Aeron wants me to go with him to Rhenna. Something's wrong.*'

'*What's happening? Where are you?*' Jondar is first to reply. Con is struggling out of sleep, out of a nightmare and into another.

'*We're flying over… the Cornith forests I think? And… that's the Rondet chamber.*' They're heading for the lake and the mountain where they hid before. Aeron spirals in to land. '*It's the cave where they hid. Where Art left them.*' He left them to die. Them and a number of high ranking Cuorean nobility and Anthaese of all stripes. I try not to think about that. He didn't know what he was doing at the time. Another of those many things we're going to have to sort out. And not just for my brother. There probably isn't a family unaffected on Anthaeus.

Aeron lands so abruptly amid the rubble on the shelf-like ledge at the mouth of the cave that I'm jolted out of his grasp. It's not a good look for a queen, sprawling in dust and stones.

'*Bel? Are you okay?*' Con's alarm is sharp, like acid in the back of my mouth. He's afraid and feeling completely helpless.

'*Yes. But this is not a good way to travel.*' It's an attempt at humour but I already know it falls flat. I glare back at Aeron and Favre who are completely unrepentant. Sometimes I think they see us as nothing more than servants. It grates. '*I'm at the cave. Rhenna came back here.*'

It's strange to see it now, with my own eyes instead of hers. She was so tired, so defeated when I was here with her, part of her. I walk back, aware how much bigger the cavern looks now I am just human and not encased in the body of my crystalline guardian. We didn't know then that the Coparius was sucking the life out of her, out of all of them. Now the sleeping sickness has passed, why would she come back here?

Except, she'd said she liked it here, in the smaller, crystal-lined cave at the very back.

I crawl through the narrow gap. How she got in here I can't begin to imagine.

'*Rhenna?*'

The colours are astounding. Blues, pinks, purples, mauves, all the crystals with their hues flowing into each other. And Rhenna lies curled up in the middle of the mass of colour, reflecting each shade and tone, purring gently to herself.

And beneath her, in her nest, there are globes of perfect energy, of raw life. *Eggs*, I realise. She has a clutch of eggs.

Eggs. She's nesting and there are eggs underneath her.

'Rhenna!' I gasp. I don't know what else to say. It's a moment of pure joy. They're a dead race suddenly reborn. 'Why didn't you tell them?'

She opens one eye and looks at me.

'*Why? They didn't do anything.*' She yawns and stretches, so catlike it's comical.

I sit down in front of her cross-legged, amused and caught up in wonder. They're beautiful. They glow like she does, rippling with light. There must be seven or eight of them.

'Well,' I purse my lips to suppress the smile. 'They must have done *something.*'

Rhenna stretches her neck out and presses her face up to mine so I can stroke her nose just the way she likes. 'You humans, you're so... binary. They have nothing to do with this. *I* did this.'

Oh, the xenobiologists are going to have a celebration. And write a thousand papers. And they'll probably all be wrong.

'How long have you known?'

She shrugs. '*I was tired. I thought it was the Coparius at first. Perhaps it was. But then, afterwards it didn't go away. So I came back here. I like it here. The colours are calming, the energies are right. When I sing—*' She purrs again, a delicate hum which vibrates in rocks all around us, returning in harmonies which are more beautiful than anything I've heard before. '*You see?*'

'Why didn't you tell them?'

She shakes her head. '*You can tell them. It has nothing to do with them.*'

'They're terrified, Rhenna. They think there's something wrong with you.'

'*Oh,*' she says, as if it's a huge surprise. '*Oh. Well, I should tell them then.*'

She doesn't include me in that moment. It isn't my place anyway. But I hear their reaction, the trumpet of triumph and delight from them both.

It's almost as delightful as the moment I tell Con.

*

The days pass slowly with still no word from Petra and my big brother. I'm uneasy, unable to relax. It's like I'm waiting for disaster and when Jondar appears at the door, I know he has bad news. Really bad news.

'We have a problem.'

Of course we do. We always have a problem. I glance at Con. He's listening intently, waiting. 'What sort of problem?'

'We've lost the ship.'

'But… it has cloaking technology. That could be it, couldn't it?'

'I made Art give me the readings for the cloak. I should be able to track it. Thom says it was there until—'

'Where's Thom?'

'On the Valiant. I think he likes it up there.'

Con shakes his head. 'Not more than he likes it down here, Jondar. Don't worry. Keep scanning for them. I'll put in a call and get us some help.'

That's how we end up talking to my father. And Con is charming and diplomatic, the perfect monarch. That's how we get permission for Thom to take the Valiant off into deepest space to look for them both. And that's how, in spite of my reservations, my father, King Marcus of Vairian, invites himself to Anthaeus.

Chapter Thirty-Seven

Petra

I wake up an unknowable amount of time later when the Valiant picks up the shuttle floating in space on minimal power and basic life support. Apparently there was a distress beacon but I have no memory of activating it. The last thing I recall is Zander shooting me. With Con's stunner, as it turns out.

The first face I see in sick bay is Thom. He looks so worried that I'd laugh if I didn't ache everywhere. I do not like those stunners. Whoever gave Con the idea it was a more humane option needs to be shot with one a number of times in succession. A large number of times.

But it is still more humane that being dead, I suppose.

I close my eyes and I see Zander standing there, shooting me, his eyes full of panic and despair, but unable to do anything other than obey. Is this his life now? Is this all that is left to him? Perhaps it would have been easier as a Mecha. At least then he wouldn't know what was happening to him.

'I need to get to a coms station,' I tell Thom, as I attempt to push myself up off the bed. 'I need to track the—'

If Teel didn't find it. If he didn't disable it or put it somewhere to send me on a wild goose chase. If—

My head spins and I want to throw up. I can't think that way. I just can't. I will not allow it to end like this.

'You're going to have to let me help,' Thom says. 'Tell me what happened.'

'There isn't time, Thom. I need to—'

'*Kel*, report!'

I can't help but snap to attention, even if that's impossible lying down. He has the tone of voice down pat. 'Kaeda de Lorens and Teel, that's what happened. It was her ship on Kelta. They probably never came on the whatever it was called. Or at least she didn't. They were her Mechas, her tech. And Teel stole Con's inhibitor chip. He used it on Zander. They're taking him to Cuore.'

He swears and helps me to stand.

I don't dare to hope. The things Teel said – not all of them made sense. What was the Passionflower? And he must have seen which weapon Zander had. Who rigged a beacon if not him? Kaeda certainly wouldn't have done me a kindness.

'What's happening on Anthaeus?' I ask.

'All's well. I left with the Valiant when the word came through that your ship wasn't responding. When you missed your window to return, Bel was worried.' Worried? Furious, probably. 'That's when we picked up the signal.'

'What signal?'

By the time we make it to the bridge of the Valiant, I'm almost back to myself. At least the effects wear off quickly enough once you're moving. Thom is still standing close in case I wobble. Daria's in the command chair. She gives me one of those looks.

'Permission to...' I can't think of the words with my scrambled brain. I wave my hand towards the central coms unit.

'Permission granted, General Kel,' she says. 'You have a plan?'

'I have an idea.'

'We followed your signal this far, so I hope your idea is a good one.'

'My signal?' I ask.

Thom points at the readout on the com's unit as I slide into the seat.

Kel, it reads. *Follow the star.* Nothing else. It just repeats. Over and over again.

'What the hell?'

'That's what I said. Great minds. It was on our emergency frequency so we followed it to you. And this is embedded in the signal.'

He leans over and his fingers dance on the controls. There's a picture of a flower. The oddest damned flower I've ever seen. It's blue and white, with a circular fringe of soft lavender coloured spikes around a selection of green and purple lumps in the middle. It's peculiar and not exactly pretty. I've seen it before, but I don't remember where.

'What is it?' I ask. 'And where's it from?'

'It's from the Firstworld, originally. Called a passiflora. As to what it means…'

In the gardens, on Anthaeus, Teel, lifting it towards me so I could smell the scent.

'Passionflower,' I blurt out.

Like in the Passionflower on Cuore, Teel had said. What the hell was the Passionflower on Cuore?

I start three searches at once. One for Teel and Kaeda's ship – a pointless exercise, I know, but it's worth a try. The second is for the necklace with its distinctive signal. The third is on the feeds, for Passionflower and Cuore. A ship, maybe? A shop? A bar?

He was always bound to wind up in a brothel somewhere…

My fingers fly across the screen.

'Petra? Why are you looking up brothels?' Thom's voice is no more than a rush of air beside me.

And it comes up. Not on Cuore. Nowhere near Cuore. But there's an orbital station attached to a mining world on the edge of central space, just outside Imperial jurisdiction where anything goes. Anything. It's so well known for lawlessness that they even renamed it Deadwood after an old Firstworld story.

And there's a brothel on it, called the Passionflower.

At the same moment the tracking signal is located. In exactly the same place.

'Get me there,' I tell Daria. 'Get me there now.'

*

They aren't cells, not as such. They're more like kennels, small windowless rooms, lavishly furnished and securely locked. When I finally find him, Zander is sprawled on a bed, arms wide, legs splayed and his eyes staring at the flaking gold paint on the ceiling. He's wearing little more than a loin cloth and a collar. He's also stoned out of his tiny mind.

'Ancestors,' I gasp and my hand closes on the metal gate that shuts him in there. 'Open it.' It has a physical lock, a huge clunking metal thing like a brick. Part of the aesthetic. It also can't be hacked.

The facilitator fumbles with the keys and sets to work. I grab the ring out of his hands when he isn't fast enough and Thom shoves him out of the way.

'I don't understand... the gentleman was most particular. We were to keep him. No one was to touch him. We have taken very good care of him. I swear to you, madam, no one has broken trust here. The merchandise is in perfect order.'

The merchandise. Ancestors, I add him to the growing list of people I want to pulverise as soon as I get Zander to safety. When the lock gives, I shove the keys at Beq. 'Get the others out. All of them. If anyone complains shoot them.'

And then I stumble into the cell. There's incense or something everywhere. The air is cloyed with it. At best it's a soporific. It's probably addictive too. Anything to get the punters coming back. And the merchandise subdued.

I cough as I kneel down beside him. 'Zander? Can you hear me? Wake up.'

He stirs, thank every ancestor I know and all those I don't. I'm going to light so many candles of thanks it'll be a fire hazard. For a moment, he just moves his mouth as if trying to moisten it, or figure out how it works. Then he lifts his head like it weighs a ton, opens his bleary eyes and attempts to focus on me.

'Petra?' he says. His voice sounds hoarse. 'He said you'd come. I said it's no place for you. It'd make you angry.'

Angry. Right. Relief makes me giddy instead. I hope it's relief and not the sweet and sickly smoke.

'Did you? And a crown prince fits right in here, does he?'

I help him to sit up. Thom comes to my aid and together we haul him out of there.

'My head hurts.'

'I'm sure it does, your Highness,' Thom says. 'But right now we need to get you out of here.'

'That bastard, Teel. I'll kill him,' I mutter.

'He said you'd come,' Zander insists. 'Just said to wait. Just said… Petra, the drinks here are funny.'

'Yes, Zander,' I tell him as patiently as I can. 'Because they're spiked with Kenhenol and you have clearly had a lot.'

I summon one of the other Vairian guards – good, loyal and discrete men and women handpicked by Daria, who are clearly as appalled by this as I am. And yet, just thankful to have him back unharmed.

I round on the facilitator. 'Who paid you?'

'I don't – I don't understand, madam.'

My temper finally snaps. I grab his throat and slam him back against the bulkhead. 'Stop calling me that. I'm General. Or, if you piss me off any more, I can be your personal version of Death Incarnate. Who. Paid. You?'

'A – a man. Very fine. A Lord. From an Imperial ship. He said to keep him here. That he was marked for one person alone and we were to keep him sedated and untouched, unharmed. We had offers, you know. I swear. No one touched him. We were just to hide him and wait until either he returned or his agents or—'

I lift him from his feet before I slam him against the wall again.

'So you were just to dress him as a sex slave, drug him to high heaven and keep him here for collection?'

'Please, madam… General. Please I'm just a—'

I don't wait. I don't want to hear any more. I'll get a description out of him later. Or maybe I'll hand him over to Daria. She'd like that. I don't really need to hear the description. I already know.

Teel. It was Teel. This is exactly the sort of situation he would find hilarious. How he pulled it off, I don't know. And part of me doesn't care. Zander is here. I have him now. He's safe.

'He left this too,' the weasel-faced little man scrabbles at his pockets and I slap his hands away. 'He said if a woman came – a very *angry* woman – to give you this. You're Petra, aren't you? He said… he said not to make you angry…'

There's a crushed and stained envelope. It's clearly been steamed open and resealed poorly. The paper is think and cotton rich. You don't get more expensive than this. It has an Imperial crest on the back, Teel's crest.

I let him go, snatch it from him, and then, just for good measure I punch him until I hear a satisfying crunch.

He folds up at my feet.

Zander is gazing at me in adoration. He turns his face to Thom and says, very solemnly, 'Shh. Don't make Petra angry.'

*

I don't open the envelope until we're back on the Valiant. With Zander having his system flushed out in the sickbay there's nothing for me to do. I'm only in the way. That doesn't mean I leave him.

He lies on the cot, unconscious, thankfully covered by a sheet and I sit there with him for some time. The collar is still around his neck, a stark black band which marks my crown prince as property of a whorehouse. Something in me finally unwinds enough that I sink forward, head in my hands and I groan. This could have been so much worse.

The collar feels like a personal affront, so I carefully unbuckle it, my fingers fumbling against his burning skin. Underneath it, pressed so firmly into his flesh it has left a mark, is the necklace. The tiny star-like diamond Teel gave me, which I planted on Zander and which led me back to him. Teel must have helped him hide it. Which means he knew it was there all along.

I leave it there.

Kel. Follow the star.

The chip, however, is gone. Zander is himself again. He smells of cheap perfumed oils and incense but I can't see any injuries on him. He'll probably have a hangover as bad as mine when I woke up after the stunner. I forget myself and smooth his hair back from his face. His eyes open, catch on mine and he smiles a sleepy, drug addled smile.

'Hello, Pet.'

'Hello, Zan,' I whisper and my voice chokes in my throat.

'He promised you'd come.'

I sigh. I'm suddenly exhausted. 'Maybe he does keep promises after all.'

'Maybe.'

The medic comes back and I finally have to leave him. Even though it's the last thing I want to do. Exhaustion is catching up on me. If I stay, they'll check me in again and I have had enough of infirmaries of every kind.

I go back to the tiny cabin that comprises my onboard quarters, sit on my bed and stare at the envelope for a long time.

When I finally open it, there's a note, and some pieces of broken metal and crystal which once might have conceivably formed a small ornate disk reminiscent of a maze. The handwriting is flamboyantly beautiful of course, the type of script it takes years to master and is good for nothing except showing off the education, artistry and skill of the writer.

'*My dearest General Kel,*' I read.

Forgive me. I had no choice if I was to rescue him. By now I am long gone, exiled or executed. If Kaeda has her way, I'll be thrown in the darkest hole on Cuore and never seen again, but I doubt it will come to that. I have always had the talent of talking my way out of difficult situations. If you hear nothing, know that I'm out there still. But our Zander is meant for no one but you. Keep him close.

    Teel.

There's a post script.

Please return the shards to the Anthaem with my apologies. No one should have this technology, especially not those who would misuse it.

That's it. That's all he said. No more apology than that for Zander and me.

Our Zander is meant for no one but you.

If only.

I pack everything away again and secure it. I'll return the remains of the chip to Con with Teel's message. The rest, I'll keep to myself.

When I fall asleep, fully clothed, I don't even dream. At some point I'm aware of the Valiant making course corrections, the engines revving and slowing. It's like sleeping in heart of a great beast swimming through space. I missed this, I realise. I feel unaccountably at home. Safe.

*

When I wake, there's a marked change to the atmosphere on board. I can't put my finger on it at first. The communiqué from Thom waiting for me is the only warning I get.

'*His majesty, King Marcus of Vairian, boarded at eleven hundred hours. Full honours. Anthaeus informed of imminent arrival.*'

There a group of royal Vairian guard waiting for me outside my quarters but they don't seem to be in any particular hurry. I take my time to shower and to change into plain black kit. I tie my hair back in a neat pony-tail, mainly to get it out of the way. I look like a soldier again. Not an Anthaese general. A raw recruit perhaps. But I need to do this. It's the only armour I have left to me.

I almost look presentable.

I'm marched along the corridors of the Valiant, the royal troops surrounding me like an honour guard. Or maybe like I'm some kind of prisoner. The dangerous kind.

At best, I'm about to get the dressing down of my life.

King Marcus of Vairian sits at Zander's desk. There's no sign of the crown prince. I lock my disappointment down deep inside me. He's probably still in the sick bay. It's not his fault. But I wish he was here. Just this once. I wish I could rely on him as I keep briefly thinking I can. But every time – *every* time – this is how it ends.

The king studies the screen before him. In his expression I can see more of his daughter than his sons. Bel frowns the same way. But I can also see the man Zander will become. The king he will be.

'We have a problem, Petra,' he says in that deep measured voice which inspires such trust for his people. And such dread in me. 'I want it cleared up before we reach Anthaeus. I want no confusion over this matter.'

'Yes, your Majesty.' There's no point in playing dumb. I knew this was going to happen. I knew it all years ago and I know it now. I am fully aware of who and what I am.

'My son has informed me that he intends to marry you.' He looks up then. His grey eyes are not unsympathetic, but they're not exactly kindly either. 'In fact he has informed me that he's *not* going to marry anyone else.'

He has? He said he loved me. That was all. What was he thinking? A grand gesture? An ultimatum? He couldn't possibly take a diplomatic route or at least talk to me about it first. I can imagine the argument. He must have got his legendary stubbornness from somewhere. They all have it. All the Merryns. It's more than the traditional Vairian strain. Theirs is something extra special.

'Your Majesty,' I respond because he's clearly waiting for some sort of reply even though he hasn't asked a question. I don't know what else to say. I'm in an impossible situation really. All I can do is try to ride the wave of this latest tsunami. The truth is probably the best thing.

'Do you love my son, Petra?'

Oh.

I tighten my shoulders and stare at the wall behind his head, just past his ear. My eyes sting because I know what's coming. I just know. And I can't show weakness now.

So, the truth then. Whatever the consequences.

'With all my heart.'

There's a long pause. 'That's… unfortunate.' He looks down at the tablet again, reading something, as if he has lost interest in me now. I watch his eyes moving. I wait. 'You understand that this relationship is impossible, don't you?' Oh ancestors, he's trying to be kind and reasonable about this horror show. It's worse than I imagined it would be. If he commanded, threatened, or exiled me, it would be easier. I can handle anger and grief, I can rail against injustice. But not this.

'Y-yes, your Majesty.' Why argue? He's right. A crown prince of Vairian could never marry the daughter of Levander Kel. 'By your leave, I'll return to Anthaeus as soon as possible. Until then I'll keep to my quarters. I trust the Valiant can still take me there.'

'Granted. We're on the way already.' Given that I'm sworn to Con and Bel rather than him, he can't actually deny me passage back. But he could put me off on the nearest asteroid and let me hitchhike home. Just like that, it's over. All my stupid hopes, in spite of what I knew all along. 'It is a shame, Petra, and I am sorry he let it get this far. He should have known better.'

It's like a slap to the face. *He* should have known better? *He* shouldn't have let it get this far? Like I had no part in this whatsoever?

No. I can't leave it at that. Not with pity and regret. Not from him.

'It was not just your son, your Majesty. I wasn't just some random girl he led on. You know me, you know who I am. I would have done anything for Zander. Anything. I still would. I almost died for him. I chased him across three systems and found him when everyone else would have given up on him. You were all willing to surrender him to the Empress but I never was. I'd marry him in a heartbeat if I thought it would stop her, but she'd just kill me, wouldn't she? I don't need forever with him. I don't expect it. And I certainly don't want a crown. I see what your wife saw. The crown always comes first doesn't it?'

His eyes narrow. 'Tread carefully, Petra.'

Maybe mentioning Yolande Astol is a mistake. Maybe. But I've made so many it really doesn't matter any more. Everything is crashing and burning anyway. I might as well take it all down with me.

'Don't pretend I have never cared as much as he did. Or that I wouldn't die for him. I've proved that time and again. Not just for him. For Bel too. You underestimate them, your Majesty. They aren't your pawns, they're your children. And you misjudge how much other people love them. Even Teel did everything within his power to protect Zander from the Empress, did you know that? If he's still alive, he's going to be on the run forever. You don't realise the devotion others feel to him.'

He plants his hands flat on the desk with a slap and uses them to lever himself up. 'So you – and the notorious Valentin Teel apparently – love my son more than his own father?'

'Of *course* I do. Like Yolande loved you. And would she have just given up and walked away?'

'If duty commanded her? Yes. Yes she would have.'

Duty. It always comes back to duty. Like that's all we are. Vairians and their duty… Oh I'm not in the mood for this. Not at all.

'Would you have *let* her?'

He laughs. He actually laughs. It's a slow, sad sound, devoid of joy, and now I really regret bringing her up. Ancestors, I should have known better. I am a prize idiot. That asteroid he kicks me out on to had better have breathable atmosphere.

'You are very like her, you know?'

I'm panicking so much I almost don't hear him. I need to get out of here as soon as possible. Before I do any more damage. And the panic is turning to rage. I'm furious with him, furious with myself and oh so furious with the amazing invisible Zander.

'I'll take that as the highest praise, your Majesty. Am I dismissed?'

I just need to get out of here and lock myself in my quarters for the rest of the journey back so I can have my breakdown in private.

And then I hear his voice.

'I told you,' Zander says from behind me. 'And I'm not prepared to settle for less. No more than you were, Father. I'll give up the crown and follow her to Anthaeus if I have to, or to somewhere else at the end of the galaxy. And there's not a thing you can do about it.'

Has he been there the whole time? Listening to me? Hiding back there somewhere and listening to me pour out my heart, and insult his father, and bring up his dead mother, and—

The words he just said finally sink in and I turn, unwisely, to look at him in horror.

'I mean it, Petra. I'm not going to let you go again.'

I bolt. It's the only word for it and I have no shame in that. I push past him and sprint down the corridor, decorum be damned.

People throw themselves out of the way. They see me coming and just fold back out against the walls. I hear him running after me, but I don't look back. I can't. I reach the small cabin assigned to me and hit the door controls as hard as I can. Sealing him out.

'Petra, let me in!' I hear him trying to control his voice but he can't. It's shaking wildly. 'Please, I need to talk to you. Let me in. Please, love.'

I struggle to breathe but it just comes out in great gasping sobs. It's not fair. It's just not fair. I sound like a child, like a spoilt brat who doesn't understand how the universe works. And I know. I know it better than anyone. Nothing is fair. Shit happens.

And life… life and love… are just horrible.

'Petra,' he says again, more softly now. 'Pet.' I can picture him, leaning up against the door. I put my hand against it, and then lean in, as if I'm leaning against him instead, as if we're pressed together without that thin sheet of the door between us. 'I meant what I said, Pet. Every word. If it means giving up everything, I don't care. It won't matter, without you.'

'Don't—' I try to say. But that one word just spurs him on.

'I mean it, Petra. I'll go with you back to Anthaeus. Bel will probably give me a job. Don't you think?'

Zander with a job. Trying to obey his little sister. Would she give him a job? I wouldn't. Except… except of course I would. And even if not, I'd look after him. Doesn't he know that?

But still…

'Zander, it's… it's impossible…' Even I'm not sure what I believe any more. 'The Empress won't stop, you know? She'll kill me eventually. And if she doesn't someone else will. Kaeda still has her twisted Mecha technology.'

'Then I'll stop them. All of them. If… if you don't do it yourself.'

'Zan, I'll embarrass you at every turn. I'll shame Vairian.'

'You'll *never* do that.'

I drag in a breath. He just won't stop. He'll never stop. 'But the alliances and the compacts with all the other worlds—'

'That's my father talking, love.' Then he pauses and barks out a bitter laugh. 'No, actually, that isn't my father. That's the King of Vairian, a politician and a diplomat, a player of Imperial games.'

'Games which you'll need to play too. What will people say? You can't do that with me at your side.'

I press my hand up against the door, in front of my face, my fingers splayed wide. Is his hand on the other side? Is his face pressed against mine? His lips so close and yet so far away?

'Why not? I can't do it without you. I don't care what people say. I never have. I need you. Only you.'

But our Zander is meant for no one but you. Teel said. *Keep him close.*

My hand moves against all logic. I press the door control and the sometimes crown prince of Vairian stumbles through the sudden gap.

I catch him before he can fall. Just like always.

'Zander, your father—'

Zander smiles as his arms encircle me. 'Do you want to know what my father told me? Not the king. My father.' He breathes in, smiles that magical smile and I can't take my eyes off him. 'My father told me I'd better not let you get away again.'

'But Zan…'

'Stop arguing with me, Pet. Just for once.'

And then he kisses me so thoroughly that I forget how to argue at all.

A Letter from Jessica

Thank you so much for reading *The Stone's Heart*. I hope you enjoyed it as much as I loved writing it! If you'd like to keep up-to-date with all of my latest releases, you can sign up at the following link. Your email address will never be shared and you can unsubscribe at any time.

www.bookouture.com/jessica-thorne

Petra Kel was one of *those* characters. She started off in the background. She wasn't meant to be particularly important. She was there to look after Bel, kick down some doors and kill some bad guys. She certainly wasn't going to have her own story.

But Petra – being Petra – wasn't going to stay in the background, was she?

Not in *The Queen's Wing*. And when time came to write *The Stone's Heart*, I knew she had to be front and centre. Her history with Zander and his history with Teel complicates her life when really all Petra wants to do is her duty, her job. She's determined, and faithful, and, mainly because of the Merryns, her life will never be easy. As a possible future Queen of Vairian, she's not what anyone would expect. But she could be what they need. Just like Bel.

And of course, Bel was not going anywhere either. Because Vairian stubbornness is notorious.

A sequel is a funny thing. We return to characters we have loved and cherished, we see their lives moving onwards, see new challenges and dangers. It also leaves the question of what next? What's going to happen in the future to these people and their worlds? Space Opera is about adventure and excitement, it's about other worlds and great ships in the vastness of space. It's fantasy out among the stars, on other worlds, with other beings. But most of all it is about the characters.

What is going to happen next? We'll have to find out.

If you have time, I'd love it if you were able to let me know what you thought of the book and write a review of *The Stone's Heart*. Feedback is really useful and also makes a huge difference in helping new readers discover one of my books for the first time.

Alternatively, if you'd like to contact me personally, you can reach me via my Website, Facebook page, Twitter or Instagram. I love hearing from readers, and always reply.

Again, thank you so much for deciding to spend some time reading *The Stone's Heart*. I'm looking forward to sharing my next book with you very soon.

With all best wishes,
Jessica

www.rflong.com/jessicathorne

JessThorneBooks

@JessThorneBooks

Glossary

Anthaem – Ruler of Anthaeus, selected from among his or her people by the Rondet, noted for their ingenious technology, peaceful nature and great beauty

Anthaese – The people of Anthaeus, human colonists who left the expanding Empire to settle there

Anthaeus – A colony world ruled by the Anthaem, independent of the Empire. It was previously home to the Rondet and a great deal of their buildings and marks of civilization remain

Camarth – An Imperial world, noted for its religious nature

Cuore – Central world of the Empire, seat of the Empress

Duneen – Rural area near Elveden on the planet Vairian

Elveden – Bel's home, now the new royal capital of Vairian

Falcons – Vairian flying machines designed specifically for combat

Firstworld – The original world from which all colonists set out

Gravia – Homeworld of the Gravians

Gravians – Ancient enemies of the Vairians, an alien race who worship a death goddess. Their dying world means they need to seek out other worlds to exploit

Higher Cape – The former royal capital of Vairian

Kelta – The moon of Anthaeus, source of powerful energy crystals which are mined there

Limasyll – Capital of Anthaeus, mostly built by the Rondet and adopted by the Anthaese when they colonised the planet. Known for its beauty, the citadel which houses the palace and the elaborate gardens

Maestre – Honorary title of male member of the Rondet

Maestra – Honorary title of female member of the Rondet

Mechas – Human-machines, created by the Gravians by grafting technology onto the dead to fight as cannon fodder in their many wars

Melia – An Imperial world, known for food and wine

Montserratt – A region of Anthaeus

Rondet – Ancient beings who guide the Anthaem as a council

Vairian – Bel's homeworld, independent of the Empire but closely aligned to it through a military alliance which sees Vairians as the military might of the Empire

Wasp – Vairian flying machines

Acknowledgements

My thanks to everyone who helped me bring *The Stone's Heart* to life, for your faith and support. Thanks to Kathryn, Jennifer and everyone at Bookouture, and to Sallyanne and Max at Mulcahy Associates. My eternal thanks to and for the Naughty Kitchen, the Romantic Novelists Association, my Lady Writers' social club and all the amazing writer friends who offer so much help on a daily basis.

And finally to my family, and Pat, best husband ever.

Made in United States
North Haven, CT
18 May 2023

36710188R00232